A wall of darkness loomed, blocking out the stars along the horizon, rising higher as it approached. The monstrous seething thing extended across the whole southern horizon. Now Kerrick understood the light breeze from the north. He had encountered the same phenomenon with a few other ocean storms. Before the weather struck, it moved through a swath of low pressure, actually sucking air, water, and boats *toward* the front.

This was a storm like none he had ever experienced before.

"*That* looks kind of interesting," the kender observed.

DRAGONLANCE NOVELS BY DOUGLAS NILES

Chaos War Series

The Last Thane
The Puppet King

Preludes

Flint the King (with Mary Kirchoff)

The Lost Histories

The Kagonesti
The Dragons

The Lost Gods

Fistandantilus Reborn

Icewall Trilogy
Volume One

Douglas Niles

THE MESSENGER

Distributed in the United States by St. Martin's Press. Distributed in Canada by Fenn Ltd.

Distributed to the hobby, toy, and comic trade in the United States and Canada by regional distributors.

Distributed worldwide by Wizards of the Coast, Inc. and regional distributors.

Made in the U.S.A.

Cover art by Brom
First Printing: February 2001
Library of Congress Catalog Card Number: 00-190760

9 8 7 6 5 4 3 2 1

UK ISBN: 0-7869-2026-2
US ISBN: 0-7869-1571-4
620-T21571

U.S., CANADA,
ASIA, PACIFIC, & LATIN AMERICA
Wizards of the Coast, Inc.
P.O. Box 707
Renton, WA 98057-0707
+1-800-324-6496

EUROPEAN HEADQUARTERS
Wizards of the Coast, Belgium
P.B. 2031
2600 Berchem
Belgium
+32-70-23-32-77

Visit our web site at **www.wizards.com/dragonlance**

Dedication

To Pat McGilligan,
editor, teacher, friend

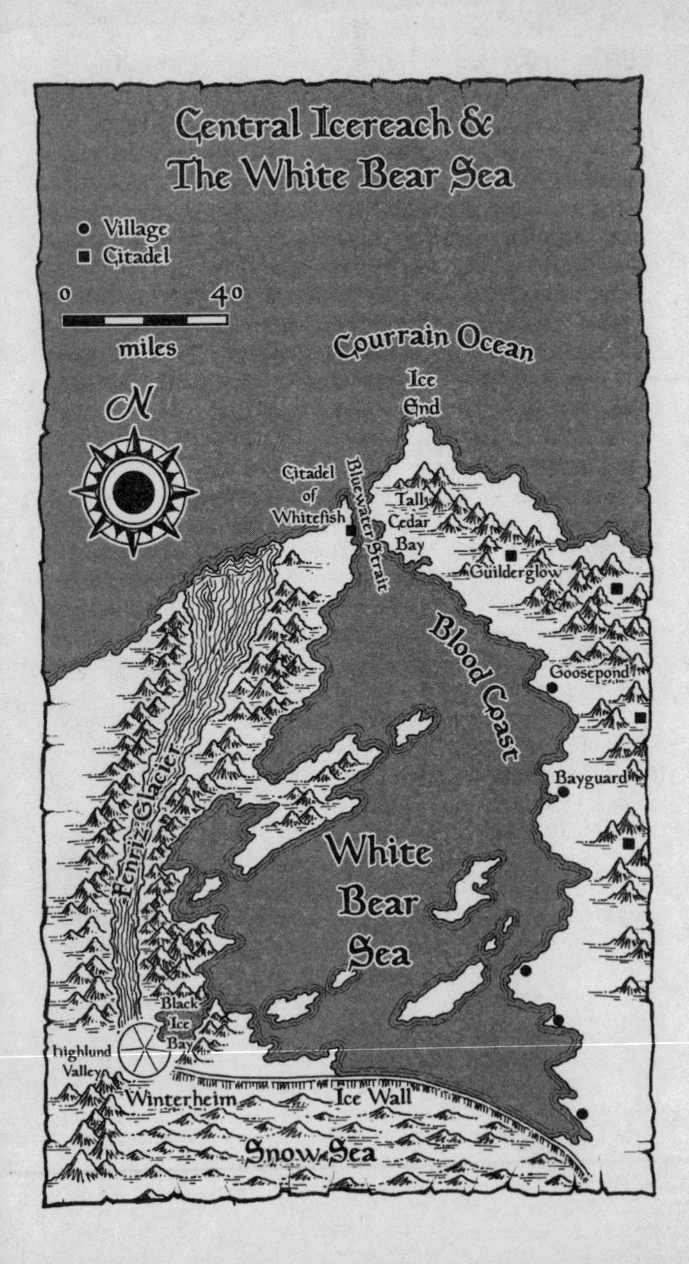

Central Icereach &
The White Bear Sea
Village
Citadel
0
40
miles
N
Courrain Ocean
Ice End
Citadel of Whitefish
Bluewater Strait
Tall Cedar Bay
Guilderglow
Blood Coast
Goosepond
Bayguard
Fenriz Glacier
White Bear Sea
Black Ice Bay
highlund Valley
Winterheim
Ice Wall
Snow Sea

1

Hunters on the Blood Coast

I can throw a harpoon as far as any man and hit the target twice as often!" Moreen knew that her voice was getting loud, but right now she didn't care. How could her father be so Chislev-cursed *stubborn*? "You know it's true! So why can't I take a kayak out with the rest of the hunters?"

"You're my daughter, and you will stay in the village with your mother!" growled Redfist Bayguard, his swarthy face darkening into the flush of deep anger.

The young woman opened her mouth to speak, but the chieftain trampled over her objections without hesitation. "I have already given you too much freedom! Do you know there are those who speak ill of me because I let you learn how to cast a harpoon, how to track a bear and build a fire on the tundra? They say I cannot control my own child—how can I be expected to manage the affairs of the Arktos?"

Moreen felt her own temper slipping away, knew that she should bite her tongue, but the words spilled out in a voice that reached far beyond the sealskin walls of the little hut. "Maybe people should worry more about their *own* affairs," she snapped.

"You will be silent, now!" roared the chieftain, rising to his feet and trembling in such rage that the daughter momentarily feared his clenched fist. She stood up too, glaring, challenging him, all but daring him to strike.

He turned and pushed through the leather door, stomping into the misty dawn.

Striding after him, Moreen caught the flap of door before it closed, then stopped, quivering from her own anger but unwilling to press the fight. She saw the blue-white sky, the flat waters of the bay, and, closer, the villagers going about as if they hadn't heard the argument. It was early morning, but early morning in the time of the midnight sun. The sky was already fully bright after the short, ghostly interval of midnight.

"I know that you don't want to humiliate him, but that is what you do."

Her mother spoke from the shadows beyond the cold firepit. Inga Bayguard sat crosslegged, looking at Moreen with her dark eyes soft and sad.

"How can he be so unfair?" the younger woman demanded, even as a small voice inside of her suggested that it was she who was being unreasonable.

"If you had asked him to take you along when he was going hunting by himself, you know that he would have gladly let you accompany him. How many times has he done just that? Remember, not four years ago, he took you hunting in spring, and the two of you paddled as far as Tall Cedar Bay? But today . . . this is the great hunt of Highsummer. Every male in the tribe is going along, and, like it or not, your presence would be a huge distraction."

"Well, how can it be such a humiliation for him when in the end everyone knows I obey his will?"

"Because you shout at him, corner him in arguments. Because you make certain that everyone in the village knows how you feel."

Letting the door flap drop, which enclosed the hut in a dimness broken only by the whale-oil lamp, Moreen pushed a strand of black hair back from her eyes and crossed her arms over her chest. Her mother rose and stepped around the small room to look up into her daughter's face.

"You have your father's strength, Moreen Bayguard, and your mother's—well, I want to believe you have your mother's heart. But you are your own person. As you enter your eighteenth summer you have been granted unusual respect by the Arktos—even those old hunters who have now worked you into such a rage."

"What do you mean, 'respect'? They think I'm a frivolous pest."

"Sometimes you *are* a frivolous pest," retorted Inga. "There are other times when you show skill that cannot fail to impress. The men may complain about you learning manly skills, but they have noted your talent with the harpoon. You were right—you *can* throw better than any of them. They respect your intelligence, and the force of your words. You are a true heir to your great-grandfather."

The young woman's anger softened. She looked at the pelt that stretched across one whole interior wall of the hut, the lush black fur that was far too precious ever to lie upon the ground.

"I want to be worthy of Wallran Bayguard. I really do," she said.

"I know, child," Inga replied. "As it was for your father, the legacy of the Black Bear will be a burden and an honor that you carry all your life. Wallran Bayguard hunted and slew the mythic bear as foretold in the prophecy, killed it with a single spear-cast, as had been foretold since the Scattering. That promise for the future, that our people will one day prosper and rise to be masters of Icereach, is embodied in you. It is your legacy and your future."

"My future?" Moreen replied in disgust. "My future looks like a lifetime of cooking and skinning the prey that the men bring home!"

Her mother's expression gently chided her, but the younger woman was in no mood to heed it. Instead, she pushed through the door and stomped across the village square. The Arktos hunters there, busy with their preparations, had the good sense to avoid meeting her eyes.

By the time the Arktos hunters had rigged their kayaks and collected their gear Moreen and Bruni, her best friend, had ascended to the rocky crest rising just beyond the shore.

Beyond the mouth of the bay, the White Bear Sea was a dazzling swath of silver, bright with reflected sunlight. The sky overhead was pale blue, which brightened to white closer to the horizon. The summer sun was a shining presence in the northeast, a spot of fire burning through the haze.

The huts of Bayguard nestled across the flat ground between two hills and the sheltered bay that had been the tribe's home for three generations, since Wallran Bayguard had killed the black bear that had hallowed this spot. Here they weathered the brutal onslaught of Sturmfrost each winter, and emerged each spring to, if not prosper, at least survive. The threescore structures looked neat and snug, clustered around the flat square and ceremonial firepit in the center of the village. Across that plaza rose a shape made of bundled sticks, the half-bird, half-fish image of Chislev Wilder, hunter goddess of the Arktos. Little kayaks were arrayed along the shore. For a time the two women watched the hunters push the boats into the shallows, each scrambling aboard and quickly starting to paddle.

"Do you think they will be gone long?" asked Bruni, lifting her voluminous leather skirt enough that she could sit comfortably on a large, flat boulder.

Moreen, who was dressed in sealskin trousers and a woolen shirt, leaned against another outcrop and shook her head. "I don't care," she snorted, "if the lot of them are gone until Lastsummer Day!" She watched as the kayaks bobbed through the gentle surf near the shore, each man paddling his little craft through the breakers until the boats gathered a short distance off the beach. Redfist Bayguard, his kayak distinguished by a crimson stripe, stroked into the lead and led the boats toward the mouth of the small, protected bay.

Bruni chuckled, the sound rumbling from her big body with an easy humor that Moreen inevitably found infectious.

Moreen sighed in resignation. "If luck from the past holds, they'll find seals not too far away. Even if they get after a whale—" the chieftain's daughter winced inwardly at the thought of missing that thrill—"I would think they'd be able to tow it back here within a week or ten days."

"Let's hope for ten days of peace and quiet, then," Bruni said, shading her eyes with her hand as she looked toward the dazzling sun. She was sitting up straight, a tall and round-shouldered bulk on her flat rock. Bruni's face was flat and "round as the moon," as Inga was fond of saying. Her cheekbones were prominent, and when she smiled her face took on a glow all its own. She was tall and wide, with thick arms and strong, plump fingers. Her feet were bigger than any man's in the tribe, and instead of moccasins she encased them in heavy leather boots.

Moreen, by contrast, felt like a waif. Her frame was wiry and compact, the top of her scalp reaching just over five feet from the ground. She kept her dark hair cut to shoulder length, usually tied behind her ears, while Bruni favored the typical style of Arktos women, with a lush tail of black hair that, when unrestrained, reached nearly to the ground.

A girl's shriek rang out from the hillside below them, and they saw a child race into sight, shaking droplets of water from her hair. "I'll get you for that, Little Mouse!" she cried, reaching down to pick up a fist-sized rock. She hurled the missile into the hillside where it clattered loudly. Grinning broadly, a tall, dark-haired boy dodged out of the way, then stood making faces while the girl cast stone after stone.

"Ouch!" he cried suddenly as one finally glanced off his forehead. "Okay, Feathertail, I'm sorry," he said.

"That'll teach you to douse me!" the girl declared and

flounced away. In her hand was a basket partially filled with spring blossoms.

The youth's expression turned sour as he made his way higher onto the hillside. After he had taken a dozen steps he noticed the two women regarding him, and shrugged his shoulders.

"Lucky throw," he said, rubbing his forehead.

"Not lucky enough," Moreen retorted, though she smiled enough to take the sting out of her words.

Little Mouse sighed, and his eyes drifted toward the kayaks which were now starting to round the point of the bay. In another few minutes they would be into the swell of the deep gulf waters and would make the turn to head northeastward along the coast.

"You wish you were out there with them, don't you?" the chieftain's daughter said sympathetically. "I know how you feel."

Little Mouse looked at her eagerly, and she was reminded of a puppy, frantically eager to please. He was thirteen summers old, awkwardly torn between boyhood and becoming a man. "But you—they *should* let you go!" he proclaimed, his voice cracking an octave on the last word. "I've seen you throw—why, I bet you'd get the first seal!"

Now it was the woman's turn to sigh, and she shook her head ruefully. "You'll be going on the spring hunt before I will," she said.

"Papa said maybe next year," Little Mouse admitted. "Normally I'd wait til fifteen, but since I'm the only boy my age in the tribe they might make an exception."

"I know you'll be ready," encouraged Moreen.

"What's that?" Bruni asked abruptly, pointing into the dazzling brightness of the sea. Something came across the water, distant but moving toward them, trailing a long wake that sparkled in the sun.

The boy quickly looked toward the sun. "A whale? It's too big!"

"No . . . no whale." Moreen felt a peculiar chill, awe that quickly gave way to fear. She squinted, trying to adjust her notions of scale and realized that it was a vessel, a massive hull slicing through the waters of the White Bear Sea. "It's some kind of boat, but it's as big as the village!"

As it emerged from the swath of the sun's brightest glare they could begin to make out more details. The vessel was long and slender like a kayak, with a row of long paddles. It was hard to get a sense of the craft's size, but it must be huge indeed. This was not a boat of any Arktos tribe.

"Highlanders?" asked Bruni tentatively.

"No." Moreen was certain. "The only one of them I've ever met looked squeamish at the very thought of going on the water."

"Have the hunters have seen it?" Bruni asked, with a glance toward the kayaks scattered like specks nearing the mouth of the bay. They were much closer than the strange ship but still tiny by comparison.

"Not yet." Moreen was remembering her many hunting expeditions along the shores beyond the village. "There's that headland to the east that will block their view—until they come around the point, and that thing will be right on top of them!"

"What is it?" asked Mouse, worriedly. "Are you sure it's not some kind of whale?"

"No whale. I don't know what it is, but I'm frightened. Let's get to the village!" replied the chieftain's daughter in growing urgency. "We can light a signal fire to call the hunters back."

Little Mouse was already sprinting down the hill, while Moreen trotted after, and Bruni picked her way more cautiously between the jutting rocks.

What could it be? Little Mouse's question churned in Moreen's mind, coming up with the one and only possibility, a dire explanation indeed. A mythic name, imbued with terror and doom, a threat she had never seen but that had been a part of her people's storytelling and folklore since before her birth.

Ogres.

The great brutes had not raided the Arktos in Moreen's

lifetime or during the lives of her parents. They remained a threat of legends, monstrous figures from stories told by the shaman, crabby old Dinekki, to while away the long, dark months of winter. Always in the back of the tribal consciousness, though, there was the knowledge of this brutal race that also dwelled in the place called Icereach and that might one day renew on the cruel raids that had made ancient life deadly for the Arktos since the time of the Scattering.

It was because of these legendary ogres that every child of Clan Bayguard, from the moment he or she could first walk, learned the path to the Hiding Hole, the narrow-mouthed cave notched into the hill beyond the village. They learned the first rule, as well—never go to the Hiding Hole if an ogre can see you, or you may lead the raiders to the whole tribe.

How did that explain the great boat? Always in the stories the ogres had moved across the land, marching out of the spring mists to lay waste to this village or that town, dragging off slaves, smashing buildings, leaving death and destruction and despair in their wake. Surely the building of a craft like the one they had seen was beyond the cunning of an ogre mind!

Yet who else could it be? Clearly the vessel wasn't the work of the Highlanders. Moreen had encountered a group of those human hunters on one occasion and had not been impressed. Shaggy, bearded, tall, they seemed like simple-minded savages. One had tried to approach her, but of course she had turned and fled, and he had reacted with almost comical disbelief when she gotten into her kayak and rowed away. She suspected they were frightened of any liquid deeper than the mugs of warqat they reputedly drank continually during the long months of winter.

It was even less likely that the ship carried outlanders, people from beyond Icereach. Though there were tales of lands, of humans and even stranger beings from far across the turbulent ocean, outlanders were like imaginary beings. None of these had ever come to these shores, not in the memories of the oldest elders recalling their own elders' stories.

The ogres, however, did live across the gulf in a mountain fastness. And if it had been a human's life span since their last raid, there was no doubt that they really existed—every child had been shown Dinekki's tusk and given a lesson about the nature of their ancient and brutal enemies. How many times, scolding Moreen for some infraction, had her mother threatened her with, "Behave, or I'll leave you outside where the ogre king will find you"? Always the warning brought a chill.

By the time Moreen reached the outskirts of the village, barely winded from her long downhill sprint, she had convinced herself that it was ogres coming. Little Mouse had already run between the huts, shouting an alarm, and the chieftain's daughter was met by a confused rabble of women, children, and elders.

"What is this racket?" crabbed Dinekki, as the skinny old shaman tried to tap Little Mouse on the foot with her staff.

The boy skipped out of the way, pleading earnestly for her ear. "Grandmother Dinekki, it's true! A great kayak sails the coast, coming this way! Moreen saw it, and Bruni too! We've got to light a smoke fire and bring back the hunters!"

"I saw it also!" claimed Feathertail, the girl hopping up and down beside Inga Bayguard. "It's coming toward my papa, toward the kayaks!"

Already another young woman, Tildey, was whipping a coal from her firepit into bright flame. Other women were busy grabbing logs from various woodpiles, dousing some with oil, and casting them into a great pile in the village square. Tildey touched her fire to the kindling, and quickly the bonfire crackled into a smoky conflagration.

"Are you sure it's ogres? Couldn't it be a ship of men?" asked matronly Garta with a quaver in her voice, three small children clinging to her gown.

"Not Arktos, and not Highlanders either," Bruni declared with a shake of her big head. "Can't be men."

"This tusk will tell." Dinekki's dry, brittle voice somehow cut through the commotion. The shaman held up a curved ivory tooth, one of the many talismans she wore on various strands around her neck. She removed the thong from the hole that had been drilled through the base of the object. Next she blew softly on the ivory, then muttered a rhythmic prayer in the language of the goddess Chislev. Raising the tusk, she held it in her fingertips at the end of her rigidly extended arm.

"*Ogre tusk shall show the truth—seek thy owner, lonesome tooth*!"

She released her grip on the tusk with a sudden gesture, but instead of falling straight down to the ground, the tooth spun away toward the sea, finally clattering to the stony ground some ten feet distant.

"Yes! There are ogres there," Dinekki said, pointing along the line of the tusk's flight.

"That's the direction to the great boat," Moreen said, feeling a sickening tightness in her belly.

By now the fire was crackling hungrily through the wood, and a plume of black smoke was rising high above the village. A gentle breeze curved the smoke over the land, but it rose as a clear beacon. The kayaks were beyond the point of the bay, now invisible from the square, but Moreen felt certain they would take immediate note of the time-honored signal and return.

"Everyone to the Hiding Hole!" declared Inga Bayguard. "Gather your precious things."

"I will stay here to fight alongside the men!" her daughter declared in a sudden burst of emotion.

"You will lead this tribe to the Hiding Hole," Inga replied in a clipped tone that somehow halted any attempt Moreen might have made at an argument. "Bruni, you must carry Grandfather Oilfish. You bigger children help with the youngsters—start out now, and your mothers will be right behind. Now hurry, all of you!"

The chieftain's daughter hastened into the hut. She looked at the huge black bearskin on the wall and for a moment felt a pang as she remembered Wallran Bayguard's legacy. She should take it—the pelt was a rare treasure in this land where all other bears were white. Even more, it was symbolic of her family's place, as chieftains of all the Arktos in their many coastal villages.

Nonetheless it was more than she could carry alone, and there was no time for such a burden. Picking up three of her harpoons, she also grabbed a heavy woolen cloak and a large skin of water. By the time she emerged the other women were gathering in the village square. Little Mouse was directing a file of several dozen children who were already making their way up the winding hillside path, some suppressing frightened sobs, others casting longing looks toward their homes.

"Let's go," Moreen said, coming to her mother's side.

"I said *you* will lead them," Inga replied. "I will follow when I know that you are safe and the men have seen the beacon. Until then, I will stoke the fire." Her mother indicated the signal pyre, and Moreen saw that the initial fuel had already been reduced to crumbling coals. "Now make haste—and Chislev be with you!"

Giving her mother a quick hug, Moreen gathered the rest of the women and the elders. She saw that Tildey had armed herself with a bow and arrows, while Bruni carried a stout stick.

"What about Grandfather Oilfish?" asked Inga. That elder, his legs crippled years earlier, would be unable to walk on his own.

"He refused to come—he has his harpoon and sits inside his doorway."

Inga blinked, then nodded. "Very well—now, hurry!"

Several other women had armed themselves with harpoons, but for the most part the group consisted of frightened, white-haired grandfathers and grandmothers wrapped in woolen shawls and wide-eyed hearthwives who bit their lips and, for their children's sakes, made brave efforts not to cry.

They started out of the village, moving as quickly as they could, many of the women helping the elders. Moreen cast one glance back to the sea, despairing as she saw no sign yet of the kayaks returning to the bay. Inga was tossing more wood onto the fire, and she dumped the contents of an oil lamp into the rekindled blaze. Quickly she retreated as a black, smoky cloud once more erupted into the sky.

It seemed to take forever to climb the hill, though in reality the tribespeople ascended the twisting path in just a few minutes. Moreen and Bruni brought up the rear, watching the last of their village-mates slip through the narrow crack in the rocky cliff to enter the deep, dry cave.

The shelter was perfectly concealed, for the irregular surface of the precipice curled around itself here, so that the cave mouth was not even visible to one who peered straight at the hillside. Still, as she glanced down Moreen was dismayed to see the trampled brush and dusty tracks leading up the hill.

"Here, help me sweep this away," she declared. Pulling up a brittle willow bush she moved partway down the path and started brushing away the footprints. Bruni followed, dropped tufts of greenery onto the trail until it looked no different from the rest of the hillside.

"There are the hunters," Moreen said, as she saw that the kayaks had come around the point and reentered the bay. The men were paddling with crisp, efficient strokes, and the little boats fairly skipped over the gentle swell, racing like gliding birds toward the shore.

"The great boat, close behind!" Bruni exclaimed.

Her observation was unnecessary as the chieftain's daughter, too, saw the immense vessel glide into view. It seemed to move impossibly fast for a craft of such size, for it churned around the point and surged toward the shore, closing the distance on the nimble kayaks, looming over the smaller boats like a mountain over mere huts.

"Let's get out of sight"

The big woman knelt and Moreen shrank beside her, dropping behind the cover of several boulders. She looked back quickly, saw that the mouth of the cave was still. None of the other villagers were showing themselves.

The first kayaks reached the shore. She could spot the

men scrambling out of their little boats, turning to help their fellows onto shore. The great ogre vessel loomed close behind, churning toward the beach. Golden rails gleamed and sparkled in the sunlight, and the burnished image of a great, tusked head loomed awkwardly above the bow. The deck was crowded, teeming with figures bearing tall, golden-tipped spears.

A spot of color flashed along the graveled beach and the women saw Inga Bayguard running toward the men, her dyed cloak trailing from her shoulders. She was carrying Redfist's bear spear, his mightiest weapon, as with a flurry of powerful strokes the chieftain pushed his red-striped kayak right up to his wife.

The big rowing ship churned right through some of the kayaks that hadn't reached shore, breaking a few of the little boats like child's toys crushed under heavy booted steps. Arktos hunters boldly hurled their harpoons at the hulking figures lining the gunwale of the great vessel. Moreen couldn't see if any of these casts scored hits, but she groaned as she saw big spears fly outward from the ogre ranks, easily piercing several hunters and some kayaks. A few of the boats sank, carrying their men into the chill depths.

Another overturned near shore, and a hunter flailed in the water, trying to crawl out of his leaking boat. Moreen saw that he was lanced through with a huge spear, bleeding so much that the wave breaking around him foamed into a crimson crest. Finally the little vessel rolled over, nudging gently into the shallows, the hunter obviously too weak to right his craft. The young woman felt a rush of guilt, oddly shamed that she couldn't recognize which of her villagemates was dying before her eyes.

The grinding of the rowing ship hitting shallow water was audible even up on the hillside. Surf broke to either side of the big hull. Two broad ramps dropped downward, one to each side of the bow, and big raiders lumbered down the platforms to splash into the knee-deep water.

The Arktos hunters met them on both sides of the vessel, casting harpoons, slashing in with fishing knives, paddles, anything that could serve as a weapon. One ogre bore a huge axe, and he swung it into a human, dropping the man with a wound so deep that Moreen could see the spray of blood from her lofty vantage. The raiders were monstrous, looming a foot or two over their victims. Wearing armored breastplates, heavy boots, and thick gauntlets, they seemed to merely brush aside any of the villagers' attempts at resistance.

Another man fell back, lying in the shallow water with a huge spear sticking in his midriff. Here again, and now in many other places too, the frothing surf was tinged red. An ogre howled as a harpoon struck him in the shoulder, penetrating deep into gristly flesh—but even before the brute plucked the weapon from the wound his attacker was beaten down by a pack of other ogres who surrounded him. The Arktos were outnumbered and losing badly.

"Where is my father?" whispered Moreen, as the melee spread from the shallows onto the flat beach. Here and there men established pockets of resistance, while the ogres spread out and moved in slowly.

"There," Bruni said grimly, pointing a finger.

Moreen gasped, seeing Redfist wield his spear against a huge ogre with Inga behind him. The chieftain made a curt gesture to his wife, and she finally turned and raced toward the village, sprinting past the first little domes. When the ogre attacked, Redfist thrust the tip of the spear up through the creature's great belly. With a roar, the ogre reeled sideways, and the chieftain twisted his weapon and then pulled the gory tip out of the wound. The stricken raider collapsed on the ground, kicking weakly, as Redfist turned and race in the same direction as his wife.

"So many are dying," Bruni said numbly. Moreen could only nod with heartsickness. Already the surf was thick with bodies, and ogres were advancing toward the village along the whole breadth of the beach. A few men still fought in the open, while others fell back among the skin-walled huts.

A woman—it was Inga Bayguard—screamed as burly

ogre paws grabbed her arms. She was thrown roughly to the ground as another one of the raiders rushed up, raising a large axe.

"By Chislev—no!" cried Moreen. She tried to spring forward, racing to her mother's aid, but Bruni threw her to the ground and held her there with firm pressure.

"I have to go to her!" hissed the chieftain's daughter.

"No," Bruni said, her tone gentle despite the power of her stout grip. "You cannot help her—and you would only give away the position of the Hiding Hole."

With a sob Moreen collapsed onto her stomach, still staring with horror. The ogre with the axe stumbled sideways, as Redfist raced up to jab his bloody spear into the monster's hip. It collapsed with a roar and a feeble kick, but now the other ogre reached out and seized the haft of the chieftain's spear. With a twist the brute yanked the weapon out of the man's hands. Redfist drew his long, bone-bladed knife, but the ogre used the bloody spear like a club, bashing him in the head and sending him reeling to the ground.

With casual contempt the great brute aimed the point of the spear downward, piercing Inga's body and staking her to the ground. Her hands clasped at the blood-slick haft, but her struggles quickly ceased. In moments the chieftain's wife lay still, a patch of crimson slowly staining the ground around her.

Redfist, meanwhile, had been roughly hoisted to his feet. Seeing his wife's death, he thrashed with fury, but the brute hoisted him as if he was a child, carrying him toward the rest of the raiders who were starting to gather in the midst of the village square.

"That is their chief," Bruni said, once more pointing.

The gesture was unnecessary—the leader of the raiders was clearly identifiable even from this high vantage. He swaggered forward between a pair of his fellows, awaiting delivery of Redfist. A gold breastplate gleamed across his massive chest. His twin tusks gleamed with gilded wire, tightly wrapped around the ivory stubs. Bracelets and thigh guards, also made of gold and secured with golden chains, protected his limbs. Massive boots of black whaleskin rose past his knees, and at his waist he wore a sheath and a long sword. Moreen hadn't seen this gaudy ruler in the thick of the battle, and she wondered contemptuously if he had been absent and was content to let others do his fighting for him.

"Someday we will feed him those gold chains, one link at a time," vowed Bruni, for the first time betraying bitter emotion in her voice.

Numbly Moreen pledged agreement. She was tense and trembling, but her eyes were dry, and her thoughts seemed strangely calm.

For the first time, she saw the dwarf.

He swaggered out from behind the ogre leader, his chest thrust out, straw-colored beard bristling in a self-important display. A metal breastplate, gray instead of gold, protected his chest, and a cap of similar material fitted his head, though stiff, wiry hair jutted out from beneath the rim. With manifest arrogance he stalked up to Redfist Bayguard, staring into the struggling chieftain's face, then walked past to turn toward the surrounding hillsides.

"Hear me, people of Icereach!" the dwarf cried. "Come forward and pay homage to your prince! His name is Grimwar Bane, and he is the son of Grimtruth Bane, the King of Suderhold, who rules your lands from his citadel in Winterheim. Know that you are his subjects, and you owe your lives, your breath, your homes, to his beneficence!"

Redfist twisted, tried to raise his clenched hand, but the two ogres now holding him merely exerted a little more pressure until he hung motionless in their arms.

"We know you are up there, hiding . . . watching," cried the dwarf. Even from this distance his eyes seemed unusually large to Moreen, but they were pale and empty. He brandished a dagger, a silver-hilted knife that he waved back and forth so that it sparkled in the spring sun.

"It is important that you understand the power of Grimtruth Bane, as shown here by his son Grimwar. Do not defy him."

Abruptly the dwarf spun around. He stood several steps

away from Redfist Bayguard, but he raised the knife as if he would have stabbed the man. He barked some word, a sound Moreen could not identify.

Instantly the short blade of the knife flashed into a long, slender sword. The silver tip flicked across Redfist Bayguard's cheek, scoring a shallow cut.

The chieftain came alive with a scream, a sound of pain and anguish that would haunt Moreen's memories for the rest of her life. Her father was a brave and stoic man—she had seen him pull a barbed harpoon right through the meaty part of his thigh after a tribesman's miscast—and so his eerie shriek was a shock to the young woman.

His struggles became so frantic that he somehow managed to pull away from the two ogres. With both hands pressed to his face, he stumbled weakly, bouncing off of the low stone wall surrounding the village square. The ogres watched in amusement, some of them laughing, as the stricken man staggered to his wife's body. With a last strangled sob, the chieftain dropped to his knees, gasped once more, and then collapsed beside Inga's lifeless form.

Moreen didn't have to watch any longer to know that her father, too, lay dead.

2

The Court of the Elven King

Kerrick Fallabrine met Gloryian on one of the crystal bridges arching through the shadow of the Tower of the Stars. He saw her coming toward him and halted at the rail, turning his eyes toward the lofty spire, the pride of Silvanesti and this great capital, Silvanost.

Gloryian, too, stopped at the rail, several paces away from him. For several moments the two stared with apparent interest at the lofty tower, as other elves, nobles and servants, made their way past. Finally the sound of receding footsteps told Kerrick that, for the moment, they were alone.

"Can I see you tonight?" he whispered.

"Yes," she replied in similar tones. "My brother has returned home from his duty on the Blöten frontier—there will be a feast for the early part of the evening, but I will make excuses, and slip away before midnight."

"The door on your balcony will be open?" The elf dared a sidelong glance and was rewarded by the dazzling beauty of his lover's smile.

"Naturally," she replied. She gave him a pinch as she left her spot on the railing and glided past him to continue across the bridge.

He waited a few more minutes, then wandered along in the opposite direction, lost inside a haze of anticipation, scarcely noticing the splendors of this city, the heart of the greatest civilization on all Krynn. Silvanost occupied a great island in the middle of the deep, wide Than-Thalas River. Much of that great current was visible from this lofty vantage, iridescent waters dotted with graceful watercraft. High barges, moving by oar power and often bearing the canopied pavilions of great nobles, made their way here and there, while slender galleys and deep-drafted sailing ships coursed through the main channel. Nimble fishing boats scuttled like waterbugs among the larger craft, while the heavy gunwales of the king's war galleys were visible in the fortified harbor of House Royal.

A casual glance might take the island for a fabulous grove of well-tended gardens. Many of the elven manors were towering spires of wood, rising from yards crowded with flowers, bright with blossoms, and sparkling with blue pools, crystalline fountains, trilling streams. The dominant structure was the Tower of Stars, of course, and Kerrick couldn't help but feel a sense of awe as he stopped again and looked at the looming spire of crystal and steel. Several of the lower railings were gilded, but the shortage of gold during this era of the Istarian Kingpriests required that golden ornamentation be kept to a minimum, so steel had often been made to serve.

The young elf started down the spiraling stairway connecting the great bridge to the courtyard of House Mariner, where he had his apartments. He passed a veranda where an elf was playing a lyre to a small audience of his fellows. On the road to his house he met more musicians, flautists dancing in step and playing merry tunes. With a tolerant smile he moved to the side, vaguely impatient. His mind was filled with anticipation—he would have a long bath and a steam, then a good rest while he awaited the hour of midnight.

He could see much of the city from the gate to House Mariner—the bustling shipyard where a new galley took shape, the temple of E'li with its lofty towers of gold plate, the royal arboretum with acres of flowered gardens terraced across the side of a great hill—but, as it did so often, his mind drifted to gold.

He was thinking about gold as he climbed the outer stairway to the balcony ledge outside of his quarters. Kerrick had precious little of the stuff—three coins tucked safely in hiding. A mere squire in a minor house could have no delusions of attaining any significant wealth. He reminded himself that he had everything he needed in the luxury of his appointment at court and in the attentions of a noble young maiden.

Nevertheless, gold had cast a spell over Kerrick's life. It was gold, or at least the lure of gold, that had claimed the life of his father, the famed admiral Dimorian Fallabrine . . . gold that had given his father great stature, gold that had led him to doom.

Like his father Kerrick thought too much about gold.

Later that night, at the corner where High Avenue met the waterfront, Kerrick turned for one last look at the harbor. The full moon shimmered in the water, white Lunitari rendered into clear, soft light. The ships at anchor made perfect reflections against a surface mirror-still in the windless night. For a moment Kerrick had a dizzying sensation—which way was up, which down?

Cutter stood at anchor there amidst the other vessels, and he relished the beauty of the high prow, the swept gunwales, and the single mast jutting so proudly before the low cabin. She was not as big as the king's warships, at anchor close to the mouth of the harbor, nor the mercantile galleys belonging to many of the elder houses. These gaudy showpieces displayed ornately carved bowsprits, engraved transoms, and even, to distinguish the highest ranking nobles, gilded rails and gunwales. The white moonlight sparkled into fiery orange here and there as it caught one of these surfaces of gold and reflected their light straight into Kerrick's eyes.

Beside those vessels *Cutter* was clearly a modest sailboat, but to the lone elf on the waterfront she was very much more than that. *Cutter* was the legacy of his father. She was pride and ancestry, strength and freedom . . . the key to everything he was, everything he had earned, everything he hoped to do in his life.

As Kerrick made his way up from Water Street, he thought about how fine it was to be young, to be here, in the spiritual center of elvenkind and, in his sincere belief, the center of all Krynn. A slight breeze whisked down the broad avenue, carrying the scent of blossoms and smoke, the hint of distant magic and the aroma of good food, tart wine.

Footsteps scuffed in the street before him, and Kerrick melted into a yard of lush, flowering bushes. A patrol, two elves of House Protector, ambled past, but their attention was focused on a hushed conversation and neither cast his eyes toward the shadowy ground.

They would probably be the last guards of the night, but in this neighborhood Kerrick would take no unnecessary chances. Elven eyes were keen in the darkness, capable of spotting a concealed person merely by the heat of his body. Kerrick knew that the presence of a common squire here in the heart of the city's elite enclave would be difficult to explain.

He moved cautiously across the grass and into the pathways of a formal garden. Staying low, he kept a tall hedge between himself and the street as he moved from one great compound to the next. He wormed through the hedge at one of many narrow passages, then skirted a shimmering pool. The water was bright in the moonlight and alive with flyfish that hovered above the water, snatching bugs from the air and then plopping into the depths. From here he slipped into the cover of a groomed oak grove, stepping over gnarled roots, gliding from trunk to great trunk as he kept a lookout.

As always, he felt the keen excitement, the thrilling anticipation of the supple form, the willing smile of Gloryian Diradar. She was a true daughter of the city's elite, a prize who had demanded all his skill in the taking. He had wooed her patiently for nearly a year before winning her in bed, but the months before that conquest were well worth the wait.

Her house was before him finally, a wall of rose quartz leading to a balcony and shadowed windows. Gloryian was up there, probably looking out for him already, watching from the dark of the chamber. Kerrick's heart pounded as he crossed the stretch of lawn to the trellis below her window, his familiar route up the wall. He grasped the branches, set his foot on a crosspiece, and started to climb, pulling himself up with practiced gestures.

The *crack* of breaking wood shot through the quiet night, and Kerrick, thrown by the surprise of it, felt himself falling backwards. Somehow the entire trellis had broken free from the wall! He twisted, pushing away, trying to land on his feet. When his moccasins hit the grass he lunged to the side, stumbling out from beneath the collapsing rack of sticks and vines.

Something hard hit him in the head, and he dropped to his knees, thinking groggily that a piece of masonry must have tumbled from the wall. Then he heard the voice.

"Sneaking, crawling *bastard*!"

A fist lashed at him from the side, smashing his nose. Through swiftly blurring eyes he saw an elf—no, two elves—looming over him. The nearest was a minor nobleman named Patrikan Diradar. More to the point, he was Gloryian's father, though he looked strange and monstrous now, his face contorted by an almost animal fury. Patrikan's fist lashed out again, striking the struggling elf in the ear, knocking him on his side.

"I treated to you as a friend!" said the second attacker, his voice a low growl. This one he recognized as Gloryian's brother, Darnari, a haughty young elf who had never seemed even remotely friendly to Kerrick. Darnari bent over, seized his prone victim by the hair, and punched him in the stomach. Again and again he jabbed, all the time meeting Kerrick's watering eyes with a look of pure hatred.

"You are an embarrassment to Silvanesti, to E'li himself!" snarled a third voice from behind Kerrick, invoking the elven name of the great god Paladine. A savage kick caught him between the shoulders.

Kerrick's head snapped back, and he collapsed on the rubble of the trellis, instinctively curling his knees to his chest. He couldn't escape, couldn't fight back, could barely draw a breath.

"You're not fit to sweep up the droppings of an ogre whore!" growled Patrikan, stomping on Kerrick's side with violent force. The elf groaned, felt his bile rise with the pain, and he vomited. His guts convulsed, as broken bones twisted and stabbed with each involuntary movement.

"Did you think you could get away with it?" declared the third elf, seizing Kerrick's arm, yanking him around, as he lay sprawled helplessly on his back. Vaguely Kerrick recognized this new tormentor . . . Waykand Isletter, one of the most prominent of young nobles in all Silvanesti. "You dare to *violate* the woman who will be my wife. What foolishness creeps through your pathetic mind?"

"It is only through the goodwill of King Nethas that you are still alive," Patrikan said, leaning over Kerrick with a look of disgust. He snorted contemptuously. "Our king, in his wisdom, seems to have fond memories of your time at court . . . though he recognizes that you have abandoned all claim to his protection and favor. Perhaps our liege still believes those stories about your father's heroism in the war. As for me, I knew Dimorian Fallabrine for the pirate that he was, and I can see that his dubious legacy lives well in you. Like your father, you have no sense of your proper station, no awareness of your betters."

Darnari dropped to one knee and let Kerrick see the silvery point of a dagger that waved very close to his tear-blurred eyes. "Not even the king's favor will protect you if you ignore this warning." The blade sliced through his shirt and left a burning trail of blood on Kerrick's chest. "If you go near, if you look at, if you even mention my sister's *name* again I will kill you."

"Not that you have a prayer of ever seeing her, or this place, again," declared Waykand Isletter. He had a sword drawn, and it looked to Kerrick as though the king's favor meant very little when weighed against the lord's desire for bloody revenge. "If I catch you in Silvanost, or anywhere in Silvansti, I will make it my business to kill you. So hear me well, sea-rat, and heed my words if you value your wretched life."

Waykand's sword touched Kerrick's throat and he sobbed.

"Your father, at least, knew how to conduct himself in a fight. Whatever starch he had does not live in you," declared the noble with contempt.

"Bah—his father had a lucky win in one battle," snorted Patrikan. "The rest of the time he was consorting with humans or trading with kender. Finally he sailed to his destruction on a fool's quest, leaving his progeny to befoul my daughter's honor."

"Gloryian!" The cry burst from Kerrick's throat, as his eyes searched for her up in th balcony.

"Oh, you should know this," Patrikan hissed hoarsely, rage choking his voice. "I have paid a fortune in gold to have the priest of E'li restore my daughter's virginity and to banish whatever nightmarish memories you have given her. You are like a sickness that has been exorcised from her skull, a disease from the past that she will mercifully forget. She scorns you now and forever!"

Above Kerrick saw a white gown swaying. How many times had he tenderly removed that garment ? His lover's face was lost in shadow, darkened by the moon shining with mocking allure.

"Go away," she called, and it was certainly Gloryian's voice, though somehow hardened into a steel blade. "I will never see you again!"

"But—I love you!" These words, hoarsely exploding

from his own lips, surprised him. Even through the fog of pain and humiliation he knew they were born of desperation and shame, not truth. Still, he shouted his love—his pride demanded it, required that he show these elves that his purpose was no less lofty than theirs.

He had the strange sense that his words might as well have been shouted into the sea-fog on a dark night. There was no echo, no sense even that anyone had heard. When Gloryian stepped forward to look down at him he saw the brightness of her eyes against the moonlight, and in that shiny blankness he saw nothing, no hint of the warmth or the vibrancy he had known so well.

"She has been changed, I tell you!" hissed Patrikan in his ear. "The priests have cleared the fog from her mind, so that the sight of you turns her stomach, and all knowledge of your intimacy has been excised from her memory!"

What else had they taken from her? As Gloryian turned and, trancelike, walked back into her rooms, Kerrick could think of nothing else to say, no words that would bring her back. The wraithlike image of white silk vanished into the shadows as strong hands grasped his forearms and began to drag him along the ground.

"This is how you repay me? By consorting with the first daughter of an Elder House?"

King Nethas betrayed no emotion in his face, nor did his voice reveal any trace of anger. Nevertheless, Kerrick recoiled from the words, felt a tremendous guilt. How was it that he had never imagined this, never stopped to reflect how his actions would seem to the king—to this elven patriarch who had given Kerrick shelter and direction in the years of his young adulthood, who had offered him a place to belong and thrive, when his parents had been claimed by the sea?

Now he, Kerrick, had betrayed that trust.

"I'm sorry, Sire—I—"

"Silence!" The regal elf, his eyes arching dispassionately, gestured to Waykand Isletter and Patrikan Diradar. "What punishment do you suggest?"

"He is not fit to live," declared the younger elf, Gloryian's affronted suitor, "but I know that we are not barbarians, not a people who put our own to death. So I want him banished forever. Yes, banished—brand him a dark elf!"

"I agree—his name and memory should be wiped from the People's lives. A dark elf!" Patrikan was as vehement as the nobleman.

Kerrick slumped hopelessly within the arms of his two captors. There could be no worse fate for a Silvanesti than such condemnation. A dark elf was forever exiled, and even his name was stricken from the memories of his people, never to be uttered again.

"A dark elf . . . dark indeed is his shame," Nethas declared. "Nevertheless, such a fate I would not recommend for a transgression such as his. It would cheapen the punishment to use it to address such a tawdry affair, such a pathetic malefactor."

Nethas fixed Kerrick with two eyes that were suddenly cold and narrowed, emotionless as a serpent's. The young elf saw no trace of the kindness, patience, and beneficence he had known for so many years. The king laughed, a dry and ironic sound, and Kerrick knew that he had damaged himself in ways that could never be repaired.

"You will leave Silvanesti, but not as a dark elf. No, we shall remember your family, for the folly you illustrate in so many ways. For our mistake in elevating one of such wild roots to a station above your place, for your own foolishness in thinking that your treachery might go undetected, and for the grand folly that your father showed, when he took his wife and crew and journeyed the way of the gods, all on a quest of pure madness. Now you shall be scarred in shame, shown as the outcast you are."

"Sire, I beg the honor of marking the elf, so that he may be known to all." Waykand Isleletter had his hand on the hilt of his sword.

"Do so," replied the king with a curt nod.

The steel blade whipped past Kerrick's face. He felt the tear, the searing pain, and clapped his hand to the side of his head, where blood flowed copiously from the slashed cartilage and skin.

On the ground, now a pathetic scrap, lay the pointed tip of his ear, the graceful taper characteristic of elves. Kerrick moaned, a drawn out sigh of agony that rose from his spiritual torment as much as any physical suffering.

"Enough," said the king, grimacing at the sight of the mutilated flesh, waving to a servant. "Clean this up. Set him to the sea, with his boat enchanted away from our shores and lands. He is banished from Silvanesti!"

"Forever?" croaked the bleeding elf, finally finding his voice.

The king, half turned away already, paused and looked back. He pursed his lips, and for the first time a trace of humor entered his eyes. But it was a cruel humor, and Kerrick was afraid.

"Let us say, not forever, not necessarily," said the king. "No, you shall have a condition more appropriate to your folly and to your father's legacy. Surely you have wondered, as even did I, what if he was right? What if there is a land of gold, a way for us to obtain that precious metal without gaining it at the expense of the Kingpriest's profits? It would be a worthy find, a treasure that could restore Silvanesti to the richness that is our due.

"So you shall have this chance, this condition: If your father was right, and *if* you can prove the same, then, and only then, may you return to Silvanesti." The king nodded, a tight smile relishing the private joke of his wisdom. His last words came over his royal shoulder, as Nethas started back to his chambers.

"So go to sea, Kerrick Fallabrine—and bring me the secret of your father's gold."

3

A Prince of Suderhold

nock down the walls—break up the tools and the kayaks—slash the hulls and search the huts. Load anything of value onto the galley. The rest, we burn!"

Grimwar Bane's voice roared through the village as the ogre prince strode among the low, round huts. Everywhere his brutal raiders hurried to obey, a hundred hulking warriors scattering through the community, while at Grimwar's heels the dwarf Baldruk Dinmaker all but jogged to keep up with his master.

"Here, at least, the human scum showed some fight," said the prince in satisfaction as he looked over the ragged bodies, many of them still bleeding, scattered haphazardly across the flat, gravel beach where they had died.

"It is indeed a great victory, Majesty. I would go so far as to say that the Arktos people have been destroyed for once and for all."

The ogre drew a deep breath and snorted through his broad nostrils, knowing he should be satisfied but aware that there was still a vague sense of unease lurking in his mind. Impatiently he shook his head and flexed his long, muscular arms.

He reminded himself that he was a a mighty ogre leader,

heir to a kingdom that had survived five thousand years. His lineage could be traced to a time when Krynn had been ruled by his proud race, when humans and elves were mere irritants on the carapace of a world belonging to Grimwar Bane's ancestors.

The prince of Suderhold was a splendid example of that heritage. A strapping bull ogre, Grimwar was tall and broad bodied, with fists like hammerheads and legs as sturdy as tree trunks. His mouth was exceptionally wide, a trait of favor among ogre males, boasting a lower jaw jutting proudly forward to display two magnificent tusks. Each of these ivory cones was fully four inches long and inlaid with golden wire. Across his shoulders was a cloak of white bearskin, a long pelt covering his upper arms and extending all the way to the ground. His boots were black, made from thick whaleskin and rising higher than his knees.

He wore a golden plate across his chest, a metal disk so heavy that a strong human would have buckled under its weight. That breastplate was secured by four chains of thick golden links, extending over and under his shoulders to meet in the middle of his back. At his side, suspended by another heavy chain of gold, hung the Barkon Sword, sacred weapon of his ancestors. This keen blade, five feet long, had carved human and elven flesh since long before the First Dragon War.

"Here, my prince," declared one ogre, coming out of a village hut, a domicile slightly larger than the others. He bore a huge, dark pelt in his arms. "It is the skin of a black bear."

"A black bear?" Grimwar was fascinated. "Never have I seen the like."

The raider held up the fur, which trailed onto the ground even from the height of his upraised arms. The pelt was lush, luxuriously shiny and thick, so much so that the burly ogre strained from the weight of the massive skin.

"It must have been a splendid animal," the prince acknowledged. "That skin shall go in my cabin."

"Perhaps a trophy for the king?" Baldruk suggested.

Grimwar snorted. "My father already has his trophy—a young wife!" He glowered at the thought.

The dwarf smoothly adopted a new tack. "The prisoners of the Arktos from the other villages have spoken about their chieftain . . . he who bears the Black Bear cloak," Baldruk Dinmaker reminded him. "The walrus-man said that this was the village of the chief. No doubt this robe is their talisman. Your capture of it is symbolic of your utter triumph."

"The tusker chief spoke truly," said Grimwar. "The chieftain was slain here today, along with his warriors. We are told this is the last of their accursed villages, are we not?"

"Yes, by the tusker, Urgas Thanoi."

"I believe he speaks the truth," the prince said with a grim chuckle.

"He'd better. Holding the tusker's wives as hostage was a stroke of genius on Your Excellency's part," chortled the dwarf.

"Indeed it was." If the ogre prince had paused for reflection, he would have remembered that Baldruk Dinmaker had been the one to make that suggestion, but such introspection was not in Grimwar Bane's, nor any ogre's, nature. Instead, he cared only to bask in the glow of another successful raid. He turned and roared to two of his warriors standing at the foot of the galley's ramp. "Bring me Urgas Thanoi!"

In moments the walrus-man was hustled onto the shore. Urgas plodded across the beach on his great, flat feet. His tiny dark eyes glowered from the deep folded skin of his face. Two great tusks jutted from his mouth, but he made no move that could be taken as a threat. Even from five paces away, Grimwar Bane smelled the fishy stink of the barbaric creature. How he would be glad to be rid of that smell!

"You have served me well," acknowledged the prince. "I am glad that I spared your tusks. You know, I gave serious thought to having them sawn off.

The thanoi scowled, his leathery face creasing into deep

wrinkles. "It would have been a sentence of death—my tribe would never let me return, thus shamed."

"I have decided to release you back to your tribe and let you return to your stronghold as chieftain. Take care that you remember who is your liege."

"How could I forget, Your Majesty?" If the tusker was being sarcastic, Grimwar couldn't tell. "My wives . . . they will be released, too?"

Grimwar nodded. He had no desire for the company of the three fish-eating cows—they had spent the spring and summer in chains and were a bother to feed.

"I have your assurance that this is the last of their villages, here on the Icereach coast?" the ogre prince asked.

"Yes—you have seen that the shore of the White Bear Sea is but sparsely settled. For all my life, my people have explored in the wilds along here, watching, spying, waiting for a campaign such as you have waged to rid this coast of human scum."

"You have helped us," the prince acknowledged. "The Arktos are finished, and your people shall be rewarded with the right to stay for all time in the citadel set aside as your own."

"Your Excellency is most gracious," said Urgas, with a bow so deep that his tusks touched the ground.

"Yes." Grimwar had several practical reasons for allowing the walrus-men to maintain possession of the ancient fortress across the strait. For one thing, they would harry the few surviving humans, and for another he would have a stronghold of allies on the point of land at the terminus of Icereach.

"With your permission, Sire, my wives and I shall depart at once. We will swim across the strait and bring word of your greatness to the rest of my tribe, which awaits me there. Naturally, we desire to get there well before the release of the Sturmfrost."

"Very well." The prince was secretly relieved. He would have feigned a celebration with the tusker chief and his wives in his mountain fortress, but he could only imagine how bad the place would smell, what with hundreds of oily walrus-men now dwelling there. This was an ally from whom he would be glad to keep his distance. "You may make your departure at once."

The thanoi chieftain waddled away, padding on his flapping feet, while the ogre prince turned his attention to the hills rising above the coastal village.

"We found only men here, hunters and warriors. There must be survivors, their families, up there, somewhere," said Baldruk Dinmaker. The dwarf stretched as he leaned back to look slyly up at the ogre prince. His hand, still holding the deadly weapon he so jauntily named "Snik," gestured toward the rocky hills rising beyond the little coastal village.

"Bah," Grimwar Bane snorted. "We killed enough men. Let the women try to survive through a winter if they wish. It's not worth the trouble to pursue them. Besides . . ." He chuckled at a thought that made him feel rather clever. "If some of those wenches are taken in by the Highlanders, they will spread the tale of our raids. I would like for the rest of these humans to fear me."

"Fear you they shall, Excellency," agreed the dwarf. "I daresay the name of Grimwar Bane will bring terror into human hearts for generations to come."

The prince scowled. It was his deepest desire that there be no more human generations, no humans at all—except for slaves of ogrekind—in this great expanse of land that was his ancestral kingdom. To this end he had embarked on the brutal campaign that had lasted these past four months, a series of lightning attacks and several particularly satisfying massacres, culminating in this bloody landing that had so thoroughly shattered the main camp of humans.

He knew, though, that, even though the coastal-dwelling Arktos had been decimated, more of the humans lived in the inland hills and mountains. These warlike Highlanders dwelt in fortified towns and were beyond the reach of his galley. He vowed to himself that they, too, would eventually be exterminated, but that would require long, grueling years of war.

Now his thoughts turned to home, and he pictured his own wife, the stern high priestess Staric ber Glacierheim ber Bane. What dire prophecies, what bleak warnings, would she have for him when he returned?

Another thought—the voluptuous new bride so recently taken by his father—brought a deeper frown to the prince's face. When this kind of temper swept over him all of his underlings except Baldruk Dinmaker left him alone. The other ogres drifted away, and the prince of Suderhold stood alone with his dwarven adviser in the village center, watching with vague displeasure while his minions went about sacking and destroying.

"Search among the fallen! Find me one who still lives!" the ogre prince called impulsively. "I would question a prisoner."

As if he had been waiting for just that suggestion, one of the ogres gave a shout as he stooped to enter a hut. Cursing, he backed away and plucked a harpoon out of his thigh. Fortunately, the weapon had been thrust weakly, barely puncturing his skin. With an indignant snort the ogre bent double and reached into the small abode. A moment later he rose with a squirming, pathetic figure held in his arms. The prisoner was an old man, and when the warrior brought him to Grimwar and set him down the fellow collapsed weakly to the ground.

"An old human, Majesty," reported the raider proudly. "'Was hiding in that little hut—legs don't work."

The poor cripple tried to crawl away from Grimwar, but the younger ogre kicked him around so that the wretch could only stare upward piteously at the prince. Grimwar knew that he made an impressive, even awesome, sight to a human. He puffed out his massive chest, feeling the solid weight of the golden breastplate, allowing the dazzling metal to reflect pale sunlight into the human's eyes.

"Have you seen any elves here?" demanded the prince.

For a moment the man looked blank, then scowled and shook his head. "Who ever heard of an elf in Icereach?" he demanded.

The ogre who had captured the man cuffed him across the head, a blow that knocked him prone. "Be silent when you answer the prince!" he roared.

Grimwar suppressed a sigh, but didn't point out the illogic of his underling's command. Instead, he waited for the man to push himself back to a sitting position. The prince couldn't help being impressed by the fellow's spirit—even after such a blow, the human glared with defiance. Though he was an old man, he still had a warrior's glint in his eye.

"You know nothing of any elves?"

The man's laugh was dry and humorless. "If you mean, 'have I ever in my life seen an elf?' I can tell you 'no.' Nor have I heard of any elf in this part of the world—they live far across the sea to the north, as any fool would know."

The prince held up his hand before his raider could land another blow as punishment for the man's insolence.

"Tell me about precious stones, then. Why are you people so poor? There have been but a few coins, buckles, and the like among all your wretched villages! Why, do you have so little care for things like gold?"

"Gold? Do I look like I have any need of gold?" The man contemptuously cast his hands over himself, and the prince took note of his ragged leather clothing, the lack of any ornamentation. He didn't even have a belt buckle—his pants were supported by a belt of frayed rope, tied in a knot at his waist.

"No, for gold you must seek the Highlanders. Talk to their king—he will tell you of gold mines, and then, undoubtedly, he will kill you!"

Grimwar turned away. The first answer pleased him. The second did not. He nodded at Baldruk, who was already holding Snik at the ready. The prince stalked toward the beach, the prisoner already forgotten. Moments later the dwarf, huffing into a jog, caught up with him.

"Where did the damned clouds go?" snorted Baldruk, using his hand to shield his eyes from the sun he hated so much.

This was something the ogre prince had never learned to understand: How could someone hate the sun? He himself pined for a mere glimpse of it during the span of winter, three to four months of frigid night that always seemed to last longer than the whole rest of the year combined. When he was outside, under the open sky, Grimwar resented every shred of cloud that blocked the precious brightness. This dwarf, born in the distant underground realm he called Thorbardin, was forever griping and shading himself.

"Again we hear of this Highlander king," mused the prince. "Perhaps it is true that the humans in the mountains know of more gold mines."

"Indeed, Sire. They would be worth a campaign in a future year."

"Yes. Perhaps we will commence that next spring. And for now, there is no sign of any elf. That is good news."

"You are still worried about the prophecy made by the high priestess, your wife, aren't you?" guessed Baldruk.

"Do not discount the wisdom and the warnings of Gonnas the Strong," Grimwar warned. Especially as interpreted by the stern high priestess Stariz ber Bane, wife of the crown prince, he added to himself.

"I would never imply disrespect to the god of your ancestors," the dwarf said hastily, "but perhaps the warning refers to a threat that has already been neutralized."

"My wife did not think so," Grimwar noted. With a little shiver of nervousness he pictured her in full ceremonial regalia. Stariz ber Bane was a forbidding woman physically, as large as the prince himself at fully four hundred pounds and seven feet of height, his equal in short-tempered stubbornness. When she wore her obsidian mask with its tusked, bestial visage, when she was surrounded by smoke and incense, her appearance was as frightening as anything Grimwar had ever seen. As high priestess of the ancient ogre god, Gonnas the Strong, who was also known as the Willful One, she was prone to casting stones and working auguries, announcing various predictions from a fierce and vengeful deity.

Furthermore, these divinations had a way of proving surprisingly accurate. It had been Stariz who predicted that Grimwar's father, the king, would banish his first wife, the Elder Queen, to distant Dracoheim. And she had seen that he would then, quickly, take a beautiful young mate in her place. These events, as Grimwar knew only too well, had come to pass. He asked himself silently, why did that young wife have to be Thraid Dimmarkull?

However, it was a recent prophecy that had been on his mind this summer.

" 'Beware the Elven Messenger,' my wife told me, 'for he brings your doom to Icereach.' I would mock her faith, and mine, if I took her warning lightly."

"Of course," the dwarf agreed unctuously. "But look, Sire, the tide has turned. Shall we put to sea?"

The king nodded, still struggling with a vague discontent. He looked at *Goldwing*, knowing that the great ship's hold was crammed with slaves—hundreds of humans they would take back to Glacierheim, many of whom had been imprisoned below decks for months. Their numbers made this the most profitable campaign against humans in the memory of any ogre. Yet when he paused on the ramp leading to the galley's deck, his eyes involuntarily shifted back to the land, and followed the rugged crest of mountainous horizon rising a dozen miles behind the beach.

In his mind he saw Highlanders and elves, gold and more humans, and war.

4

Moreen Seal-Slayer

She held the harpoon against the ground and remained utterly silent, completely still. Her quarry, a sleek, fat gulf seal, was sunning itself on a flat rock above the lapping surf, an instant's wiggle away from deep water. Moreen knew that she would get one cast, and success or failure would determine whether sixty people had a substantial meal tonight, or—once again—would have to make do with a few greens plucked from the banks of the coastal streams and whatever shellfish and mussels they could scrape off the flat beach.

What would they do in the winter when the Sturmfrost descended upon them and survival out of doors became all but impossible? That question, had come to dominate her thoughts, but she roughly pushed her fears aside. Later she would try to find an answer for the future. Right now, she had to worry about tonight's dinner.

With deliberate motions she advanced her right hand and the harpoon, then the left hand, then each knee in turn, crawling closer to her prey. Abruptly the seal lifted its head, dark eyes alert, one seeming to fix itself on the human woman who was still fifty feet away, too far away for an effective cast. Moreen heard barking from up the beach, other seals out of sight behind the rock, squabbling and complaining.

Finally her intended prey laid down its head once again to bask in the warmth of the midsummer sun. The huntress resumed her cautious approach, watching the tundra before her, careful not to scrape a rock or crush a brittle willow twig. The soft wind came off the sea, safely carrying her scent away from her quarry.

Inch by inch, foot by foot, she wormed her way closer . . . forty, now thirty feet. The flat coastal ground was so wet that water soaked right through her leather pants, and her knees felt cold and sodden. Her neck grew stiff from holding her head upright, but her alertness paid off. She froze just in time as the seal again lifted its head. This time, when the animal settled into its drowsy repose, she was ready to act.

Gradually, she rose up to a kneeling position, until her back was straight, her throwing hand cocked. The smooth stretch of the harpoon, with its keen ivory tip floating almost weightless before her, was parallel to the ground, at the same height as her ear.

Now all of her care, all of her skill, her hunger, her desperation, came into sharp focus. The target seemed to grow before her, a warm heart pulsing beneath that black, shiny coat, and for just a moment she felt a powerful connection, almost as if the seal's blood was flowing through her body. She made a soundless prayer to Chislev, a whisper of gratitude for this opportunity, and a plea for steadiness and true aim.

She let fly. The harpoon sailed through the air even as the animal, alerted by the sound of her throw, flipped toward the water. The ivory head pierced the wriggling body, and Moreen sprang to her feet and hauled on the thin line wrapped around her wrist, the sturdy cord attached to the barbed head of the harpoon.

The seal was gone by the time she reached the rock, but when she looked in the water she saw that her aim had been true. The animal floated, lifeless, in a murk of blood. Quickly she pulled upward, wincing as the animal's dead weight came free from the sea.

"Eighty pounds, I'll bet you are," Moreen said. "Thanks be to Chislev Wilder. The Arktos will eat well tonight."

Only then did her eyes fall on the beach exposed behind this seal's rocky perch. She was not surprised to see dozens of seals there—the sounds of their barking had suggested as much to her already. Surprisingly, though, several of them were very close to her vantagepoint. This seal had been killed cleanly and had died without barking a warning.

Swiftly she lowered herself to the ground, out of sight of the animals. Methodically she started to coil the cord. Taking only the time to clean the head of her harpoon, she started crawling forward again.

"Five more seals?" Bruni's broad face split into a disbelieving grin. "Praise to Moreen Seal-Slayer!"

"They're all gutted—about a half a mile up the coast, behind a big flat rock," Moreen said, staggering under the load of the one animal she had carried back with her. Exhausted, she dropped the cleaned carcass and collapsed to the ground, suddenly feeling weak in every limb, every muscle.

"Rest yourself—we'll get the others," Bruni said cheerfully. "I'll carry two. C'mon Tildey, Garta, Little Mouse. Let's go get dinner." The big woman pushed herself to her feet. Accompanied by her three willing helpers, she started up the shore at quick pace. From her waist, hung the heavy stone hammer she had found in the rubble of the village after the ogre attack. Since that day Bruni was never seen without her favorite weapon close to reach.

"Did you really get six seals?" asked Feathertail, wide-eyed, as she came up to stare at the gutted animal.

Moreen nodded tiredly. "Would you like to learn how to skin it?"

A cluck of sound drew Moreen's attention. Dinekki was hobbling toward her, shaking her head and making a *tsk-tsk* noise over and over.

"She has to learn sometime," Moreen said, wondering what the elderly shaman wanted.

"Well, of *course* she does," Dinekki agreed readily, "but there are plenty of us who can teach her that. Why, I myself used to know how to use a skinning knife, before my hands got all knotted up like a sun-dried cord." She inspected her wrinkled and knobby fingers with a scowl.

"Can I learn how to skin the seal?" Feathertail asked tentatively.

"Didn't I just say you could?" snapped Dinekki, though an affectionate light in her eye softened the rebuke. "Hilgrid, you have a sharp knife, don't you?"

Hilgrid, who was stretching out a pelt from the seal Moreen had killed yesterday, smiled and nodded. "Just a minute, Feather. I'll show you how to do it. You know, if Moreen keeps hunting with so much success, I'm going to need to teach someone how to preserve these pelts also."

"You," Dinekki said, glaring down at Moreen, who wanted only to close her eyes and loll on the soft tundra for the last hour of daylight. "You must come with me."

Knowing better than to argue, the huntress pushed herself to her feet and followed the shaman up a gentle slope, toward the small niche in a cliff wall, where the Arktos had collected the few meager belongings they had brought with them away from ravaged Bayguard.

Moreen sighed as she entered the scant shelter beneath the overhanging rock. She saw a pile of straight sticks off to the side, next to a stack of sealskin pelts, the few that had been overlooked by the ogre raiders. There were some skins full of fresh water, a couple of clay pots containing whale oil, a pile of ivory harpoon and spearheads that the survivors had scavenged from the broken weapons left behind by the attackers.

Just outside the shelter, three sealskins were drying on racks, pelts that had been cleaned and mounted by Hilgrid from animals that Moreen had stalked during the past two weeks. During that time, ever since the tribe had abandoned their ancestral home and moved to this rocky enclave ten miles up the coast, they had managed to increase their reserve of food supplies. Moreen's hunting prowess,

Tildey's skill with the bow, and the wealth of bounty from the sea and beach, had yielded perhaps twice as much provender as the tribe needed for the short term, but it was still not enough for the long, hard winter ahead.

"How are we ever going to last the winter!" Moreen declared, trying unsuccessfully to keep the despair out of her voice.

"There are some who say we should go back to Bayguard, try and make shelter from the ruins of our houses," Dinekki said, neutrally. "Or go live in the Hiding Hole."

Moreen's face flushed, and she shook her head violently. Her mind burned with the memory of her mother, staked to the ground by an ogre spear, and of her father whimpering and thrashing and dying.

"That place is cursed forever!" she snapped. "The ghosts of our ancestors will stalk the winter night there!"

Dinekki nodded, still noncommittal. "Truly, the ogres left us so little that I can see no benefit to returning there, even if the ghosts choose to leave us alone."

Moreen turned to look outward, her gaze falling across the Arktos who were gathered across the flowered hillside below. The blue water of the gulf sparkled beyond. Here and there young children played, while several women stood along the banks of a nearby creek, fishing spears raised. A few of the elders scoured the beach, collecting such clams and crabs as they could, protein-rich morsels that would add variety and nourishment to the tribe's diet.

"We're finding enough to eat, day by day," she said quietly. "Now we'll have some extra seal-meat—some to smoke and preserve for winter. But I would have to kill six seals *every* day to store up enough food for the winter, even if we manage to find shelter from the Sturmfrost. You and I both know what our chances are like!"

"Yes, we know these things, and other things as well," replied the shaman. "We know that it was a very good thing that Redfist Bayguard taught his daughter how to hunt. We know that we were fortunate that you were up on the hill, that you saw the ogre ship in time to for many of us to reach the Hiding Hole—"

"Time for what?" demanded Moreen. "So that we can starve and freeze in the cold season, instead of perishing swiftly under ogre spears?" She saw the old woman stiffen and she immediately regretted her harsh tone. "I'm sorry, Grandmother," she said meekly. "I do not rebuke you, I rebuke myself."

"A good thing that is," clucked Dinekki, "else I should be tempted to rebuke you back, and I am getting too old for such foolish exertion."

"You asked me to come up here. What did you want?" Moreen said, feeling weariness wash over her again.

"Fill this bowl with water, clean water," Dinekki said, gesturing toward one of the ceramic vessels, "and bring it over to me."

By the time Moreen had followed the shaman's instructions, Dinekki had started a small fire, using nothing but rocks for fuel. Her fire-magic was a gift of the goddess Chislev, Moreen knew, and it was a power that the tribe relied on heavily in their unforested land, where wood was precious and rare.

The old woman sat cross-legged before her blaze, her eyes closed, her toothless gums mumbling some kind of chant that seemed more like half-chewing and half-grunting. Moreen sat down on the other side of the fire, holding the water bowl patiently, knowing enough not to interrupt Dinekki's concentration.

"What is your question?" Dinekki asked abruptly, without opening her eyes.

"My question?" Moreen was caught off guard. "I have lots of questions!"

"What is your *question*?" repeated the shaman, holding out her hands, swaying her head back and forth while she continued chewing and grunting.

Moreen handed the bowl across the fire, letting the flames warm her hands for a moment, and thought carefully before she replied.

"How can we make ourselves safe before the advent of the Sturmfrost?"

Instantly Dinekki inverted the bowl, sending the water cascading across the fire to spatter and sizzle on the rocks. A cloud of steam billowed up, moist warmth enveloping the two women, wetting Moreen's skin and suddenly obscuring her vision.

"Look!" urged the shaman. "Look into the vapor. Tell me what you see!"

Moreen wanted to cry out, to object that all she could see was a cloud of stinging steam, but then her eyes discerned vague shapes, white tufts of vapor bending and curling unnaturally. The steam flowed away, formed a column trailing up the coast. "It's heading north, I see," she said. She saw a wrinkled face glaring at her from inside the mist, brutish eyes perched above a broad snout and two long, curling tusks. "I see a thanoi," she added quickly.

"A direction, and a warning," Dinekki said grimly. "There is danger on our path, danger from the walrus-men. Look more, and remember what you see!"

"I see a wrinkled line, bending around, twisting this way and that. It's a pathway, water on one side, hills on the other . . . this coast!" Moreen recognized the bay where she had lived all of her life, where she had watched her parents die, and, following the line of shore northward toward their shallow cave, she noted the flat beach where she had just slain the seals.

"What is the coast telling you?" Dinekki pressed.

Straining her eyes to see into the murk, the younger woman watched an image take shape. "The picture . . . leads northward along the coastline," she said. "To the farthest hunting grounds ever mapped. . . . I see trees . . . a whole forest of them. . . . It must be Tall Cedar Bay! My father took me there, once."

"Keep looking. Do you see all the way to Ice End?"

Ice End was the legendary end of the world, the place where the rocky terrain of Icereach plunged into deep gray ocean waters, leading only to limitless and uncharted roiling waves.

Even as these thoughts assailed her, she realized that the magical image was not taking her so far north as that terminus. "I see a sparkle of yellow, golden light on the coast . . . a glimpse of a smoking mountain. Farther down, I see sparks of red, flaring here and there. And more . . . steam?" She blinked, trying to clear her vision, but it wasn't steam she was seeing. "No, it's a picture of steam, of warmth rising up from the ground!"

Dinekki nodded. With her *harrumph* the vapors, the steam of the shaman's casting, faded into the air, wafting from the shelter on a tiny breath of breeze, leaving Moreen feeling strangely hot and breathless. She looked at the older woman quizzically.

"What does the vision mean?"

"It means," the shaman said with no trace of hesitation, "that you must lead us northward along the coast. Our hopes for survival will be found where you saw the golden light."

"Steam coming out of the ground? What is that supposed to mean?" Moreen had never heard of such a thing.

"Remember the old legends," Dinekki chided. "The tales you learned as a little girl."

"I remember the tale of Ice End, the stormy point at the end of the world. Another story says Ice End is *not* the real end of the world but the beginning of something else. Is that what you mean?" Somewhere to the far north, according to the legends of her girlhood, there was vast land, a place where ogres and humans lived among dwarves, elves, and giants, all squabbling for control. "How can Ice End save us?"

"Yes, how?" echoed the shaman.

Another childhood story came back to her, a vague legend dismissed by some elders. "I remember hearing about a place, a citadel where the Arktos once dwelled, protected from ogres by a gate, by hall walls . . . a place that was warm even through the long winter, snug and safe against the

Sturmfrost. That was the place the people once lived, long before the Scattering."

"Brackenrock," Dinekki confirmed with a pleased nod. "The place that was heated by steam, steam that burst forth from frozen ground."

"Surely that place isn't real?"

"Better to ask, where is this place?'" the shaman retorted sharply.

"Are you saying that it really exists—a place where we could be warm, even in the depths of the Sturmfrost?"

"Aren't you listening?"

She tried to think. "I remember the old song. It was something about serpents breathing fire. Yes—crimson monsters flying from the sky. They came and claimed Brackenrock for themselves, and the tribe fled, spreading across all of Icereach."

Finally Dinekki's lips crinkled into a hint of a smile. "Yes. I sang that song to you and some of the others when you were but babies. I had hopes that you, of them all, might remember my song."

"How did the song go? Was there really a place called Brackenrock, where monsters drove our ancestors away?"

Dinekki nodded. "They were called dragons, dragons of red scales. They came from the north, and claimed the fortress Brackenrock for their own, as comfort against the Sturmfrost. They breathed fire and killed many of our people. The rest, ancestors to you and me, they drove from the ancient citadel, scattering them across Icereach. This is a true song."

"No one alive has ever seen these red dragons!"

"Nor white dragons or dragons of any other color, either. Yet it is believed that at the time of the Scattering there were other dragons here, as well . . . dragons of white. Such serpents relished the cold and were the masters of Icereach until the red dragons, which were even mightier in power, came."

"If these red dragons mastered the whites and drove our ancestors from Brackenrock, what makes you think it would be safe or wise to go back there?"

"Because," Dinekki said with a wink, and a sly smile, "I think there are no more dragons. I think they are gone from the world. All this was long, long ago."

Moreen snorted skeptically, but she was intrigued. "Why do you think this?"

"Well, there are many beasts of legend recounted among our people. There are stories of ogres, that we know to be true. The Ice Worm, called Remorhaz—my own father saw one—it killed his brother and two companions. Also we know of great bears—even have a proof of the black bear, slain by your own great-grandfather. But dragons? Even old Chantarik, who was an ancient shaman when I was a girl, had never heard of anyone who had glimpsed them. Oh, to be sure they existed, once. They must have, from all the stories and songs, but by my reckoning they vanished from Krynn many lifetimes ago."

"Are you sure enough to lead us to this legendary place?"

"Oh, you will do the leading. Brackenrock is a real place, and closer to here than Ice End. There might be danger there, and we might never reach the place, but it is a worthy goal, worth the chance."

"And the dragons?"

"In my spell I sought dragons, and found only ancient bone and scattered remains of scales. Chislev revealed to me that there are no dragons in Brackenrock. I do not know about the rest of the world."

"But . . ." Even as she spoke, Moreen knew that she had already accepted Dinneki's challenge. "What about the thanoi?" she asked.

Dinekki shrugged. "There will be danger. We will know more about the danger when we encounter it. Now, the question is this: Are you prepared to lead the Arktos on such a march to Brackenrock?"

"Yes," Moreen declared with sudden, honest hope. "Yes, I am."

For the time being she did not speak of their ultimate destination but instead encouraged the tribe to simply keep heading north. Everyone knew there were groves of trees in the north, and with the goal of Tall Cedar Bay as shelter—and as a source of limitless firewood—the Arktos continued their journey with all the speed and enthusiasm Moreen could desire.

The little tribe made its way roughly parallel to the coast, sometimes marching inland to follow hillcrests around the boggy salt marshes that were so common along the Icereach shore. At other times they came down from the heights to march along the smooth beach. The months of the midnight sun were waning. Though daylight lingered for many hours each day, the sun remained close to the northern horizon, the light often filtering through a haze of clouds and mist.

A few of the women—usually Moreen, Bruni, and Tildey, though a score of others took turns in this job as well—proceeded the tribe by a half mile, roaming with care, searching the route for signs of danger. Seven days after departing their temporary cave, they had encountered nothing more belligerent than an aggressive bull seal that didn't care to allow trespassers on its beach. That brief combat yielded a dinner of rich, fresh meat and a large, handsome pelt to add to the tribe's growing bundle of furs.

Spirits were high. The day after they battled the big seal, they came upon a small group of Arktos, survivors from the Goosepond Clan. These told a tale much similar to the Bayguards—the ogres in their great rowing ship had set upon them from the sea, killing many, carrying others away as prisoners. The fifteen Goosepond women and children were nearly starved and gratefully accepted the comfort and company of Moreen's clan. After partaking of a fine feast, they joined in the northward trek.

"We're lucky, in a way, that the ogres left us so little,"

Dinekki said with a wry chuckle as she joined Moreen on a rocky headland and gazed ahead at the approaching stretch of shoreline. "Otherwise, how would we carry it all?"

Though she hobbled awkwardly, her posture bent, her weight supported by her staff, the old shaman never showed signs of slowness or age. The coast was rugged and precipitous, and again and again they had to curve inland to avoid the steep-walled ravines that regularly plunged to the sea.

Moreen looked back at the file of her people, carrying their waterskins and few weapons. They carried dried meat suspended on sticks, while some of the stronger females carried bulky bundles of furs, in addition to the few spears and harpoons they had saved.

They started along a pathway that followed the edge of a high bluff. Moreen's eyes drifted toward the horizon, where the setting sun lingered. All too soon, she knew, that warm orb would vanish for the long, dark winter, and within days of that disappearance they would face the brutal, lethal onslaught of the Sturmfrost.

She couldn't help but wonder: Would the Arktos ever see another spring?

Bruni came up to join them, the big woman actually dwarfed by the great pack on her shoulders. Still, she climbed the hill with an easy, rolling gait and pointed inland as soon as she joined her two tribemates. "Look there," she said, with an urgency that broke through Moreen's reverie.

"What?"

"Men . . . six of them, just coming onto the next summit."

Moreen saw them now, little spots of movement with pale, heavily bearded faces and fur cloaks that blended smoothly into the brown terrain. "Highlanders!" she guessed, as one of the men raised a hand in a slow, ceremonial wave. "They want to parley."

The man who had gestured broke away from his companions and hastened down the slope of the hill with one of his fellows advancing a few steps behind. The other four remained standing, watching from the summit.

"Come with me," Moreen said, starting down from their own elevation at a pace she calculated would meet the Highlander at the shallow stream below. Bruni descended too, as her escort. As the strangers drew closer, Moreen saw that the first man was wearing a large wolfskin cloak. The head of the creature, with jaws split to bare white teeth, rested as a cap on his skull. Eyes of golden nuggets gleamed from the animal's sockets, while the man's face was masked by a beard of rusty red. His hair, in two long braids of the same color, dangled from beneath the wolfjaw cap all the way down his muscular chest.

The Highlander halted on the bank of the opposite stream, and Moreen came to a stop just across the quiet, shallow waterway. The second man, who bore a heavy spear and a shield, stood a few paces behind his leader, while Bruni quietly took the same position behind the chieftain's daughter.

"Greetings. I am called Lars Redbeard of Guilderglow." The Highlander's accent was thick but intelligible, his tone friendly but neutral. "I bring you salutations from Strongwind Whalebone, King of Icereach."

Moreen snorted contemptuously at the thought of anyone arrogant enough to consider himself king of all the known world. "I am Moreen Seal-Slayer of the Arktos. What does Strongwind Whalebone have to say to me?"

Lars bowed stiffly. "Strongwind Whalebone has heard of the sufferings faced by your tribe. He knows of the ogre cruelty, and he wants you to come to him in Guilderglow. He commands an audience."

"Commands?" Moreen's temper flared. "Who is he, to give me commands? Tell your 'king'—" she spat the world with clear mockery "—that I take orders from no one, not ogre nor Highlander."

"No!" Lars Redbeard looked dismayed, and shook his head. "You don't understand. He wants to talk—"

"He can talk all he wants to!" she replied, infuriated,

"but he should not dare to presume I will listen! We are proud Arktos and Goosepond people. Now, get out of our way—and let us continue on our path!"

"I cannot tell him this!" the emissary protested.

"Tell him to come here, and I will tell him myself!" snapped Moreen. Trembling in rage, she turned her back and left the Highlander gaping in disbelief.

5

A River To Exile

A vague grayness seeping through his swollen eyelids suggested that the hour was past dawn. Kerrick felt the gentle rocking of the deck, but for a blessed moment couldn't recall how he had come to be aboard his boat. Even without opening his eyes, he knew this was *Cutter* beneath him—perhaps it was the smell of the fresh varnish or some subconscious awareness that he was, at least for the time being, safe.

He tried to open his eyes and failed, the effort sending jolts of pain stabbing through his forehead. When he lifted his arm he groaned aloud at the agony, a broken rib jabbing him in the side, and with that sensation his memory, his anguish, came flooding back.

Finally one eyelid cracked open. It was daylight, and he lay on deck, though a heavy overcast thankfully muted the full painful glare of the sun. Without moving, he became aware of a gentle shift in orientation, as the boat spun gradually in the arms of an inexorable current.

"The anchor?" He croaked the words aloud, realizing he was adrift. The resulting sense of alarm was enough for him to push himself upward to a sitting position. Each movement provoked overpowering sensations of pain, but at last he could rest his head against the bulkhead and look across the deck, out over the waters of the Than-Thalas River.

He quickly realized that it wasn't the sky that was overcast, for the gray haze extended down to the water. Instead, something else was obscuring his vision. It was not a cloud, or even a thick fog—rather it was like a heavy layer of gauze draped across the world. Wincing, he rubbed his eyes, breaking dried blood free, finally opening both and blinking.

Everything was masked by a bizarre gray haze.

Magic! He remembered then: the king's wizards, chanting powerful words, weaving spells with their supple fingers, wrapping a cloak of sorcery around the sailboat as she stood at anchor in Silvanost Harbor. Kerrick had lain on the deck, gasping. Somewhere in the distance Waykand Isletter was laughing, taunting, jeering at the young sailor while the enchanters worked their arts.

Just before that he had been heaved into the waters of the harbor by guards of House Protector, a group of rough-handed fellows who had hauled him down from the palace. They chose to douse him close to the fishing sheds, in water that was foully polluted. Somehow he had bobbed up amidst fish guts and scales and slime, his broken rib hurting with each flailing movement. Kerrick had no memories of climbing aboard his boat, nor did he recall who had cut the anchor. A glance toward the bow showed him that the iron weight had been hoisted aboard. Perhaps he had done so himself in a daze.

Peering toward the riverbank, he could barely make out a horizon of lofty towers, crystalline bridges, and verdant, rolling hills crowned with marbled mansions. He knew there were brilliant flowered gardens cascading down those hillsides, though the magical cloak around his boat seemed to sap the view of every hint of vibrant color. Somehow *Cutter* had drifted out of the harbor, and the current was carrying him away from the island of Silvanost, a disabled passenger on the river's eternal course toward the sea.

Grimly, gasping in pain as tears stung his eyes, the elf

forced himself to his knees and finally, with his hands clutching the cabin for support, onto his feet. Already he was several miles below the city, moving into water surging with implacable force, propelled vigorously as the two branches of the river reunited below the island city. The Than-Thalas was nearly a mile wide here, and he seemed to be roughly near the middle of the expanse. With each pain-wracked breath, the city that he loved was falling farther and farther behind.

"No!"

He all but screamed the word. They wanted him banished, exiled from their lives and their land, but maybe he could fight them! There were many places he could come ashore, countless small villages in the great forest where no one would know him, where he would be able to recuperate among his own kind. Somehow, someday, he would figure out a way to return to the city—but at least, until then, he would be close by. Lunging into the stern, he grabbed the tiller in his hands, and tried to shift the steering lever. But the gods-cursed thing was stuck—he couldn't get it to budge.

That exertion proved costly, as his guts suddenly heaved. He leaned his face over the side, retching into the blue-green water barely a foot below his face. With each convulsion the broken rib jabbed at him, until Kerrick fell sobbing and exhausted and flat on his back. All he could see now was that strangely hazy sky, with the tall mast poking like a naked tree trunk straight into the air.

The sail! Again he forced himself to his feet, for the first time noting that there was a significant breeze pushing up from the south. If he could raise some canvas he could capture that wind, use it to slow or divert his course. Yet once more the agony seized him, twisted his insides, rendering him all but immobile.

Doubled over in pain, he thought about the weight of the sail, the lines he would need to hold, and he realized the effort was beyond his strength.

Stumbling toward the cabin, he pulled open the hatch

and plunged into the small compartment, staying low as he moved past the cramped galley. His eyes adjusted to the darkness, as, again exhausted by the effort, he slumped onto a bench. It took all of his effort just to hold his eyes open against the pain thudding into his skull, rippling through his body.

His bunk occupied the forward quarter of the compartment. To his left was a table holding his charts and documents, but which was just as likely to be used as an eating place. He craved a steaming pot of his precious Istarian tea, but the stove was cold and he didn't have the energy to start a fire.

Kerrick's sword, in its light leather scabbard, hung on a rack above the table, next to his longbow and several quivers of arrows. On the right was the sea chest, his bins of coal, charcoal, and firewood, and several small cupboards containing all of his worldly possessions.

At least, all of those possession that he hadn't left behind in his palace apartment. He snorted, thinking of the favorite things still ashore, of a particular red silk cape, doeskin boots, chains of silver locked in a box of cedar, feather caps and embroidered tunics. With regret he thought of the precious coins he had saved during his decades in the city: three gold pieces in a little pouch, hidden under a floorboard in his house—gone to him, now.

He also remembered the small collection of ladies' gloves under his bed. All right-handed gloves, dainty and perfumed and freely bestowed upon him by his lovers. Gloryian's glove was the prize of his collection, but when he thought about it now the smell of her perfume blurred almost indiscriminately with the fragrances worn by all of his other mistresses.

Oh, he had been quite the rake of Silvanost, at least for a while. He winced as he remembered that life, suddenly and forcibly confronting the fact that he might never be going back there.

Once more he shivered, and he realized that he was still wearing the clothes he had donned for his tryst with

Gloryian Dirardar. They clung to him, scratching and chafing, smelling vaguely of fish entrails. Wrinkling his nose, he kicked off his moccasins, pulled off the silk hose, shrugged out of his woolen shirt and vest. Each movement hurt him, but he took almost a pleasure in the pain, in the shedding of these garments that were like a skin on an earlier body.

He opened his sea chest and laughed bitterly, spotting a red silk cap with its black and white eagle feather sitting carefully atop his practical clothes. He recalled that he had worn that cap recently, when he had brought Glory out to the boat. Afterward, her servant had returned her to shore in the dinghy while Kerrick had napped. When he was ready to go ashore himself, he had swum. Not wanting to damage the plumed hat, he had left it here.

As he dressed, Kerrick relished the comfort of sturdy, dry seafaring garb. He slipped into brown woolen trousers and supple boots, then encased his upper body with a loose cotton shirt. He eschewed the leather gloves and the woolen overshirt—such clothes were essential when he sailed the southern sea, but in the Silvanesti summer they would only be stifling and heavy.

At the bottom of his sea chest was a small strongbox, unlocked, with the key jutting from the latch. He popped it open and regarded the two objects within. One was the ring of gold left to him by his father, the only other legacy, besides *Cutter*, of Dimorian Fallabrine's life. Kerrick touched the wreath of oak leaves emblazoned so meticulously into the curved surface. He had never donned the ring—his father's warning still resonated in his memory—but he treasured it and saved it, and wondered. Someday, if Dimorian had spoken truly, that ring might save his life.

The other thing in the box was a small ivory tube, with a scroll of parchment inside—a scroll with writing he had committed to memory. Absentmindedly, he took the scroll tube and slipped it into his pocket. Still aching, he decided to brew some tea. An hour later, after nursing two mugs of thc pungent, invigorating draught, he wondered if it might be possible to raise the sail.

He still felt pain, but it was manageable, no longer crippling. Once more he stepped through the hatchway onto the deck, shutting the portal tightly behind him.

He felt himself moving easily, was able to forget the fact that he was injured and bruised. With barely a grimace he lifted the lid of the sail locker and was rewarded with a sharp twinge from his broken rib. More carefully he reached inside and hooked the line to the top of the mainsail.

With practiced gestures he began to pull on the line. He enjoyed the sight of the blue canvas rising slowly from the locker, climbing up the tall mast. He paused to attach the base of the sail to the boom, then continued hoisting away. The sail snapped and fluttered in the breeze, and he began to feel some hope, some confidence in his own experience as a sailor, and in the remembered seaworthiness of this fast, dependable boat.

For now he let the boom trail over the water and the canvas flap loosely, and soon the sail was fully aloft. With a firm gesture, he pulled on the steering line, bringing the sail against the wind, waiting for the push that would show him the boat was firmly under his control.

Instead, the breeze came hard and *Cutter*, without veering from her down-river course, heeled sharply, lurching and almost pitching the elven sailor into the water. Kerrick let go of the rope and threw himself down, hands grasping the rail as the boat quickly righted herself, its sail flapping loosely off to the side. Gasping from the sudden pain, he looked around, and again that gray haze filled his eyes.

The spell! He understood it fully, then: He was trapped by the king's will. His knuckles whitened on the gunwale and he stared wildly around him at the gray murk, comprehending beyond all doubt. The king's sorcerers had surrounded the boat with a spell that kept him on a southward course, no matter how he steered or the wind blew.

With a glance over the stern, Kerrick saw that Silvanost had already vanished behind him around a bend. He felt heartsick—he had missed a last look at the most beautiful place in all Krynn. Anger swept over him, the sense of a great injustice that had been done to him and frustration in his inability to strike back at his tormentors. From somewhere in the depths of his memory Waykand's taunting laugh echoed.

Then came despair. Would life be worth living if he had to live it away from Silvanesti? He gazed longingly at the verdant bluffs on the distant shore. A gleam of color, washed pale by the haze, arced over a deep, tributary canyon. This was the Rainbow Gorge, he knew, the shadowy vale where wizards maintained a permanent and brilliant pattern of rainbows, bright even in darkest night. When he sailed northward from the sea, he had always used the Rainbow Gorge as a sign that he was drawing near to home.

Now it seemed only a mocking reminder that he would never feast his eyes upon their pure beauty again. Slumping in the hull, he at last gave way to a hopelessness so deep and wounding that he could not even weep. He only sat numbly, watching as the gorge and its precious rainbows slowly receded in the distance.

A froth of water caught his eye, and he glimpsed a great trading galley churning northward through the river channel. Banners of silk, in red and blue and green, the colors muted by the magic haze, trailed from every mast and post. Double banks of great oars propelled the big ship upstream against the current. Kerrick drifted close enough that he could make out the faces of the elven captain and his mates, saw them leaning casually at the rail. It had been a successful voyage, to judge from the many pennants, and Kerrick wondered fleetingly how many times his father had made just such a return to this great land, had brought back cargoes of dwarven stone or Tarsian horses or—after the Istarian War—precious gold to make rich the coffers of the elven king.

As the great ship cruised on past and he studied the officers and their laboring crew, he came to a realization that only deepened his unhappiness. For these elves were looking in his direction, admiring the shoreline, but they made no acknowledgement of his presence, even steering dangerously close to him.

"They can't even see me!" The wizards' magic not only locked him onto a course of exile but shrouded his very existence from those he encountered on the way down the river and out of the elven nation.

As he crumpled against the transom, he was reminded of the scroll tube he had placed in his pocket. Kerrick took it out, pulled the cork from the end of the container, and slid the sheet of silken paper into his hands.

Even now, in the depths of his misery, the words brought back a measure of the pride he had felt when his liege bestowed it upon him:

> *These are the words of the King, for the eyes of all elvenkind:*
>
> *Know that a young sailor of Silvanost has made the arduous journey from the Than-Thalas estuary to Tarsis, and then returned, crewing his sailing boat,* Cutter, *entirely by himself.*
>
> *This solitary voyage ranks high in the annals of elven seamanship, and Kerrick Fallabrine is to be known to all of Silvanesti as a Friend of the King.*
>
> *Speaker of Stars*
> *Nethas Caladon of*
> *House Silvanos,*
> *Fifth King of Silvanesti*

A gust of wind carried drops of water across the gunwale, splashing onto the page and causing the ink to smear. Strangely, though this scroll had been one of his treasured possessions, Kerrick wasn't concerned. His mind wandered, drifting away from the boat, across the water with the wind, free of this bobbing vessel and its magical geas. He remembered his first voyage, not in *Cutter,* but in his father's fabulous galley, *Silvanos Oak*, a vessel that would have dwarfed the splendid ship that had just passed him.

Of course, Dimorian Fallabrine was the king's admiral and a victor of many noteworthy sea battles. He had made himself a name and a fortune during the Istarian War, when navies of that human empire had attempted to block the elves from trading with the many human nations flourishing to either side of Silvanesti. The Kingpriest had sent his ships by the score, great, deep-drafted galleons that sailed with impunity back and forth across the mouth of the Than-Thalas, blockading the ships of elves and humans alike, keeping all from entering or departing from the elven kingdom.

The roots of the conflict were ancient but could be boiled down to one word: gold. That precious metal, ever in short supply among the civilized nations of the world, was the historical symbol of Istarian might. The Kingpriest claimed that every ingot, every flake of the precious stuff belonged, by gods-given right, to him. However, elves coveted gold, too—not only for its beauty, but because it was necessary for the working of great magic spells, such as the sustained beauty represented by the Rainbow Gorge.

Many elven noblemen, dashing sailors who fancied themselves epic heroes, dared to try and slip past that blockade, but their ships were always caught, the crews put to the sword, nobles held hostage against exorbitant ransom. It was Dimorian Fallabrine, in a small trading galley, the *Southcoast Elm*, who successfully challenged the Istarian fleet. The tale of his exploits would later be made into a court poem and national song, and the recounting of his accomplishment never failed to fill Kerrick with pride.

With his ship crewed by an unusual mix of races, Dimorian faced two Istarian galleons in a long battle. Fire arrows filled the sky with smoke, and the ships rammed and counterrammed all day, breaking timbers, masts, and oars. The Kingpriest's cleric shouted spells of protection and blessing until an elven wizard killed that priest with a crackling bolt of magical lightning. Eventually, one of the Istarian ships was sunk in a tangle of rigging, wreckage, and drowning men. Another ship was trapped against the shoals and captured with her entire crew. When *Southcoast Elm* towed the prize upriver to Silvanost, Dimorian Fallabrine was accorded a welcome reserved for the greatest heroes.

Kerrick's father was awarded an admiral's commission by King Nethas, together with a purse of gold allowing him to build the mightiest vessel afloat. The result was *Silvanos Oak,* a ship propelled by nearly two hundred oars, with a hull enchanted against damage and a ram of deadly steel. Dimorian next sailed down river with a force of a dozen galleys, and *Silvanos Oak* as his flagship. He led the final campaign against the blockade, a campaign so constant, so costly in terms of ships and lives lost, that finally the prideful Kingpriest was forced to acknowledge the failure of his plan.

The resulting treaty allowed Silvanesti free access to such gold as the elves could obtain by trade and mining, and involved settlement of a significant amount of gold paid directly from Istarian coffers into those of King Nethas. For a time there were rumors that Dimorian would be accorded rank as a minor noble, but in the end the monarch instead rewarded the bold sailor with a payment of riches and a vow that all of his offspring would be entitled to training in the royal court of Silvanost.

Kerrick was born shortly after the war ended, and by that time his father had established a great manor on Silvanost's exclusive Harbor Hill. His wealth granted the family privileged status in the city, though he was never fully accepted by the nobles of the Elder Houses. Still, Dimorian was able to provide for his son a comfortable childhood, with nurses and nannies and plenty to eat.

The young elf's earliest memories were of the water. He used to gaze southward from his father's manor tower, eyeing the broad river, dreaming of the endless ocean beyond the elven realm. How many hours had he wasted up there in the tower? Happily he awaited the *Silvanos Oak*, each time the sleek galley returned from some profitable adventure.

Upon each homecoming Dimorian produced fabulous gifts—dyes of unique hues, wines, fruits, and grains of exotic origins, teas from as far away as Istar, and, once, an ornately modeled sword of tin that had been hammered out by a Tarsian craftsman.

Most mysterious of all was the tiny box that Dimorian showed to his son, when Kerrick was still a lad of twenty-five. It came with a whispered promise of magical powers. It was a rare treasure obtained in trade with a mysterious wizard.

"You will have it, my son, a golden prize when you have reached your adulthood, and it may give you the strength to face the trials that will inevitably come your way. But always treat it with caution and respect, for it also has the power to weaken and destroy."

Before Kerrick could attain that mystical rank—"adulthood," to an elf, came some time in the seventh or eighth decade of life—he entered the palace of House Royal to begin his studies in earnest. Setting aside the toy sword of his childhood, he said farewell to his mother. He could still remember her carefully restrained tears as he passed through the gates of the great capital to begin service as a page in the court of the great King Nethas. How eager he had been to go—he was too quick to break off those final embraces, too much in a rush to race across the drawbridge and enter a new world.

For three years he had lived the courtly life, learning of Silvanesti's heralded past, her station as the greatest nation in the history of Krynn. He thrilled to the tales of the great dragon wars in which ogres, even more than the great winged serpents, threatened the existence of his homeland. The most recent of these had been barely four centuries earlier, when the elven armies—with some aid, admittedly, from the human hero called Huma—had turned the tide of evil and preserved Krynn for the enlightened races. At that time, the eternal plague of the world, dragons, had been banished forever, and a new age, marked by human ascension, swept over the world. For the reclusive elves of

Silvanesti, life returned to the pattern of yore. They neither traded with nor worried about the humans beyond their borders.

In the royal palace the masters of House Protector also taught him and the other pages the vital art of swordsmanship. Kerrick excelled in weaponry and was eventually awarded the fine steel blade now hanging in his cabin. Upon his promotion from page to squire even the king took note of the pleasant young elf. Nethas remarked that Kerrick was proving to be a worthy inheritor of his father's name. Following that ceremony, which Dimorian and his wife attended, his father had announced that he was embarking on a great quest, pursuing a mystery as ancient as Silvanesti.

Was there a fabled land of gold somewhere over the sea? One of Dimorian's mates had convinced him that the question was worth a vigorous quest. So he bade his son farewell and embarked, seeking gold in the name of his family and his king.

There came a long year, and after that, a cold and sunless progression of winter after winter after winter. Kerrick had been reluctant to face the truth, though others whispered it and some, cruel and arrogant young men of Waykand Isleletter's ilk, had spoken it boldly to his face until reality could no longer be denied.

Dimorian Fallabrine would not be coming home.

For twelve years there had been no word, nothing, though even then Kerrick refused to accept the worst. One day, however, he was told to meet someone in the garden below his apartment. He could still remember the dour figure of Tartaniad, master of the royal squires, waiting near the central fountain. The water splashed like raindrops as Kerrick halted, then approached the elf who had been a teacher, mentor, and friend to him, in the king's court.

Tartaniad held out a small circle of gold, though at first Kerrick didn't understand.

"This was something your father left. He wanted you to have it as you reached manhood."

"A ring?" Kerrick said, somehow forcing out the words.

"Yes."

The elf reached out to take the circlet. He recognized the pattern—oak leaves—carved into the surface, felt the heavy weight of the heirloom as he cradled it in his palm.

"From who? How did you come by it now?" he asked.

"It was left in the temple of Zivilyn Greentree by your father before he departed on his last voyage. The high priest was instructed to hold it in trust for Dimorian, until the event of his return. Or until such time as his auguries indicated that your father would not ever be coming home."

He had looked at the ring, seen the intricate pattern of oak leaves, felt the warm enchantment that he would come to associate with the band of thick, yellow metal, and at last he had accepted that his father would never return.

"Your father insisted that, should the ring be given to you, it must also be delivered with a warning," Tartaniad noted.

"What warning?"

The courtier drew a breath and closed his eyes, remembering the exact words. "You must not wear the ring, unless your life is in imminent danger. It can give you the strength to survive great peril—but if you wear it too much, it can also sap your life."

"I understand . . . and thank you," Kerrick had said, though in fact he wasn't sure what his father meant. He took the warning seriously, resolving to cherish the ring but never to wear it unless, as his father had said, his life was in "imminent danger."

He was restless in his grief, and finally he sought and received the king's permission to embark in *Cutter*, the small boat that had been his father's first vessel. For a time he made his way back and forth on small coastal voyages, until finally he set himself on the solo voyage to Tarsis, a journey that took him more than a year to complete. When at last he returned to the palace, he was welcomed back to court and rewarded by the king's proclamation.

His eyes fell again upon the silken sheet in his hands, the

ink smearing, the lettering even more obscured by drops of water. Whether this was spray coming over the side, or tears dropping from his own eyes, he could no longer be sure.

How many times had he tried to imagine his mother and father in the depths of the Courrain Ocean? How much had they suffered? Had pirates slain them? Or had some ravenous sea-monster brought them to doom? Perhaps *Silvanos Oak* had merely gone down in a storm, though he found that unthinkable.

He had wondered about all this countless times before. Whenever he was alone in the boat such questions seemed to bubble up from the depths. On his voyage to Tarsis—that "*solitary voyage ranking high in the annals of elven seamanship*" as the king himself had proclaimed—there had been times when he felt as if his father was at the tiller right beside him. He had often imagined his mother busy at the cookstove. Once he woke up to the smell of oats boiling and leaped up to throw open the hatch—only to be confronted by an empty galley, a cold stove, nobody.

Perhaps the long months on that lonely journey had changed him. In any event, after he returned home and received the king's honor, he found himself drifting into a new, irresponsible kind of life. He laughed off the slights of those who fancied themselves his betters and allowed himself to be drawn into the lively circle of Silvanost's high society. His good looks, newly won and slightly notorious reputation, along with his demeanor of cool calm, attracted many women, and he enjoyed romances with a long string of willing lovers. His conquests included certain wives of other elves as well as many a virginal maiden—though few were as appealing as Gloryian Diradar. Their affair had lasted better than half a year, at a pitch of high passion until—he snorted in wry amusement as he remembered—it had been ended in passionate acts of a different kind.

Did he hate Patrikan Diradar, and Darnari and Waykand? Not to mention Gloryian herself for her utter reversal of affection? He supposed that he could, but now it seemed like too much work to muster up any emotion.

Indeed, every action was tiring. Even his head seemed like a leaden weight. He was exhausted, woozy. Once more pain suffused him. He forced himself to rise, enter the cabin, and collapse on the bunk. He saw the little strongbox and remembered the proclamation from the king—he had left it in the cockpit, beside the tiller.

He remembered right where he had put it, but when he left the cabin he could see that it was already gone—probably snatched away by a gust of wind. Surprisingly enough, he didn't care about that, either.

6

Warriors of Bayguard

Tuskers! I saw a whole tribe of them on the beach!" Little Mouse came sprinting up, his voice breaking with excitement. He was panting and staggering by the time he halted before Moreen and Bruni.

"Where on the beach?" asked the chieftain's daughter. "How far away?"

"Two miles, maybe more," gasped the youth. He pointed to the north, toward the rim of coastal hills that stood between the little band of Arktos and the blue waters of the White Bear Sea.

"What were you doing over there?" Garta demanded, coming up behind the other two women. "You told me you were looking for berries in the marsh downstream!"

"I didn't find any," the lad said defiantly. "And, well, I just kept walking and looking. I wanted to see where the stream went, and maybe I hoped I'd find some berries farther down. So I went to the shore."

"All the way to the *beach*?" Garta's stern face was locked into a ferocious scowl. "If you remember, one of the reasons Moreen took us inland was so that we could scout these upcountry marshes for food! Why, if your father was here—"

Little Mouse still had that defiant look, but suddenly he blinked and sniffled, looking down. "I'm sorry," he said, to no one in particular. "I know it was careless—"

"Also pretty brave," Bruni said, clapping a hand on the boy's shoulder. "In truth you did us a favor, finding those brutes before we wandered past them—or right into them. Your father"—she cast an accusing glance at Garta—"would be proud."

"Did they see you?" Moreen asked.

"No—I don't think . . . I'm sure they didn't," Mouse replied, his swagger returning. "I saw them from the cut where the stream flowed out of the hills, but I stayed up on top. I did try to get a little closer to count them and see what they were doing."

"What did you find out?" asked Bruni.

"There are a dozen of them—big ones. They look like warriors—they have spears and axes. They were cutting up a whale that they had pulled up onto the beach. They just got started. Mostly it still has the skin on. I think it will take them a few days to finish."

"Good work," replied the big woman, while Moreen nodded in confirmation.

The chieftain's daughter was trying to absorb the news, remembering Dinekki's prophecy—which had warned of tuskers. She turned to look at her people, who were going about the business of preparing the evening meal. Several small fires, kindled from the brush in the nearby marshes, glowed in shallow pits, and the old women were stringing pieces of seal meat onto sticks for roasting. Augmented by a few fish, meat from a big turtle, and some berries, they were preparing the same meal that had sustained the Arktos every day for a month, since the day Moreen had sent the Highlander emissary retreating back to his "king."

She knew that she would have to kill dozens more seals before she could come close to the amount of meat they could strip from a single whale. Of course, under their own devices, lacking kayaks and many skilled hunters, they had no way of even looking for a whale, much less bringing one to shore. But now, perhaps, Chislev had seen that someone else had taken care of the first part of that job.

"There were tuskers with the ogres that sacked Bayguard." Bruni pointed out, although the thought that had already occurred to Moreen. "I would like the chance for revenge."

"I would too," agreed Tildey, who had come forward to join the trio.

"I can show you where they are!" Little Mouse offered enthusiastically. "We can sneak up really close on the hill, and charge down to take them by surprise!"

"A dozen of them?" The chieftain's daughter tried to be realistic. "We have barely that many spears among us and not many people who are strong enough to throw one and to fight." Privately, she doubted the warrior abilities of any of the women, save perhaps Bruni and herself. A full-grown thanoi warrior was a formidable opponent. Surely the safest, the sanest, thing was to pack up their camp and move deeper inland, giving the walrusmen a wide berth.

But Moreen was surprised to realize how badly she desired that whale and how much she hated the thought of barbaric thanoi on this, the Arktos' shore.

Dinekki, her wobbly legs aided by the support of a slender staff, came up to them. Moreen was acutely conscious of the rest of the tribe, the women and the elders and the children, all watching the group of leaders with interested, concerned eyes. She recounted what Little Mouse had seen when the shaman cut off further words with a sharp gesture.

"Tuskers, eh?" she grunted, with a smack of her toothless gums. "I thought so—could smell that fishy stink from clear over here. So what're you going to do about 'em?"

She asked the question directly of Moreen, and in that instant the chieftain's daughter understood: It really *was* her decision to make. The tribe, those who survived, looked to her. A glance at grim-faced Bruni and Tildey told her that they wanted to follow her into a fight. What would the others think? How would they fare?

She thought of the winter that was drawing inevitably closer, the lightless, implacable Sturmfrost that would roar out of the south as the sun vanished for the season. Already it was autumn. The nights were as long as the days, the hours of darkness characterized by a penetrating chill. Her dream of Brackenrock had kept her going, driving her people on toward the north, but they remained woefully unprepared for winter. What would happen if they bypassed the tuskers, and the walrus-men, some time later, came upon the Arktos, surprised them as they had the option to do now.

"We don't have any choice," she declared curtly. "We'll attack them. Tonight."

She lay on the crest of the hill, staring with unblinking intensity at the beach below. Bruni, Tildey, and Little Mouse were beside her, while another score of tribeswomen, burdened with their unfamiliar spears and harpoons, waited farther down the slope in the shelter of a narrow ravine.

Despite the busy presence of the menacing walrus-men, Moreen's eyes were drawn irresistibly toward the carcass of the whale. It was a medium-sized gray, but it dwarfed the tusked warriors. Not even half skinned, the giant mammal presented a flank of gory blood and fresh, sumptuous meat. The tuskers had apparently spent the day cutting back the skin, and had not yet begun to carve away the actual flesh.

"Bah—they don't even know how to dry the hide," Tildey whispered contemptuously. "We've got to get down there soon before it starts to rot."

"I think the tuskers themselves are a more immediate problem," Moreen said wryly, trying to cover up her nervousness with an air of calm.

She looked out to sea, toward the northwestern horizon. The sun was low, only a handspan above the world's rim, but during these days of early autumn it would descend at a gradual angle, moving farther west as it finally set. Even after it disappeared from view, a bright twilight would linger for a long time, leaving another three hours before full darkness.

Moreen tried to think. Counting three women from the Goosepond tribe and Little Mouse, there were twenty-four in her battle troop—twice as many humans as tuskers. However, as she watched a monstrous figure stroll around the whale's head, she was reminded of the strength and fierceness of their foes.

The brutes were each as tall as a huge human and walked upright with long, clawed toes on webbed feet. Their arms were muscular and dangled almost to the knees. The only clothing on their streamlined bodies were strips of whaleskin around the loins. Most hideous of all were their bestial faces. Even from her distant vantage Moreen shuddered as she noted their broad nostrils, sloped foreheads, and beady, shadowed eyes. She could see clearly their vicious tusks, twin prongs of ivory that curled down and forward from the beasts' upper jaws.

"There are their weapons," Little Mouse whispered, pointing to a patch of beach ten paces inland from the whale's body. They could see a bundle of sticks, tipped with stone heads, that were the tusker spears. Next to those were several axes, also headed with stone, mounted on stout handles.

Moreen nodded. Already she had considered and rejected several plans, and now she had seen everything she needed to see. "All right," she replied softly. "Let's get back to the ravine."

"Are we going wait to attack them until it's darker?" asked Tildey.

"No." Moreen shook her head, noting the disappointment on her companion's faces. She explained further. "No. We're going to start this fight just as soon as we possibly can."

A half hour later, Dinekki finished dabbing ritual paint on the faces of the warrior women.

"How many arrows do you have?" the chieftain's daughter asked Tildey.

"A full score," she replied, "but it will take a lucky shot to kill one of those creatures, at least from the hilltop."

"You don't have to kill them, at least not at first," Moreen explained. "The important thing is that you get their attention."

"That, I can do," agreed the archer.

"Now, does everyone have a weapon—a spear or a club?" asked the chieftain's daughter.

"I don't," Little Mouse piped up, "but that's okay—I'll just grab a spear from the first dead tusker."

"You'll do no such thing!" snapped Garta, who looked decidedly unmotherly with a great, knobbed club clutched in her plump hands. "You'll do as we discussed and wait back here until we're finished."

"How is that fair? I'm the one who found the tuskers!" Mouse protested.

"Who said life had to be fair?" retorted Moreen, thinking that she suddenly sounded very much like her father. "Garta is right—you can't be up close where you might get hurt."

"Well, at least let me come to the hilltop," pleaded the youth, his black hair hanging almost in his dark eyes. "I can keep a lookout behind you—and I'd be just as safe there as hiding back in this stupid ravine."

Garta looked at Moreen, and again the cheiftain's daughter made the decision. "All right, you can come that far with us. No closer, and don't you dare get in the way."

"I promise!" agreed Mouse.

"I'll keep an eye on the boy," Dinekki said curtly. "Now, aren't you forgetting something?"

"Yes, Grandmother," Moreen said gratefully. "Will you ask for the blessing of Chislev Wilder upon our endeavor?"

"That is the purpose of the paint," explained the shaman, who by now had daubed each of the women with a band of red coloring under each eye and across the forehead. "Now, take each other's hand in a circle, all of you—and let me in, too!" she snapped.

"Chislev Wilder we beseech you . . . give us strength, to see our need through." Dinekki chanted the words, creating a strange, choppy rhythm Moreen found entrancing and exhilarating. "Grant your skill, give weapons might . . . honor courage, in the fight."

Moreen felt a buzzing in her arms, a lightness in her feet, an energizing power. Chislev was all around them, their goddess was smiling up at them from the green grass, could be heard in the buzz of the hive-bound bees, the splashing of the fish in the nearby stream. For Chislev Wilder was a deity of nature, and her power and beauty lay in all of nature's aspects, including blood and death.

"The goddess will steady your aim and lend strength to your blows. Now, go and do battle in her name."

With Moreen and Tildey in the lead, the Arktos she-warriors filed up the steep chute and, staying low, emerged onto the crest of the coastal hill. The blessing of Chislev felt like a warm blanket around them. With the sun still visible, low in the northwest, the women, in their brown leather vests and tan leggings crouched and did a reasonable job of blending into the brush-covered ground. As they came over the hilltop, Moreen motioned to them to get down, and as a band they dropped to their hands and knees and began creeping forward.

"See that rocky outcrop?" the chieftain's daughter whispered, pointing. The promontory jutted above the beach, looming over the tuskers and the carcass of the whale. "We've got to crawl out there without being seen."

The others nodded grimly. Moreen saw the fire of determination in Tildey's expression as the archer bent and strung her bow, the scowl of anger that burned across Bruni's brow, the tremulous fear blinking in Garta's eyes, and the faces of Nangrid and Hilgrid and Darna and so many others. They all looked to her with hope and at least a show of confidence, and she was determined not to let them down.

She had gone over the plan in detail, and there was no

need for further discussion. Pointing to Little Mouse, she held up her hand in silent command for him to stay, then started along the narrow ridge of land. Crawling, staying low, she was able to remain out of the line of sight. Soon she had reached the shelter of the rocks and looked to see that the women of the band were following, one after another, along the elevation. Little Mouse was a small blur against the hilltop a long stone's throw away.

Moreen herself carried three harpoons. Her sinewy cord was looped around her wrist, ready if she needed it, but for now she would not tie it to any of the weapons. She laid two of the harpoons behind a rock and hefted the third, as Tildey leaned forward and nocked an arrow into the string of her bow. On the other side of the archer Bruni crouched expectantly, the heavy, stone-headed club balanced in her hands. The rest of the warriors crowded around them, all of them keeping low and out of sight of the thanoi.

Moreen saw that the tuskers seemed to be finishing up their labors with the whale carcass, at least for the night. A few of them had flopped onto the ground to rest, while others were seated up the beach, busily gnawing on great, crimson strips of raw meat.

Tildey looked at Moreen, who nodded and pulled back until she could barely see their enemies through a crack between two boulders. The others remained still and hidden.

Standing up, drawing the butt of an arrow back to her cheek, Tildey took careful aim. She released the string with a soft *twang*, and the feathered missile hurtled toward the beach.

The nearest thanoi, a great brute sitting with its back toward the humans, lurched forward with a grunt, dropped the piece of meat it had been holding, and sprawled onto the ground. The shaft of Tildey's arrow jutted squarely from its broad back, right at the base of the neck.

"Nice shot," whispered Moreen, impressed. Her hand closed tightly around the haft of her harpoon as she watched the nearby thanoi leap to their feet with a chorus of barking and growling.

The archer was already preparing a second arrow, drawing a careful bead and shooting in one smooth motion. This missile punctured the thigh of a standing tusker, spinning the creature fully around before it dropped to the ground with a howl of outrage.

Now Tildey had been seen, and the thanoi rushed toward the base of the rocky knob where she was positioned, snatching up stout spears, heavy clubs, and wicked bone knives lying on the beach.

Moreen saw Garta and Nangrid look at her, wide-eyed and tense, but she shook her head vehemently, pleading for them to remain hidden. Obviously nervous, they nevertheless stayed low, fingers clenched around their unfamiliar weapons. With another glance through the crack in the rocks, the chieftain's daughter saw that the tuskers had started up the hill, though—as she had planned—they found the going tough on the steep and boulder-strewn slope.

A third walrus-man grunted in pain as Tildey shot again. This tusker was caught full in the chest and rolled backward to lie still at the bottom of the hill.

"Here they are," Tildey said coolly as she set another arrow against her string. Moreen saw a brutal face looming just on the other side of her rock, dull eyes glaring balefully, wicked tusks swaying back and forth.

"Now!" she cried, leaping to her feet, the harpoon steady in her hand as she drew back for a throw.

The barbed head of the harpoon pierced the thanoi right in the throat and its wide jaws gaped soundlessly as the brute dropped its spear to claw desperately at the weapon. With a frantic, lashing twist the tusker spun around and tumbled away, knocking down one of its still-climbing fellows from the force of its fall.

Moreen heard whoops and screams as the other women also rose and launched their attack, bashing and poking and shouting in the face of the stunned tuskers. Bruni smashed her stone hammer hard into the broad snout of a walrus-man, and the beast fell, clasping both hands to its bleeding maw. The big woman smashed downward again, killing the creature. Nangrid also pierced one, driving the metal point of her spear clear through its sinewy torso, then shaking her weapon free. The tusker, groaning and bleeding, flopped helplessly on the ground at her feet.

Other women hurled rocks. Several good-sized boulders clattered down among the thanoi, knocking them backward or bouncing down the slope, forcing the other thanoi to dodge out of the way. The sudden onslaught caught the monsters by surprise, and those that weren't struck down immediately hesitated in their ascent, piglike eyes flashing as they confronted this horde of screaming, wild-looking attackers. Moreen had encouraged the Arktos to make a lot of noise, and—whether because of her instructions, or the fierce, panicked energy that seized them at the moment of battle—the tribeswomen were whooping it up like a crazed band of berserk warriors.

One of the walrus-men, a huge beast with long, curling tusks and an ornately feathered spear, shouted something Moreen could not understand. It was obviously a command, and the surviving tuskers wasted no time in scrambling back down the hillside, slipping and stumbling in their haste.

"After them!" cried the chieftain's daughter, snatching up her second harpoon. Tildey's bowstring twanged again, as Moreen cast her weapon, and the twin missiles took the tusker leader through the belly and shoulder.

Garta was shouting something unintelligible as she lunged after a particularly slow thanoi, snapping off one of its tusks with a wild sweep of her club. The creature jabbed back with its spear and the Arktos woman cried out, falling backward, blood running from her stomach. The walrus-man lunged, jabbing a tusk toward her heart—but Garta, kicking frantically, managed to hold the monster at bay until Bruni kicked it away, then crushed its skull with a hard blow of her club.

Moreen hefted her last harpoon and started picking her way down the steep slope.

"Remember—none can escape!" she shouted, as the

other tribeswomen, too, started in pursuit. Spears flew, most of the weapons clattering harmlessly across the rocks, though at least one other tusker fell, pierced through the leg. Nangrid stepped on the squirming thanoi and, with a quick flick of her skinning knife plunged deftly between the tusks, slicing its throat.

A trio of the tusked brutes had reached the beach, with a few more, badly wounded, limping along behind, or still working their way down the hillside. The thanoi wasted no time in starting for the surf, two dozen paces away, though one fell before it took two steps, punctured by another of Tildey's lethal arrows. A few Arktos cast spears, and a second tusker tumbled and thrashed, pierced in the hamstring by a lucky throw.

Moreen was on the beach now, sprinting past bleeding, dying walrus-men as she raced in pursuit. One thanoi moved with surprising speed, flat feet slapping across the stones as it lunged toward the water and plunged into a breaking wave with a smooth dive. The chieftain's daughter halted at the water's edge. With a practiced movement she took the end of the cord from her wrist and slipped in through the eyehole in the weapon's haft. Then she pulled it back, held the shaft beside her head, and squinted into the sun-brightened surf.

All around her she heard the groans and shrieks of wounded thanoi, the beasts grunting and snarling as the women raced among them, using their sharp bone knives to finish the work they had begun with spear, club, and stone.

There! The rounded head of the beast broke the surface, two dozen paces from shore.

"Just like killing a seal," Moreen told herself, and let fly. She didn't aim for the head, but sought to hit the muscular body.

The sleek harpoon shot into the water, and the thanoi bellowed in pain and instantly dove under. Planting her feet, Moreen grasped the cord and set her weight in anticipation of the creature's power. Even so, the tug on the line pulled her off of her feet, and she was dragged across the rough stones of the beach. An icy wave washed over her as she was pulled into the sea.

Bruni was beside her, her strong arms wrapped around Moreen's waist, pulling her—and the wounded tusker—back to land. The chieftain's daughter climbed to her feet, and they both tugged, hand over hand, reeling in the monster. Soon it was in the shallows, rolling in the surf, then suddenly, surprisingly, it sprang upward, lunging toward the women, wet, slick tusks jabbing like spears.

Tildey was standing nearby, with one more arrow pulled back, and her aim was true. The walrus-man froze, an arrow suddenly protruding from the middle of its face. With a sputtering groan it wobbled, then flopped downward. Blood washed into the water lapping at Moreen's feet.

"You did it, Moreen, Chieftain's Daughter!" Little Mouse was at her side, jumping up and down in excitement. "You led us into battle, and we won!"

She looked around numbly. "Garta?" she asked, looking back at the rocky knoll.

"Dinekki's helping her—she's going to be all right," the boy assured her.

"Mouse is right," Bruni said, placing a big arm around Moreen's shoulders, steadying her as her legs suddenly grew weak. "Except perhaps we shouldn't call you 'chieftain's daughter' any more."

"No," Tildey said, nudging the floating, bleeding tusker with her toe. "I think you are Moreen, Chiefwoman, now."

7

Winterheim

The knocking on the cabin door slowly penetrated Grimwar Bane's awareness. The ogre prince snorted, stirred, and tried to claw his way out of a dream. In that dream he had been wandering through a fog, seeking something, a person he could know, trust. Faces floated around in the murk. His mother was there, her face soft and round and warm. Now she was gone, replaced by his father, King Grimtruth. The prince saw Baldruk Dinmaker's bearded face, followed by the image of his own wife, Stariz ber Glacierheim ber Bane.

Finally came an image of the king's young bride, the voluptuous ogress Thraid Dimmarkull. That last image was a pleasant one, one that filled him with longing, with aching desire. She, too, disappeared, and again he was confronted by the forbidding visage of his father. Eyes bleary, breath reeking of warqat, Grimtruth raised his fist for a blow, and the son was powerless to fend him off.

He awoke. With a sense of relief he recognized his cabin, this ship, where *he* was the master. He grunted in acknowledgement, knowing that his crew wouldn't awaken him for any trivial reason.

"Lookout reports that Ice Gates are in sight, Your Highness!"

Mumbling gruffly, the great ogre swung his feet out of the sea bunk, ducking his head as he reached for his boots and cloak. The captain's cabin in *Goldwing* was the most spacious enclosure on the ship, but even so Grimwar felt cramped and confined. Part of it was the monotony of the long months at sea, he knew, and so the announcement that awakened him was good news.

Still, he was in a foul mood as he pushed open the door and emerged onto the deck of the massive galley. His eyes immediately fell upon the massive palisades that marked the approach to Winterheim.

The Ice Gates were twin mountains, massifs bracketing the mouth of a narrow fjord, rising so that their icy summits seemed to scrape the very heavens. Each was draped in cascading glaciers, blue-white sheets of ice spilling downward in a chaotic jumble of precipice, chasm, and snowy cornice. Here and there a rough shoulder of bedrock showed, black rock glistening in the sunlight, in stark contrast to the frozen surroundings.

Now, in early autumn, streams still cascaded downward among the glacial faces, plumes of water spilling into long streams of spray, sparkling like a million diamonds in the pale sunlight. At night these streams would freeze into elegant icicles, only to liquefy again under the heat of the next day's sun.

It was impossible to tell which of the two peaks was greater. From sea level each loomed impossibly high, spires of rock that seemed to challenge the laws of gravity. The mountains were so close together that the entry to the fjord was all but invisible to enemy vessels. The ogre helmsman, Barelip Seacaster, guided the galley with skill, however, and Grimwar stood and watched, knowing what was about to unfold.

The ship approached the shoreline and veered to port. Gradually, as they drew close, the shoreline became visible in clear relief. Finally the shade from the low sun cut a swath across the mountainside, and the ogre prince could see the opening of the narrow channel.

Barelip Seacaster hauled on the great tiller as the drumbeats slowed and the rowers settled their pace. The ship followed a smooth curve, moving with stately grace, easing toward the entrance. When they passed behind the looming shoulder of mountain the shadows embraced them chillingly, a sense of frost that penetrated through Grimwar's heavy sea cape and brought visible mist to each royal exhalation.

They moved through utterly still water, oars dipping, pushing, rising to drip across the calm surface, before once more gently immersing for another stroke. Each side of the fjord was close enough that the prince could have struck it with a well-thrown stone. The wall emerging from the deep water sloped steeply upward, slick with ice and glowering dark stone. Every time he passed through here the hulking ogre felt small and vulnerable.

"By Gonnas, it's good to be going home," Grimwar noted as Baldruk Dinmaker joined him in the prow.

"Aye—and 'tis a fair pleasure to bid goodbye to that cursed sun, Your Highness," agreed the dwarf heartily. "Will we see the city before nightfall?"

"I hope." The prince had been through this channel on many occasions, but he didn't dare make a prediction. Sunset occurred earlier with each passing day, the season waning so fast that he wasn't sure. Still, he *hoped* they would get a glimpse of Winterheim while there was still light, for there was no finer view that he had ever seen in his life.

There, an hour later, it was. The galley slipped from between the close walls of the fjord and emerged into a watery bowl called Black Ice Bay, an enclosure that was completely sheltered from the sea except for this dangerous approach. The shadows were long, the water inky dark and still, but Grimwar's eyes were drawn to the alabaster façade sprawling across the full stretch of the southern horizon. The clear sky, rich with the deep indigo of twilight, brought the snowfields, cornices, and glaciers into splendid, purple relief.

Winterheim was a city, but it was also a mountain. If the Ice Gates were towering pillars, Winterheim itself was a monument of sublime wonder that dwarfed every surrounding elevation.

Fading sunlight glimmered with phosphorescent brilliance along the crest of the great mountain, a corona of white light sparkling along an arcing ridge of pristine snow. Fresh powder blanketed the upper palisades. Even in summer, such precipitation was an almost nightly occurrence, and now already the darkening days of autumn crept closer.

The King's Wall circled the summit perhaps two-thirds of the way up the lofty slope. This palisade of sheer stone was more than a hundred feet tall and looked like a belt of gray around the mountain's lumpy midriff. A multitude of towers jutted from the slopes, many of these strung along the upper ramparts above the King's Wall and across the highest shoulders of the edifice. Other spires dotted the lower slopes, and from these—as well as in great windows and doorways in the mountainside—a multitude of fires hove into view, sparks of light brightening the massif as the shadows of sunset inexorably thickened.

To the right a ridge extended into a great, flat surface with ornate columns, these pillars rising up to merge with the base of the King's Wall. On this field the king's troops drilled, and his people gathered for such celebrations as occurred outside the city walls. Grimwar recalled with a thrill standing up there and watching King Grimtruth drive the pillars into the ice during the Icebreaker Festival, which took place at the end of the long, sunless winter.

To the left of the mountain appeared a great, frozen cliff of solid ice. This was the Icewall, the dam holding back the Snow Sea. In a few months that wall would be shattered by the king himself, in a ritual as old as Winterheim. When the sun finally vanished for the winter, a strong male slave would be offered in sacrifice, and his blood, together with the enchantment of the high priestess, would provide the power to break the Icewall, and release the Sturmfrost to dwindle across Icereach.

Barelip Seacaster called out to the drummer, who picked up the pace. Grimwar felt the galley surge beneath his feet, and he thrilled at the power of the great ship, of a hundred and twenty slaves responding to a single command.

Darkness settled across Black Ice Bay, but the prince of ogres didn't budge from his post. Instead, he watched the sparkling lights of his home, remembered the smells of scented oil, of roasting whale meat, and the day's catch of fish. A slit of brightness appeared in the base of the mountain, where it merged with the dark water. The gap slowly widened as the Seagate, operated by hundreds of slaves turning great capstans, trundled open. His ship had been spotted, and the ogres made ready to welcome their prince and his crew. Grimwar thought of the slaves, the throng of captives crammed below the deck, of the victories that had marked the campaign along the Icereach coast.

He hoped his father would be pleased.

"You call these slaves?" King Grimtruth Bane snarled. His massive fists were planted on his hips as he stood next to his son on a landing above Winterheim's great harbor. The massive chamber had been excavated in the base of the lofty mountain. The great stone slabs of the Seagate were still rumbling shut, though the galley had been docked for nearly an hour.

"Why, they're scrawny as skeletons! It's a wonder they could even row the galley back to Winterheim!"

Beside the king a fat nobleman, Quendip, laughed in sycophantic amusement, but Grimwar's eyes were drawn past that obese ogre, to the more sympathetic gaze of the king's young wife, Thraid Dimmarkull. She wore a woolen gown and her long hair was loosely bound. Like the king, she had been roused from bed to greet the prince and his ship. Indeed, the smile that had brightened her face when he stepped off of *Goldwing* had been the highlight of this homecoming.

Now the prince, slumping under his father's criticism, took heart from the kindness he saw in the eyes of the ogress queen, who, though she was his stepmother, was several years younger than himself. He looked to Baldruk Dinmaker, saw that the dwarf was quietly standing behind the king. Naturally, he took no chances of falling under Grimtruth's stern gaze and any subsequent recrimination.

Grimwar Bane sighed. His mistake, if it could be called that, was arriving home at midnight, after the king had quaffed his fiery warqat and then fallen asleep. Of course, he had been rousted when the prince's galley returned, but he was inevitably ill tempered, bleary eyed, and thick tongued with drink.

"Of course they're scrawny," the prince retorted, indignance overcoming his better judgment. "They've been cooped up, some of them for three months! We didn't have enough to feed them, but now they'll fatten up again." He wanted to add that only two of the slaves had died during the months of confinement, but he decided not to waste the words.

The king leaned close, his bloodshot eyes squinting as he peered at the humans huddling on the wharf, now starting to file up the ramp toward the lower level of the ogre city. "What about wenches?" whispered Grimtruth, his boozy voice carrying easily to his young wife's ears. Thraid flushed and compressed her thick lips as she looked purposefully away.

Grimwar winced. Certainly Grimtruth would not be the first ogre bull to pleasure himself with a human female, but the king should at least have had the decency to discuss the matter at some other time, in some other company.

Grimwar found himself wanting to remind the young queen that the son was not the father. Instead, he met the king's leering stare and noticed a spittle of drool now dripping from Grimtruth's protruding lower lip. He abruptly vowed, privately but solemnly, that when he inherited the crown he would take every effort to avoid slobbering in public.

For now, he couldn't avoid his father's question.

"Yes, of course. We brought some wenches, some fair

and big-boned. Of course, we mostly need slaves to work in the mines, to row the galleys, to open the harbor gates, and so forth. So most of the prizes are men."

"Prizes?" The king snorted, but at least his thoughts had been distracted. He squinted at the queen, who was standing around in obvious embarrassment. "Why don't you run off to bed, my lady. I will see to the debarking of the prisoners."

"Of course, my lord," said Thraid meekly. Whatever she was thinking, she kept her thoughts to herself and turned to depart without another look at her husband or his son.

Grimtruth went to the stone parapet at the edge of the balcony and looked down at the column of humans. His son joined the ogre king, and for the first time noticed exactly how bedraggled, how filthy and scrawny and unkempt, these pathetic people looked.

"These were the best of the lot?" Grimtruth asked.

"We raided a dozen villages. Yes, these were the finest specimens. The tusker told us of each place where the humans had settled, and we hunted them there. In the first battles we took many slaves, but halfway through the campaign the galley was filled to bursting with extra humans. After that, we just killed them."

"All of them?"

Grimwar shrugged. "All of them that posed a threat. No doubt some women escaped and old ones too feeble to survive the winter. We left them no shelter, and polluted the wells and streams with the dead."

"Good tactic, that," Grimtruth acknowledged. "It would seem you have done well. I suppose some of this rabble will regain enough strength at least to till the fields in the Moongarden." Even in his praise he sounded so restrained that the prince couldn't help but feel insulted.

Once again the king's eyes scanned the disembarking slaves, who shuffled numbly into the dark cavern of Winterheim's Undercity. He pointed. "That one—bring her out of the line!"

Immediately an overseer hustled the woman forward.

She cried and struggled, flailing with arms that were practically skeletal, then clasping the pathetic remnant of a cloak around her body.

King Grimtruth looked hard before he spat, the spittle catching on his tusk. He took no note of it. "Bah, who could enjoy one of those stick-females? I'm off to my chambers—you will report the details of the campaign in the morning."

"Yes, Sire," Grimwar Bane said. He watched his father lumber away and wondered how the king, who was married to the most alluring ogress the prince had ever seen, could even think about turning to the affections of a human woman.

He looked back at *Goldwing* and saw that young dockworkers were boarding the ship. She would be scrubbed and painted, new gold plated onto the rails, fresh caulking added where the timbers were showing signs of wear.

It occurred to him that he already he missed the sea, but even then he knew that what he really missed was the mastery of a place, where he heeded the command of no ogre, no being of any kind, especially his fool of a father, the king.

As he rode the icecart up toward the Royal Quarter of Winterheim, Grimwar reflected glumly on his own wife. It was ironic to think that the prince was married to a female older than his father's wife by a full decade. Whereas Thraid Dimmarkull was a beautiful trophy, selected by a powerful king as his second wife, Stariz ber Glacierheim ber Bane had been matched to the crown prince because of her powerful family and the even mightier connection she had demonstrated to Gonnas the Strong, the god of all ogrekind.

His wife had not come to greet him at the dock, of course, though the king himself had been rousted from his slumber. No, Princess Stariz would doubtless be wallowing in deep prayer, seeking in the auguries of her god such messages as could be divined by the time and state of her husband's return. These revelations would inevitably be revealed to him in painstaking detail, as soon as he reached his apartments.

Grimwar leaned back in his seat, a wave of melancholy breaking over him. The icecart rumbled through the steeply inclined tunnel, climbing steadily, its magical vibrations lulling the prince.

The lower part of the cart was a large block of ice, glowing softly from an ancient enchantment. Upon this frozen base rested a cart such as might have been found on a grand carriage. Two huge, bearskin seats faced each other across a space large enough to hold a table or another pair of benches. Since the ride took the better part of an hour, it was not uncommon for a royal passenger to enjoy a repast during the climb or descent. The cart passed through a long tunnel that was fully encased, floors, walls and ceiling, in ice. The only illumination came from the magical ice that formed the base of the cart, an intentionally soft and pleasing glow.

Riding alone, Grimwar pulled the fur, a great bearskin, closer around him. His father and Thraid would have returned already, but since the prince had stayed to see the offloading of his own booty he had taken a different icecart back to the palace. Again Grimwar wondered—how could his father have such a treasure in his bed and yet fail to appreciate his good fortune?

Thraid Dimmarkull was not new to Winterheim. The daughter of a minor noble family, she had grown into ladyhood on the fringe of the circle familiar to the crown prince. Indeed Grimwar had noticed her, had seen that she received the right invitations, was placed near the royal table at banquets. He had spoken to her, and her smile had spoken in return. Certainly she sensed his attentions. Very quickly she had changed her style of dress to favor gaudy, low-cut gowns that favored her voluptuous figure. She made a startling contrast to the typical dour ogress clad in tentlike robes with the typical ogress face that seemed as likely to catch fire as to break into a smile.

Unfortunately, the king himself took notice of this vision of ogre femineity. Thraid had cheeks as round and red as apples, a wide mouth with full lips and dainty twin tusks, breasts that swelled with every movement. Her waist was slender, by ogre standards, and her legs long and muscular.

Grimwar had watched jealously as his father had made his desires known. During his decades on the throne, the king had grown tired of his first wife, Hananreit ber Fallscape. Abruptly he ordered her exiled to the remote island of Dracoheim. After a brief farewell to her only son, the galley had taken Hanareit away at the first crack of spring, three and a half years ago. There, so far as the prince knew, his mother still spent her days in the dark, sky-piercing castle on that fortress isle, pining for the luxurious life she had known in Winterheim.

Thraid had been summoned to the royal chambers barely a week after the Elder Queen's departure. Shortly thereafter the Grimtruth had taken her as his Younger Queen. And as if to emphasize his ultimate power, the king at the same time had arranged for the daughter of the baron of Glacierheim to marry his son, the royal heir. Stariz had been brought to Winterheim, and father and son had each been joined to a mate in a double ceremony at the Neuwinter Rites.

The icecart's rumbling gradually slowed. The narrow corridor opened into a vast chamber, illuminated with a hundred torches. Looming far above the prince saw the great gates of the palace. He was home.

He suddenly felt a terrible longing for *Goldwing*, and the sea.

"The auguries are positive, for now." Stariz Ber Glacierheim reported, as a human slave woman removed Grimwar Bane's boots and several others filled a great marble tub with steaming water. "You came back with many slaves, and you won great victories over the humans."

"Yes, these are truths," the prince said, trying to suppress his irritation. He could have told her these very facts! Yet he had long ago learned that it was best not to act impatient with his wife's prognostications. Her words had a way of turning very ugly very fast if she sensed his devotion was wandering.

Stariz began to recite a remarkable litany of his landings, the tactics he used to capture each human village, numbering the captured and the dead. This recounting, Grimwar suspected, was intended to serve as a reminder that she could keep magical tabs on him wherever he roamed. Whether she had a spy in his crew or actually learned through the medium of her arcane powers, the prince did not know. Her information, as always, proved impressively accurate.

Stariz mentioned the name of an ogre who had been killed in the second raid, where more than a hundred humans had fought courageously. She droned on. Despite his good intentions to pay conspicuous heed to her words, the prince found his thoughts following their own path. He gazed curiously at his wife, studying her as if he was observing a picture, an image completely detached from the words she was saying.

Stariz had never been a beauty. Her body was stout and squarish, like her face, possessing all the grace of a craggy, ice-splintered boulder. Ropy strands of hair dangled past her shoulders, forever unkempt. Instead of the full lips that added such beauty to Thraid's visage, Stariz's appearance was dominated by an exceptionally large nose, and two prominent tusks that were nearly as big as a young male's.

"And in the final battle you killed the men, but allowed the women to escape!" Stariz concluded. There was a hint of a questioning in her statement.

"Yes. It was no different than I had done before. What use are the wenches with no men? I suspect the lot of them will die over the winter."

"I would not be so sure," she said, with a tone of warning.

"What do you mean?"

"You remember my prophecy, the words I said to you in spring?"

"Yes," Grimwar replied. "I must beware an elf. He will be a messenger, *the* messenger of the Bane Dynasty's doom. My princess, Baldruk and I were forever interrogating prisoners, and always we asked about an elf. The humans of Icereach know nothing of any elves—they think they are creatures of myth!"

"Would that were true," muttered Stariz.

"Aye, praise to Gonnas," Grimwar agreed. He had been well schooled on the events of Krynn's history over the past five thousand years, since the rise of humans and elves had driven his own people, once masters of the world, into remote enclaves such as Icereach.

"But here we are strong—the Kingdom of Suderhold endures, even when the rest of ogrekind is on the wane!"

"Yes, that is true . . . so far," Stariz mildly agreed. The prince was surprised and a little unsettled to see a hint of real fear in his wife's eyes.

"The auguries show great danger in the future," she continued. "The warning about the elven messenger came to me again, writ large in words of fire. The god tells me that a human woman may be the agent of his might and our doom."

"I'm tired," Grimwar objected, suddenly fed up with all the complications of this homecoming. "Tell me the rest in the morning." He rose, bypassing his waiting bath on the way to their cavelike sleeping chamber and its warm hearthfire.

"I will tell you now," Stariz said sharply, rising to follow him. "Even so, I fear I may be too late."

8

The Castaway

The horizon was gray, angry cloud, and gray, angry water. A gray, angry mist swirled through the air. Now, at least, the murk and tumult was proof of real weather, not the enchantment of elven sorcerers.

Cutter was bearing due east, parallel to the coast of Ansalon, which was somewhere out of sight a hundred miles to the north. The mainsail billowed overhead, angled sharply across the deck, filled with the canted forces of a northerly wind. The topsail and jib remained in the locker, at least for now.

Three days earlier, Kerrick had been borne by the Than-Thalas through the lofty Towers of El'i. He was blocked from returning to his homeland, but the moment he turned *Cutter* toward the east a strong tailwind had risen, and his boat fairly flew along. His aches and bruises were healing, and his broken rib too. He quickly fell into a comfortable routine with his boat. Now, surrounded by the freedom of the ocean, he had finally begun to feel a little bit like his old self again.

In this weather he wore his leather cloak, a good thing, too, as spray constantly blew over the gunwale. Throughout the long afternoon his course didn't vary. He was navigating by compass since he could see little of the sun through the murk of clouds. Only the gradual darkening of his surroundings told him that evening approached. He decided to take in some sail for the night so that he could rest a little during the hours ahead.

He set the tiller in place and went forward. He hauled on the line, reducing the mainsail. The boat still made good headway but no longer such rocketing speed.

Pitch darkness had descended when he finally noticed a break in the overcast. He was sitting on the bench atop the cabin, sipping a small, scalding hot cup of Istarian tea, when he saw a single star, bright with a hazy shade of green, sparkling just above the bow. He knew then that Zivilyn Greentree had emerged from the heavens to guide his voyage.

Kerrick felt a sense of connection with that iridescent blur of emerald. Zivilyn was a wandering planet, unfixed in the heavens, and to spot it now, directly on his bearing, could only be an omen. That star had been the patron god of his clan since the dawn of elvenkind. Most of the Silvanesti elves saved their highest allegiance for the great E'li Paladine, but the Fallabrines and many other elves of House Mariner traditionally made their devotions to Zivilyn Greentree. It was an odd choice, in a way, for a clan of sailors. As a wanderer, the star Zivilyn was of little use in navigation, and its sporadic pattern meant that it was often absent from view for years, even decades, at a time.

As the sky cleared, his eyes swept the rest of the constellations—the great Draco Paladine, the five-headed serpent of Takhisis, Gilean and his open book, and the rest. Only at sea could the stars appear so bright. They were like familiar landmarks on a highway, symbols that told a sailor his bearing and the number of hours until dawn.

Far to the south another bright speck of light caught his eye. This was tinted yellow, and he recognized Chislev Wilder, the symbol of a nature goddess cherished by many humans, especially barbarians. As he watched that star drifted visibly lower until it was finally obscured in the mists lying close to the horizon.

He brought his bedroll into the cockpit and tied off the sail to steady his course while he slept. With the tiller planted easily under his arm, he leaned back, let the green light of Zivilyn spill across his face, and went to sleep with a prayer on his lips.

The hull smashed into something solid, and Kerrick was thrown forward. *Cutter* heeled crazily, and he heard the sound of a rough, solid surface scraping past the hull. Groggy and face down he tried to collect his thoughts—collision! With what?

"Hey, slow down there!"

The high-pitched voice was so childlike that the elf felt certain he was dreaming. Sometimes the solitude of sea gave him dazed visions.

"Wait for me!"

Now Kerrick forced himself to his knees, still hearing that awful grating against the hull. The boat had slowed, but was still moving. Gray light brightened the surroundings, and he knew that it was near dawn. He sat up, blinking, rubbing his forehead where he had banged it against the cabin bulkhead. Through blurred eyes he saw something fly through the air, then heard the sound of a body landing on deck.

"Thanks for nothing," sniffed his visitor. "You could have at least circled around or something. I almost landed in the water! Do you know how long it takes to dry out this topknot?"

"Topknot?" Kerrick gaped at the diminutive person standing lightly on the cockpit bench. The elf's head was still aching, and he couldn't think—couldn't even *imagine*—what he had collided with so far out to sea. Sure enough, though, a kender had somehow materialized aboard his sailboat.

"Coraltop Netfisher, at your service," said the fellow with a deep bow, embellished with a wide flourish of both hands. The kender hopped down from the bench and sauntered over to the elf. "Say, you're bleeding," he observed with a cluck of his tongue. "Have an accident or something?"

Kerrick pulled his hand away and groaned at the slick redness he saw. "Who are you?" he demanded. "And what, by all the gods, did I hit?"

"Well, *that*, of course." The kender pointed off the stern. "I should have thought it was obvious, but then you *did* get a nasty bump on the head. You're probably still confused."

The elf wasn't listening any longer. Instead, he was staring at a great, barren mound rising from the placid ocean. The shape was much too broad to be the barnacle-encrusted hull of a capsized ship, which was the only possibility that entered the elf's mind.

He suddenly became aware of the sound of rushing water. "We've been holed!" he cried, and threw open the hatch to the cabin. In there it was dry. "Farther forward!" he said, sprinting along the narrow catwalk, leaning out over the gunwale.

He quickly spotted the damage, several planks along the starboard side, scored with ugly cracks. Coraltop Netfisher had scrambled right behind him, stretching out far over the water for a good look.

"Say, that doesn't look too healthy," the kender said. "Do you think this boat will sink? That happened to the last boat I was on. Purely accidental of course, and I'd just as soon not have it happen again."

"Here!" Kerrick threw open the small hatch in the prow. "Climb down there and have a look—if you see water coming in, take some of the canvas you find there and try to plug the hole."

"That sounds like fun!" agreed the kender cheerfully. In an instant he dropped below, feet first.

Kerrick went back to the main hold and pulled open that hatch. Quickly the sound of gurgling water reached his ears, and he whispered a fervent prayer to Zivilyn Greentree, pleading with the god for enough time to patch the boat before it went under. He plunged into the darkness, reaching for the bucket of tar and a swath of spare canvas.

"That was sure exciting!" Coraltop Netfisher told him an hour later. *Cutter* wallowed in the thankfully gentle swell. All of her sails were furled, and the kender and elf had managed to reduce the water pouring in through several holes to a trickle.

Kerrick flopped on the deck, exhausted. "I'm not sure I could have done it without your help," he admitted. "Now, we've got to pump for the rest of the day, and we might just find that we're seaworthy again. Here, I'll show you how to work the pump, while I make some caulk and try for a more permanent repair."

For the time being he had to admit he didn't mind the kender's company, though he was sure he would have cause to regret that feeling. Among all the peoples of Krynn, there was no more vexing and troublesome race than the small, fearless, and eternally curious kender.

Kerrick finally had a moment to inspect "his kender," who was smiling at him guilelessly. Coraltop's long red hair was bundled into the typical knot in the middle of his scalp, with a glossy tail hanging loosely as far as his waist. He wore a green shirt of some kind of mesh, gathered in at the waist by a belt of the same material. His feet and legs were bare, and he bore no apparent possessions.

After a minute of coaching, Coraltop was cranking the pump handle with a look of real delight. He squinted at the bellows mechanism, and the tip of his tongue protruded slightly from his lips as he set himself to the work with a look of real concentration.

"Hey, look at the way the water comes shooting out this hose!" he cried in delight as, moments later, the contents of the bilge started spraying over the side. "But it's all getting wasted into the ocean—here, we can use it for a shower." Quickly he pulled the nozzle around so that cold water washed over the elf. "You can go first," he said graciously.

"This is no time for joking around," snapped Kerrick. "Do you want to stay afloat or not?"

"Stay afloat," pouted the diminutive passenger, but he followed the elf's instructions.

Kerrick made his way forward again, and ducked into the main hold. The saturated canvas he had jammed into the cracks was leaking badly, and he wasted no time in plastering caulk over it. By the time he was done his muscles ached, and his hair was stuck to his face with a mixture of sweat and caulk. With a sigh he came back up on deck and sat on the bench next to Coraltop, who was still pumping. A short distance away, rising in a great dome above the surface of the water, he could spot the dark shape of the massive obstacle that had almost doomed his little boat. He was just about to ask the kender about it, when his passenger preempted his question with a query of his own.

"What happened to your ear?"

The elf froze. His hand went to his scar, feeling the scab, the strangely rounded flap which once been a long, slender, elegantly tapered ear.

"I had an accident," he said curtly.

"I've had *lots* of accidents," Coraltop replied proudly, before frowning. "I never got half my ear cut off, though. That must have really been some accident! Tell me what happened. Don't leave out any good parts."

"No." Kerrick slumped. He thought about raising the sail, but it seemed like far too much work. Instead, he leaned his head back against the gunwale and remembered Silvanesti. Closing his eyes, he imagined that he could smell the blossoms of the royal gardens, hear the songs of the flautists in their towers and the lyres of the wandering minstrels as they sang their way down the city's winding streets. It seemed unthinkable that he was exiled from the center of his world. He missed Silvanesti with such inexpressible pain that, for a few moments, he actually toyed with the thought of throwing himself over the side, of ending his suffering right here. He knew he had had to fight the wave of self-pity that was washing over him.

"So, where are we going?" asked Coraltop. "Wouldn't we get there faster if we put up the sail?"

Kerrick groaned inwardly and cracked open one eye. Again he saw that great, floating mass off to the side, already black against the growing darkness.

"How'd you end up on that thing, anyway?" he finally asked. "And what is it exactly?"

"Well, my last ship sank, and I would have sunk too, if I wasn't a pretty darned good swimmer. 'You swim like a whale,' my Grandmother Annatree used to say. But of course whales swim better, probably because they have more practice. I wouldn't mind being a whale, except for all the drawbacks. Of course, like my grandmother used to say, 'Life isn't fair—unless you're lucky.' Do you think I'm lucky?"

"I think . . . well, you must be, yes." The elf chuckled dryly in spite of himself. Kender might be utterly fearless to the point of stupidity, but they were amusing. Well, he could use some laughs in his situation.

"What *kind* of ship were you on?" he persisted.

"It was a Tarsian trading galley," the kender replied. He seemed almost sorrowful. "The captain was really nice. I met him just two days out of Tarsis, when I woke up from my nap and went on deck to say hello. He said he going to tie a stone to my foot and throw me in the water to see how well I could swim." Coraltop sighed. "His wife was there, and she was even nicer. She pointed out that I couldn't very well swim with a stone tied to my foot—although I can surprisingly well—she made me her cabin boy, and as long as I stayed out of the captain's 'dang-blasted way' I got to roam all over the ship and see how things worked."

Kerrick knew the kind of ship Coraltop was talking about. Indeed, the sturdy trading vessels were probably the most common large craft along the coast of southern Ansalon. Occasionally one would stop and visit Silvanesti, though the royal tariffs were exorbitant and insured that only elven captains made much profit bringing goods to or from the great port of Silvanost.

"What happened to the galley? How did it sink?" He knew that the trading galleys were famously seaworthy and offered a brief prayer to Zivilyn in memory of the doomed sailors.

"We got smashed up by a dragon turtle," Coraltop replied cheerfully. "Boy, was *that* exciting! It had fins the size of your sails, and a mouth as big as a castle gate! Why, it bit that galley right in two. Some of the sailors got eaten up, I'm sorry to say. The rest of them tumbled into the water, but they didn't swim as well as I did. Fortunately I was holding onto a barrel—it turned out to be a barrel half full of water, which is a good thing because you can't imagine how *thirsty* a person gets—"

The kender prattled on, but Kerrick wasn't listening any more. Instead, he was staring at the vast, domed shape wallowing in the waves, looking at it with a sense of dull horror.

Dragon turtle! He had never before seen one—nor had he ever spoke to a sailor who had encountered one of the legendary ocean monsters. They were the stuff of nautical folklore, horrors of the deep that could reputedly crush a ship with one bite, scattering its crewmen into the sea, allowing the monster to leisurely gulp down the hapless adrift sailors.

That, he suddenly realized, was what the *Cutter* had rammed. With new wariness, he looked out at the floating blob, noting the knobs on its rough surface, gaping at its huge size. Yes, dragon turtle it was—and if he was lucky, it was stunned or sound asleep.

"Get to the mast!" hissed the elf. "We're going to raise the sail!"

Was it his imagination or had the great shape twitched? He looked for a sign of a scaly head or a vicious, lashing tail, claws like iron battering rams.

A wave splashed against the hull, breaking to either

side. Now the head was rising, a visage of ugly leather, crusty with barnacles except for a sharp, beaklike snout, impossibly, monstrously huge. Water spilled from the flat skull, a sheet of brine pouring like a waterfall. The monster craned its neck and yawned, revealing a slick, pink maw surrounded by a pair of serrated jaws wide enough, it seemed, to swallow the *Cutter*.

"The mast is that big pole, right?" Coraltop asked, standing up. "I'm becoming quite the expert sailor. What do you want me to—"

"Quiet!" whispered Kerrick, seizing the kender and yanking him down into the cockpit. His eyes just barely above the level of the gunwale, the elf watched the great dragon turtle, trying unsuccessfully to suppress the trembling that seized his limbs. The creature's face was primitive, saurian. The one eye turned lazily toward the sailboat was black, cold, and easily as big as the elf's armspan.

"Oh, we're hiding?" Coraltop guessed, with an exaggerated whisper. "I like this game!"

Kerrick's full attention was focused on the dragon turtle. The legends had spoken of a shell as long as *Cutter*'s thirty feet, but this monster was three times that, at least. The great armored plate slowly began to swivel towards him. Water churned, and the elf saw two huge webbed and taloned feet kick into the air. The shell angled down, and a large wave churned as it surged toward the sailboat in a rolling crest.

The beast dove, vanished. A long, scaly tail thrashed the air and followed into the depths, leaving a vortex of frothing water swirling on the surface. Kerrick and Coraltop clutched the gunwale as the wave heaved *Cutter* upward, rocking them violently back and forth as it passed on until, once more, they bobbed on a placid, featureless sea.

"Lucky for me—as my grandmother used to say—that it never did that while *I* was sitting on it," Coraltop said.

The elf's head was spinning. "You were riding on that dragon turtle." He glared furiously at the kender, straining to keep his voice low. "I thought you said you were clinging to a barrel."

"Oh, I drank almost all the water that was in that keg, I remember, and I was starting to get kind of hungry. Then the dragon turtle surfaced, and I think it fell asleep. Say, do you have anything to eat?"

"Yes—but first let's get some canvas up. I want to be away from here before that thing surfaces."

"Not much chance of that," said Coraltop Netfisher. "It'll be coming up real quick now, like it did when it ate my other boat. First you see it, then you don't, then bang!" He leaned over the gunwale, stretching down so far that his nose was bare inches from the gentle swell.

The elf wasted no time staring into the depths. He scrambled past the cabin and started to unlash the sail from the main boom. If the dragon turtle had sounded merely to rise up and smash his boat, they would never get away in time. If it had dived for reasons of its own, they still had a chance.

His hands shook so badly that for a second he could only fumble with the lines. Forcing himself to be calm, he at last freed the ropes, one after the other, that bundled the sail onto the long timber. He was reaching for the mainsail guyline when Coraltop Netfisher's voice, incongruously cheerful, reached him.

"Here it comes!" chirped the kender, pointing into the ocean deeps.

Kerrick felt the boat slide sideways and grabbed onto the mast as *Cutter* tilted violently. He swung into space, certain they would capsize, but the little boat spilled down the water rushing off of the great carapace. The dragon turtle's great head broke from the surface, rising past the boat, one eye glaring coldly. Its jaws were wide, blue-green brine gushing out, as the elf tumbled, getting tangled in the sail. Coraltop fell sprawling on the deck of the cockpit.

"Look out!" shouted the kender, his narrow face split by a wide, toothy grin, as he tried unsuccessfully to lift himself up.

"Zivilyn Greentree protect us!" the elf prayed fervently, lost in the folds of the sail, clutching the mast and feeling the impact as the sailboat spilled off the shell and plunged back into the ocean.

The bow and half the hull vanished into blue water, but in another instant *Cutter*'s sharp prow rose up out of the sea, water pouring off the deck. The elf swung wildly, free of the sail now, still clinging to the mast, then slamming into the boom and feeling—*hearing*—his arm snap. He saw the monster's rough, scaled shell rolling past, looming out of the water like a mountainous horizon, then following the head, which had already plunged into the depths.

The last thing he saw was the spiked tail, long and wicked as a dragon. It lashed overhead, striking the mast and boom with a sickening crack of timber. Kerrick was buried under a wave of billowing blue canvas as a hard beam smashed him in the skull.

The blue faded to black.

9

Strongwind Whalebone

How many more days?" Garta asked Moreen, as the tribe broke camp on a drizzly fall morning. The wind was light, fortunately, but dampness permeated every one of the Arktos, and there was no wood to spare for a breakfast fire. "Remember, Little Mouse said he found a cave yesterday. Wouldn't it be a good idea to at least have a look at it before we go any farther north?"

"I did have a look at it," the chiefwoman replied, with a shake of her head.

"When?" the matron inquired, surprised. "You were still up when I got the last of the children bedded down, and that was halfway into the night!"

Moreen sighed. "I went up there early this morning, before the rest of you stirred. Mouse was right. It was pretty big, and it was dry—but not big enough for all of us, unless you want to spend the winter standing up. It had a wide mouth facing south, so it wouldn't provide any shelter against the Sturmfrost."

Garta blanched and drew a deep breath. It was an awareness they all shared—the onslaught of the Sturmfrost was less than three months away, now.

"Well, we have to find something better then, don't we?" she said with forced cheerfulness. "How far can it be to this Tall Cedar Bay you told us about? Surely we must be getting close?"

Moreen nodded, once again wondering if she should share her secret, her hope of finding safety for the tribe in ancient Brackenrock. Instead, she changed the subject. "Our food situation is very good, now."

They had plenty of food, thanks to the black whale. Immediately after the battle with the thanoi, the women had set to work with skinning knives, carving long strips of flesh from the meaty carcass. For two weeks the elders tended low fires and suspended the strips of meat on makeshift racks made from the weapons recovered from the slain walrus-men.

Garta's hand came to rest on Moreen's shoulder. "I don't mean to question your judgment," she said softly. "You already know how hard this is on the little ones—"

"And the elders, yes." The chiefwoman looked at the hobbling grandfathers and grandmothers, most of them accompanied by a child or toddler. She saw the women hoisting great backpacks, the bundles of dried whale meat that weighed them down so much they couldn't move any faster than the elders.

"Up the coast again today?" Bruni asked cheerfully, coming up to the pair. The big woman carried a pack twice as large as anyone else's, with a bundle of harpoons and spears lashed crossways to the top that gave her the appearance of some great, antlered beast.

"Yes. A few more days, maybe a week, along here."

Bruni narrowed her eyes shrewdly. "My grandfather told me once of an old ruin, a place built by the Arktos in generations past. What was it called, again?"

"Brackenrock?" Garta said in surprise. "You're not taking us *there*, are you?"

Moreen sighed. "The thought had crossed my mind."

"But—but even if it exists, it was taken over by monsters! Dragons!" Garta's round face was a picture of astonishment, then she blinked and lowered her eyes. "I mean, I'm not trying to question your judgment, but what are you *thinking*?"

"First, I believe Brackenrock exists. Dinekki saw it in a vision, and we have to trust the guidance of Chislev Wilder. Dinekki could see it, up on the hills above the water. Steam was rising from several vents, so perhaps the legends are true, and Brackenrock stays warm all winter, even through the Sturmfrost."

"What about the dragons? What about the Scattering? What about the risks of going there?"

"Dinekki also says that there are no dragons there. I trust her. Chislev protect us—we'll find a way to make it."

"Moreen! Come quick!" Little Mouse was running towards them along the hilltop above the beach.

"What is it now?" she snapped, more irritably than she intended.

"It's that Highlander. He's back again, with two dozen warriors. He wants to talk to you again."

Lars Redbeard again wore the great wolfskin cloak, with the lupine head, jaws agape, resting like a crown on his scalp. He was waiting for Moreen on the next hill, with his band of fur-clad spearmen.

Little Mouse and Bruni accompanied the chiefwoman, who stopped twenty paces short of the sub-chief and crossed her arms over her chest.

"I bring you greetings from Strongwind Whalebone, king of Icereach."

"Send the 'king' my greetings in return." She couldn't keep the irony out of her voice. Who was this Strongwind Whalebone, who thought he was a monarch of all Icereach?

"Hear me, Moreen Seal-Slayer."

"She is Moreen Chiefwoman now," Bruni chided. "Daughter of Redfist Bayguard, and heir to the Black Bearskin."

Redbeard's eyes widened, and he bowed stiffly from the waist. Moreen wasn't sure if she was being mocked or not. "I bring you another invitation from Strongwind

Whalebone—he desires that you come to Guildgerglow to meet with him."

"My answer remains the same," Moreen retorted. "My tribe is here, and they need me. If Strongwind Whalebone wants to meet with me, he should come to the coast. We will not walk too fast for him to catch us," she added with a snort.

"We realize that we insulted you before, that we erred with clumsy words. Strongwind Whalebone admits his mistakes and tries to learn from them. To this end he has authorized a gift, something he alone can offer."

Lars Redbeard gestured, and one of his men came forward with a small, but obviously very heavy, box. He set it down on a flat rock and lifted the top to reveal a stack of gleaming gold coins.

"This treasure is considerable, enough to justify a noble rank among our people. My king offers it to you as proof of his honor and his good intentions. Will you accept his gift and accompany me to his castle?"

"What need have I of the yellow metal?" snapped Moreen.

Lars Redbeard did not seem to take offense. "Why, *everyone* has a use for gold," he replied earnestly. "You can use it for barter or for ornamentation!"

"It's too heavy—it would make more sense for you to give us food," replied the chiefwoman.

"Oh, I think we might accept the king's gift," Bruni said gently.

Moreen looked into the strongbox, impressed in spite of herself. The yellow metal had a beauty, a purity, a seductive gleam, she had to admit. She felt angry at her weakness, glared at Bruni, and once again shook her head firmly. "No—thank you."

The emissary stiffened and cleared his throat. "It is important. You *must* come with me."

"Why, you big wolf!" snapped Little Mouse, stepping between Bruni and Moreen to glare up at the Highlander. "You can't talk to my chiefwoman that way!"

He took another step forward as Lars Redbeard narrowed his eyes menacingly. Despite the bulk of her heavy pack, Bruni leaned down and snatched the lad by his tunic, pulling him back.

Moreen was glad for the momentary distraction. She felt trapped, uncertain.

"I know you are concerned for your people," Lars continued. "I give you my word—they will be safe. They will be under the protection of my warriors." He gestured behind him, though his eyes never left the chiefwoman's face. "Look, we have brought food and furs, enough to greatly improve the comfort of your tribe."

For the first time Moreen noticed the large bundles that were sitting on the ground just beyond the party of Highlanders. She saw sheepskins and several large white bear pelts. There were a number of stout casks, as well as bags bulging with what she supposed must be grains or dried food. She had spoken too rashly. Surely these were well-intended gifts.

Her eyes also took in the strangers' clubs and axes, the stout spears and several great longbows outfitting the band. Finally she made her decision.

"Let me see the bounty you have brought," she declared imperiously, striding past Lars Redbeard to look at the food and furs scattered on the ground.

She knelt and touched a sheepskin. The wool was soft and clean, the leather expertly tanned—this one pelt alone might mean the difference between life and death for one of the Arktos children. She quickly saw that the sacks were full of edibles. She smelled barley, saw the pebbly outlines of dried berries. Two of the casks had the glossy sheen and briny stink of fish oil, another valuable commodity, while a third, with a distinct smell of its own, undoubtedly contained warqat, the pungent brew the Highlanders reportedly consumed by the barrelful to while away the boredom of winter.

If this was a trick, it was a very generous one.

"Very well," she declared, standing up and looking

frankly at Lars Redbeard. She was surprised, and secretly pleased, at the palpable relief flooding his features. "I will visit King Strongwind Whalebone of the Highlanders. You may tell him that Moreen Bayguard, chief of the Arktos, agrees to be his guest."

As soon as they came through the pass on the inland ridge, Moreen knew that "village" was a clear misnomer for the Highlander stronghold. Indeed, she had never seen, nor even imagined, such a sprawling and solid-looking community. Most of Guilderglow was concealed by a lofty stone wall, but she could see towers, several smoking chimneys, and a great blockhouse of a building all rising beyond the rampart. The near slopes were scored with regular terraces, autumn brown now but showing the last hints of summer colors. The shallow valley before them sparkled with ponds and streams. She paused, not just because she was out of breath but to take in the view and wonder, once again, whether she was doing the right thing.

"Quite a place, don't you think?" Lars Redbeard said.

"I know I've never seen the like," Bruni admitted, saving Moreen the task of muttering her impressions.

The two women had been escorted here by four of the Highlanders, while the rest of Redbeard's band had stayed with the Arktos. They agreed to keep moving northward while she took this detour inland, a trek that had required four days, most of the journey uphill.

"We'll rest up here for a bit," Strongwind's emissary said. "That climb up to the pass takes a lot out of even a veteran Highlander. I admit, the two of you did very well."

Moreen, who wanted nothing more than to collapse on the ground and gasp for breath, nodded gravely. "I can see why these are called the Highlands," she said, then immediately wished she hadn't said anything so obvious and foolish.

Indeed, they were surrounded by an array of dazzling

mountain peaks. Some of the summits rose like stony needles into the sky, with great slabs of bare cliff plummeting down every side. Lofty cornices of snow curled like graceful decorations upon their unattainable heights. Other mountains were domed and more gradual of slope, but every bit as high in their elevations, often laced with dazzling snowfields and great, crevassed swaths of glacier. The autumn sun was low, but even in the limited light the effect was nearly blinding. She could only imagine this vista under the brilliant glare of summer's sun.

It seemed strangely incongruous to see such a wintry landscape and at the same time wide pastures and irrigated fields below the walls of Guilderglow.

"Those are the Scarred Rocks."

Lars pointed to a tangle of dark stone on the valley floor. The route down from the pass led into the maze, where it twisted and curled this way and that before emerging to climb terraced slopes on the far side.

"Our first line of defense," the Highlander said. "Any army coming to attack us must force its way through traps and ambushes and many other obstacles."

"I will remember that, in case my meeting with your king does not go smoothly." Moreen was immediately aware that her words were bluster. Seeing Guilderglow she could think of Strongwind Whalebone as a king, and her fears were reawakened.

It amazed her to observe white specks dotting the pastures—*thousands* of sheep, all within her field of view. Lower down, where the ground was marshy, she spotted herds of large brown cattle. How much firewood did it take to account for the black columns of smoke rising from so many chimneys?

"Are you rested, ready to go the rest of the way?" asked Lars Redbeard solicitously.

"Yes," the chiefwoman replied, wishing desperately that she had her grandfather's black bear cloak or some visible symbol of her leadership status. She felt very plain, ordinary, but there was nothing to do but continue onward.

"Yes," she repeated. "Let us go and meet the king of the Highlanders."

Shaggy, fox-faced dogs ran everywhere, chasing children or being chased in return. The stink of manure and sweat and soot permeated the air, the walls and, apparently, the people. It cloyed so thickly in Moreen's nostrils that she knew she would be smelling it for days after she left Guilderglow.

From a great, blocky building she heard hammering and shouting, and Lars told her this was a smelter, where men broke up coal for burning, and extracted gold from precious ore. The great city gates had opened wide for their approach. The chiefwoman was acutely conscious of the stares of bearded scowling men and suspicious scowling women who thronged both sides of the narrow street or looked down from the balconies that seemed to line the front of every house.

The road crested a little hill, then descended steeply to cross a shallow stream over a stone bridge. On one side of the bridge loomed a tall mill, waterwheel churning, while the other had a porch with many benches and tables. Here Highlanders, all of them men except for some serving wenches, sat hunched over mugs of warqat. They watched her pass with unreadable expressions.

Looking down, she noticed that the shallow water below the bridge was brown, spotted with refuse. Every space of land within the city walls seemed crammed with overuse: tiny, walled yards filled with linens hanging in the sun; houses that crowded together and loomed surprisingly high, with frail balconies leaning over the muddy street. From the gutters the stink of sewage was abominable.

They reached the next crest and she saw, lying ahead, the castle of King Strongwind. It occupied a low knoll in the midst of the city's rolling terrain. Its wall was higher than the city wall, though it had several wide gaps revealing the courtyard and royal buildings. Judging by the scaffolding, the great stacks of stone already cut into blocks, Moreen deduced that the royal domicile was a work in progress.

The little party strolled through the uncompleted gate in the castle perimeter, and the chiefwoman was stunned as she caught sight of the huge doors leading into the keep.

"Are those solid gold?" she asked, in spite of her determination to keep her amazement to herself.

"Solid gold. Each weighs many tons," Lars said proudly. "Strongwind Whalebone had them carved with his own crest."

That crest, she saw, was a long-hafted battle axe crossed with a great spear, the combination crowned by the antlered head of a massive elk. However, the raised pattern on smooth metal was crudely rendered. Moreen had seen Dinekki, even after her hands had become gnarled with age, do finer work on an ivory carving.

The mighty doors rumbled outward on tracks that vibrated with enough force that Moreen could feel it underfoot. They parted to reveal a great hall, with a lofty, arched ceiling and a dozen or more stout wooden columns lining each wall. These pillars held several sconces, and bright oil lamps were suspended from each, combining to cast a brilliant glow through the middle of the great chamber. The far end remained shadowed.

Many people stood behind these columns, watching with the same surly expressions she had sensed from the folk in the city. The main difference here was that these people, in dyed woolen capes and gowns, feathered caps, oil-polished boots and sandals, were much better dressed than those she'd encountered amid the city streets.

The center of the hall was empty, except for a carpet of white bearskin extending like a line into the shadows at the far end. Her eyes were drawn to a lofty chair. More lights flared into existence—magical globes that floated in the air, ignited perfectly on cue, to reveal the great man himself, sitting high up in his thrown and looking down upon the small party advancing along the bearskin carpet. A great helm, with a rack of elk antlers crowning a metal cap, adorned his head, and his yellow beard was thick, with the ends braided into twin strands. He wore gold chains around his neck, gold bracelets on his wrists, and his boots were bright with gold buckles.

Everything about this place, she suddenly realized, was designed to flaunt his greatness, and she found herself wondering: How great can he really be that he needs this exaggeration to awe me?

She came to a stop below the lofty throne. She was only vaguely aware that Lars and Bruni had stopped somewhere behind her. Her mounting irritation, as it so often did, found its way to her tongue.

"Are you Strongwind Whalebone?" she demanded. "I can hardly see you way up there!"

She heard gasps and mutters from the surrounding galleries, and footsteps behind her indicated that Lars Redbeard was hastening forward. Those footsteps ceased when Strongwind held up a hand glittering with gold rings. Moreen was startled to see amusement sparkling in his eyes, which—now that she looked closely—were a rather appealing shade of light blue.

"I had better climb down, then" he said mildly, scrambling out of the big chair and down the several steps to the floor with surprising ease—surprising, considering the full weight of gold that was draped about his person, his wardrobe, including the massive, antlered, solid-gold-seeming helm. "I greet you, Moreen Bayguard, chief of the Arktos."

There were some snickers at his words, but the king—she couldn't help now but think of him as a king—glared sternly into the galleries, and the rebuked fell instantly silent.

"And I greet you, Strongwind Whalebone, King of the Highlanders."

"Thank you for coming to see me," he said, and he sounded genuinely grateful. "I know this has been a tragic year for your people, and I want you to know that you have my sympathy and my support."

Moreen was suddenly glad she had come. To her, the

Highlanders had always been strange and vaguely frightening beings whom the Arktos had encountered only rarely. Sometimes these meetings resulted in trade, sometimes in violence, but never had she stopped to consider that the Highlanders were humans like herself.

"Please, may I have the honor of showing you my castle?" inquired the king, with a tone of utmost respect. He gestured toward a door in the side of the great hall.

"I would be greatly interested," Moreen replied sincerely. He extended his arm and, after a moment's hesitation, she put her hand on his elbow. The courtiers in their path scurried out of the way as he led her away, and the door closed behind them. She felt stronger, somehow, emboldened by the fact that they were now beyond the hostile scrutiny of his citizens.

They went down a long, partially open hallway, meeting only a few servants who scuttled, eyes downcast, out of the way. To their left was a series of columns, beyond which lay a small courtyard. Moreen took in an array of laundry tubs and saw a large cage where dogs barked and yelped, scampering back and forth as they spotted the king.

"My pack," the king said proudly. "They pull sleds over the snow in the winter and chase game during the warmer months." He indicated the antlers that hung so ostentatiously from his helm. "It was my dogs that brought this stag to bay, though I myself took it with a spearcast."

They went into a square, stone-walled building where he proudly showed her his mint, where molten gold was poured into molds, shaped into small bars with the emblem of the weapons and antlers embossed on each. This was a dark, sooty place, with a scent of smoke that stung Moreen's nostrils, but she listened politely as he showed her the melting vats and the great, coal-fired furnaces that melted metal. The woman had not seen coal before, but she nodded and watched as the firetenders shoveled the stuff into the great roaring maw. Even from across the room she could feel the tremendous heat, knew that this was a blaze hotter than any fueled by wood or charcoal.

"We mine gold from the highland valleys above Guilderglow," explained Strongwind. "We possess the richest orefields in all the Icereach."

"This gold is why you call yourself king of Icereach?" Moreen asked bluntly.

The monarch scowled, momentarily irritated. "No! It has helped me to ensure that the other lords appreciate my status," he admitted. "Here, let me show you something in my map room."

He led her into a large chamber, with a mosaic of tiles and several small pieces of gold set into the floor. Much of the floor was blue granite, which met the more detailed tiles along a twisting and irregular line. Other tiles were green, white, or black.

"Here is Guilderglow," Strongwind proclaimed, indicating the largest of the gold markers, one that had been stamped into the shape of a star. He stepped to the side, straddling the smooth sheet of blue stone. "This is the White Bear Sea, upon which shore your people have made their villages. Here is the place you called Bayguard."

Moreen was startled to see how accurately her world was portrayed. She recognized the land enclosing the small bay and the rugged coastline to the north.

"This white stone is glacier and permanent icefield," the king was explaining, now walking around the floor and indicating a portion of the map showing terrain to the east of his city. "These lands I do not think you know, as your people have stayed near the coast."

"Where is the place called Ice End?" she asked.

Strongwind paused to take two small glasses from a servant who had entered, quietly, bearing a small tray. "Please, will you try our beverage? It is called warqat."

"Uh, I have heard of warqat," Moreen admitted, taking the glass and sniffing. She blinked in surprise—never before had she smelled anything so pungent. It burned, in an admittedly pleasant fashion, all the way down her throat.

"It is brewed from grain, steeped in the ice of a secret glacier."

"All of your people drink it?"

The king shrugged. "For us, it is the Winterfire. It takes the place of the sun during the long, dark months."

The Highlander drank his entire glass in a single gulp, but she took only one more sip and set her drink besides Strongwind's empty glass on the servant's tray. Yet it was warm in her belly and seemed to bring a pleasant lightness to her mood.

"Now, Ice End?" she repeated, finding a smile coming easily to her lips. Still, she remained alert. In the back of her mind she was wondering about Brackenrock. Though she looked along the northern reach of the map she could find nothing suggesting such a ruined citadel.

"Yes, of course. Here is the extent of Icereach," Strongwind replied, pointing. She saw a narrow peninsula marking the terminus of the land. Somewhere just south of there, she suspected, the Arktos might find their ruin.

Moreen indicated another mass of land, across a narrow swath of blue. "What's that?"

The king shrugged. "You would know better than I what lies on the far shore of the White Bear Sea. The narrows here I have heard called the Bluewater Strait, but as to the western coast, only a boat could visit there."

"Indeed." Moreen agreed, though she had never taken a kayak far enough to see the opposite coast of the gulf of Bayguard. At the strait, of course, it looked much narrower. She remembered her visit to Tall Cedar Bay—there she and her father had seen a rugged horizon across the sea. Now, looking at the map, she could see how that coastline extended south, making a long shore on the other side of the White Bear Sea.

One more question occurred to her. "What of monsters called dragons?" she asked. "Are they known to you?"

The king looked surprised, shaking his head. "Do you not know the legend of Huma and the banishing of dragons? That happened four centuries ago, so my teachers claim. I have no reason to dispute them." His eyes narrowed. "Why do you ask?"

Moreen did not want the conversation to turn toward legendary Brackenrock, so she merely shrugged and pretended to study the gold inlays, each of which, the king quickly explained, symbolized one of the many clanholds of Highlanders.

"Come—I have much more to show you," Strongwind said, again extending an arm. Once more she walked at his side.

Next they arrived at a large courtyard, where dozens of young men were launching arrows at targets across a wide space. "These are the new recruits of my archer regiment," the king boasted. "Young men, all. By the time they are finished with their training they will be able to hit the target with ten out of ten shots."

"Impressive," Moreen murmured. That was no greater accuracy than Tildey could claim, but she was keenly aware that her tribe had but one Tildey, while the Highlanders were training numerous archers—and these would swell the ranks of a band that already counted only Chislev knew how many trained bowmen. How weak the Arktos were by comparison!

"What is that across the way—that image of a bear?" Moreen gestured to a statue, taller than life, of a great bear rearing onto its hind legs.

Strongwind's eyes widened in surprise. "You do not know Kradok, the Wild One, god of all Icereach?"

Moreen's jaw clenched stubbornly. "We give proper worship to Chislev Wilder, and she sees to our lives with good care!"

"Please, I did not mean to offend." From somewhere the king had picked up another glass of warqat, and he casually tilted that into his mouth. "There are gods—and problems—enough for all people," he said with a reassuring laugh.

She was offered a look into the royal armory, a vault with walls lined with spears, wooden shields, axes, and hammers. A few of the hammerheads were dark and exceptionally hard, made from the metal called iron which

Moreen had seen only a few times in her life. There was one man on guard at the door of the armory, and on the way out the king paused to introduce him to Moreen.

"This is Randall Graywool," Strongwind said. "I present Moreen Bayguard, chiefwoman of the Arktos."

"The pleasure is all mine, my lady," declared Randall. He was smaller than most of the Highlanders she had seen, and his beard was trimmed neatly short. He smiled bowed to kiss Moreen's outstretched hand. "I hope we will all be seeing much more of you."

"Perhaps," she said noncommittally, unsettled by something about the man's dark, flashing eyes.

As they continued on, the king leaned over as soon as they were out of earshot. "He's called Mad Randall," Strongwind said. "Believe it or not, he is the most fearsome berserker among all the clans."

"Berserker?" she asked, again confused—and angry with herself for her lack of sophistication.

The king seemed only too glad to explain. "When he goes into battle he . . . well, he 'loses himself in the fight', as we say. He shows no fear and has the strength of ten men. I myself would not care to fight him—and you should know that Strongwind Whalebone fears neither man nor ogre!"

"I well believe you," Moreen replied, casting a glance back. Randall was leaning against the armory door, his eyes on the drifting clouds, whistling.

Next they passed a great smoking shed from which the alluring odor of roasting beef reached her nostrils and provoked an unintended growl from her belly. If the king heard, he was polite enough to make no comment.

"That is my royal smokehouse," he pointed out. "Many kinds of beef and mutton are brought here for preservation. Of course, the best cuts are fresh. I trust you will come to enjoy the taste of steak. I know that it is not a staple of the Arktos diet."

"No, we are fishers and hunters of seals." She wanted to add that her people gathered clams and crabs and lobsters and other delicacies along the beaches, but suddenly the memory of those long days of foraging seemed somehow embarrassing when contrasted against the industry and productivity so obvious around here.

"Sometimes we will take a whale," she added tentatively, "harpooning from our kayaks."

"That must be a cause for feasting," Strongwind said politely, although his tone caused her to bristle.

She was thinking now, and as they climbed the steps to a tower parapet she stopped and disentangled her hand from the king's arm. "What did you mean—I will 'come to enjoy the taste of steak'? And why did Randall sound as if he expected to see a lot more of me?"

Strongwind Whalebone took a step away from her, so that he came to the battlement at the edge of the tower. He raised his eyes and looked into the distance, toward the fertile valley, over the Scarred Rocks, onto the craggy mountains that formed a bowl around this citadel of Guilderglow. When he turned back to her his blue eyes were soft, and strangely penetrating.

"Guilderglow is the heart of my kingdom," he began, "and my kingdom is destined to be the greatest realm in all Icereach. I know there is an ogre stronghold, far away from here, where the brute ruler fancies himself a king in his own right."

"King Grimtruth Bane in Winterheim," Moreen supplied, strangely anxious to display that she had *some* knowledge of this land that was her home. "It was his son who destroyed my village."

"Yes. He raided the whole coast of the Ice Gulf, over the last few summers. Every one of the Arktos villages was struck, destroyed, the people slain or carried into slavery."

"Every . . . one?" asked Moreen. She had never imagined the devastation was so extreme, and yet somehow she believed—she *knew*—that Strongwind was telling the truth.

"A few escaped, like yourselves," the Highlander said. "Not many, and hardly a warrior among them. The Arktos survivors are women, for the most part. That is why I was so anxious to meet you again and to have you see, with your own eyes, the glories of my realm."

"What do you mean, again?" Moreen's voice was calm, but she felt violent emotions rising in her heart, her mind.

"I saw you once, when you were hunting, and I was doing the same!" Strongwind forged ahead in a torrent of words. "I tried to talk to you, but you jumped into your kayak and paddled away."

"That was *you*?" Moreen remembered the incident. Now she recalled the blue eyes of the man, the intensity of his voice as he pleaded with her to stop, to return to shore.

"Of course, it was easy to find which village you came from—my scouts simply observed your boat from land. When they summoned me to Bayguard, I could see that you dwelled in the great hut in the center of the village. Obviously, you were daughter of the chief!"

"But, why? Why would you go to all this trouble?" Moreen wondered how often these shaggy men had observed her surreptitiously, spying from the surrounding hilltops.

"Because I could see right away that you are different, different from the wenches around here, from any woman I have ever seen. You are strong and proud . . . and so beautiful!"

Moreen shook her head, angry and a little afraid. "Why are you saying this?" she demanded.

"I mean to say, that you should come to Guilderglow—you *must* come here. I have need of a wife, and you are the leader of the Arktos. Arktos and Highlanders—we are all humans, the natural enemies of the ogres. You and your people will swell our numbers—you have many women of childbearing age, and that will increase our population. We will breed a great nation of warriors, you and I and our people, and within a generation we will be ready to strike at Grimtruth Bane, ready to attack Winterheim itself."

Moreen stepped backward, felt the cold stone of the parapet meet her back. She gaped at the king, felt the flush of humiliation wash over her face. Apparently Strongwind

Whalebone did not recognize the signs, for he advanced, hands outstretched.

"Think of it, Moreen Chieftain's Daughter! You have seen the wealth of my realm—there will be homes here for all of your people. Many of my men will be eager to take a second wife! Within two years our children will be crowding under our feet!"

"And me?" Her tone was icy enough that the king stopped short. "Will I be a *second* wife? Or perhaps a concubine, given a luxurious apartment so that I can make babies for you?"

"Oh, no!" Strongwind looked relieved, apparently concluding that he could give her the answer she desired. "You will reign here as my sole queen, having the rights to all the bounties of my realm! I have no wife, but I want one. I want you!"

Moreen stood as tall as her slight frame would allow, turning the full force of her glare on the king. "Let it be known that I am not a commodity to be harvested or minted—not like your wool and your gold and your beef and your hounds. I am the chiefwoman of the Arktos, and I will not be summoned to become anyone's wife. Not even for a king who wears stag's antlers on his head. Incidentally, did anyone ever tell you how ridiculous they look?"

The king's jaw dropped in an almost comical expression of shock. He reached up to touch the broad rack extending to either side of his scalp, and for a moment a strange emotion—a wounded sense of hurt—flashed in his eyes. That expression of vulnerability vanished, and those blue eyes darkened to a color like that of a boiling sea.

"Think about what you are saying," he declared grimly. "Do you really think your people will survive the Sturmfrost, much less the coming years, without men to protect them? I am offering you that protection, and you would be wise to—"

"I would be wise to make my own decisions!" snapped Moreen, turning to start down the stairs. She spotted Bruni, waiting below in the courtyard, looking upward with a curious expression.

"Do not do this—do not shame me thus!" hissed the Highlander, his hand seizing her arm in a vicelike grip. His expression was so dark and furious that Moreen, for the first time, felt a twinge of real terror. But that could not overcome her stubbornness.

"Shame?" she spat back at him, fiercely twisting her arm away. "What greater shame could there be, than to sell myself, sell my whole tribe, for the chance to eat steak?"

"You will regret this mockery," growled the monarch. He shook his head, astonishment obviously tempering his rage, giving him a moment's pause. "I tell you again—*do not do scorn me*!"

"Know this, Strongwind Whalebone, king of the Highlanders," she replied. "I am chiefwoman of the Arktos, and I shall do as I please. No man, be he slave or peasant or king, will order me otherwise!"

Her fury did not abate as she hurried away. Bruni joined her, hastening to keep up as she stalked out of the castle, down the city streets, and finally through the gate and away from the citadel called Guilderglow.

10

Courrain Currents

For a time, Kerrick knew nothing, and when awareness returned it was with the reality of head-splitting pain, agony that threatened to blanket his entire existence in miserable torment. He tried to open his eyes, but something seemed to be holding them shut. His swollen tongue filled his mouth, all but choking him, and he groaned and thrashed and tried to lift himself up.

He couldn't move. From somewhere he felt cool water trickling between his lips, and he drank greedily. His pain remained, and his blindness, but with his thirst somewhat quenched merciful oblivion returned, and he slept.

The next time he returned to vague consciousness he became instantly aware of the pain trying to crawl its way out of his skull. It seemed almost a living thing, a serpentine enemy that coiled through his brain, rubbing up against every nerve, hissing through his body. One of his arms, too, seemed a seething furnace, the pain searing his flesh. For a moment he wondered if he was dead, then decided no—death couldn't possibly hurt this much.

With that realization came the first return of memory. He wasn't rocking in a cradle, he was aboard a boat, most probably *Cutter*. He was suffering the residue of terrible injury . . . an assault that should, by rights, have shattered him and his boat and ended his life. An image loomed in his mind: That great, spiked tail lifting from the sea, trailing great sheets of brine as it swept through the air and lashed into the mast and boom of his sailboat. He remembered the snap of breaking wood, something smashing into his skull with brute force, and then oblivion.

How long had he languished? The only thing he remembered was a wet rag somehow finding its way between his lips, again and again offering him a few drops of moisture, at least sufficient to keep his tongue from curling up, to allow his throat muscles to work through a few reflexive swallows.

He realized that only his arm was immobile. The rest of his body he could move and flex ever so slightly. So thick was the fog in his mind that it was a very long time before he realized that someone was tending him, offering him the lifesaving moisture, over and over again. Oh yes, there was that kender who had leaped from the back of the dragon turtle into his boat . . . that was who it must be. Coral Fisher . . . something like that . . . some kind of nautical name . . . that much he remembered.

The elf awoke and shifted in his bunk, peering into the grayish light seeping through his eyelids. He turned his head toward the open cabin door. Searing pain shot through his head, but it was a welcome sensation for it was proof that he wasn't permanently blind. He all but sobbed with relief, before turning his head away and collapsing back onto the bunk.

This was the cabin of *Cutter*, he realized. Somehow the little boat had survived the attack of the sea monster. He tried to speak, and though the sound that emerged was a mere croak, he took encouragement from the fact that he could make and hear the noise.

"Did you say something?"

The kender's voice chirped from the entranceway, and then Kerrick felt the warmth of his companion's presence seated on the edge of the bunk beside him. Coraltop Netfisher—that was his name! Once more the elf dared to open his eyes. He looked into a small face, old beyond its childlike shape, eyes dark with concern. The kender's green shirt smelled damp and, vaguely, of seaweed.

"What happened?" Kerrick asked—the words sounded like "Wuh ha'n?", and the kender's face broke into a broad smile.

"What happened? Well, the dragon turtle swam away luckily, but unluckily its tail knocked into our boat. It broke that wooden thing off, and that wooden think conked you on the head. Just about broke your skull, too. I don't think the turtle actually saw us, I mean, you and me. It doesn't eat ships usually, you know, just sailors. When you got all tangled up in the sail, I fell down in the back. I think the big dumb dragon turtle looked around and decided there was no food here. The tail just kind of whacked us almost by accident when it swam away."

"It broke off the mast?" At least, that's what he tried to say, as he struggled to keep up with the kender's rapidfire explanation. "Ih oh off uh ass?"

"Well, yes, it just snapped off. I tied it to the boat, so it's kind of floating along next to us, but I didn't know how to fix it."

Now the despair returned, deeper than ever. Without a mast *Cutter* was simply a cork bobbing in the current. The boat was directionless and uncontrolled, at the mercy of the first storm that came along. Certainly the harsh currents of the Courrain Ocean would doom them, would carry the boat farther and farther from land, into the trackless and icy southern end of the world. For a moment the elf wallowed in self-pity, wishing that the broken mast had in fact crushed his skull and brought him to a quick, merciful end. All the time he had been kept alive in the cabin had merely postponed his deserved fate.

That raised another question. "How 'ong 'a' I 'in 'yin' 'ere?"

"How long have you been lying there?" The kender squinted in concentration. "Let's see—there were seventeen days before you even twitched. I don't mind telling you it wasn't much of a twitch either. It's like my Grandma Annatree used to say: 'If it looks dead and acts dead, well, then, it just might be dead.' Then you started to grunt and groan a little bit, here and there. That went on for—don't worry, I made a mental note—let's see, twelve more days. Then it was five days ago that you looked like you were trying to move. You've been getting slowly but steadily better, no doubt about it."

Kerrick wasn't feeling better—in fact, he was numbed by disbelief. He tried to force himself into a sitting position. That only resulted in spears of pain shooting through his spine, his back, and both arms. He immediately collapsed. "'Oo oo 'een I 'in 'ere 'or a 'ole 'onth?" he croaked in disbelief.

"Why yes, four days *more* than a whole month, actually. The weather's gotten quite cold and gloomy. Do you know, that's a very long time for me to go without having someone to talk to. Well, of course, I could talk *to* you, but you really couldn't talk back, which isn't so bad come to think of it. It was like talking to a wall, or a fish, or talking to the ocean. I don't mind a little talking to the ocean, but it *does* get boring."

The elf felt the darkness rising, unconsciousness surging from the depths to wrap his mind in sticky, obscuring fingers. He tried to fight, tried to stay awake. As he slipped beneath the surface of awareness he heard the kender, still talking to the ocean.

He was glad Coraltop Netfisher was there.

"That's not the mast—it's the boom," Kerrick said two days later, when he had finally, with much pain and extremely slow movements, crept through the cabin door to collapse in the cockpit.

"The boom . . . oh, I'm sorry," Coraltop said, chagrined. "When you said 'mast'—well, it sounded more like 'ass'—

and I thought I had better humor you. Seeing as how you were near death and everything."

Despite his pain, Kerrick couldn't help but chuckle. "Don't be sorry. This is very good news. If the mast had broken off, we'd be doomed. The boom I might be able to repair."

He leaned back, shading his eyes with a hand while he gazed at the pale sky. He couldn't see any clouds, but even so the color seemed more white than blue. The sun was very low on the horizon, and the water, slate gray, was almost preternaturally still.

How far had they drifted? He knew, like all experienced sailors, that the prevailing current of the Courrain Ocean would carry them south, away from any known mass of land toward uncharted waters reputed for their lethal storms and dark, icy winters. It seemed almost unthinkable that he had lingered, all but comatose, for some five weeks, and that during that time they had not encountered a ship-killer storm. In fact, when he had asked Coraltop, the kender had shrugged and replied that it had never even gotten very windy or rained. "Boring weather," said the kender.

That raised another concern, and Kerrick painfully made his way past the cabin to check the level of the water barrel. As he had feared, it was nearly empty—perhaps a handspan of water sloshed back and forth deep within the container. He realized that the kender must have been very shrewd in doling out the precious liquid. Normally in this part of the world there would be rainstorms enough to keep them well-supplied with fresh water. In the event of a long dry spell, he would typically put in to shore, refilling his stock from one of the freshwater streams common on the coast.

How far away was that coast, now?

"Are you sure about how much time I was unconscious?" he asked the kender.

"Look. I marked it on the deck," Coraltop replied proudly. Sure enough, the tiny hash marks added up to thirty-four days. "That's not counting the days since you woke up," added the little fellow.

Suddenly dizzy, the elf sat down. His whole body ached, and he felt weak as an infant. His left arm was in a sling. Coraltop had informed him that he had set the broken bone right after moving Kerrick to the bunk. The kender had done a surprisingly good job. The limb was straight, and seemed to be healing well if slowly.

"Let's pull the boom aboard and see what we can do with it," the elf suggested. Yet as soon as he tried to lift himself, Kerrick knew that even limited activity, not to mention complicated repairs, was beyond his abilities.

"Let me try," Coraltop suggested, kneeling and clutching the rope at one end of the boom. He pulled, but when the stout shaft started to rise out of the water he groaned, and the beam splashed downward. "It's too heavy," he admitted.

As Kerrick leaned back, despairing, he felt a breath of wind against his cheek. Raising his eyes in sudden alarm, he saw that the northern horizon was dark, obscured by a wall of cloud that could only mean an approaching storm.

"That doesn't look too good," the kender observed.

"Not too good at all," Kerrick agreed. He felt hopeless and angry—why had he survived this far, suffering all this pain, only to face a storm threatening his crippled boat? Doom was inevitable if he couldn't repair the boom and raise some semblance of a sail.

Only then did he remember the little strongbox, the gift from his father that might, one day, save his life, when he was in "imminent danger."

He gasped out directions to Coraltop, and half a minute later the kender had returned from the cabin with the little box. Naturally, he had already opened it and was exclaiming in delight over the circlet of gold, holding it up to the sky, peering through the ring with curiosity.

"I need it," Kerrick whispered, too weak now even to try to grab it.

Coraltop handed it over agreeably, and the elf, at last,

held his finger up to the ring. He saw the pattern of oak leaves, winking in the daylight already fading under storm-clouds, and he pushed the metal band onto his finger. It felt warm and tight.

The warmth began to spread, a tingling sensation of energy that drove back his pain, tightened his sinews. Even his broken arm felt whole, strong, and limber.

He shucked off the splint and, accepting the enthusiastic help of the kender, was able to guide them through the job of heaving the boom back onto the deck. The breeze continued to freshen, rocking the boat slightly as he examined the break and planned the hasty repair.

The end of the post had been badly splintered, but by sawing off the broken wood and then reattaching the bracket to the freshly hewn end of the boom, they were able to once again mount it onto the mast. "It's a foot shorter than I'd like, but we can live with that," Kerrick announced, when the work was done. The wind was lashing spray across the surface of the sea, and *Cutter* was bobbing unpredictably in the rising swell. "Now, let's see if we can get some canvas up."

"Hooray!" cried Coraltop. "I knew you—we—could do it."

Kerrick smiled wryly. "We make a good team," he admitted. He turned to the sail locker, pleased to recall how neatly he had stowed the canvas, after their frantic and makeshift repairs. The ring was a powerful ally. His father's warning, the notion that this enchanted ring might eventually sap his life, nagged at the back of his mind. Kerrick brushed the concern away, and in another five minutes they were ready to face the storm.

"You've got lots more sail!" Coraltop shouted over the howling of the wind. "Why don't we put some more of it up?"

Kerrick grimaced as he leaned on the tiller and guided

Cutter's sharp prow through a black wall of rising water. Spray broke over the deck, churning into the cockpit, giving him a chill despite the protection of his slicker and woolens. He still wore his father's ring, and he needed the magically induced stamina to steer the boat amid the violence of the southern storm.

The elf shook his head. "More canvas up there and the wind would rip it away. If it didn't, it would push us so hard that we could capsize."

"Oh, good point. I think I've had my fill of capsizing," said the kender, bracing himself for the jolt of another wave, this one rising from the port beam. "Hey, that's a *really* big one!"

The elf hauled on the tiller, bringing them around so that the breaker crashed over the port bow. The sailboat staggered sideways, wind and water tearing in opposite directions, but slowly she broke free of the heaving brine and clawed her way up another slope of the churning sea.

That was one of the worst things about these southern ocean storms, Kerrick realized. The waves seemed to come at them from every direction, and whatever way he steered the boat they were assaulted from fore and aft, from one side, then the next. The long twilight had faded into a night as dark and tempestuous as any he had endured. Only the slightly phosphorescent crests of the waves gave him momentary warning of the next crushing onslaught. Where the water lay smooth in a trough of the boat, it was black, eerily lightless.

He was piloting the boat more by instinct than rational thought. The sail, as Coraltop had pointed out, was deployed into a small triangle, efficiently capturing the gale roaring out of the north, but every time the wind smashed into the canvas and pushed the boat forward they had to hold on for dear life. Kerrick's clothes were wet, clinging to his body. He smelled of soaked wool. When his body was racked by an involuntary shiver, he didn't even notice. His wounds were a vague and distant discomfort, unimportant when weighed against the primal struggle he now waged.

Something loose flapped near the bow, canvas or rope streaming along the deck, whirled about by the storm. Kerrick knew that he would have to get up there and fasten it down, a daunting task in this tempest.

"Take the tiller!" he shouted to the kender, who was seated on the bench beside him. Despite his chattering teeth and obvious discomfort, Coraltop had declined Kerrick's earlier suggestion that he bury himself in the cabin for a while.

"Great, it's the biggest storm ever, and you finally let me steer," he said, with a slight pout. "Don't worry, I've got a lot of experience—"

"Don't pull on it!" yelled the elf. "Just hold it steady until I get back."

"Oh, of course, don't pull," sniffed his companion. "That'd be obvious to a gulley dwarf. . . ."

The rest of his remark was lost in the din of the storm, though Kerrick looked back to insure that the kender had the tiller clenched firmly in both hands. Limping past the small cabin, the elf turned sideways to ease along the narrow catwalk. Carefully, grabbing hold wherever he could to avoid losing his footing, he inched ahead to the bow, where he saw a corner of the jib sail flapping outside of the forward locker.

The ship pitched into another wave, and Kerrick held on as cold water poured over him. Without the strength provided by the ring he would certainly have been swept away. As it was, he was sputtering and gasping by the time the boat once again fought itself free of the clutching wave. With a swift gesture he pulled open the lid of the locker and wasted no time in jamming the sodden stretch of sail inside.

Clinging to every bracket, rope, and rail, he cautiously made his way back to the cockpit, at last tumbling onto the bench beside Coraltop Netfisher. The kender's teeth were clenched as he blinked away the ocean spray, but he flashed the elf a delighted grin as *Cutter* sliced across the face of a huge wave and then glided into the momentary smoothness of the next trough.

"This is *lots* more fun than drifting along without any mast and stuff," announced Coraltop.

"Yeah, fun." Kerrick sighed, feeling the weariness creep over him, the enchantment of the ring fading. A new wave rose astern and caused the boat to lurch sharply forward. He cried out as he caught himself on his mending arm, then clenched his teeth and held on grimly. The swells were larger than ever, and wind whipped the whitecaps.

Times in the past he had found a storm invigorating, a challenge to his boat and his seamanship. But this was a monstrous assault of nature, a threat of death. The gale seemed to be attacking him personally. The breakers grew taller the troughs deeper. The wind stung. All of a sudden *Cutter* heeled, and for a sickening moment Kerrick thought she was going over and under. He braced his feet and reached out to seize the tiller that was still clutched under the kender's arms.

"Pull!" he shouted, leaning into the bar, feeling Coraltop throw his own wiry strength into the maneuver. Kerrick ignored the pain shooting through his arms and back, knowing that if the boat capsized here, they had no chance.

Rising swells heaved under the stern, before cresting and pouring away at a shallow angle. Mountainous black seas rose to port and starboard. Straining together on the tiller Kerrick and Coraltop managed to pull the vessel and use the last bit of its speed to turn her tail into the wind.

The biggest breaker yet crashed against the stern, and water rushed into the boat, surging around their legs. As it drained slowly *Cutter*, heavy with the extra weight, lumbered like a drunk, slipping sideways into a deep yawning trough. The elf tried to pull the boat around but his weakened hands slipped right off of the tiller, and again the boat teetered on the brink. The ring . . . he had been wearing it so long that he had reached the limit of its power. He felt all but impotent, paralyzed by fatigue.

Coraltop showed good instincts as he pushed the tiller away from himself, giving just enough steerage to start the boat, nose first, down the slope of the wave. In seconds they were plunging with headlong speed, and a moment later the prow sank deep into the opposite wave. Water gushed across the deck, but the little boat was sturdy, and they held their balance. Once again the *Cutter* managed to slice through the briny barrier and claw her way back atop the crest of the next wave.

"You steer! I'll work the pump!" Kerrick shouted. His arms were limp and stiff, but he could crank the bailer by foot, and he set himself numbly to the task. The gale roared and they raced with the wind, headlong to the south. Again Kerrick was hit by a different kind of wave, the fatigue that threatened to consume him. Soon the simple device was shooting a steady jet of water over the side.

For more than an hour he cranked the footpedals, maintaining pressure in the hose, slowly emptying the hull as Coraltop guided them through the continuing tumult. As she grew lighter *Cutter* became easier to handle, riding higher in the water, skimming the crests of the worst waves. Kerrick pumped automatically, leaning against the cabin, barely conscious of anything except the rhythmic motion. Finally, when his head dipped forward to slump against his chest, he lost all awareness. Only when he fell sideways and sprawled in the chilly waters of the cockpit did he awaken.

It took Coraltop's help before the elf could force himself up. His surroundings swirled, a mist thicker, more permeating than the foul weather. Gradually he realized that it was his own mind that was foggy. His strength was utterly gone, he could barely keep his eyes open.

The ring! He remembered his father's warning words. It took all of his strength to draw his right hand over to his left, and then he could barely claw the circlet of metal from his finger. Finally he fumbled with the leather flap and slid the ring into the secure pocket inside his belt.

The darkness of the night surrounded them. The icy water penetrated his bones. However, the kender turned out to be a surprisingly worthy crewman, and the boat was solid. As they plunged deeper and deeper into the southern ocean, Kerrick slipped into a profound slumber, dreaming that they would survive.

The wind held firm over a full day, during which the kender guided the sailboat on a straight course, and Kerrick slumbered. He awoke just before the second dawn broke. Immediately he checked the compass, which showed their course to be just west of south. The clouds had shifted enough to reveal a familiar star, Zivilyn Greentree, sparkling once more directly over his course. Kerrick had never known it to lie this far to the south. For the second time on this voyage, the sight filled him with awe.

Dawn suffused the northeast with a gray, reluctant light, and the elf guessed the sun would remain low for a few short hours before vanishing again.

At least they would behold another day.

Coraltop Netfisher slept within the cabin, and the gray ocean rolled to the far horizon in every direction. Kerrick could not recall a more violent storm or a more perilous night at sea. He touched the pouch at his belt, where the ring was securely hidden. The fatigue was fading.

During the long hours of darkness they had been driven relentlessly south by the force of the storm. Now sunlight had come, not directly but filtered through the gray haze. The wind had settled somewhat. Still, he had little choice but to hold the tiller steady and let the wind continue to bear *Cutter* south.

"Aw, the big waves are calming down," Coraltop Netfisher griped, popping open the cabin door and squinting ruefully at the mountainous swell. "It's gonna get boring."

"I'll take 'boring' anytime you want to offer it," Kerrick said with a laugh, glad his companion had emerged to join him. He was used to sailing alone, but it surprised him to realize how quickly he had accepted the kender on this trip to wherever the storm took them.

"Do you want some fish and flatcakes?"

The elf's stomach grumbled. "Yes, I'm hungry."

Coraltop went forward to the fish locker and came back with a long fillet. "There are five more left," he reported.

That was ration enough for barely another week, yet Kerrick was strangely unconcerned. Perhaps he was still dazed, giddy with the aftereffects of the ring. Perhaps they would find a school of fish and spend a day casting the net. Maybe something else would happen in this trackless ocean.

He froze, squinting across the stormy wavetops, looking south, straining to make out something on the horizon.

"What is it?" the kender asked, noting the intensity of his gaze. Coraltop scrambled onto the cabin and looked forward. "Say, I see it too. Is that what I think it is?"

Kerrick could only nod, awed and thrilled and frightened at the same time. There was supposed to be no land here, nothing but dire weather and trackless ocean. Yet there was a definitely solid shape in the distance, a rugged horizon above the sea, outlined in snow and rock. Suddenly Kerrick felt a sense of destiny, as if Zivilyn sat upon his shoulder and, in his wisdom, guided tiller and sail. Still holding his south by southwest course, he stared in the distance and watched as the land mass grew in size.

"Yes," he said, finally answering the kender's question. "That's what you think it is—a mountain. Many mountains."

11

Snow Sea and Prophecy

The King's Hall of Winterheim was a great chamber at the very summit of the city's lofty mountain. Huge panels of enchanted ice gleamed high upon the arching walls and ceiling. During the summer these admitted the light of the sun, while in wintertime they emanated a light of their own, a magical spell cast upon them many generations before, at a time when the ogres boasted powerful mages and sorcerers among their ranks. Grimwar Bane had frequently wondered how long that enchantment was likely to last, for if it faded he knew that they would never find similar power among the ogres of contemporary Winterheim.

He was wondering about that right now, in fact, as he and Princess Stariz joined the king and queen and several other nobles, for a late breakfast in the vast chamber hall. Of course, it was still dark as they came along the outer balcony leading toward the royal hall. The span of daylight was by now limited to a few hours around noon. Beneath them, Grimwar could sense the contained power of the Snow Sea, the great drifts and swells heaving restlessly. Through the enchanted panels the rim of the Ice Wall was barely visible, a band of blue-white extending until it vanished in the distancc

The smells of fish and bread surrounded them as they entered and took their seats at the long table. The king and queen and the other lords were already there, but the prince knew he and his wife's tardiness would be excused. Everyone knew that Stariz went through an elaborate prayer ritual upon awakening, and none wanted to offer any offense to Gonnas the Strong.

"We are going to inspect the mines later today," announced King Grimtruth, a buttery fillet of salmon dangling from his lower lip. He slurped loudly, and the strip of fish, a good eight inches long, vanished into the royal maw. The king fixed a stern eye upon his son. "You must conclude your studies in the morning."

Grimtruth's attention shifted to Baldruk Dinmaker, the only non-ogre at the table. The dwarf was seated on a tall stool, though he was still overshadowed by Princess Stariz, on one side, and the obese Lord Quendip on the other. "How fares the prince's learning?" the king asked Baldruk. "Do you remember that he must recite the royal lineage at the Neuwinter Rites? I will not tolerate a disaster such as occurred four years ago!"

Grimwar wanted to declare that yes, the dwarf certainly remembered that fact, as he had been drumming names and dates relentlessly into the prince's head since their homecoming several weeks earlier. Instead the younger ogre merely turned his attention to his own pile of fillets and let the royal adviser answer for himself.

"In truth, I believe he will be ready, Sire, but the task is not an easy one, for the prince's mind has a way of wandering." The dwarf, his beard bristling, glared at Grimwar.

"You know how important that recitation is!" joined in Stariz, in the tone that never failed to creep up the prince's spine. "You must show honor to our ancestors, to the kingdom—to the Willful One himself!"

"Do not concern yourself, I will master the names!" Grimwar retorted, his growl rising nearly to the level of a roar. It was sufficiently forceful that most other ogres would have recoiled, but not his priestess-wife. She merely stared at him, as if evaluating the truth of his answer. Finally she snorted, returning to her breakfast.

"I'm sure you will do very well," Queen Thraid said encouragingly.

The king harrumphed skeptically, but before the conversation could continue Lord Quendip ordered the slaves to bring another platter of fillets. "Perhaps you should bring some for the others, too," he noted without irony, smacking his thick lips.

For a time they ate in silence. Grimwar brooded upon the tedious tasks of the coming day while the others, apparently, were lost in appreciation of the sweet fish harvested in such plenitude this season. Once Thraid flashed the prince a sweet look, and he brightened a little, but then he saw Baldruk Dinmaker, his pale, cold eyes narrowed suspiciously, and Grimwar quickly returned his attention to his plate.

"The days grow very short," the king announced, finally pushing himself back from the great table. "But I see the dawn has broken. Come with me, and behold the majesty of the Snow Sea."

The others stopped eating, though Quendip slid a few oily fillets into the pouch of his leather vest, as the party rose. With the king leading and the prince following closely, they headed for the golden doors, which were whisked open by slaves. Immediately the icy wind swept in, as the ogres and the dwarf marched outside.

From the lip of the massive precipice, standing in a parapet, they saw immediately that the Snow Sea had risen to a high, probably unprecedented level. Vapors rose and swirled from a surface of drifts, huge swells that shifted and tossed hypnotically. In the graying light the vast swath of snow roiled angrily. Here and there the mists spun into whirlwinds, and against the barrier of the Ice Wall, a quarter mile below, the snow smashed and crested like powerful, icy breakers against a rugged coast.

Grimwar felt awe at the spectacle, and imagined the day when his father would wield the Axe of Gonnas and part the Ice Wall at the Neuwinter Rites. The great basin of snow was many thousands of feet deep. Over the sunlit months the snows swept steadily from the polar distance, massing and heaving and swelling behind the dam of the Ice Wall, waiting for the release provided each year by the ogre king's rite. Legend claimed that should the ritual go awry, the pressure would increase until Winterheim, Black Ice Bay, and everything around was swept away by epic explosion and avalanche. It was the duty of the Suderhold King, most recently those monarchs of the Bane Dynasty, to ensure that never happened.

This ritual was always followed by the sacrifice of a slave, the pouring of blood onto the glacial face. The Axe of Gonnas struck the wall and released the storm that drove the ogres back into their citadel, wrapping a blanket of ice and darkness over all Icereach.

"We will leave for the mines at noon, to use such daylight as we can," King Grimtruth announced as he abruptly took his leave. These words were largely for his son. "Be sure you are ready on time."

Before the prince could reply, two slaves had slammed the great golden doors behind the departing king.

"The standard of the Death Hawk flew over all Ansalon at the height of the Foundation Age," Grimwar recited, stalking around the tutorial chamber as he tried to remember the elusive facts of his history lesson.

"What were the major capitals?" snapped the dwarf, who was seated in a soft chair, leaning back with his eyes closed. Snik was in his hand, and Baldruk absentmindedly cleaned his fingernails with the lethal magical dagger.

"There was Kern in the east . . . Narakid to the north. . . ." The prince paused, forcing his mind to work. "Far west was Dalitgar, with Parlathin in the northwest."

"The south! You can't forget the south!"

"I was just getting to that," snorted Grimwar, who had,

in fact, forgotten all about the south. "That was Blöden Khalkist, heart of the empire and birthplace of the Death Hawk line."

"How came the ogres to Icereach?" pressed the dwarf.

"It was King Barkon who set sail after the Heresy of Igraine," Grimwar continued, once more feeling on firm ground. "He acted upon a prophecy given to him by Gonnas himself, who saw Igraine's folly."

"What was that folly?"

"He showed kindness to humans, even releasing some of his slaves. Those humans would breed in freedom, and Barkon saw that their spawn would be the ruin of our race."

"Go on."

"King Barkon's slaves built him a hundred galleys, and he loaded his wives, and his army, and many slaves and craftsmen, wizards and priests, and set sail from the southern shore of Ansalon. Following the guidance of the Willful One, he came to these shores, to the land called Icereach."

"How long ago?"

"Fifty-five centuries," the prince said with certainty. "King Barkon departed Ansalon twenty-eight centuries before the elves founded their ancient kingdom."

"What is that elven kingdom called?"

Gonnas curse him—why did the dwarf always have to ask the questions that Grimwar wasn't prepared to answer? He had been studying *ogre* history, not the lore of the accursed elves! "I can name my own ancestors," he growled, "going back five thousand years!"

"That is not the question—name the realm of the elves!"

"Silver . . . silver . . . east . . . silver something," he started lamely, then roared. "I don't know that one!"

"Well, you *should* know it!" snapped the dwarf, sitting up and confronting the prince with those pale eyes opened wide, a pale and watery stare. "Your father, the king, *wants* you to know it! It's 'Silvanesti'!" he added contemptuously.

"I was going to say that," growled the prince, who felt

that he should get credit for at least being close. "Why in the name of all the gods should I be concerned with a place that lies across the sea, a place no ogre of my kingdom has seen for thousands of years?"

He knew he had made a mistake. This kind of challenge Baldruk Dinmaker couldn't help but answer. Though Grimwar had heard it all before, he slumped into a chair, resigned to the lecture he knew was coming.

"You must always be vigilant against the elves," began the dwarf, "because it is the elves who have been the bane of ogrekind throughout the rest of the world. Those great capitals you mentioned, most of them are gone now, sacked by elven armies and inhabited by human rabble and worse."

"Yes. I remember your lessons. Neraka is a land of men, and the great ogre port of Parlathin has become the place humans call Palanthas. Daltigar, too, is now in human hands, while Blöten and Kern are small, backward kingdoms, mere shadows of the empire that had once united all the world. But those places that have fallen are now claimed by humans, not elves, so why do you insist that elves are still our greatest enemy?"

"Because humans are like cold clay: They can be shaped by artisans of many kinds. Here in Icereach we are shaping them to serve us. Can you imagine what Winterheim would be like, without your human slaves to do all the work?"

In truth, Grimwar couldn't imagine that. Everything from farming to smithing to mining and building was done by the men and women enslaved within the ogre kingdom. If those humans were gone, the kingdom—or at least the life that Grimwar had been born to know—would cease to exist.

"That simply means that we have vanquished the humans here—we have been strong enough to prevail."

"Because the humans of Icereach are few, and they are barbarians. They know nothing of the elven civilizations that have spread to other corners of the world. You must understand this: In the First Dragon War, the army that broke the ogre power on the central plains consisted of ninety-nine humans for every one elf. Yet it was an elven army, an elven king—Silvanos himself—who won that victory, in a battle that sealed the fate of the ogre realms on Ansalon."

"But not here." Grimwar was anxious to prove that he had been paying attention.

"No, because *there are no elves* here!"

"I know that!" Grimwar shuddered inwardly, remembering the prophecy of his wife, the message from Gonnas the Strong. "Did we not search every village, interrogate every prisoner, on the summer's campaign? The humans know nothing of elves, and as you said yourself, men are fit only to be our slaves."

"That is not what I said. You would do well to pay closer attention," the dwarf said in disgust. He glanced at the window. The short period of full daylight had arrived, and Baldruk shrugged. "That is all we have time for, today—we don't want to keep your father waiting."

"These are fine bears," Grimtruth Bane said proudly. "The best I have bred."

The prince, riding beside his father in the large, open cart, could only agree. Four massive ice bears lumbered in harness, pulling the royal sled along the vast curve of Fenriz Glacier. The bears' motley white pelts matched the dirty ice of the path, and the animals lumbered along at an easy trot. Golden muzzles caged each fierce maw, but their long claws were bare, necessary to hold the smooth, hard path.

Baldruk Dinmaker and Queen Thraid were seated facing the two bull ogres. Above their bench was the driver, a loyal ogre of advanced age known as Kod Bearmaster. The iron skids grated over the snow as the big bears loped along with comfortable speed.

The sun was a pale orb, low even at noon, and soon it would vanish behind the shoulder of the great mountain.

All around loomed the huge peaks of the Icereach Range, the loftiest mountains in the world—at least, according to the teachings of Baldruk Dinmaker, who had traveled far and wide. Those summits ran along both sides of the glacier, jagged teeth extending toward the far frozen south.

The glacier was a river of ice that made a splendid highway leading from the fortress mountain toward the ridges where the kingdom's richest gold deposits had long been mined. The broad surface extended northward for nearly a hundred miles, until it spilled into the gray waters of the Courrain Ocean. As they entered the shadow of Winterheim, Grimwar felt the chill penetrate his clothes and his flesh, seeping into his very bones, but he huddled even deeper under his bearskin and knew better than to make any complaint.

"We will now look at the mines in the valley," the king said, addressing the driver.

Kod Bearmaster held sturdy reins and a whip but coaxed the bears along with a series of barking commands. Now he guided them onto a steep sheet of ice that spilled down the valley between two great summits to merge onto the main glacier. All four of the bruins strained in the harness, taloned paws gripping the smooth surface firmly as they hauled their royal cargo.

In a surprisingly short time they had reached the pass between those summits, the best vantage in all Icereach for seeing into the world beyond. In places they could glimpse the surface of the Snow Sea, saw the dark waves of blizzard heaving and tossing. Again Grimwar involuntarily shivered to glimpse that power, the unrestrained might, waiting for the release that could only be provided by the king of Suderhold.

"Where did you get such an unusual pelt?" asked Queen Thraid, who was riding with Baldruk Dinmaker on the front seat.

"Yes, who ever heard of a black bear?" wondered the king.

"I found it in a human's hut, in the last village we

sacked," the prince explained. "All during the summer we had heard of this particular talisman. It was supposed to be the symbol of the high chief of the Arktos." Grimwar chuckled grimly. "He's dead now, and I have his sacred cloak."

"It is good you killed him," the king said. "I do not like to have these humans thinking of themselves as chieftains. Far better when they only have a mind for slavery." The monarch beamed, baring his impressive tusks, as the bear cart glided around a bend in the glacier. "Look. See what they can accomplish as slaves."

The prince saw the long, scarred face of mountainside, pocked by the holes of hundreds of tunnel mouths, great heaps of yellow-brown tailings strewn in fans at the foot of the vast cliff. The workers were using the few hours of daylight to make last, frantic progress before the Sturmfrost marked the end of the mining season.

The Highlund Valley was a great bowl in the mountains. Lofty, snowcapped peaks rose above the rim, but the heat of the miners' activity had melted any trace of snow within the vale itself. A dozen low, sooty smelters were at work, black smoke belching from the chimneys, huge piles of coal rising like small mountains beside each of the buildings.

The mines were linked by a grid of ledges and catwalks, some of the scaffoldings rising hundreds of feet in the air to provide access to the higher tunnels. The stink of smoke and bitter fumes was thick and a dark haze obscured the view. Hammers and picks clattered in a regular cadence, and as the bears slowed their pace and the cart skidded to a stop Grimwar could hear men shouting, ogre overseers cursing, and mining carts rumbling along the numbers of tracks that linked mines, holding piles, and smelters.

The king's driver steered them to a stop before a sturdy building of gray granite sculpted into a miniature fortress. Two ogres stood guard at the massive iron door, but they quickly pulled the great portal open as the king, queen, prince and dwarf climbed down from the cart.

"Welcome, Sire," said one, making a low bow. "The goldmaster has set out the ingots for your inspection."

"And transport is arranged?"

"Yes, Sire. They will be carted to the royal treasury in three days, when we close up the mines and retire to Winterheim for the season."

"Very well," declared Grimtruth, who beamed in fine humor as he swaggered through the entry and into the chilly depths of the great vault. With a clap of his hands—three quick slaps, a pause, and then a fourth—he brought the magical lights into being. Like those in the upper face of Winterheim's King's Hall, these panels now shone like windows filtering full sunlight.

Even Grimwar, who did not share his father's lust for gold, was impressed by the array of the yellow metal reflected by this light. The ingots, each more than a hundred pounds, were bars of pure gold, arranged in a dozen stacks that nearly filled the large room, leaving only enough space for a strapping ogre to squeeze sideways between them.

"Ah, splendid!" crowed the king. "This will make a good season's profit for my treasury, I declare." Thraid, Grimwar, Baldruk and the guards watched from the doorway as Grimtruth walked up and down the aisles between the stacks of ingots. Here and there the king stopped to pick up one of the bars, cooing over it like a baby in his arms, then setting it gently back into place.

Grimwar grew quickly bored. Hearing a soft sigh beside him, he knew that Thraid, too, had tired of watching the king count and coddle his treasure. Baldruk Dinmaker, on the other hand, stood entranced, his eyes alight, his tongue licking his lips anxiously.

"Very good," the monarch said finally, striding back through the doors and into the pale twilight of the valley. "Now let us go up to the mines."

The little party, on foot now, made its way up the slope from the vault, between a pair of smelting houses, each with a stocky chimney spewing acrid smoke. Grimwar looked up at the massive frameworks of scaffolding leading toward the higher mines. Here and there human slaves climbed up the steep ramps or carefully maneuvered heavy wheelbarrows downward. A rattle and bang attracted their attention across the valley, and they saw a cloud of dust rising from a chute where a dozen slaves were pouring a gravelly mix of ore down toward the nearest smelting house.

Soon they came to a great stockade, the gate standing wide open as a few frail-looking humans swept out a large barracks hall and stirred several cauldrons steaming over low, smoky fires.

"Sire!" cried an officious ogre, hastening out of a little hut near the barracks gate. The prince recognized Brasstusk Whipcrack, the chief overseer.

"This is indeed an honor! My Lady Queen and Prince Grimwar! Welcome to you all."

"Enough pleasantries. Tell me how the slaves are performing," the king said impatiently. "Why do I see twelve men doing the work of two, there at the ore chute?"

"A shame, Your Majesty, a true shame, I agree," declared Brasstusk sadly. "It is the new slaves, those who were brought here in the last month. They are low in spirit and so far have proven unwilling to learn even the simplest of tasks."

Grimwar groaned inwardly. His father had never ceased complaining about the humans captured during the prince's raid this past summer. The last thing he wanted to hear was yet another explanation of why his captives were inadequate and disappointing.

"Foolish wretches," snapped the king. "Take one of them down right now, and kill him. Let the others witness the deed. That will let them know that we will accept no further shirking. Warn them that my son or I will return tomorrow to see whether they have begun to perform at an acceptable rate."

"Of course, Sire," replied Brasstusk. He turned to a pair of armed warriors standing outside the stockade gate. "Guards! Bring me one of those men, the scrawniest of the lot." He pointed to the group at the top of the ore chute, who had ceased their labors to watch, intently, the royal party on the valley floor. "He shall be put to death by . . ."

The overseer turned toward the king. "How should he be killed, Sire?"

"Snik will do the job," volunteered Baldruk Dinmaker, stepping forward quickly, holding up his lethal dagger. "Bring the human before me."

Again Grimwar felt a sense of disgusted boredom. How many times had he watched the dwarf dispose of a human captive with his poisoned magical blade? Certainly his father and Baldruk never seemed to tire of the sport, but the ogre prince failed to see the fascination. Hadn't he risked life and treasure to bring back these slaves? Now his father had ordered yet another one killed, merely out of spite and pride.

By now the slaves had perceived the danger in the king's attention and were busying themselves before the two guards arrived at the high scaffold. Nevertheless, the ogres wasted no time in seizing one wretch by the shoulders and dragging him down the long ramp toward the ground.

The prince noticed that his father's young bride was looking a trifle stricken. Thraid mopped her brow with a handkerchief and glanced around restlessly, letting her eyes fall on anything except the sobbing, pleading, pitiful human captive.

"Would you like to return to the cart, my Queen?" asked Grimwar. He offered her an arm which she gratefully accepted. The king cast his son a glance of disgust, then turned away as the prince and queen started down the trail, past the smelting houses, and back toward the ice bears and the royal sled.

"By Gonnas, is it necessary to *kill* him?" Thraid asked in a low voice with exasperation. "You'd think he could be whipped or tortured instead!"

Grimwar snorted, looking at her from the side. "Sometimes we must do things . . . unpleasant things, but necessary," he said pointedly.

"Necessary?" She met his gaze, her large brown eyes flashing. He could tell she was upset. "Necessary, like marrying the daughter of a baron?"

"Or marrying a king—one who is older than your father!" he retorted.

She pulled her hand off his arm and turned her eyes forward. They walked as quickly as decorum allowed, but still they were well within earshot when the human slave, now stricken by the dwarf's slow-acting poison, began to scream.

"O Great Gonnas, show your humble priestess thy immortal will."

Stariz ber Glacierheim ber Bane bowed her massive head, averting her eyes from the blazing visage on the temple dais. She was on her knees, befitting her status as petitioner and priestess. A mask of black obsidian, carved into the bestial face as the god's own image, covered her face. The princess of Suderhold—and daughter of the baron of Glacierheim—held her pose for a long time. Grimwar knew that she was letting the awe and the wonder and the power well up within her.

The prince stood in a darkened alcove off the temple's entryway, feeling some of that awe himself. His wife did not know he was here. At least, Grimwar corrected himself, she had not been informed of his arrival, though she had ways of finding things out he had never been able to understand. For now, he would respectfully wait for her to conclude her devotions.

The image of Gonnas the Strong, the Willful One, rose in all its glory, the obsidian image of a massive bull ogre, improbably long tusks jutting proudly from the lower jaw. The great black statue, outlined in sparkling points of fire, was three times the size of the greatest ogre. It filled the whole central atrium of the temple, which itself was one of the largest chambers in the great underground sprawl that was Winterheim. The massive golden blade, the Axe of Gonnas, rested at the feet of the statue.

The high priestess was alone, except for her husband and an unimportant human slave. Even the king and queen were respectfully waiting outside. Any lesser ogre would have faced a sentence of death for daring to intrude upon her worship.

"Gonnas, source of all wisdom," Stariz intoned, tusked mask turned upward. "Gonnas, Lord of Strength . . . Gonnas the Mighty . . . Gonnas, protector of ogrekind, we seek only to do honor to your image and your name." Her voice boomed like a powerful drum. The power of the dark god was clearly in her now, as she began to tremble through her elephantine torso, neck, and limbs.

"Gonnas, Lord of Strength . . . Gonnas the Mighty. . ." Again came the Reciting of Names, the energy infusing her, slowly raising the pitch of her voice. Grimwar took a step backward, fearful of the power, envious of the frenzied joy he witnessed in his wife.

Stariz rose to her feet, arms outspread, face upturned to the black image. The voice of the ogress was a desperate plea for a sign, for some indication of the god's favor, or of his will.

Smoke and vapors thickened in the chamber, swirling around, obscuring the air so that Grimwar could see neither his wife nor the black statue symbolizing the object of her worship. Crashes and roars resonated from the murk, and the prince fought to hold his nerve, fighting the urge to flee. He stayed in place, hands clenched so tightly that his fingers hurt. The smoke stung his eyes, but he blinked away the tears and stared intently.

Abruptly Stariz screamed and stumbled out of the smoke cloud, staggering drunkenly, her hands clasped to either side of her face. The human slavewoman stepped forward only to be slapped roughly aside by an accidental blow of the ogress's flailing hand. Finally the priestess slumped to her knees, holding herself as her huge body was convulsed with deep, racking sobs.

Grimwar froze, again feeling that almost insurmountable urge to flee. He shook his head sternly, reminding himself that he was a bull ogre, heir to a great kingdom. He would not, *could* not, allow himself to give in to fear.

He went to his wife, knelt at her side, helped her pull off the heavy mask. Supporting her in his strong arms, he assisted her to the clearer air behind the temple's heart. The smoke was thick and choking but finally parted enough for him to breath easier. Nearby the human slave groaned and followed them groggily.

"What? What is it?" demanded Grimwar, as his wife's eyelids fluttered open.

"I have seen the visions of the Willful One, and they are filled with messages of doom if we—if *you*—fail to act!"

"But what—"

"The elven messenger!" gasped the princess, cutting him off, her bloodshot eyes fixing Grimwar with a look of terror that he found utterly unsettling. "He has come to Icereach! He is here! I saw more, a deeper warning. There is a human woman, a survivor of your raids this summer. You should not have let her escape! For it is as I told you—she will be his agent of destiny!"

"How?" The prince couldn't suppress his irritation. Why was she telling him this now, when it was too late to do anything about it. "What else did you learn? What other dangers do we face?" he demanded, as they came out of the temple gates to find Grimtruth and his queen watching them worriedly. Stariz staggered, leaning against the wall, slowly slumping to the floor.

Finally the high priestess, with a groan, struggled to a sitting position, legs splayed before her on the marble floor. The queen touched her arm and Stariz impatiently brushed the other ogress's hand away.

"Other dangers. Is that not enough? No, I saw none beyond those two," Grimwar's wife said slowly. But he noticed, as she spoke, that her tiny eyes shifted, narrowing with a scowl that was directed straight at Queen Thraid Dimmarkull ber Bane.

12

Tall Cedar Bay

That smoke will be visible for miles," Moreen said with concern. She, Bruni and Tildey stood atop a rocky hill, watching the camp where the Arktos were beginning to stir on this cold, misty morning. During these short days, the tribe rose before dawn and continued marching long into the hours of darkness. "Do you think there are any thanoi around here?"

"It seems like those whale-killers are everywhere these days," Bruni said with a grim shake of her head.

"Best to keep a constant lookout," Tildey remarked. She looked at her half-empty quiver. "I wish I had more arrows." After the fight with the thanoi, she had recovered about ten of her lethal missiles, but that was all she had.

"The way is probably clear to the south and east," the chiefwoman continued, thinking aloud. "I'd like to head north for another day's march, though, to scout in that direction. We must be getting close to the place my father called Tall Cedar Bay. I'd like to find Tall Cedar Bay and maybe take shelter there until we can find Brackenrock."

"Good idea," Bruni said, as Tildey nodded too. "We'll come with you."

Moreen's eyes rose from the campsite, her gaze sweeping past the strip of beach onto the gray water of the gulf.

Many days it rained now, and just yesterday an icy wind off the gulf had turned the rain into stinging sleet, forcing the Arktos into an early camp. To take advantage of the halt, they had erected racks, and continued the process of curing whale meat above slow-burning fires.

"Is it just the thanoi that worries you?" Bruni asked, her round face frowning thoughtfully.

"No. In truth, I'd feel better if the Highlanders didn't know how to find us by looking for our smoke." Unconsciously she glanced over her shoulder, across the landscape of rolling, hilly tundra. There was no sign of any of Strongwind Whalebone's men, but the chiefwoman had no doubt that some remained in the vicinity, keeping track of the slow-moving and poorly armed band.

"The cedars might give us some cover," Bruni agreed cheerfully. "Not to mention we'd be able to build some nice fires."

As if in response to her assertion, the wind picked up a notch, chilling Moreen's face, tugging at the strands of hair that broke free from her braids. "Let's go, then," she said.

Dinekki, who was overseeing the drying racks, smacked her toothless gums in appreciation of Moreen's plan. "Good. Watch out for tuskers," she said. "I'll keep an eye on things around here."

"Thank you, Grandmother. We'll be back in two or three days."

"I'm coming with you!" Little Mouse, who had been squatting near a drying fire a dozen paces away, jumped up and ran towards them.

"The ears on that boy," Bruni said with a laugh. "He could hear a flower bud, I swear he could."

"Not that there'll be much of that in the next half year," Dinekki clucked. "You, Mouse—you're needed to stick close around here. Every camp of the Arktos needs a scout, and with these three off sightseeing who else do you think I'm going to count on?"

"But—!" The youth's objection died in his throat. "A

scout? You mean, to kind of look around the area, keep an eye out for trouble and the like?"

"As I said, if not you, who?" the shaman demanded. "Would you send a little toddler out to do some scouting? How about your mother? Or maybe you think old Dinekki has nothing better to do than march up and down these hills on her old bones?"

"No, I'll do it!" Mouse declared. He raced to the tribe's small cache of weapons and picked up the spear he had claimed after the battle with the tuskers. "Nothing's going to sneak up on the tribe while I'm the scout!" he declared proudly.

"I'm glad we can count on you," Moreen said, feeling emotion tighten her throat. He looked so sincere, so brave, so young. The chiefwoman, Bruni, and Tildey had been all through the area in the past day, and she felt reasonably confident there was no threat in the immediate vicinity.

"All right—stay alert, and come and tell Dinekki if you see anything unusual."

"I will!" he promised. He slung the spear over his shoulder and started up a hill, as the trio of women armed themselves and took a few provisions and a waterskin from the tribe's supplies. The last thing the chiefwoman saw, before they started up the beach, was the black-haired youth bracing himself against the wind, long spear in his hands, earnestly peering out over the land.

"I admit I wasn't sure where we were, or that there was any hospitable land around here," Kerrick said as he and Coraltop gazed across placid water at an enclosed valley, dark green with a dense grove of evergreens. Two ridges faced by steep, rocky precipices extended inland. It seemed that trees—the first such timber they had seen on this rugged coast—thrived between the elevations.

"Oh, *I* knew we would find some place to land sooner or later," the kender said breezily. "It was just a matter of staying patient. As for me, I'm always patient. As my grandmother used to say, 'Coraltop, you are the very soul of patience.' "

Kerrick was standing at the front of the cabin and looking down into the empty fish locker. "Well," the elf said, "we timed it right anyway. We've run out of food."

For five days after spotting the mountainous horizon rising to the south they had steered along a rocky coast of exceptionally barren and apparently uninhabited terrain. The rugged skyline rose steeply only a few miles inland from the shore, and the edge of the land was in most places a high cliff of jagged, weatherworn stone. Kerrick had taken *Cutter* into a few narrow inlets, but even there the shore had been rocky and treacherous. Since the regular rainstorms had resulted in the water barrel remaining comfortably full, the elf had elected to keep sailing while searching for a more promising landfall.

At last they had come upon a strait of deep water extending between two rugged shores less than ten miles apart. Here they had veered south, hoping to find anchorage.

Now their search was rewarded, in the discovery of this bay on the eastern shore just inside the bottleneck. Kerrick studied the forest, confident they would find game—deer, pheasant, or rabbit—somewhere in the woods. His belly rumbled, and his mouth watered at the remembered taste of grilled meat. He checked his bowstring and arrows. Unwilling to leave the powerful talisman behind, the elf tucked his magical ring into a small pouch inside of his belt. Ready at last, he stood in the stern and looked for the most promising spot to begin the hunt.

The trees were barely half as tall as the pines that grew so commonly in Silvanesti, but their color was lush, and the ground showed mossy meadow and fern-bedded dale. A stone's throw away was a stretch of sand beach, backed by trees that looked especially inviting.

"How are you getting to shore?" Caroltop asked, frowning.

"*We're* going to swim," Kerrick replied.

"Good idea," the kender replied cheerfully. "Except, who will watch the boat?"

"Don't you know how to swim?"

"What kind of question is that? Netfisher practically *means* 'swimming,' in kenderspeak! But I think I could do some pretty good fishing right here, just in case your luck as a hunter is the same as your luck as a sailor."

Kerrick opened his mouth to reply when he realized that he wouldn't mind spending a few hours by himself. The kender, surprisingly enough, had proved a companionable shipmate, and of course, he *had* saved the elf's life. However, Coraltop talked a lot, even when he didn't seem to have anything noteworthy to say.

"All right. Why don't you drop a line in the water, and I'll have a hunt in the woods. Tomorrow we'll put both together and have a feast."

The elf tied his weapons and clothes into a nearly watertight bundle inside his oilskin, and slipped over the gunwale and into the chilly, slightly choppy water. He felt the cold instantly, but it was an invigorating sensation, and his spirits lifted as he tugged his floating garments along behind him and stroked toward shore.

A minute later he emerged onto the smooth, grainy sand, shivering in the breeze. The morning sun was up, but it was barely a blur low on the horizon. It seemed to offer little heat, so rapidly the elf donned his moccasins, woolen shirt, and leggings. He left his leather cloak behind a tree at the edge of the narrow beach strand, and quickly strung his bow.

Ready, he turned to wave goodbye at the kender, but Coraltop wasn't anywhere in sight. Kerrick sighed.

"You'd better catch a few fish if you want any dinner," he muttered irritatedly, suppressing his urge to shout only because he didn't want to startle any nearby game. He readied an arrow against his bowstring, relished a deep breath of cool pine-scented air, and stepped into the woods.

"That cloud across the gulf—do you notice how it's lingered there all day?" Moreen asked worriedly, as she and her two companions made their way along a ridge that ran parallel to the shore, perhaps a half mile inland.

"Yes, as if a part of the far shore is obscured," Bruni noted. "It goes away when the wind blows, then comes right back."

They were far enough north, now, that the opposite side of the gulf had come into view across the passage that Strongwind Whalebone had called the Bluewater Strait. They could see the shore when the fog and drizzle lifted enough, during the few hours of daylight. No more than ten miles away, they observed a rugged landscape of coastal bluff and steep mountains looming on the far side of the water.

"There—now the sun's hitting it. What does it look like to you?"

"It's a kind of wall!" Tildey said quickly, "and a tower, there on that hilltop over the sea. It's some kind of citadel!"

"She's right," Bruni confirmed after a moment's scrutiny. "A big one too, to show up so well at this distance."

"I think that must be Brackenrock," Moreen said, a knot in her stomach.

"The steam is coming from caverns below the city?" mused Bruni. "It makes sense to me. You were right!"

"No, I couldn't have been more wrong!" She was thinking of Strongwind's map, the fact that this ancient ruin had not been displayed there, and now she thought she understood why.

"It's way across the water, isn't it?" Tildey said quietly.

Moreen slumped down onto a rock and nodded bleakly. The truth was in plain sight: The citadel, the mythical place where the chiefwoman had hoped to find safety for her tribe, was miles away, way beyond any map, on the far side of this impassable bay.

"If we still had the kayaks . . ."

Bruni's voice trailed off and Moreen bit back her sharp retort. Not only had the ogres broken up all the tribe's little boats, but they had slashed all the sealskin shells when they abandoned Bayguard. It took a skilled builder the better part of a year to make a kayak, and one kayak could only carry one person, perhaps with one small passenger. That was no solution for the entire tribe.

"What about an ice crossing?" Tildey ventured, tentatively.

"*After* the Sturmfrost?" Moreen couldn't keep the scorn out of her voice. She wondered to herself: How many of us will even be alive, after the assault of that first, lethal blizzard?

"Well, there's no point in going back to Bayguard," Bruni said. "Let's keep going north somewhere. We might find that woods that you remembered. We have to be getting close. Being in a forest is better shelter than camping out here on the tundra."

Moreen nodded stoically and let her friends hoist her to her feet. Her mind drifted. She pictured Gulderglow, with its high walls, heat-producing coal, stockpiles of food. The Arktos could survive the winter there, although Strongwind had made the price of that shelter very clear. Still, paying that price was better than starving, wasn't it? Or leaving infants and elders outside where the Sturmfrost would certainly doom them? Suddenly the mantle of "chief" felt very heavy on her shoulders.

The three continued to make their way along the crest of a ridge toward a low hill. When they finally came over the hill, they stared in awe. Before them stretched a whole valley green with trees, lush evergreens spilling like a dark carpet across the miles of level ground between them and more rugged elevation. Down below was a small expanse of water, a sheltered cove. The surface was gray, streaked with gentle waves.

"This must be Tall Cedar Bay!" Moreen announced with relief. "I'm sure of it." The memory of her long trek by kayak with her father, the only other time she had seen this protected inlet, came flooding back. This was more wood than she'd ever imagined, a treasure of fuel and building material. So their journey hadn't been in vain, after all.

"What's that?" Bruni asked ominously, pointing toward an object bobbing near the shore. "Another ogre ship?"

Instinctively they dropped to the ground, staring at what was clearly some kind of modest-sized watercraft. Unlike a kayak or galley, it was distinguished by a long pole rising straight up from the center of the deck.

"I don't think ogres have boats like that," Moreen said. Her heart pounded with sudden excitement, and her mind whirled. Perhaps Brackenrock wasn't unreachable after all! "Let's get down there and look."

The chiefwoman pointed to a nearby ravine, a shallow-sided cut in the ridge that would allow them to descend with good cover. One by one, the three Arktos she-warriors moved in that direction and started down, working their way toward the suddenly ominous-looking beach fringed by woods.

Almost immediately Kerrick had found a game trail, a narrow track of dirt amid the pine needles and brush covering the ground. No tracks were discernible on the hard, dry surface, but he took the path with confidence. His feet made no sound as he advanced into the wind, eyes scanning his surroundings. He relished the sweet, powerful scent of pine, after his months at sea.

Sunlight filtered through the thick branches at a steep angle, but though the trees were stunted by Silvanesti standards, the forest floor was shaded and dark. Ferns and juniper clustered between large, square-edged boulders. Kerrick wondered if he might be the first person in the history of Krynn to traverse this ground.

The trail followed parallel to the beach for a while, and

several times he peered out to see his boat still at anchor, bobbing in the swells that were growing high even within the deep cove. Still, no sign of that damned kender, however.

Before long the path curved inland and the trees closed in to surround him on all sides. He found some pebbly droppings, and his heart raced. Whether it was a deer, elk, or large sheep that had left the spoor, the elven hunter felt keen anticipation. Jogging as fast as he could without making too much noise, he held his bow ready, arrow crossed at his chest.

Nor did he grow discouraged after a full hour passed with no sign of game. Several more times he spied the neat prints of small, cloven hooves. Fairly certain he was after a deer now, Kerrick's mind entertained a dozen tempting imagined recipes for venison. He wondered if he might find wild chive or onions growing near one of the small boggy wetlands he passed. The trail had taken him across the valley, toward the base of the southern ridge, and now he skirted the edge of a small pond. Cedars reflected in the still water, and the reedy shoreline showed muddy tracks, slowly filling with water. Apparently his quarry had stopped to drink here, not minutes ago.

Again the trail entered the woods, and the elf slowed his pace. He was still out of shape after all his injuries and time at sea. He came to a steep-walled ravine that swung down to cut a low rocky swath through the forest.

Across the ravine, he saw the deer. It was a doe, large and brown and rigid with alertness, staring at him with long ears upraised. In a flash it whirled and bounded away, gone before he could even raise his bow. Returning the arrow to his quiver, he slung the bow over his shoulder and found a place where he could descend the rocky wall into the ravine. Stepping on stones, he passed the narrow stream at the bottom without getting too wet, then jogged along until he found a tall pine trunk, with branches jutting like the rungs of a ladder, leaning against the opposite wall. Quickly he climbed up and plunged in the direction taken by the doe.

Every sense alert, he continued on and froze as he heard a rustle in the brush ahead. The arrow was drawn now, bowstring tight as he drew a bead on a leafy thicket. He tried to anticipate. If the deer broke from cover it could go in any direction, and he would have a split second to aim and shoot.

Instead, the rustle was repeated, but he saw no sign of movement. His whole body vibrated with tension as he advanced, one step after the next, taking care to keep his footing.

He was utterly unprepared for the attack from behind. When something solid smashed into him he toppled forward, releasing the arrow into the ground and sprawling on his face. The force of the tackle knocked the wind from his lungs, and he gasped under the weight of a heavy body.

More attackers went for his arms, pulling away the bow, pressing him against the ground. He saw leather moccasins, several sets of leggings, one foot pushed firmly down on his hand. Finally he was hauled to his knees, then pushed onto his back as the first attacker—a massive human woman with a round, curious face—sat on his belly.

With smooth movements, the other two, also human women, lashed his hands. Still without talking, they hoisted him to his feet and started pushing him through the woods.

They were heading directly for the shore, toward the little cove where *Cutter* stood at anchor.

"This is a good spot," Moreen announced, after a mile of walking along the rim of the deep, steep-sided ravine. She gestured to a small, mossy grotto above the gully. "We can build a fire back there, and it won't be seen unless someone's right nearby. Those rocks will make it all that much harder for our prisoner to escape."

"Sounds good to me," Bruni agreed. "What about you, stranger?" She looked quizzically at their captive, who returned a blank stare, giving no sign that he understood their language.

Tildey stood three paces behind them, an arrow ready in case the man made some threatening move. Thus far, however, he had merely plodded along in listless, demoralized silence.

"Tie him to that tree, and keep his wrists bound. Oh, and search through his pack, and see if he has anything in his pockets."

Bruni and Tildey went about securing the prisoner while Moreen gathered a pile of dried pine limbs. She kindled a fire, and quickly the warmth spread through the grotto area, driving back the damp chill of early nightfall. Huge, square boulders rose like walls to the right, left, and rear.

"What was he carrying?" she asked, as her two companions made themselves comfortable near the blaze. The prisoner was seated a short distance away, still illuminated by firelight.

"He had a bow and arrows, a knife—sharper than any blade I've ever seen—and this beaded waterskin," Tildey said, laying out the stranger's possessions. She held up the skin. "Nice craftsmanship."

"Maybe he's a rich Highlander," Bruni said with a chuckle, and a quick glance at the still-impassive prisoner. He was leaning backward, his straggly blond hair hanging limply down on both sides of his head.

Moreen snorted. "He's no Highlander. No beard, and his face is too skinny. Also there's something about those big eyes that seems strange to me."

"Yes, I know," Tildey said, scrutinizing the stranger. "It's as if he's got a boy's skin but much older eyes."

The chiefwoman's eyes, meanwhile, turned west, toward the coast hidden by the trees. "We could use that ship," Moreen said softly. Bruni snorted and shook her head, while Tildey gazed at the fire.

The wind swirled, carrying the smoke toward the prisoner. Unable to move out of the way, he choked and coughed, finally twisting onto his side for relief. The Arktos took no note of his discomfort.

Finally, Bruni heaved a sigh. "Why do you want a ship so bad?" she asked.

"Because we could cross to Brackenrock, before the Sturmfrost! We could be into the old fortress, snug in the steam caves, by the time the first blizzard begins."

"You can't put the whole tribe on that little boat!" snorted the big woman.

"Not all at once, no," Moreen acknowledged. "But you saw the far shore this morning—it's not such a far crossing, and we could take the whole tribe in many trips."

Bruni shook her head. "I'm not getting in that boat," she said stubbornly.

"So you'd prefer the Sturmfrost, hunkered down here in the woods? Not just you, but Dinekki, Feathertail—every one of us? The elders? The children?" Moreen snapped impatiently. "Or perhaps we should go back to Guilderglow. You could be some Highlander's concubine!"

"What?" demanded Bruni, her eyes blazing.

"*That* was the cost of shelter there," the chiefwoman continued, feeling guilty about the outburst. "They offered us . . . me . . . a place to live, for a price."

The large woman sighed, and looked in the direction of the sea. "I never cared much for those kayaks, but that's a bigger boat out there. I'll have to think about it."

"What do we do with him?" asked Moreen, gesturing to the prisoner.

"Maybe we should kill him?" This was Tildey, more of a question than a suggestion. "He may not be an ogre or a tusker, but he's not one of the tribe. I agree with Moreen. I don't think he's any Highlander, either."

It took all of Kerrick's self-discipline to feign ignorance of the language as he strained to listen. He grunted, shifted onto the rocks, half-turned his back to the women.

There was no feigning his search of a comfortable position as he twisted on the rocky ground. He couldn't move far since his hands, lashed together at the wrists, were tethered to a pine tree with only a foot of loose line. Nor could he feel much of the warmth of the fire, which was several feet away.

At first, the elf pretended utter disinterest as he tried to eavesdrop on the women's conversation. As they led him through the forest he had begun to understand some of their words: "camp," "ogre" and "fire." Their language was very similar to a coastal dialect common to humans from Tarsis to Balifor, and their accent was heavy. Still, many of the crewmen on his father's galley had used the language, and he had learned it as a child.

The big one was called Bruni, and the other two were Moreen and Tildey. Moreen seemed to be in charge.

"So we kill him?" It was the one called Bruni who at last replied to Tildey's suggestion. "What now? Are *we* ogres?" Kerrick was beginning to think fondly of this bovine human, who was in no hurry to steal his boat and now, apparently, saw no purpose in cold-blooded murder.

"No, we're not," Moreen agreed decisively. "I think we should keep him tied up and bring the tribe here, to the cedar grove. There are many mysteries here, including who he is, where he came from, and what is the nature and mission of his ship."

"Do *you* know how to paddle that thing?" Bruni asked her.

"I think he can be convinced to show us. He understands our language—can't you tell?"

Moreen had been watching Kerrick, slyly. For the first time she looked amused. He noticed the way her mouth bent into a wry smile before he glanced away, quickly.

"Why do you say that?" asked Tildey.

"He tensed up when you asked if we should kill him." Moreen continued to stare at Kerrick. "You do know what we're saying, don't you, stranger?"

He saw no point in continuing the charade. "Yes," he

replied in that same rough tongue. "At least, I think I understood the important points. You might kill me."

"Understand this: We *will* kill you if you prove a danger to our tribe, or if you prove to be uncooperative. Tomorrow we will go aboard your ship, and you will show us how it works. Do you understand?"

"I understand," Kerrick replied. He shifted around so he could better inspect his three captors. He understood something else: When the women had searched him, they had failed to find the hidden belt pouch where he had placed his father's ring. That secret, he hoped, would save him. Until the right moment, he had only to be patient, and to avoid antagonizing his captors.

"These look like ogre tools," Tildey noted, holding up his steel-headed arrows and sleek, double-curved bow.

Kerrick almost revealed his surprise but remained impassive. What could she mean? The slender elven shafts and keen steel arrowheads bore no resemblance to the crude weapons of that monstrous race.

"He's not an ogre," Bruni argued. "A boy, not even shaving yet?"

"Did you notice his ear?" Moreen asked. "One is cut and scarred, but the other is *long*. I've never seen any like it." Her tone was hard, and she gave him a cold, appraising look. Kerrick flushed, the shame of his scarring a withering memory.

"How did he come to have ogre weapons?" wondered Tildey.

"And an ogre ship?" added the big woman, who looked more puzzled than fierce.

"I don't think it's an ogre ship, and I don't think he's an ogre." The intensity of Moreen's gaze made Kerrick squirm. "No, I think he's something new entirely."

"The ogres came in a different kind of ship, I admit," Bruni mused. "His has that big post sticking out of it. The ogre ship had all those paddles on the side."

Kerrick wondered what kind of savages these were, never to have seen a sailboat before. He was not reassured by their ignorance. He wondered if they had even heard of Silvanesti or elves. For the time being he would be content to let them think he was a "boy, not even shaving."

Later, when they were sleeping and he could slip on the ring, they would learn of their mistake.

13

Pawns and a Prisoner

Kerrick was dreaming, and in his dream he was deeply ashamed. His friend was dead and it was his fault. He knew he was to blame, even though no one would say it out loud.

He was a child in a tiny boat, and he had erected a broomstick with a blanket for a sail. Wind gusted with surprising force, and he went skidding across the waters of the Than-Thalas River. Silvanost, dominated by the graceful spire that was the Tower of the Stars, sparkled in the summer sun, and the waves splashed against the little hull, cooling him with moisture.

His father's galley, *Silvanos Oak*, stood at anchor nearby and he steered under the shadow of the mighty ship. Crewmen, many of them Kerrick's friends, gathered at the rail, cheering. Then the little boat shot past the hull of the great ship, into the windier water of the open river.

A gust of wind slammed Kerrick's small boat onto its side. He heard the sound of the sail striking the water, a hard *slap*, as he tumbled sideways. Quickly the boat filled up, leaving the youth trapped by rising water. He tried to call for help but only choked and sputtered. He couldn't see anything, and he couldn't breathe. He needed air, desperately craved air.

He he found himself lying on the ground, feverish and chilled, in a forest grotto at night. He drew in great, ragged gulps of air, groaning aloud at the aching in his back and limbs. The stones on the ground felt as if some nocturnal fiend had filed their edges into daggers. Slowly his fear was replaced by a deep sadness.

"I'm sorry, Delthas," he mouthed silently, blinking back the tears that inevitably came with the name and the memory.

Delthas Windrider. Kerrick hadn't spoken that name in many years, but the memory of the young elf was never far from his thoughts, especially when he was sailing. He had learned the story in bits and pieces as he grew older. When Kerrick's little boat had sunk, several young sailors, elves and humans both, had flung themselves into the water to rescue him. Two of them had seized Kerrick's hands as he was descending into the indigo depths. Kicking hard, they pulled him to the surface, where he would be hauled onto the galley deck of his father's ship.

His rescuers climbed aboard on rope ladders, then noticed Delthas Windrider was missing. He had jumped with the other sailors, but apparently his head had struck the side of the hull. He had vanished in the depths.

No one ever told Kerrick he was responsible for the young sailor's death, but he had seen the tears in his father's eyes when Dimorian had been informed of the missing elf, and he sensed a new reserve in the looks he got from the other men.

As it always did, the dream left him exhausted and filled with despair. He tried to collect himself, to forget the dream and to consider his course of action.

The night was utterly still, windless and dark. The fire had faded to a mound of gray ash, brightened only in a few places by the lingering crimson of glowing coals. Gradually turning his head, the elf studied the three bedrolls. His captors remained still, apparently sound asleep. Now he was almost grateful for the rocks that made his own position so uncomfortable. Undoubtedly they had helped to wake him, prodding him to escape.

Kerrick had already worked at the knot that held his hands together, concluding that he wouldn't be able to loosen the tough, leathery bond. He hoped that would be only a minor impediment to escape, however. Taking care to keep as quiet as possible, he squirmed around and slipped the fingertips of his right hand into his belt pouch. With a wriggle he put on his ring.

Immediately the magical strength began to flow through him, energizing his muscles, driving the cramps and stiffness from his limbs. He snapped his bindings with a simple flex. Even his hearing seemed acute, as he listened to the regular breathing of his three captors. He rose and very carefully took a step away from the tree to which he had been tethered.

The camp was enclosed in the steep-walled grotto. Kerrick moved gingerly around the fire. His keen night vision compensated for the scant light emanating from the fire

Another few steps and he would be loose in the forest. He moved past a pile of loose, brittle firewood. Next to Tildey lay his bow and quiver of arrows. He wanted very much to take his weapons with him. He reached to grab the bundle and very gently started to lift.

There was a clatter of stones and a sharp outcry from one of his captors. Too late he saw that the bow was tied down and had been rigged with a trap of loose gravel. Abandoning stealth, cursing the loss of a fine weapon, he leaped over the pile of firewood. He came down awkwardly on a twisted root and fell. The magic of the ring hummed through him, and he bounced to his feet. Before he could take another step, however, a heavy body slammed into him, and he and Bruni tumbled together onto the forest floor.

Kerrick twisted and nearly broke free. Magical energy surged through his sinews as he grasped the woman's big hands and pulled them apart. He whipped his head back, cracking into her chin, while his feet clawed and kicked at the rough ground. Even with her weight on his back he managed to rise to his knees, then his feet. One more twist, one frantic leap, and he would be gone.

Except that Bruni's grip still wasn't broken. It felt as though a bracket of iron had been clamped around Kerrick's waist. Panicking, he kicked wildly, again feeling that pulse of magical strength. She grunted, but held him as tight as a manacle.

Moreen and Tildey stumbled toward the fracas. Finally the elf broke Bruni's grip. The big woman fell back as he scrambled forward, only to be simultaneously tackled by the other two. Before he could react Bruni was back, bashing him on the head with a heavy piece of firewood. He fell, stunned, his skull throbbing as they dragged him back to the tree.

"Be still, now," warned the big woman, shaking the log as though it was a mere twig. "I only hit you 'cuz you made me." She rubbed her chin. "You know," she admitted to her companions. "He's stronger than he looks."

"Are you sure you can keep him here?" Moreen asked Bruni. She spoke to the big woman quietly, as they stood under a cluster of cedars two dozen paces last night's campfire. Dawn's gray light filtered through the trees, creating a dim murk on the forest floor. Still, it was enough light that they could see their prisoner lying as though dead. They had bound his hands with extra loops, noting with surprise that he had apparently broken the original ropes. Tildey remained near the fire, keeping a closer watch.

"Oh, sure," Bruni agreed, rubbing her bruised chin. "He's a tough one, all right, but now that we have his arms tied real good I don't think he'll be going anywhere. We used plenty of rope, too. He's probably sorer than I am and needs a long rest."

"I hope so!" the chiefwoman snapped.

"Now, you can't really blame him," Bruni said good naturedly. "You or I would have tried the same thing."

Moreen snorted. "He's not much of a hunter, though." For some reason she was irritated by Bruni's sympathy for the unwary captive. "All we had to do was make a little noise in the brush. You'd think he expected to shoot a bull elk, the way he was creeping around."

"Well, hurry up and bring the rest of the tribe," said the big woman cheerfully. "Don't worry about us."

Still feeling those misgivings, Moreen nodded and started toward the south. She stayed on the beach, where the way was easiest, and as soon as she emerged from the cedar forest she broke into a steady, loping jog. It was a cold and murky day, but her exertion kept her warm. Curls of surf crunched into the beach, but there was no trace of the sun behind the leaden overcast.

Unencumbered by the need to explore or to accommodate slower companions, the chiefwoman made excellent time, and as the pale gray day finally slipped toward the deeper gray of nightfall she spied a familiar figure waving to her from an inland hilltop.

"Moreen! Up here! It's Mouse!"

She began to feel the fatigue as she climbed. The youth trotted to meet her.

"The rest of the tribe is just over the hill," he explained. "I've been staying close, scouting, like you told me to do."

"Good job," she said, pleased that the Arktos had made such progress on their northward trek. "Any sign of the Highlanders?"

"Well, yes," Mouse reported. "That one, the redbeard with the wolf-cape, was hanging back there, one valley over. With a dozen of his men. I spied on them from the hilltop, but they didn't see me. They know where the tribe is, though. They kept coming up to the ridge to watch."

"You did well not to let them see you," Moreen said sincerely. "Now, take me to the others." She followed the boy around the hill to find Garta and Dinekki engaged in conversation while the rest of the tribe were starting the evening fires.

After welcoming embraces, the women looked at their chief with curiosity. "You're alone, but I can tell you don't bring bad news," the shaman observed shrewdly.

"No, it might be that Chislev has smiled upon us with a rare opportunity," Moreen declared. "How tired are the people? Is there any chance they could march through the night?"

Garta's eyes widened at the question, but Dinekki all but cackled in amusement. "Of course we could!" she replied. "The walk would do us good, give us a chance to stretch those cramped muscles."

"Yes—yes, I think we could keep going, if we had to," the other woman agreed. "But we're hungry and just got good fires going. Why do you want us to move on?"

Moreen consciously avoided looking up at the inland ridge where, she felt certain, Lars Redbeard or one of his men was watching. Instead, she answered with the plan that was still taking shape in her mind. "Go ahead and build the fires. Cook dinner. I want it to look as if we're going to camp just like any other night. We won't be moving out until it's been dark for awhile, in any event."

"Just so those Highland eyes are fooled, eh?" said Dinekki with a sly grin.

"I knew you'd understand, Grandmother," the chief-woman replied.

She joined her tribe for a meal of smoked whale, water-cress, and roasted clams, making her way from fire to fire, greeting people. Feathertail proudly displayed a clean, soft sealskin she had prepared all by herself. Hilgrid showed her an ivory whistle she had been carving. To each in turn, Moreen explained her idea, and the Arktos played along, even unrolling their bedrolls in the growing darkness. By late afternoon it was fully dark but, for once the chief-woman was grateful they'd have long hours of concealment ahead.

Finally Moreen took Hilgrid, Garta, and Dinekki aside for a whispered conference. She told them of the cedar grove, describing the unobstructed route along the beach that would lead them to the woods. "It's important to make haste, as much as you can," she encouraged. "If you haven't reached the woods by dawn, keep going. Get under the cover of the trees before the Highlanders catch sight of you."

The tribeswomen gathered their possession, taking care to stay away outside the dying light of their small fires. Satisfied they would be underway soon, Moreen again consulted with Little Mouse, who directed her toward the nearby ridge where he had last seen the Highlanders.

Despite the dark and the clouds, she made her way up the rise, and was rewarded by the sight of another campfire crackling brightly barely a quarter mile away. With no attempt at secrecy she began to walk toward it, making noise by scuffing stones and treading over the crackling dry brush.

Despite the fact that she was ready, she gasped in surprise when a human form rose from the shadows ten yards away. Something white flashed in the darkness, and she knew a speartip was being waved in her direction.

"Stop right there! Who are you?" demanded a gruff voice in the crisp Highlander accent.

"Moreen, Chiefwoman of the Arktos," she replied sternly. "Who are you to accost me?"

"I . . . I am Daric Sheepskinner," replied the sentry. "I am watching the approach to our camp. You startled me. . . . That is . . . what do you want, Moreen Chiefwoman?"

"I would speak with Lars Redbeard. He is here, is he not?"

The man seemed even more flustered than before at this statement and at her obvious lack of fear. "I . . . yes, yes he is."

"Well, take me to him!" snapped Moreen.

"But . . . of course." The man turned toward the glowing fire, and she could see other forms silhouetted in the dim light, men obviously roused by the commotion. "Be careful," Daric warned. "There are sharp rocks here. It is easy to fall."

"I have walked around rocks before." She was grateful that the darkness concealed her half-smile. It pleased her to keep these burly Highlanders surprised and off balance.

"Lars Redbeard!" shouted the sentry, as they advanced toward the camp. "It is the chiefwoman of the Arktos. She has come to see you."

"Moreen, daughter of Redfist Bayguard!" Lars Redbeard exclaimed, as he hastily adjusted his wolfskin cloak. "It is indeed an honor to have you visit our camp."

"We Arktos share the honor, knowing Strongwind Whalebone sends only his most trusted advisers to spy upon an inconsequential tribe of women and elders."

Lars nodded, then frowned as he realized she was mocking him. "No, not spy," he said quickly. "In truth, we want no harm to come to you, and my king has entrusted me with ensuring your safety."

"How comforting," she replied dryly. "May I be seated?"

"Yes, of course!" Redbeard gestured to a pair of flat rocks near the fire. "Erikal, bring us warqat! Marlat, put more wood on the fire."

Moreen enjoyed the spectacle of the Highlanders scrambling to refresh their camp fire and to make her comfortable. She took her time in settling herself. Erikal brought a leather sack. Lars Redbeard poured several drams of dark liquid into two small, golden cups and extended one to her.

"I would drink from that one," she said, pointing to the cup the Highlander had kept for himself. "That is, if it makes no difference to you."

"What?" He was taken aback and clearly insulted but quickly switched around the two vessels. "No, of course it makes no difference. Here."

The scent of the draught was pungent in her nostrils. She remembered the strong, bitter sensation from the drink offered to her by Strongwind Whalebone. Reminding herself to stick with small sips, she felt the fiery warmth slide across her tongue, then sting the rest of the way down her throat. It took all of her effort not to reveal her discomfort, but she made no sound and lowered the cup to her lap with dignity.

"Thank you," she said, surprised as the word came out

breathy and forced.

Now it was Lars Redbeard's turn to smile smugly. "That draught is from the royal cask itself. It is renowned for its smoothness."

"Obviously," replied Moreen, her voice returning to normal. "Now, tell me, why does Strongwind Whalebone take such interest in our little tribe? Surely you and your men would be more comfortable in Guilderglow, not camping on the damp tundra as the winter winds begin to blow harsh. Despite his offer, I have made it clear to him that I will not be his wife."

"You told him that?" The Highlander's eyes opened wide with amazement.

"Yes. He didn't take it well."

"My liege is worried about those same winter winds. He fears that your tribe will suffer unduly when the snows come, and he wants it known that you are still welcome in his city."

"Yes, but on what terms?" Moreen said sarcastically. She managed to hold her temper in check by reminding herself that she was not here to provoke an argument. "In fact, you may tell the king that I have been thinking about his—" she wanted to say "demand," but she bit her tongue. "—offer."

"Strongwind Whalebone will be delighted to know that," Lars said sincerely. Flames rose from the fire and as the emissary glanced to the side he brought his wolfshead cap directly into line with Moreen's gaze. She imagined that she saw cunning and amusement reflected in that lupine visage.

"Perhaps you will carry my message to him, as soon as possible?" she suggested quietly. "If he was to come to this valley, I could speak with him. It may be that we could arrive at an understanding on matters that eluded us in our previous conversation."

"It would be my pleasure, Lady Chiefwoman!" pledged Lars. "In fact, I will dispatch a runner to him at first light."

"First light?" She sighed in disappointment. "Of course,

the night is dark, and there are many dangers abroad. Very well, I understand that your man cannot depart until dawn."

She heard mutters of displeasure from the other men, who were hanging politely back but close enough to hear the conversation. Lars looked pained at her words, and she felt a momentary stab of guilt. She took another sip of the warqat, acknowledging a certain pleasant heat to the stuff as it trickled down her insides.

"I will go immediately!" one of the Highlanders volunteered to Lars. She looked up and smiled at the sincerity of the sentry, Daric. "There is no threat in this night that should delay a warrior of Guilderglow!"

"No, none!" came the chorus of agreement.

"You are right," Lars said firmly. "Daric, begin at once. Take provisions for two days, and do not rest until you reach the castle."

"Remember, ask the king to come here, to this valley," Moreen said.

"It shall be done!" Daric promised. The sentry made his preparations with impressive speed, nodded a farewell to his companions, bowed to the chiefwoman, and trotted away into the night.

"Would you like an escort back to your camp?" asked Lars.

"No!" Moreen replied, more sharply than she wanted. "No, I came up the hill in the dark. I can make my way back down it as well."

"Very good," Lars replied. "We will see you in the morning."

"Of course." She spoke the lie easily, knowing that she ought to be miles away by dawn.

14

A Partnership

"What manner of people are you?" Kerrick asked. "What is your tribe?"

"We are the Arktos," Bruni replied. She was leaning back, picking her teeth with a bone from one of the grouse Tildey had shot. After some muted discussion, the two had agreed to share their food with the prisoner, releasing one of his hands to allow him to eat.

The elf had been unconscious for most of the day following his ill-fated escape attempt. He had managed to remove the ring, dropping it onto the ground and pushing enough pine needles over it to conceal it from view. He had only worn it for a short time, but even so the magic had left him drained, sapped of energy.

Now food had restored some of his strength, and he knew his captors didn't plan to kill him. He had shifted around enough to pick up the ring and slide it into his boot. Tildey remained suspicious and jumpy, her weapons near to hand, but Bruni seemed willing to talk and answer his questions, asking a few of her own.

"You aren't a Highlander or an ogre," she observed bluntly. "Who *are* you, and where do you come from?"

"I am a sailor, son of a sailor, and I come from Ansalon," he answered. "That is a land to the north of here, across the sea."

"A sailor, but not a human sailor." He was startled to see Moreen emerging from the woods. She stood with her hands upon her hips. "I've been thinking about it. You're an elf, aren't you?"

Kerrick saw that Tildey was equally surprised by the chiefwoman's return. The archer leaped to her feet and hugged Moreen, who seemed shorter and more wiry than he remembered. He noticed that her black hair was unkempt and that she gazed at him with a wry smile, as if he intensely amused her.

"Of course I'm an elf," he admitted easily, wondering why that was such a revelation to these people. "I imagine you've seen elves before, haven't you?"

"Never," replied the chiefwoman bluntly. She turned to her fellow Arktos. "The tribe is here, on the outskirts of the grove. They marched all night to get here, but everyone made it."

"And the Highlanders?" asked Bruni.

"I think we gave them the slip. It will take four or five days, I hope, before Strongwind Whalebone even learns that we've moved north. Then they'll have to come up the coast, so that's another day before they catch up with us. Still, I want us to move fast." She looked at Kerrick again. "Now, get up, elf sailor, and come with me."

"Should we tie his hands?" Bruni asked, as she loosened the bond that had secured Kerrick to the tree for the past two days. He stretched, standing awkwardly, feeling with his foot the comforting presence of the ring in the bottom of his right boot.

"I don't think he'll go far, not without his boat," Moreen replied. Her words sent a twinge of fear through the elf.

"What have you done with *Cutter*?" he demanded. "If you've damaged her, so help me Zivilyn, I'll . . ." His words trailed off as he saw they were all staring at him.

"*Her*?" Again Moreen gave him another look of wry amusement. "I didn't know you and your ship were so attached. Is it usual for elves to treat ships as their wives?"

Kerrick glowered at Moreen. "*Cutter* is a sailboat, not a

ship—though perhaps to you barbarians they're the same thing!"

He was startled by the fury that suddenly darkened her features. The smile was gone, and somehow a knife had sprung into her hand. She trembled as she held the blade toward him, speaking in a low, brittle voice. "The last ship I saw was filled with killers, brutes. I have no reason to believe that your boat has brought anything different to our shores. Now, keep your mouth shut, if you want to keep your tongue."

The elf said nothing. He sensed that his words had wounded Bruni and Tildey, too. All three humans were in a dark mood as they roughly pushed him along the forest trail. Not long afterward they entered a small clearing, brightened by glimpses of the gray sea through the trees. Scores of people huddled under the cedars, watching him with wide-eyed curiosity. There were frail, white-haired elders clutching babes and toddlers, and several tough-looking women holding spears. A number of children watched him with unabashed interest, and one—a tall youth with a shock of dark hair hanging over his forehead—fingered his spear, as if he would cast the weapon at the slightest provocation.

"Come this way," Moreen said curtly, leading him through the band toward the shore.

Kerrick quickly realized that, except for some frail elders, there were no men among the group. He remembered Moreen's words, about a ship filled with killers. How long had these people dwelled here in ignorance, pathetically surviving in this icy and forgotten corner of Krynn? They hadn't even recognized him as an elf—at least, not until Moreen had had several days to think it over.

A few more steps brought them to the edge of the woods, where the chiefwoman halted beneath the cover of a dense cedar. He was relieved to see that *Cutter* bobbed at anchor where he had left her. For the first time in hours he thought of Coraltop Netfisher, wondering at the fact that there was still no sign of the kender.

"You are going to ferry my tribe across the strait," Moreen said. "On your she-boat. It may take several journeys, but you must land each group on the far side and come back for more."

Kerrick squinted across the water. He could make out the murky outline of a distant horizon, the shoreline obscured by fog. The wind was blowing from the north, and the surface of the open water had risen into steep, choppy swells. The mission would be challenging, especially since so much of it had to be done in the darkness, but it appealed to the seaman in him. At the same time, he realized that he had no choice.

"I refuse," he said.

"What?" Moreen's lips tightened in anger, her dark eyes flashing. "Do you want to be killed, right here, right now?"

"No, I don't," he replied. "But you don't want to kill me, either . . . not unless one of you knows how to raise a sail, how to steer through an ocean swell."

The chiefwoman's face was white, and she was trembling with rage. He wondered if he had miscalculated. Moreen stomped away from him, then whirled back, her bone knife again in her hand. "Do you have a high tolerance for torture?" she demanded.

"No—but I have even less tolerance for slavery. I am Kerrick Fallabrine of House Mariner, and I am my own master." He braced himself, ready to parry a thrust of that knife, to show these barbarians that elves knew how to fight!

He was utterly unprepared for her reaction. Her whole body slumped, as if her willpower had been drained. Her eyes, inflamed with rage a moment ago, now swam with despair. "Don't you understand? We *have* to get across the strait!" she said.

He was surprised by how quickly his own tenseness faded. "And I could take you in my boat," he said. "But not at the point of a spear! And those are *not* ogre weapons!" he added as an afterthought, looking at Tildey sharply.

Moreen scrutinized him. "You are a stranger, an enemy.

It is only good sense for me to guard against treachery and betrayal."

"Where I come from, it is not necessarily assumed that a stranger is an enemy," Kerrick replied gently.

"Should I just let you go to your boat and *trust* you to come back for my tribe? Is that how your people treat strangers? I'm thinking you must come from a land of great fools!"

The elf sighed. Good manners, apparently, were not a cultural trait of these people. He shook his head, forging on. "Perhaps you could *hire* me, arrange a barter for the service of my boat. In my land, such arrangements are made all the time."

"Indeed I offer you such a trade—your life, for the use of your ship." Moreen's chin was set, her eyes still hot.

"I tell you, that is slavery, and I am no slave!"

"What do your ship-people barter for?" This was Bruni, her broad brow furrowed.

Kerrick shrugged. "Lots of things. Food, furs, wine, cut stone. Steel is a common currency and gold the most precious of all." As if these savages would know anything of gold!

"Gold!" Moreen's eyes lit up, and she looked at Bruni. "Do you still have . . ."

"Of course," said the big woman with a grin.

Her big pack was sitting on the ground, and Kerrick watched with interest as she untied the flap and reached inside. With some strain, she pulled out a small strongbox and set it on the ground. Moreen reached down, undid the clasp, and pushed open the lid.

"Here is gold. Will you accept it in trade for carrying my tribe across the strait?"

It was only with great effort that Kerrick kept his mouth from dropping open or held back from lunging at the mound of coins. There were more than a hundred of them there, thick and crudely stamped but undeniably pure gold. With a display of deliberation, he knelt and picked up one of the gold pieces. Just to be certain, he put it into his mouth and tasted it, biting down, feeling the malleable metal.

"Is that enough?" Moreen said worriedly. "We have some furs too, and I suppose we could spare some of our food, as well."

Finally the elf trusted himself enough to speak. "Oh, that's . . . enough." He could spend a hundred years hauling passengers up and down the Than-Thalas and never come close to seeing this much gold.

"Yes," he said firmly, standing and meeting Moreen's eyes. "I will accept your offer and ferry your tribe in exchange for this gold."

"Very good," she said, with obvious satisfaction. "Now, how did you get from the boat to shore?"

"I swam," Kerrick said.

"That won't work. We'll have to pull it up onto the beach."

"*That* won't work," the elf replied. He explained about the keel. "She needs at least four feet of water to stay afloat."

"What about this rock," the woman said, gesturing to a flat boulder jutting into a little cove off the bay. "The water is deep next to it, and we can step from the rock onto the boat."

"The stone might damage the hull. Can you have your people gathered many cedar boughs? Perhaps they can weave them into a bumper, to surround the edges of the rock. That just might work. I'll swim out and bring in the boat, and we can try."

Moreen snorted. "What if you just get aboard and sail away?"

The elf considered the fortune in gold that was sure to keep him here, but he didn't want to let her know how much he valued her barter. Instead, he shrugged. "What do you want to do? Swim out there with me?"

She thought about that, as the icy wind bit through their cloaks and a spray of precipitation—snowflakes, now—whisked past. Finally, she nodded. "Yes. I will."

"Huh? Suit yourself." That surprised him, but he

shucked his cloak, shirt, boots, and leggings. Moreen watched hesitantly as he walked out in the water, naked, to the flat rock she had chosen for a dock. He felt every snowflake strike his skin, each gust of chilly wind, but he suppressed his misgivings.

"Come along whenever you're ready," he shouted over his shoulder, and leaned forward to dive.

"Wait!" she cried, but he was already gone, plunging cleanly into the choppy water, gasping as the icy brine coursed over his body. With strong, churning strokes he began swimming to *Cutter*, and once there seized the ladder at the transom and quickly pulled himself up and over the rail. Shivering, with his teeth chattering uncontrollably, he pulled open the hatch and grabbed the first woolen blanket he could find. He came back out, turned, and waved to Moreen, who still stood, fully dressed, hesitant, on the flat rock.

Only then did he think to himself: Where is Coraltop Netfisher? The cabin was unoccupied. Nor was the kender in the cockpit or anywhere else on deck.

"Bring the boat here!" came the shout from shore, and he saw Moreen glaring at him, her hands on her hips.

He waved again and checked the wind, which was blowing out to sea, and the tide, which was almost at its high point. He took only enough time to slip on dry clothes before hoisting the anchor. Using his single, long oar, he stood in the cockpit and laboriously propelled the boat toward the makeshift dock.

The Arktos, meanwhile, were gathering boughs as he had asked, and by the time he had guided the sailboat to the rock, it had been circled by a thick bumper of pines.

Moreen and Bruni assisted a group of hesitant elders and overeager children to scramble over the gunwales. He sent as many of them into the cabin as would fit, then posted some of the more able-bodied around the deck. In all, he was surprised to find that he was able to get some twenty people aboard. Tildey, who still had Kerrick's bow and arrows—grudgingly pronouncing his weapons far superior to her own—posted herself atop the cabin, where she had a clear shot in any direction. Including at Kerrick, the elf realized. Moreen announced she would linger behind with the rest of the tribe.

"Where do you want the passengers landed?" asked Kerrick, making the last, hurried preparations before debarking.

"There is a ruined citadel high on a mountainside above the water. If you can't see the place itself, it might be marked by a permanent cloud—hot springs supposedly warm it, even through the winter. If that is the place I hope it is, there will be some kind of sheltered cove at the foot of the mountain."

"Okay, I'll look for a site around there," Kerrick said. "But you should know there aren't a lot of good anchorages along this coast."

"Do the best you can. The tribe will stay together on the shore until all of us are over there."

"It's going to take me all night to make that crossing, and there's no telling how hard it will be to find a place to land your people. As short as these days are, it will probably be pitch dark by the time I get back," the elf continued. "If the wind is up, I'll have to wait offshore until first light. If you can build a small fire here, one that's visible out to sea, I might be able to make it at night. It will depend on the weather, of course."

"Of course," Moreen echoed. He could tell as she gazed at the sail that she was just beginning to comprehend how *Cutter* was powered across the water.

"The payment," he reminded her, as they made ready to push off. "It would be customary to give me a portion now and the rest once the job is completed."

"It's all there," Bruni, who was going to wait with Moreen, said. She pointed at her fur-bundled pack resting next to the cabin.

"Let's get it below deck," Kerrick said, trying to sound calm as he imagined a wave carrying that treasure overboard. As they drifted away from shore the strongbox was stowed in the cabin, and the tide turned. With wind and water propelling them, they quickly moved away from the little cove.

The elf, for his part, was too harried to entertain immediate thoughts of treachery. After he raised the sail the *Cutter* took off like a living thing, racing out of the bay. Immediately, the north wind sweeping across the full breadth of the Courrain Ocean smashed into them from starboard. The boat heeled sharply, drawing screams from some of the Arktos, but Kerrick had anticipated the gust and posted a half dozen of them on the high gunwale. Their weight was enough to keep the boat from capsizing.

Night descended, and Kerrick sailed with all possible speed, heading directly toward the far shore. In the stormy straight he sailed by astrolabe and dead reckoning, holding tight to the tiller during the length of the wind-lashed night. A few of his passengers nodded off at the rail or on the deck, but most of the Arktos clung with wide-eyed fright to their handholds. The elf had no doubts but that they were praying to their wild goddess.

Whether it was Chislev Wilder or Zivilyn Greentree or Kerrick's own seamanship that carried them through the night, he couldn't know, but as dawn grayed the storm-tossed sea he was gratified to hear the sounds of crashing surf warning him of the proximity of rocks and reefs. Further daylight revealed a stony bank rising high before them. Unfortunately, the land plunged straight downward into the sea, and he saw no sign of any potential landing spot.

"Go that way," Tildey suggested, pointing south. The elf saw the heights there obscured by a clinging cloud and concurred. His passengers were miserable, cold and, seasick, but they held on uncomplainingly as the daylight swelled. For three hours he raced along that forbidding shore, riding south with the wind, constantly seeking some sign of a potential landfall.

"Look—beyond that pillar of rock, there," Tildey suddenly said, standing on the cabin roof and pointing. "I think there might be a cove."

Kerrick steered toward shore, noting a pillar that rose like a signpost at the mouth of a sheltered inlet. Nearby rose a rugged cliff, and other elevations rose steeply to three sides, creating a sort of deep bowl that opened, through a narrow gap, to the sea.

"Let's land there," Tildey declared, "and quickly."

Fortunately this shallow cove was even better sheltered than Tall Cedar Bay, with a smooth fringe of sandy beach at the foot of the rugged precipices. They happily noted several caves right beyond the beach.

The air was clammy here, different from the frigid open sea. Kerrick was heartened to see several small clumps of cedars in the hollows. A plume of vapor rose from the mouth of a large cave, quickly diffusing into a sky now almost fully dark.

"See that steam?" Kerrick asked Tildey. "I bet there are hot springs in those caves, at least in one of them."

"That'll be a fine shelter for the time being," declared one old woman, who—because of the many necklaces and talismans she wore—Kerrick judged to be a shaman or priestess.

No flat rock offered itself as a dock, so Kerrick glided *Cutter* as close to the beach as he could go. He was grateful for the calm water and the sandy bottom as, at last, he felt the keel slide against the shore. By letting the adults scramble overboard first, then passing the children into their arms, he was able to disgorge all of his passengers within minutes, watching them hastily wade from the chilly water onto the beach. Insisting upon going last was the frail old shaman, leaning on her staff in the waist deep water.

"Get some wood together and build a fire!" Kerrick called. "It'll take me at least a day to get back here with the next group, but if you can keep it bright, we'll be able to land in the dark."

The old shaman nodded and barked instructions to several children, who hastened to collect wood. Tildey was the only one who remained aboard. She had declared that she would sail back with him.

They angled into the wind, *Cutter* pitching and rolling through the growing swell. Tildey offered to take the tiller so that Kerrick could get some rest, but he shook her off.

The brief daylight dwindled before they were halfway back, but a few hours later the elf saw Moreen's people had followed his instructions. The signal fire made a beacon that guided them back to Tall Cedar Bay, and by midnight he glided into the forest-fringed cove. The wind had calmed slightly, and he was easily able to pull up to the makeshift dock and load another twenty passengers. Once more he started on the crossing, noting with concern that the north wind had picked up.

Dawn found him in the midst of the strait, the wind having swelled into a full gale. Each breaking crest cast spray across the deck, and the six sturdy Arktos women leaning on the high rail were soaked through with icy brine, as was Kerrick in the cockpit. Deftly he pulled the tiller, feeling the fatigue now with each gesture but guiding the bow between the worst waves.

A surge suddenly rose right before him, and the keen prow sliced into a wall of gray water.

"Hold on!" cried the elf, as the sea engulfed the bow. Clinging desperately to the tiller, he gasped for breath as the boat slowly struggled to right itself.

"Mergat and Kestra—the sea took them!" cried one of the Arktos, pointing astern.

Kerrick saw that only four women were now clutching the rail, and he wrenched the tiller around. "Come about!" he called to Tildey, who ducked below the swinging boom and anchored the line like a veteran sailor as the boat heeled through a sharp turn.

Seeing one of the women, frantically splashing in the water, the elf steered beside her. Even without his orders the other Arktos had snatched up a rope. "Catch this, Mergat!" shouted one.

As *Cutter* surged past they draped the line through the water, and the swimmer somehow managed to wrap it around her arms. The boat's momentum pulled her through the water as her comrades strained to pull her aboard.

"Come about again!" Kerrick shouted, knowing that another woman had fallen into the sea as well. Once again he and Tildey changed course, but when he scanned the surging sea he saw nothing except water.

Mergat was stretched out on deck, coughing and wretching and being tended by one of her comrades. The rest of the women and Kerrick scanned the sea. The sailor knew that no one could survive more than five or ten minutes in that frigid water, but even so he searched for an hour until the tragedy was undeniable. Once more Kerrick set a course for the sheltered cove and its steamy cave.

It was a grim and shaken party that at last escaped the storm's fury. Guided through the night by the roaring fire, he finally debarked his passengers on the beach.

"We lost Kestra," he told the old shaman woman, his eyes cast downward.

"Go!" she said angrily. "Don't waste any more time talking."

Once more he and Tildey made the long, dark crossing. This time he returned to Tall Cedar Bay in the pale gray dawn, loading most of the rest of the tribe. He only left Moreen, together with the last dozen of her women-warriors. When he told her about Kestra, she was even angrier than Dinekki and refused to believe that it wasn't his fault.

Soon he would be rich, he consoled himself. Moreen and most of her tribe would be safe. Again he wondered: where was Coraltop Netfisher?

"The Highlanders!" Little Mouse blurted excitedly. "And it looks like they brought their king!"

"They can't be here already. It's too soon!" Moreen declared. She leaped to her feet and cast a glance across the bay. The waters, white-capped and restless in the dawn, showed no sign of the triangular sail that would mark the third return of the elven sailor. Her gamble was perilously close to failure.

"Where are they?" she asked the youth, who was still catching his breath from the long run from his watchpost to the beach.

"Up on the ridge, south of the valley," he replied. "Some of their warriors came down to the trees, but they're a mile inland of here. It didn't look like any of them were coming toward the shore, at least not yet."

The chiefwoman looked around. In addition to Mouse and herself, there were ten women waiting here in the clearing. Her eyes locked upon Hilgrid's. "When the boat comes back, get everyone aboard. Then wait for dark. If I'm not back by then, sail without me."

"But—" The woman bit back her words when she saw the expression in Moreen's eyes. "All right."

Mouse led the chiefwoman to the edge of the forest, and she found herself looking up at the same rounded hill where she, Tildey, and Bruni had first discovered Tall Cedar Bay. Now a sparse fog had drifted in, obscuring the upper heights from view. If and when the elf returned, the Highlanders would have difficulty observing his arrival.

"Some of them went into the woods over there," the boy said, pointing to the left. "Most were still up on the hill when I came to get you."

"You did the right thing," Moreen said. "Now, I want you to get back to Hilgrid and the rest. When the sailboat comes back, you climb aboard too."

"Shouldn't I stay here—in case you need me?"

"No!" She made her sternest face. "Do what I told you!"

"All right." Crestfallen, the lad made his way back into the forest. Moreen watched until he was out of sight, then started climbing the long hill. Wind lashed at her skin, and the snow stung. She knew that the Sturmfrost could not be many days away.

By the time she was halfway up the hill, she could spot a crowd of Highlanders watching her approach. She saw the wolf cloak of Lars Redbeard, then the golden chains and white bearskin that could only mean Strongwind Whalebone himself was there.

The king of the Highlanders stood, arms folded across his broad chest, watching her approach with a grim scowl. By the time she crested the rise she saw that he had more than a hundred men here, that they had established a camp with tents, pickets, and a large bonfire.

Deciding she had best tread carefully, Moreen offered her most winning smile as she advanced to the royal party. "Strongwind Whalebone, king of the Highlanders, it is good that you have come and a pleasure to see you again."

"A pleasure you seemed anxious to postpone," he snorted, though his scowl softened in the glow of her smile. "Or did my adviser Redbeard lie to me when he sent word that I should meet you in the valley, which happens to be a day's march south of here?"

"I am sorry about that misunderstanding," she replied. "No, Lars Redbeard spoke the truth. It was only the discovery of these trees that brought my people northward, so that they could camp in comfort. I expected to see you here, though not for another day or two."

The king snorted. "As you can see, my warriors are capable of a very fast march. We Highlanders have been known to cover twenty miles a day, though the ground be snowed with drifts as high as our heads!"

"Impressive," Moreen noted. "I regret that I neglected to inform your adviser of our hasty change in plans."

"Regrettable, indeed. So you tell me that your tribe is down there?" The king looked across the valley. The trees at the bottom of the slope were visible, though the full extent of the grove was lost in the murky fog.

"Yes, we needed to find some firewood and shelter from the wind for our elders."

"They will have excellent shelter in Guilderglow," Strongwind declared. "You and your tribe will come with me, now. We must return to the city before the Sturmfrost."

"Yes, of course," Moreen said, thinking fast. "I see that

you have made yourself comfortable here. Perhaps you will permit me to go and bring them back."

She turned, ready to start back down the hill, when he stopped her with a word.

"No! I do not trust you. You have spurned me once, lied to me once. I would be a fool to let you go now."

Moreen's eyes widened, an image—she hoped—of bemused innocence. "Where would I go? Undoubtedly you can see that the far side of the valley is a wall of cliff. How would I get away? Would I swim to join the walrus-men?"

"Nonetheless I have no desire to wander around in those woods looking for you," growled the king. "No, my men and I will accompany you to your tribe."

She shrugged casually, as if his decision made no difference to her. All the while her mind was racing, trying to evaluate risks, to form a plan. Fortunately, it took more than an hour for the Highlanders to break their camp, and that was enough time, she gambled, for Kerrick to have returned with *Cutter*. The scheme she conceived was utterly desperate but might, with luck, work.

With the chiefwoman in the lead, the humans made their way down the hill and into the woods. Moreen led them, however, not directly toward the beach, but into the center of the grove, where they came to the deep ravine that divided the forest in two.

"This way," she said, scrambling down the steep slope, stepping across the stones in the shallow streambed. Strongwind Whalebone might have been her shadow, so closely did he hover by her side.

They followed her along the gully floor. "Good forest, here," Strongwind Whalebone said conversationally. "You found it because you saw it on my map?"

"Oh, yes—of course," Moreen replied, remembering the patches of green tiles—flint or jade—on the mosaic. Unfortunately, she had neglected to ask what they signified, but now she knew.

They made their way to the place where she had watched the elf emerge from the ravine on his hunting expedition. As she had hoped, the knobby pine trunk was still there, leaning against the cliff, and she started to climb up to the top.

"Wait," declared the king, putting a strong hand on her leg as she hoisted herself higher. "One of my men will go first."

This she could not allow. Keeping her tone light, she replied gaily, "I'm a very good climber! Here, you'll see it's no trouble at all."

With a smooth gesture she pulled away, smiling down to see the king glowering upward. "When you are my wife, you will learn to curb that rebellious nature!" he snapped, though he let her climb. Quickly she made fifteen feet to the top of the ravine.

She turned and took the trunk in her hands. With a sudden gesture she pushed it to the side, watching as Strongwind leaped out of the way when it crashed to the ground. "May you find a wife with such little backbone as you require!" she snapped. "Know that she will *never* be me!"

She raced through the woods, hearing the cries of shock and outrage from the Highlanders gathered in the ravine.

She didn't have much time, but she knew where she was going. Branches slapped her face, and she twisted and turned, making for the beach. Soon she heard shouts and footsteps pounding behind her, branches breaking, but straight ahead was the cove. Even in the dark light the cove shimmered, lashed by wind and snow.

There it was! That beautiful boat with her warriors, and the elven sailor, aboard, looking toward shore and the sounds of commotion. Moreen broke from the woods at a full sprint, hearing the snapping and cracking of branches behind her, the roars of enraged Highlanders lumbering in pursuit.

"Push off!" she shouted, racing toward the rock. "Get away!"

Immediately Hilgrid, Little Mouse, and the elf responded, shoving against the boulder. The floating hull drifted away, two, six, nine feet. Moreen jumped onto the rock and leaped through the air, tumbling into the arms of the tribeswomen on the deck. Somehow the elf had hoisted the sail, and the offshore breeze instantly took hold, nudging *Cutter* into deeper water. Snow pelted her skin, and the wind whipped her short hair.

In moments the shore was lined with cursing Highlanders, brutal men shaking their weapons and shouting at her. For a moment she feared a volley of spears but saw the boat was moving too fast and was already safely out of range. She saw Strongwind Whalebone, arms crossed again, standing impassively in the midst of his agitated men.

For a moment she met his cold blue eyes with a sensation both elated and terrified. Unable to help herself, she sent him a jaunty wave and turned to watch the sailboat make for the open sea.

15

Brackenrock

Cutter emerged from Tall Cedar Bay onto ocean waters that were surprisingly, ominously calm. The band of enraged men—Moreen had called them Highlanders—had mercifully been swallowed by the darkness and the weather. A light snow was falling, and there was just enough breeze to keep the boat moving west, across the dark strait. Checking his astrolabe, Kerrick aligned the boat toward the Signpost rock and the bay where he had debarked the rest of the Arktos on his three previous crossings. He went forward to set the jib and made sure his passengers were safely arrayed on deck.

Making his way back to the cockpit, Kerrick finally sat on the bench beside Moreen, who clung to the tiller with the ferocity she had shown when she threatened him with death. Her teeth were clenched, and snowflakes speckled her bronzed skin and collected in the thick tangle of her black hair. There was no trace of fear in her expression, just that grim determination to meet and vanquish the challenge raised by the ocean.

The elf was content for the moment to let her steer while he stood and studied the lines of his boat. Tildey still sat atop the cabin. Bruni crouched with several other Arktos amidships, while Little Mouse stood in the bow, clinging to the forward line and shouting gleefully at the snowflakes—at least, until one of the women shouted something, and he reluctantly joined the huddle before the cabin.

"It will be another long night," Kerrick said, returning to the bench. "I haven't used my hourglass, but I swear the sun hasn't stayed up for two hours these past few days—that is, if we could have seen it behind the clouds."

"In a few more days we'll bid it farewell, for three months," Moreen noted.

"Really?" In fact, Kerrick had wondered if the days could keep getting so short that they vanished altogether, but he had discarded the notion as ludicrous.

"You didn't know?" Moreen looked at him curiously. "That doesn't happen in your part of the world?" She blinked in astonishment, then asked, "Do you know about the Sturmfrost?"

"What's that?"

"It comes every year, right after we have seen the last of the sun. From the south, like a wall of wind and ice and freezing cold, it washes over land and sea. It will not be long now—a matter of a few days."

The elf felt a premonition of that awful chill as he considered this. "How long does it last?"

She shrugged. "A month. Five or six weeks, some years. When it passes, the world is frozen, buried under snow piled higher than your—or even Bruni's—head. It's still dark for another month or two, though after the Sturmfrost is gone you can see stars like Chislev Wilder, the goddess of my people."

"Even the ocean freezes, is covered by snow?" That possibility had never occurred to him, though the lapse in imagination now made him feel a little foolish.

"You can't see where the water ends and the land begins," she confirmed. "The gulf is like a flat plain, with great drifts of snow everywhere."

"Sometimes in Silvanesti the winter gets cold enough to freeze fresh water," he said, "though I've never known it to happen on the ocean, or the coastal harbors." His mind was racing faster than his words. He knew that boats had to be pulled out of lakes and streams before the pressure of the ice would inevitably snap wooden hulls into kindling.

"You say this Sturmfrost is coming in a few days. Do you know exactly when?"

"Dinekki will know. I could only tell you if I had seen the sun, and, well, the clouds haven't broken in weeks."

Kerrick made up his mind on the spot. He had enough gold in his cabin to make him a rich man, but it seemed that his boat faced certain doom if he remained here. As soon as he dropped off his passengers, he would set a course for the north, relying on seamanship and good fortune to outrun the imminent storm. Since there was nothing like the Sturmfrost known in Silvanesti or Ansalon, he had to assume that it dissipated over the Courrain Ocean. It would just be a matter of sailing far enough to get out of its path.

"You know, we owe you our freedom—our very survival," Moreen said. "By carrying us across the strait, you've given us the chance for a new life."

Kerrick thought of the chest of gold, felt an uncomfortable flush at her words. "The crossing wasn't without cost . . . I still feel terrible about Kestra."

Moreen sighed and suddenly looked smaller as she huddled on the bench. Then she looked at him, then put a hand on his arm. "I'm sure you did everything you could. Again, we can only thank you."

"I . . . I hope things are good for you on the western shore," he said. "Your tribe has found shelter in a cave, with a lot of firewood nearby."

Moreen was silent for a long time, and Kerrick fell into the easy routine of steering his boat. "What do you know of dragons?" she asked suddenly. "Are there such creatures in your world?"

He shook his head with fervent conviction. "They were banished from the world when my father was but a lad, some four hundred years ago. It was after a great dragon war, the third such conflict, when the serpents of good and evil battled and came close to destroying all Krynn."

"That's what I thought," she said. "There was a great hero, a man called Huma, was there not?"

Kerrick was surprised that Moreen knew of this conflict, isolated as her people were from the rest of Krynn, but he nodded. "Yes, the humans played some role, but it was mainly the elves and the good dragons who won the victory."

"Good. I am glad the dragons are gone," she said with relief.

"As are most people," the elf agreed.

"I see the fire!" Little Mouse called from the bow.

Kerrick was surprised. The crossing had passed very quickly, considering the light wind. He stood and took a bearing on the signal, saw that his reckoning had carried them on a direct line toward the mouth of the sheltered bay.

Moreen stared intently into darkness that even to elven eyes was impenetrable except for the speck of brilliance.

"Look for a tall pillar—I called it the Signpost," said Kerrick. "Behind that is a nice cove, with what looked like a big cove on shore."

"There it is," Mouse said excitedly. "Just to the left."

"That's, 'Just to port,' " Kerrick corrected good-naturedly. He gently steered *Cutter* toward the opening between the Signpost and the tall rocky promontory that marked the other side of the narrow cove entrance, using the fire as his beacon.

Moreen climbed down to sit on the cockpit bench. Her breath puffed into visible vapor, and she pulled her fur jacket tightly around her torso. "The temperature is still dropping," she observed.

The elf sensed that her words were offered in friendship, but he was still distracted by her description of the Sturmfrost and only grunted in reply.

"You said your name was Kerrick Fallabrine?" she said after a silence. "Does it have a meaning?"

"Of course. All elven names have meaning, most of them dating back to the clans that were awarded titles at the first Sinthel-Elish. That was nearly three thousand years ago," he added with a hint of smugness, steering into the cove, gliding toward the fire that was now flaming brightly, even reflecting from the surrounding cliffs.

"Well?" She was looking at him but not in anger. Instead, one corner of her mouth turned up, and the other tilted down in that bemused half-smile.

Kerrick felt a little foolish about his pompous answer. "Oh, my name means that I am a son of House Mariner, Silvanesti. We have been sailors since the dawn of our clan. My namesake, Kerrick, fought against ogres in the First Dragon War."

"Kerrick." She rolled the word around on her tongue. "Very exotic."

He didn't know what to say to that and was spared the necessity of response when Little Mouse shouted from the bow, "Ice!"

"Take in the sail!" he called, steering the boat sharply into the light wind as Tildey, who had learned a bit during her four crossings, hauled the line. *Cutter* turned gently in the light wind and coasted to a stop, while Kerrick stood on the gunwale and looked toward shore.

The fire was barely a long bowshot away now, and the flames clearly reflected a surface of smooth ice between the boat and the shore. It hadn't been there on his last visit, ten or twelve hours earlier, so he knew that it couldn't be very thick. Still, they would have to crack a path all the way to shore—a frustrating delay, with the vivid image of the imminent Sturmfrost holding his full attention.

Impatiently he cast his eyes along the shore and noticed a bright expanse of water glimmering a short distance to the side. This was not the brightness of light, however. Instead, his elven senses perceived a place where the liquid was significantly warmer than the rest of the little bay.

"Hot springs!" he guessed, encouraged. "There must be a stream flowing out of the cave, and it's warming the water all the way into the bay." Indeed, as he looked farther, he could see the vague outlines of a little creek, hazy in the distance but emerging from the wide-mouthed cave. The waters were pleasantly warm to his sight.

"Give me some canvas," he called to Tildey, and she quickly deployed the sail.

He had to tack away from shore, then come about in order to line up with the stream. Soon they were passing between sheets of ice to port and starboard, following a clear, liquid path until the keel scraped gently on the sandy bottom. By this time they could see many of the Arktos. The tribespeople had sheltered in the large cave, but with the boat's approach they came down to the shore. One by one the passengers dropped off the bow into the waist-deep water and quickly slogged their way to emerge, dripping and shivering, onto the beach where each was hastily escorted to the vicinity of the fire.

Tildey, Moreen, and Bruni were the last of the Arktos on the boat. Kerrick eyed them warily, wondering suddenly if they would try and take back their gold. He looked toward the cabin, deciding he might be able to race back and snatch his sword before they grabbed him.

Moreen seemed to have other concerns and looked at him seriously.

"I am sorry that we took you by force. Your boat has given us new chance of survival."

"Because you could escape those warriors, the Highlanders who chased you on the far shore?"

She shrugged. "In part. Here we are on the land that once belonged to our ancestors. That an ancient fortress city, up there, was long-abandoned by our people. We were forced out by dragons. We will claim it again and gain shelter from the winter. If you sail back into these waters, you will be welcomed as our guest."

"Thank you," Kerrick said. He found himself hoping that the Arktos would find the comfort and shelter they desired. "As for myself, I intend to be far away from here before this Sturmfrost hits."

"Good luck." She held out a hand and he took it, reciprocating her strong grip.

"And to you," he offered.

He watched the trio wade to shore, then, using the oar,

propelled his sailboat back through the channel between the ice sheets, noticing with concern that the passage was narrower than it had been only an hour ago. His breath frosted before his face, and the snow came harder.

From the open water of the bay he looked back to shore and saw the Arktos plodding back to the dark cave mouth. Steam rose from that opening, and he hoped the hot springs would provide enough warmth for them, at least until they could move into the ruin.

The breeze fluttered past his cheek, a little stronger than before, and he deployed his mainsail, anxious to move. The boat leaned slightly under the force of the wind, and he steered a course out of the cove, onto the gulf and its pathways to all the oceans of the world.

"Moreen! You did it!"

The chiefwoman was surrounded by Arktos, all of them trying to hug her. Gently she pushed through the throng and made her way to the fire, which swelled under the addition of numerous dry pine trunks. Her leggings, which had frozen when she emerged from the water, began to steam, and she relished the warmth seeping back into her bones.

"Right here there's a splendid cave," Hilgrid said. "Big and deep and mostly dry, except for a few springs of real, truly *hot* water!"

Moreen gestured to the looming height, the mountain rising just back from shore. She remembered her view of this place from across the strait, and the glimpse of walls and towers she had seen above. "What about a route up there? Brackenrock cannot be far away."

"There's a path, you can see in daylight," Hilgrid explained. "It's covered with rocks and scree, but at one time it must have been a real roadway. I think this cove the elf found might once have been the harbor of Brackenrock. There's a stone shelf on the other side that looks as if it must have been a dock once."

Moreen felt a thrill of awe and discovery. This was surely the place, the ancient home of the Arktos! To think that Chislev had favored them enough to lead them here.

"We'll rest until we start to get some light, then go up there, a party of us, to see what we can find. I hope we'll be able to bring the whole tribe up there before Sturmfrost."

"We'd better not dally," Dinekki said, hobbling out of the darkness. She looked at Moreen with pride, then clucked in concern. "I just cast the stones—a bit of a trick when you can't see the sky—but the goddess spoke to me. I can tell you that the Sturmfrost will be here in no more than three days' time."

"That should be enough," Moreen said. "Remember, at first light we go to find our home."

"Boy, it's cold down there. Can't we build a fire or something?"

"Coraltop?" Kerrick, at the tiller of his boat, gaped in surprise as the kender sauntered around the side of the cabin to join him in the cockpit. "But . . . where were you? How did you get back aboard?"

"I just took a nap," replied the little fellow, plopping down on the bench. "You know, I'm really hungry. Did you have any luck in your hunt?"

The elf was flabbergasted and for a moment couldn't even muster a reply. "You mean you were here all along?" he finally sputtered. "You were *sleeping*? While I was captured? While we carried seventy-five people across the bay? And raced away from the Highlanders and broke through the ice?" He shook his head in utter disbelief.

"I dreamed that it got kind of loud there," the kender said cheerfully. "I suppose if you carry seventy-five passengers you have to expect they're going to do some talking. Not very polite of them, though, when I was trying to get a little nap."

"A little nap? I haven't seen you for a week!"

"I was tired."

"How could you sleep that long? By Zivilyn, I looked for you. I was worried! Where in Krynn *were* you? I hunted all over the boat!"

Coraltop waved dismissively. "I didn't want to be a bother. I lay down on one of your spare sails in the hold and pulled the other one over me."

"For seven days?" sputtered the elf.

"It was probably this sleeping potion," the kender said brightly, producing a small, silver flask. "I traded a gnome for it in Tarsis. I had, oh, I don't know, something pretty valuable, and I gave it to a gnome who brewed this potion. He said it would help me rest real good. I guess he was right."

Kerrick swore an old sailor's oath. "Let me see that," he declared, snatching the flask out of Coraltop's hand. Cautiously he removed the stopper and sniffed a seductively sweet aroma.

"Careful," warned the kender. "All I did was wet my fingertip and lick it."

The elf quickly stoppered the flask and handed it back. "Your timing was terrible. While you napped I got beaten up, tied up, chased by bearded barbarians. I carried a tribe of *different* barbarians across this strait, on three trips, fought through a storm, and found a harbor on a barren shore!"

Indignantly he remembered the kender's earlier question. "No, I didn't have any luck hunting. You were going to be fishing while I was gone, right? I don't suppose you even remember that."

"Well, I was going to do some fishing, after I slept, but I just woke up now. Speaking of impolite, I think it's a little rude for you to do all this yelling when I still barely have my eyes open!"

Kerrick groaned in exasperation. In any event, he had bigger problems than an extra passenger, and his mind quickly returned to those concerns.

Most significantly, he had all three sails deployed, and yet *Cutter* barely moved through the water. The waters of the gulf were unnaturally still, barely shifting with an almost imperceptible swell, so dark gray they were almost black. Snowflakes fell, making a rasping hiss as they touched the still water.

Against this placid stillness it was hard to imagine the violent Sturmwall described by Moreen, yet Kerrick had often know periods of almost miraculous calm to lie across the ocean a mere hour or two before the onset of a savage gale. Even if the brutal blizzard didn't come, he pictured the ice encroaching, slowly but inexorably, until *Cutter* was locked in a frozen grasp. The ice would tighten, pressure expanding, smashing against itself, inevitably crushing anything so frail as the hull of a sailboat.

"Can't you go a little faster?" asked Coraltop, frowning over the water. "This is kind of pointless, don't you think? I mean, I know you're doing the best you can—of course you are!—but I like it better when we go shooting up the waves and stuff."

"Do *you* see any waves?" the elf asked tersely.

"Well, it's morning, at least. Maybe that will help."

The kender was right. A vague illumination suffused the white-gray sky and the gray-white sea. The increasing light brought no corresponding increase in wind. If anything, the sails hung even more slackly than before. Such air as did move came listlessly out of the north, from the exact wrong direction, if Kerrick were to have any hope of getting away from the Sturmfrost.

In the spreading light, which brightened to no more than a twilit murk, he stared across the gulf, looking southward, wondering about the winter's violence stewing there.

Knowing they would never be able to sail out of its path.

"There it is—Brackenrock!" Moreen couldn't keep the delight from her voice. After the dangerous trek, the escape from the Highlanders, and finally a perilous climb up a steep, twisting pathway, her hopes were confirmed.

The place was a ruin, clearly, but it was the ruin of what had once been a mighty citadel. High, smooth walls merged into the cliff top, blocking a view of the interior of the place, except for several towers that jutted into view. The tops of these were crumbled and eroded, denoting long decades of disuse. A wide gateway at the upper terminus of this path yawned open and dark. Whatever slabs of wood or stone that had once blocked that entrance were now gone. Steam swirled in front of the place and rose from within, a clear indication that the hot springs for which Brackenrock had once been fabled were still warm.

This path seemed to be the only approach, for the fortress stood atop a steep-sided crag. Before it the cliff plunged hundreds of feet straight down to the gray waters of the sea. Behind it towered a peak streaked with snow and ice, flanked by impassable cliff. Only the narrow trail, which wound its way along a narrow ridge crest, allowed access.

"What a fortress," Tildey said under her breath. "I can see how it stood against the ogres for so long. There's no other way to get in, and two dozen skilled archers could make sure any enemy coming along the trail never made it to the gates."

Moreen looked at her warriors. She had made this ascent, which had required more than two hours, with twenty Arktos, all veterans of the Battle of the Black Whale, as they had come to call their skirmish with the thanoi. Now each held a spear or a stone-headed axe and turned a face of grim purpose toward the chiefwoman.

The rest of the tribe remained in the seaside cave, which had proved to be a spacious and, because of a surging hot spring, surprisingly warm shelter. It lacked comforts, and the gaping mouth allowed the wintery wind to penetrate with cruel persistence, but Moreen was confident that the rest of her tribe was safe enough for the time being. Once they explored the ruin, the whole tribe could come up here.

"Why don't I go ahead and have a look," Tildey suggested. "If it's clear, I'll wave the rest of you forward."

"No," Moreen said, shaking her head firmly. "We'll go together—if we find some ice bear making a den in there, it will be better to have twenty spears than one bow and arrow."

No one dissented, so the chiefwoman led them over the crest of the little pass where they had stopped to make their observation. She looked up at the citadel, now rising to fill the whole view before them, and felt a vague sense of misgiving. There were dark holes all along the walls, and she couldn't shake the feeling of menace, that something was staring down at them, watching, waiting. She wished that Dinekki was here to cast the spell of blessing she had bestowed before they attacked the thanoi, but the chiefwoman had decided that speed was important, and despite the shaman's sturdy legs, it would have taken her much longer to make the climb to this elevation. Now, at least, they still had a little daylight.

Her misgivings were just nerves, she told herself. It was important to remember what this place offered to them: a real home, defensible against Highlanders or ogres, a place where her little tribe could not just survive but perhaps, one day, return to a life of peace and prosperity. Furthermore, after her conversation with the elf, her worries about dragons were finally laid completely to rest.

The path turned sharply to approach that great, gaping gate. They could see an empty courtyard, walls, and buildings rising beyond. A great stairway rose from the ground, providing access to the ramparts atop the wall and to a whole row of compartments—merely vacant doors and windows—that had apparently been excavated directly out of the mountainside.

Tildey and Nangrid carried bows and arrows and now, as if responding to an unseen command, each nocked and readied an arrow. Moreen's hand tightened around her harpoon, while she checked to insure that the two extra weapons strapped to her back were still there, and easily accessible. She picked up her pace, trotting through the aperture of the gates and moving toward the center of the large courtyard. The walls rose on all sides, except for that gate, giving her a sense of being down in a well, looking upward for a glimpse of gray, leaden sky.

A few snowflakes scudded past, driven by the rising breeze. She sniffed, smelling the onset of winter, tainted by the smell of stale fish. Probably seagulls, she guessed. There were numerous openings leading into buildings placed all around the walls, though none of them had doors or shuttered windows in place.

"Look here," called one of the Arktos warriors, Sanga, probing with her foot into a blackened pit near the gateway.

It was a fire scar, with chunks of burned logs sitting amid a heap of flattened, soaked ashes. "Cold," she said, reaching down to touch the debris. Sanga pointed at the charcoaled logs, which still showed cracks from a not-terribly-distant burning.

"But this was a fire sometime over the last summer."

"Be alert," Moreen called. "Let's stay together."

She led them across the courtyard toward the wide stairway they had noticed from beyond the gates. With Bruni and Nangrid at her sides, the chiefwoman started up the steps, the rest of her warriors following in a loose formation.

"There!" hissed Tildey, pointing with her bow toward a shadow doorway across the courtyard, on the lower level. "Something moved."

"All right. We'll back down the stairs and check it out," Moreen said.

Bruni, on the bottom step, now took the lead. Moreen cast a glance above, at the rim of that rampart. Her harpoon was light in her hand as she waited until the others had started down. Safely on the courtyard, the big woman started toward the door Tildey had indicated. Nangrid and Moreen started to descend backward, still facing the upper terrace.

In another instant attacking creatures were everywhere, woofing and roaring and charging, spilling out of every door, each shadowy alcove. The chiefwoman saw tusked faces, mouth gaping. Thanoi spilled across the upper terrace, lumbering toward the top of the steps, big feet slapping the flagstones. A big bull came first, pausing above to wave his heavy spear and roar. Moreen threw her weapon, catching the brute in the belly. Nangrid shot her arrow at another, grazing the beast's shoulder, giving it a momentary pause before it started down the stairs.

Thanoi charged into the courtyard, a dozen or more coming from each of the two towers flanking the yawning gate. Tildey shot, dropping one, while Bruni raised her voice in an ululating yell and charged right at another of the growling tuskers. Her stone-headed axe came down hard, crushing the monstrous skull. Recovering quickly, she spun around and bashed another walrus-man aside, while Tildey calmly fired more arrows into the mob.

Now the tuskers were charging down the stairs in a great mass, three score or more, perhaps a hundred of them. Moreen threw her second harpoon, then skipped out of the way as the tusker pierced by her cast tumbled and writhed down the stone steps. Nangrid shot again, holding her ground as the chiefwoman started downward.

"Come on!" Moreen cried, and Nangrid turned to run. Spears clattered around them, a volley cast by the tuskers who roared down the steps toward them. Abruptly the archer's eyes grew wide and she fell forward. Moreen reached to catch her companion but Nangrid toppled right past her, the stout shaft of a tusker spear jutting cruelly from her back.

The thanoi were right on top of her now, and the chiefwoman stabbed and thrust with her last harpoon, unwilling to cast it away. The attackers halted for a moment, and she backed down, past Nangrid's motionless body. Moreen reached out a hand, but the tribeswoman made no move. A swath of crimson blood spilled from her chest, fanning out and slicking the stairs in a gruesome waterfall.

Biting back a sob, the chiefwoman stabbed again, slicing open a tusker's belly. She cried out in rage as the brute fell atop Nangrid's body, but she had no choice but to keep backing down the steps. More of the monsters charged, starting to move past her on both sides. Another spear flew from below, piercing the thigh of a huge walrus-man, and Moreen sprang down the last few steps to join her comrades on the floor of the courtyard.

They fought their way toward the gates, a desperate knot of Arktos in the midst of a teeming mass of enraged thanoi. It was only Tildey's alarm that gave them any chance of escape. If the band of humans had reached the top of the stairs before the attack, they would have been surrounded and overwhelmed, for by far the greatest number of walrus-men had been waiting on the upper terrace.

Bruni led the way through the smaller throng of tuskers in the courtyard, bashing her axe first to one side, then the other. The thanoi attacked fanatically, but many of them fell, skulls or faces or shoulders crushed by her powerful blows, and gradually the rest fell back in the face of her inexorable onslaught. Tildey launched the last of her arrows and slung the bow over her shoulder, hacking and stabbing with her long-bladed knife.

Another Arktos fell—Marin, Feathertail's young mother—and she too was lost in the mass of pursuing thanoi. Moreen thrust the harpoon again and again, clattering against tusks, puncturing leathery skin. Somehow she held the throng at bay, aided by the spears of several comrades.

They were through the gates, those who still lived, and here for a moment the Arktos arrayed in a dense line, spears and harpoons bristling as a wall. Moreen dreaded a massed charge, knowing that the tuskers could quickly overwhelm them with a sudden, brutal rush.

It seemed, though, that the monsters were content to have driven them from the citadel. At least, they hesitated for precious moments, many clasping hands to bleeding wounds, growling and snapping at the humans. Here and there knots of walrus-men clustered around ragged bodies, and Moreen's eyes blurred with the awareness that six or eight of her warriors had perished in this shockingly sudden, brutal battle.

Finally the surviving warrior women turned from the gate, moving down the path at a trot, eyes warily watching the citadel for signs of pursuit. Still the walrus-men held their ground, jeering and snorting, clattering their spears together, slapping their flat feet against the ground.

The sounds were mocking and cruel, and they rang in Moreen's ears all the way down the twisting, mountain trail.

16

Rites of Neuwinter

The wind howled across the vast expanse of the Snow Sea. The frigid blast of air came from the southernmost end of the world, and it roared through the deep mountain canyons. This part of Krynn had already lost the sun, and for weeks it had been freezing in a lightless, lifeless glacial winter storm.

Tornadoes preceded each phase of the storm, picking up snow, ice, pieces of monstrous debris and strewing them across the land.

A wall of ice blocked the northern advance of the storm. On one side rose the mountain called Winterheim. The storms could not defeat that steep, lofty slope. Beyond the mountain was the great, frozen dam, a barrier extending a hundred miles or more across the wasteland of southern Icereach.

The monstrous storm hesitated at the Ice Wall, reaching with frigid fingers over the top, sending snow and rock tumbling down the face of the dam before falling back. Growing ever more powerful, ever more angry, the Sturmfrost held back like a living, sentient beast, watching . . . and waiting.

"Are you certain that you are prepared for the Reciting of Ancestry?" Stariz asked Grimwar. The high priestess wore the black robe of her station, and held the obsidian mask before her as she scrutinized her husband.

The prince had the strange sensation that he was being studied by two powerful ogres. One he had married, with square-block face and protruding jaw. Beneath her was the image of Gonnas, carved in black stone, vacant eye-slits dark and menacing.

"Yes!" he declared. "How many times must I tell you that?"

"Until you have completed the ritual," she growled back. "I truly wonder if you realize how important it is . . . how much of the future rests upon your shoulders. I was not here, in Winterheim, during the debacle of four years ago, but even in my father's remote barony in Galcierheim, the displeasure of our god was respected and feared."

"I understand," he said, wishing that *she* would understand. Huffing in irritation, he pulled on his great bearskin cloak, buckling the golden clasps that held the garment around his bull neck and massive chest. He was tired of reminders, tired of all the preparation for the future that had filled his days since his return from the campaign. It was time to be done with it, done with it all!

"I do not mean to badger you, my husband," Stariz said with sudden, surprising gentleness, still holding the mask as she came to sit beside him. They were alone in their royal apartments, their slaves having withdrawn to allow the couple some privacy. "In truth, my spells have been full of dire warnings. I fear for you, and for our kingdom. This is a winter's night of grave portent. You must be alert, watchful for danger." Her eyes narrowed, a look that penetrated to his core. "Or opportunity," she concluded.

"Bah—Suderhold is in fine hands!" he snorted indignantly.

Even as he spoke, the words sounded hollow. When he thought about his father, he, too, felt dire concern for the future. How could the realm prosper, under a king who was only concerned with counting his gold, and punishing his slaves? It had been many years since King Grimtruth had embarked upon a campaign. The last time, the prince remembered, his father had returned home with a paltry dozen slaves, Highlanders taken when the ogres had come upon an unfortunate hunting party. Though the king might insist that his son recite the names of their ancestor, back for a hundred generations, Grimwar had little faith his father could perform the same trick. Indeed, for the past three years it had been Stariz, in her role as high priestess, who had performed that ritual.

His wife seemed to sense his unease, but she only glared at him. He hated that look, just as he hated the attention, the privilege that was his father's due. He hated the knowledge that, so long as Grimtruth reigned, Grimwar Bane would be a mere footnote in the continuing history of Icereach, and the Kingdom of Suderhold.

"My preparations are completed," he said abruptly, rising to his feet. "I will take in the view from the King's Promenade while we wait for the rites to begin."

"But our prayers—" Stariz looked up in surprise as he rose.

"Speak to Gonnas for me," Grimwar declared, feeling a little better as his wife bit down on her lower lip. She drew the black mask over her face, but he avoided looking back as he stalked through the door that was whisked open by a slave.

The King's Promenade was a circular hall at the heart of the Royal Level of Winterheim. The central atrium of the mountain was open before him, the shadowy cavern plummeting thousands of feet. Far below, he could see the still waters of the harbor, reflecting the light of the magical ice panels. *Goldwing*, already refurbished from the summer campaign, gleamed beneath the atrium, gilded rails shimmering like metal fire, oiled decks smooth and perfect.

"It is a beautiful ship."

He was startled and pleased when Thraid spoke from his side. She stepped up to the stone parapet and peered with him into the depths beneath the great city. "Despite what the king says, I think you did very well to bring back so many slaves . . . hundreds of them, was it not?"

"Three hundred and twenty-seven," he replied with a proud smile.

"Did the humans fight hard?" She asked the question absently, as if thinking about something else.

He chuckled, reflecting on the mild skirmishes at the various Arktos villages. "Mostly not," he allowed. "They seemed almost not to believe we were there." He was about to go into detail when he realized that Thraid was looking at him with a peculiarly intense gaze.

"What?" he asked, feeling suddenly stupid and apprehensive.

She began to sob, quickly clapping a hand over her mouth. "It is no life—this fate of mine!" she said, crying softly. "He is a monster! And you choose to allow it!"

"I do not!" Grimwar protested in bewilderment. "He makes all the decisions. I have no power, but to obey his commands!"

"How . . . how could you give in to him about this?" Her voice was a rasping whisper, reaching his ears alone. "You knew how I felt—about *you*. How could you let your father . . ." Thraid shook her head and turned away, drawing a deep, ragged breath.

The prince grew increasingly confused. Couldn't she *understand*? Surely she knew what it was like, to live a life determined by the whim of one's father, a king who seemed incapable of thinking beyond his own immediate pleasure!

He glowered, feeling his face grow hot, then shivered with a sudden chill. Turning, he saw Stariz approaching, wearing her obsidian mask and looking as fearsome as Gonnas himself.

He grunted a farewell to Thraid, who glanced up through narrowed eyes to nod to the high priestess. Stariz returned the nod contemptuously, her small eyes glittering like beads through the narrow slits in the mask. She reached to take the prince's arm, accepting her husband's escort toward the great feast that was about to commence.

The Rites of Neuwinter combined somber religious ceremony with ribald feasting, a lavish banquet in a vast, warm chamber with the brutal onset of winter, a solemn commemoration of Suderhold's dynastic history with blood sacrifice and the release of primeval power. The festivities traditionally began in the huge room known as the Hall of Blue Ice, a massive chamber carved from a huge portion of the mountain's eastern shoulder and protected from the outer weather by a wall-sized window of frost, the deep azure color giving the hall its name.

The chamber was a massive, semicircular vault, with one side a series of tiers rising high into the mountain's interior. The outer wall was the vast sheet of blue ice, now murky and obscure because of the lightless night yawning beyond. Just outside the window was the juncture where the massive Ice Wall met the flanks of Winterheim. The sweeping dam extended into the far distance, and, beyond that, the surging Snow Sea.

The entire population of Winterheim, ogres and human slaves alike, gathered in this massive chamber. The ogre masters were arrayed around the three lower tiers, seated at huge banquet tables, all facing the vast window of blue ice so that they could see the climax of the rite. They were ranked in order of status, the royal clan and fellow nobles on the first tier, the warriors and merchants on the second, commoners on the third. The temperature in the hall was cosy for now, but each ogre had brought plenty of furs and blankets, for they knew that when the window melted away, the full fury of winter would surge into the chamber.

Above the ogres, the humans gathered in a silent body. Their involvement in the feasting was limited to their role as preparers and servers of food. Those humans who were not working remained on the upper terraces, silent faces turned downward, watching and waiting. All were required to attend, and they, like the ogres, would witness the death of a chosen slave that would mark the culmination of the rites and the release of another bitter, sunless winter onto the tundra, mountains and seas of Icereach.

At one time, the hall would have been filled with one hundred thousand ogres, the long-ago population of Winterheim, each ogre accompanied by chosen slaves. Now, in the reign of King Grimtruth, there were barely twelve thousand ogres in all the city, and perhaps that many human slaves. The upper chambers of the hall remained silent and empty.

Lord Hakkan, the protocol chief, emerged onto the upper platform and signaled the trumpeters. The human slaves raised their golden instruments and a fanfare quickly resounded through the hall. Rustling and rumbling, the ogres turned their attention upward.

Prince Grimwar Bane, Princess Stariz ber Glacierheim ber Bane on his arm, entered to the sounds of the triumphant processional. He marched down the long, inclined aisle from the upper section of the hall, to the royal table far below. He wore his golden breastplate, with the Barkon Sword encased in a bejeweled ceremonial scabbard at his belt. His tusks were fully coated with gleaming gold. Around his shoulders was draped the pelt of the massive black bear, a fur so large that the forelegs descended to his belly, and the tail all but dragged on the ground behind him.

The crown princess was an equally awe-inspiring sight. Stariz, wearing her obsidian mask, carried the mighty Axe of Gonnas, the golden blade extended before her. The ghastly visage of the Willful One was the same tusked, snarling face carved into the huge temple statue. Turning her head this way and that with regal grace, she cast her masked, searing gaze across the entire assemblage. There was none, ogre or human, who did not feel as though the powerful god looked directly into his soul.

Grimwar led his wife Stariz to their ceremonial chairs at the great table that stood directly before the sweeping pane of blue ice. Baldruk Dinmaker was already there, standing behind the chair he would occupy between the prince and the king. The trio remained standing while the trumpets blared again, this time announcing the arrival of the king and queen. The royal couple, too, started down the long procession.

Later, it would be Grimwar's task to invoke the names of all his ancestors, calling upon them to melt the icy blue barrier. Only then would ogre and human alike feel winter's deadly kiss, only then would the king release the Sturmfrost across the land.

Grimwar could hear the mournful wail of a cyclonic wind. The tumult was pure, frigid winter, churning with sleet and icy snow. The levels of snow had risen dangerously high, threatening the ice wall. Now, in this ceremony dating to the origins of time, the ogre king would once again release the storm onto the wider world, and Winterheim would be protected for another long, cold, sunless winter. Grimwar glanced toward the vast sheet of blue and was startled to see Balrduk Dinmaker glaring up at him, the dwarf's expression somewhere between contemptuous and pensive.

"Prepare yourself!" hissed the royal adviser, before turning his attention to the royal couple, now but one tier above them.

The princess sniffed disdainfully at Grimwar's side, and he glanced at her and her impassive mask. "She could at least wear a decent covering," Stariz hissed. "Like too many others, she does not understand the sacredness of the event!"

Grimwar looked up at the young queen. Thraid wore a gown of white bearskin, cut low across her impressive bosom, gathered tightly to display the unusual slenderness of her waist. Rouge brightened her cheeks and her lips, creating an effect that the prince found altogether appealing. As she walked serenely, Thraid Dimmarkull ber Bane clutched King Grimtruth's arm, clear proof to all of her position. Her eyes caught the prince's as she approached, and she met his gaze with a hurt expression. For some reason, the emotion cut Grimwar deeper than any display of fury.

Angrily, he pulled his eyes away from the young ogress. The king himself, his father, Grimwar thought, looked downright disgraceful. Of course, he was dressed in the traditional white robes of his station, with the Crown of Cospid gleaming on his head, his black boots polished to a bright sheen. His slaves had seen to all that. As to the king's person, his eyes were bloodshot, narrowed suspiciously, and a strand of drool dangled casually from one of his tusks. Those tusks were also circled with golden wire, but the monarch had not bothered to have slaves polish either the metal, or the ivory of his teeth. From the unsteadiness of the big ogre's gait, the prince suspected that his father had begun celebrating early.

Nevertheless, the king reached the table without incident, and soon they, and all the other ogres of Winterheim, were seated. Stariz intoned a prayer, asking for the blessing of the Willful One. Baldruk raised the first toast, and the king took a gulp from his goblet that left warqat shining, slick and oily, down his chin.

A procession of slaves came forth with slabs of beef, whole salmon, great wheels of cheese, iced sturgeon eggs, and cask upon cask of pungent warqat. Throughout the hall ogres began to eat and drink.

To Grimwar, everything tasted like ash.

Baldruk Dinmaker rose again from his seat between the two mighty ogres. He cleared his throat, bringing the crowd to silence.

"It has been my great honor to serve the Bane kings for two generations—three, if we count the crown prince who, some day, will prove himself worthy of this throne. . . ."

The dwarf shot Grimwar a glance before continuing—again, that look half of disdain. The ogre heard none of the rest of the words. Instead, he flushed with a feeling of rage that started at his toes and spread upward through his entire body. *Someday?* He looked past the dwarf to the king, who was slurping noisily from his goblet, paying no attention to the speech, until he sensed that Baldruk was reaching his conclusion.

". . . has applied himself with diligence to the learning. May it please the gods of us all—let the Rites begin!" Once more the trumpets, played by the human slaves who stood on the high rampart, brayed through the Hall of Blue Ice.

"The crown prince will now recite the Names of Dynasty!" proclaimed Hakkan. The lord of protocol, rigid and serene in a long green robe, stood before the royal table, his back to the king's family as he bellowed his announcement through the Hall of Blue Ice.

"Are you ready?" hissed Stariz, who had sat through the dinner without eating, since to do so would have meant removing her tusked mask and risking the displeasure of her god. She rose to follow her husband, bearing the Axe of Gonnas as was required by her role.

Grimwar tried to concentrate on the names that were marching through his skull in dynastic progression. Baldruk leaned over and glared at him intensely. "You know what to do," he said. Putting down the empty mug of warqat, which he had nursed through the long meal, the prince rose to the cheers of all the assembled ogres. Barely hearing the accolades, he was making his way past the king's seat when Grimtruth seized his son's hand and pulled him down closer.

"Do not embarrass me again."

His father stank of warqat and sweat, both equally repugnant. Angrily, Grimwar pulled himself away and lumbered toward the massive window of blue ice.

Lord Hakkan was standing by to escort him, but the prince marched past without halting. The great sheet of frost, the window to the glacier and the Ice Wall and the

Storm Sea, rose before him. Now Grimwar halted in the prescribed position. The names of his ancestors were ready, about to trip off his tongue, when his mind veered backward, to the humiliation of four years earlier.

"He's a fool!" roared Grimtruth Bane, rising from his chair and lunging around the banquet table. The young prince stood paralyzed, speechless. For a long time he had been standing there, silent, unsuccessfully willing the names from his subconscious. He looked back, saw his mother, Queen Hannareit, looking at him with an expression of pleading . . . then Grimtruth Bane filled his vision, storming toward his son, face twisted by fury and warqat.

The high priest, Karn Draco, tried to stop the king, but Grimtruth would not be deterred. "Give me that!" he demanded, snatching the Axe of Gonnas from the priest's hands.

"No—the window must melt before the Names!" protested Draco.

With a single blow from the golden axe the king shattered the blue ice. Shards of glassy frost exploded, and instantly winter's vortex had swept into the hall. The first gust sucked Karn Draco into the frosty wasteland. Tables were tossed about, humans and ogres swept away by the lethal force of wind.

Grimtruth Bane seized a nearby slave, one of the hapless servers who had been working at the royal table, and, still carrying the Axe of Gonnas, marched out to the brink of the Ice Wall. Throwing the blubbering human down, he killed him with a single blow of the axe, so that his blood soaked into the dam as required by the ancient ritual.

That sacrifice was made without the full ceremony, however, without the blessing of Gonnas. When the Sturmsea erupted that year, it did so capriciously, tearing away a great part of the city and burying a valuable gold mine in the process.

Everyone blamed Grimwar Bane. His father arranged the marriage to Stariz, whose tutelage, it was hoped, would see that the prince maintained a properly studious, devoted outlook on life. She came to Winterheim and replaced the fallen high priest and, for the past three years, it had been she who had recited the names.

Now, again, had come the time for the prince to prove himself.

"O Gonnas the Strong, Gonnas the Mighty, the Willful One . . ." Stariz intoned the names of the god. "Grant us your favor. Melt the Blue Ice, and let the king of Suderhold come forth to unleash your Sturmfrost upon the world!"

The watchers, ogres and humans alike, held their breath as Grimwar Bane took a step forward and began to speak.

"King Barkon, Barkon I, brought the clans to Winterheim, in the first year of Dynasty," Grimwar began, "and reigned until year 63. It was then that his son, Barkon II, took the throne, until the year 91. Barkon III came next, in dynasty, to year 147. These were the Barkon kings, the founders of Suderhold.

"The Icetusk dynasty commenced in 150, with Garren Icetusk, who ruled through 212. . . ."

Surprisingly, the names seemed to burst forth with a will of their own. The Icetusks were easy—they had ruled for more than a thousand years, and it seemed that each date was inextricably attached to their name. When Grimwar said Icetusk VII, for instance, the years 503 and 571 loomed clearly in his memory. So, too, with the rest of that hallowed line.

He did not dare to look behind him, to examine the blue ice. He knew that Baldruk Dinmaker was watching, together with Stariz, the king, Thraid and the rest. But it helped when he imagined that it was only for Thraid's benefit that he spoke. Still the names rolled and tumbled off his tongue. He continued, through the kings of the

Whaleslayers, the Goldcrowns, the Manreapers. He noted the short and tragic reign of King Dracomaster who, it turned out, had taken his name quite prematurely. He passed through the Glacierlords and, finally, he arrived at his own clan.

"The Bane Dynasty was born, in 4370, with Grimword Bane ruling until 4426. His son, Grimstroke Bane took the throne, and was king until 4502 . . ."

Now he was speaking of his own family, and each name came with a face, and the memory and words that much clearer.

He reached his grandfather and spoke firmly. "Grimsea Bane ruled until the year 4875."

He paused, and he sensed everyone drawing a breath, waiting for a grand conclusion. He would now speak of the last king to sit upon the throne of Suderhold. But the words, the name, suddenly caught in his throat, refusing to emerge. His frustration, his fury built up until finally he spat the words, in tones that might be mistaken for contempt, ringing through the hall.

"Grimtruth Bane, King of Suderhold from 4875 until now."

The blue ice surface was slick and wet, water pouring down the shimmering face, pooling and splattering on the floor. The great window sagged visibly until, abruptly, it trembled and fell away like shattered glass.

"Gonnas hears and is pleased!" cried Stariz exultantly.

The prince was assailed by frigid wind, stung by particles of icy snow. The gale swept into the chamber, and all the ogres reached for their furs as they watched, awestruck. The humans in the higher reaches huddled miserably together but they, too, appeared rapt. Grimwar Bane stepped forward into the gale, then turned to watch as the king, accompanied by two warriors and a human slave, hurried forward. Baldruk remained at the table, but the dwarf's face was lit by an expression of exultation.

"Do you mock me?" growled Grimtruth as he passed his son. "If so, your insult will not be forgotten."

Grimwar's own temper flared as he and Stariz followed the procession. The slave to be sacrificed this winter was a strapping human male. Certainly the slave knew that he was doomed, all the more reason why he showed little spirit.

The wind howled now as the small group made its way to the very brink of the Ice Wall, where the dam of frost met the solid stone of the mountainous balcony. This place, where the great dam merged with the mountainside of Winterheim, was a precipitous shelf poised over the surging Snow Sea.

Stariz held the golden axe, while the two guards stretched the human slave over the rim of the balcony. Grimtruth Bane stepped forward and took the hallowed artifact.

"O Great Gonnas!" cried the priestess, the roar of her voice carrying into the wind, rising over the gale in power and force. "Grant us your blessing and share your might! Let this blood sanctify your pleasure, and open the Ice Wall! Let your Sturmfrost surge forth and scour your enemies from the world!"

Now the human seemed finally to grasp the inevitability of his fate. He began to scream and struggle, to kick and thrash. The big ogres held him without even straining. Grimtruth Bane took the axe and stepped up to the man, holding the golden blade above the terrified human's chest. The victim was stretched prone on the rim of the Ice Wall, a thousand feet above the face of the dam.

The king twisted about to cast a scornful glance at his son. "This is the mark of power!" he roared. "*This* is the deed of a king! By Gonnas, you have shown that you will *never* be worthy!"

The slave made one last, desperate attempt at escape. With a frantic effort he pulled one arm free and twisted outward. The king, his mind foggy with warqat, chopped, but the blade missed the slave entirely, cutting into the top of the Ice Wall and quivering in the grip of frost.

Then the human was swinging free, dangling below the

balcony, suspended only by one wrist held by the second ogre guard. The Snow Sea surged and raged below, black tendrils of gale reaching upward, hungrily, pulling at his feet, coiling about his legs.

"Hold him!" roared the king.

The guard's grip slipped. With a hideous scream, the slave vanished into the tumult, twisting in the air for a moment before disappearing.

"Fools! Wretches!" roared the king, spittle flying, eyes bulging. He wrenched the axe free and swung first at one, then the other of his guards. The first one fell after the doomed slave. The second screamed and clawed as he also plummeted into space down the long, barren cliff.

Grimtruth whirled upon his son. "See what you made me do?" he roared, advancing with the axe upraised.

"Wait!" screeched Stariz, though she made no move to step between the two ogres. "We will get another slave."

The prince was in no mood to give ground. The Barkon Sword was in his hands now, no longer merely a ceremonial weapon. Baldruk Dinmaker's word—*someday*—echoed in Grimwar's mind. He raised the great weapon tentatively. It felt good in his hands.

"You dare to draw steel against your father, the king?" snarled Grimtruth, taking another step forward. "You worthless spawn, you are your mother's milksop, a disgrace to my line!"

Before anyone could say anything else, metal clashed, and sparks flew. The weapons met again and again, propelled by all the strength of two bull ogres. A haze settled around the prince, and he hacked and charged, parried and smashed. The king was a huge ogre, and his axe was formidable, but his son was fast, and he felt driven by years of pent-up rage.

The great hall fell silent, the ogres gaping in awe and the humans in fear as the king and the prince battled. Thraid's cheeks were flushed, her white-knuckled hands clenching the table. Baldruk Dinmaker licked his lips, stared, drew his breath in a great hiss.

Axe met sword in another ringing clash, and both ogres strained. The king's weight and his huge weapon bore down on the prince, who suddenly backed away. The Axe of Gonnas cut deeply into the stones of the mountain balcony. Grimwar stabbed, his sword grazing the king's shoulder, and Grimtruth roared in fury as he pulled his weapon back and struck anew. The younger ogre barely dodged.

Again and again they clashed and broke apart. First one held the advantage, then the other. Grimwar's thigh bled from a deep gash, while both of the king's wrists and arms were scored with cuts. Each wound seemed to drive his father into a wilder rage, while Grimwar, for his part, found himself growing calmer and more determined. Strangely he found himself thinking of the beautiful queen watching this fight, of the dwarf, and the masked high priestess. He knew what would happen, what he had to do.

Cautiously Grimwar circled his opponent, pressed him back against the rim of the balcony at the very edge of the Ice Wall. There was a measure of fear in the king's eyes now as he lost strength and flailed wildly, no longer pressing the attack, merely holding his son at bay. He parried desperately, and Grimwar stabbed at the monarch's exposed hands, driving the blade deep, forcing the axe out of the royal grip. The king sprawled backward, shrieking, to lie fully across the wall.

"The axe—you must draw blood with the axe!"

Grimwar heard the words over the gale, knew that his wife was speaking to him, uttering the awful truth that he already recognized. The rite had been sanctified by Gonnas, but the axe was needed to fulfill the ritual. The prince dropped his sword and picked up the artifact, raising it high over his head. The king, his father, this monstrous drunken cur of an ogre, was blubbering pathetically, trying to scramble away.

Grimwar Bane chopped down with all the strength of his powerful body, angling the blade toward his father's bulging gut. The Axe of Gonnas sliced royal flesh, and Grimtruth gazed stupidly at the crimson liquid spurting from the great, gaping wound. The blood gushed across the ice, sinking into the white frost. The prince stood numb, watching, until Stariz grabbed him and pulled him back through the melted window, into the shelter of the Hall of Blue Ice.

More of the fallen king's blood soaked into the frozen dam, and the power of the Sturmfrost surged and exploded, while all Icereach quailed at the threat of killing cold.

17

Sturmfrost

A massive crack spidered its way across the Ice Wall, beginning at the spot where Grimtruth Bane's blood soaked into the dam of frost. The sounds of fissuring ice split the air like staccato bursts of thunder. The Snow Sea surged against the multiplying cracks.

A huge slab of ice broke free from the crest of the wall to tumble down the sheer face. Other pieces were jarred free as the huge chunk crashed and shattered. More great sections tumbled. Finally the first real crevice appeared, and the Sturmfrost burst through with a shriek of gale force, an eruption of furious wind and snow.

That initial finger of storm tore at the gap, widened it until other pieces of the Ice Wall spun away. The whole vast surface quivered and expanded, additional fissures opening everywhere, gouts of storm erupting. Sounds of crashing ice made a roar to shake the world, as a thousand geysers of blizzard simultaneously exploded and cascaded.

At last the Ice Wall fell away along its entire length. The Sturmfrost hurled away mountainous pieces of the dam. Many crashed far away into the White Bear Sea, raising huge spumes of water. As the wind whipped past the water, they froze into fountains of ice, picked up again and hurled farther, rocketing through the sky with monstrous force. Winds screamed with hurricane power. The black waves billowed and surged with frigid violence.

As the storm spilled out of the Snow Sea, it spread, fan-like, to the east and west as well as covering the north. In the blackness of the Icereach night an even blacker face churned on its path, shaped and driven by the cold and vicious wind. The front was a mile high and utterly light-less, full of destructive energy, large enough to swallow anything and everything in its path.

"This is really boring."

Coraltop Netfisher slumped on the roof of the cabin, chin resting in his hands. "No wind, no waves, nothing. I hate to complain, but at least when I was rowing it was more fun."

Kerrick bit his tongue and didn't break his rhythm of gentle oarstrokes. Back and forth he plied the single-bladed paddle, propelling *Cutter* slowly toward land. Listening to his shipmate's complaints, he was tempted to invite the kender to take a swim. Coraltop's attempt at rowing had involved turning a wide dizzying circle in the placid waters, and Kerrick was still trying to make up for the lost time.

They were far out at sea, in the middle of a still, starry night, and the weather was preternaturally calm. There was not even a whisper of wind. No ripple marred the mir-ror-still surface of the water.

"How far do you think it is, back to that steam cave?" Coraltop Netfisher wondered.

"I don't know . . . maybe a mile, maybe less," the elf replied. Because of the faint glow of starlight, he could make out the the strait, he thought, but he wasn't sure how far away it was. He was startled to see, low in the west, a green star sparkling above the place where he remembered that cove to be.

"Hey, there's Zivilyn Greentree," he said. "Once again, right over my bearing."

"Who's Zivilyn Greentree?" asked Coraltop.

The kender listened and nodded as the elf explained about the god of his family tree. "It can be a good thing to trust in your god," Coraltop observed.

A breeze stirred the air. Ripples marked the slick water, and the sail puffed and fluttered, filling slightly.

"It's a bit of *north* wind," Kerrick noted, perplexed. "It ought to be coming from the south."

"Should we try for the ocean again?" Coraltop said, sauntering to the mast, ready to pay out the line. "Like my Grandmother Annatree used to say, 'If you're going to ride a horse, you should already be sitting in the saddle when it starts to run.' "

Kerrick was torn. He had decided to head back for temporary shelter with Moreen and her people. This fresh wind was coming from the wrong direction. Should he head back or sail on? Curious, he glanced to the south. What he saw filled him with foreboding.

A wall of darkness loomed, blocking out the stars along the horizon, rising higher as it approached. The monstrous seething thing extended across the whole southern horizon. Now he understood the light breeze from the north. He had encountered the same phenomenon with a few other ocean storms. Before the weather struck, it moved through a swath of low pressure, actually sucking air, water, and boats *toward* the front.

This was a storm like none he had ever experienced before.

"*That* looks kind of interesting," the kender allowed, noticing the wall of Sturmfrost as it churned closer. "How far away is it?"

"Too close!" Ten miles or twenty, and the gap would certainly narrow in the next few minutes. "Raise the topsail!" he shouted.

He took the tiller and turned toward the faint firelight and the little cove, catching the gathering wind to push them along. Whether he sensed the urgency or was just glad to have something to do, Coraltop efficiently deployed the topsail and jib, and the sailboat began to cut through the fast rippling water with surprising speed.

When Kerrick next looked to the south, it seemed as though the dark wall had grown to block the sky. Tendrils of cloud reached from the mass, stretching, grasping, embracing, snuffing out all starlight. Now he heard it: more like a battle than a storm. The keening of wind was a supernatural noise, a constant violent wail mingled with a cacophony of crashing and banging.

The pillar and the cliff bracketing the entrance to the cove materialized before them. The temperature was dropping rapidly. Already the dampness on the deck had frozen into slick ice, and each breath they took solidified into droplets.

"There—that's the signpost rock!" the kender shouted excitedly.

The wind whirled chaotically. Kerrick fiercely maneuvered the boom and the tiller as the sails alternately puffed and sagged. He tried to head toward shore, toward the remembered patch of warm water. "Bring in the sails!" he cried, and the kender leaped to obey.

Something heavy fell into the sea, raising a wave that sent the boat careening wildly. Kerrick saw a great slab of ice, shining slickly, and was stunned to realize that it had dropped right out of the sky.

The wind struck like a hammer. Coraltop had barely stored the jib and topsail when the main sheet ripped away and swirled into the darkness. The ocean heaved, and a wave hoisted *Cutter* and held her, poised in the air, seemingly for minutes, as if ready to hurl its brittle hull against the unforgiving rock.

Garta's hand had been chopped off by a thanoi battle axe, and Moreen was certain the woman would bleed to death before they could reach the foot of the mountain. Despite the fact that she feared tusker pursuit, the chiefwoman stopped to rig a tourniquet.

"The rest of you—keep going!" she insisted. "I'll bring Garta down."

"Not by yourself, you won't," Bruni said. The big woman's deerskin dress was soaked with blood, her long hair was tangled across her shoulders and down her back. With her face locked into a frown and the big hammer resting easily in her hands, she planted her feet and looked up the path toward Brackenrock.

"Well, we're not leaving the two of you here alone," Tildey said. "I still have a few arrows left. I'd like to see one of those tuskers come into range."

Moreen sighed. In the dark night the walrus-men would be right on top of them before the archer could launch any arrow. Still, she was warmed by the loyalty of her companions and griefstricken over the brave Arktos they had left behind.

"Dinekki will be able to patch this up for you when we get back," she said with forced confidence, not even sure Garta could hear her. The matron was white-faced, shivering. Her lips were pale, and her eyes, although they were open, did not focus. The chiefwoman lashed a strip of leather around the stump of the wounded woman's wrist, and when she cinched it tight miraculously the wound stopped bleeding.

"Can you stand up?" Moreen asked. "We'll help you."

Garta lay on the rocky ground, her breath coming in short gasps. She made no sign that she understood or even heard the question.

"I'll carry her," Bruni said. She handed the heavy hammer to Moreen and lifted up the injured woman as though she was a babe. "Let's get down to the cave, now."

Moreen and Tildey brought up the rear, imagining thanoi lurking in every shadow, behind every boulder on the mountainside.

"How many did we lose?" the archer asked, too softly for her voice to reach the others.

"I saw Nangrid fall, and Marin . . . and Carann and Anka were surrounded on the stairs. I don't think they got out." Moreen tried to speak dispassionately, but each name caught in her throat and tears burned her eyes. "I don't know how many more!"

"Maybe some escaped," Tildey said. "You kept us together and led us to the gate. Otherwise we never would have made it."

"Why did I lead us *in* there with no idea what we were going up against? Dinekki's spell—she saw the place and said there were no dragons there! But she never said . . . I never *asked* . . . about tuskers! Why?" Sobs choked her words. She couldn't blame the shaman, couldn't blame anyone but herself. *She* made the decision, and at least four brave and good tribemates had paid for her mistake with their lives.

So immersed was she in self-pity that she almost bumped into Bruni who, still cradling the semiconscious Garta, had halted in the midst of the steep trail.

"Listen," asked the big woman. "Do you hear that?"

The moaning sound reached them first on a primal level, as something they felt in their bellies, through the soles of their feet. The rumbling permeated the air, the ground, the whole world. The import of what they heard was clear to Moreen, to all the Arktos, in a flash.

"The Sturmfrost!"

"Yes . . . it has been unleashed."

"Go! All of you, hurry!" cried the chiefwoman, as the ragged file of weary Arktos hurried as much as they could in the darkness, on the steep and rocky pathway.

How much farther to the bottom of the mountain, to the cave where the rest of the tribe was waiting? Moreen didn't know. They were lost in darkness on the trail. Tildey tripped over a rock, cursing as she went down in a tangle, then bounced right back to her feet and jogging along. The wailing of the storm grew louder, a roar that shook the air and sent tremors rippling through the ground. A glance to the south showed that the sky was blacked out and the storm was surging hungrily north toward them.

"There's the fire!" someone cried, and Moreen saw

flames at the base of the cliff, the dark outline of the cave mouth just beyond. Now the noise of the wind had risen to a pitch, and they felt it swirl around them, blasting their exposed skin with needles of ice and snow. The signal fire vanished, swallowed up by the storm. Chunks of ice flew, splintering rocks free from the mountainside, bruisingly bouncing off flesh.

Moreen heard a loud smash and a scream. Stumbling blindly forward she tripped over a body, bent down to see Banrik, a young woman of seventeen years. The back of her skull, where a boulder-sized piece of ice had slammed her, was a crushed, gory mass. Her eyes were open but she was mercifully dead.

With a desperate shout, Moreen pushed ahead toward the remembered shelter. She was vaguely aware of Tildey and Bruni close to her, other women too moving through the chaos of the Sturmfrost. Her skin seemed frozen, and she was surrounded by deafening noise. She followed the downhill slope, felt the level ground at the bottom of the cliff. Finally, the cave walls were around them, and they could find refuge from the wind, slipping inside to stand near a raging fire that Dinekki and the others were tending, several bends past the cave mouth. The storm roared and wailed as they escaped it but the wind couldn't reach them here.

Moreen slumped defeatedly against the wall, sinking down to sit on the floor.

"Where's Little Mouse?" asked Garta, suddenly opening her eyes and sitting up. They looked around in panic until the youth, his cheeks pale and his hair caked with frost, stumbled in from the cave mouth. He was shouting and gesturing.

"No, stay here!" cried the chiefwoman, too exhausted and discouraged to care what he said. The lad shook his head, as if he hadn't heard.

"It's that elf and his sailboat!" he announced. "They were almost to shore when the Sturmfrost hit. Now I think they're going to be smashed to death on the rocks!"

Cutter heaved and pitched, riding high on the waves crashing against shore, as Kerrick let out an involuntary sob of despair.

"Hey—look sharp there!" Coraltop Netfisher was on the deck near the bow waving the long oar. Feet braced against the safety line, he wielded the long shaft of wood so that, somehow, just as it seemed the boat would hurl itself against the rock and splinter to bits, the kender shoved it away.

Cutter bobbed back out to sea, carried by an eddy twisting into a curl. Again the storm roared and the waves surged, and Kerrick knew that the kender's desperate maneuver wouldn't save them twice.

Something crashed against the deck, and he saw a chunk of ice bigger than his head shoot past, shattering in the well of the cockpit. Another piece, as big as a house, plunged into the water next to the boar, drenching him with freezing spray. Fortunately, the berg had splashed down between the boat and the shore and raised a wave that tossed *Cutter* farther from the jagged rocks.

All the wetness froze instantly. Kerrick felt as if he were wearing plates of heavy armor. His hands, though he wore two layers of gloves, were numb. The sails trailed in tatters from the mast. Once more he wore the ring from his father—he had donned it once the storm hit—but even magical strength seemed a pale contrast to the fury of this storm. He could barely hold the lurching tiller.

Again, however, he spotted the rock and point of land he had dubbed the Signpost. The beach was a hundred yards away, although in this storm it might as well be a hundred miles.

The storm eddied again, and the boat whirled dizzyingly. More chunks of ice crashed down, hail the size of small boulders. The wind, trapped amid this bowl of cliff, moaned like a suffering thing.

"Hey! I'm going to try to rope the rock!" Coraltop Netfisher stood at the bow, a ridiculous grin on his face. He wore nothing over his favorite green shirt. He must be freezing, thought Kerrick. The kender, who had the anchor rope coiled about his shoulders, pointed gleefully at the signpost rock. "Watch this!"

"Zivilyn protect you!" Kerrick prayed, the words a rasping whisper vanishing instantly into the heart of the storm.

The bow rose on another wave, and *Cutter* leaped through spray and snow and icy water. Still holding the anchor rope, the kender sprang or was catapulted toward the rocks at the base of the pillar of stone. More waves rolled in, spray whipping in the wind, yanking the boat away, before Kerrick could yell or do anything. The kender was gone.

"Coraltop!" shouted the elf, scrambling forward, skidding on the icy deck. He saw the rope trailing from a deep pool of roiling water. There was no sign of his shipmate.

Hoping that the kender might still be holding on to the other end of the anchor line, Kerrick seized the rope and pulled. At the same time, another crest of water surged beneath the boat, lifting the deck, twisting him around, sending the elf over the rail headfirst into the surf.

The rope was still in his numbed hands as he kicked to the surface and gasped a lungful of cold air. Some part of his mind registered the odd fact that the water wasn't cold. Something smashed his hip, and he knew the rocks were right beside him. As the wave lifted him higher he kicked and clawed, somehow forced himself into a safe area between the coastal boulders.

He still had the anchor rope, but *Cutter* had surged past the promontory now. She was heading toward the cove, pushed inexorably toward the beach. Kerrick almost sobbed in frustration as the rope slipped through his hands, bearing his treasure, his pride, his very *life*, toward certain doom. Even the ring, magic pulsing through his flesh, was not enough to help him brace against the storm's relentless power.

He felt strong arms wrapping him in an embrace, and he was certain his mind had snapped. Someone . . . two hands . . . not his own, grasping the anchor rope, slowing the sailboat's course toward doom. He grabbed the line again, feeling hope.

"Bruni!" He looked up into her round face, her lips compressed in a determined frown. Desperately his feet clawed at the slick rocks, as the big woman leaned into the rope with all her might. Still *Cutter* was pulling away away toward the rocks.

Somehow Bruni lodged the anchor in between two stones on the shore, and the line, stretched as taut as a bowstring, held. The wind roared with implacable force, trying to pull the boat away from the Signpost, trying unsuccessfully. For now, she would hold in deep water.

"Coraltop!" shouted the elf. "He's out here somewhere—we've got to find him!"

Another wave crashed over the two of them, and Kerrick's knees buckled. He lay, shivering helplessly on the ground until Bruni hoisted him over her shoulder.

"Your friend is lost," she said bluntly. "You will be too, if we don't get you inside."

The Sturmfrost churned across the vast concourse of the White Bear Sea. The surface of the sea froze quickly, often in the shape of grotesque waves, storm-tossed swells, and hardened spires. Cyclones of lethal snow swept down the mountainsides, moving across the landscape with brute force. Many creatures, whales, birds, and seals, had long since departed for temperate climes. Any animals that remained here cowered in snug dens, secure against the wind and snow if not from the deadly cold

Those people who survived had also taken shelter in dens. So it was with the Highlanders in their cities and castles, the ogres in the great fortress of Winterheim, the thanoi in their Citadel of Whitefish, the place the humans called Brackenrock. So, too, with the surviving Arktos and a lone elf, who cowered from the storm in the depths of a large, seaside cave.

"We will survive!" Moreen declared with renewed pride. "We have enough food here to last for half the winter. By that time, the Sturmfrost will have waned, and seals will come onto the ice. We'll be able to hunt again."

"This cave, in truth, is better than any hut I've ever seen," Dinekki observed optimistically. "Where else could we gather like this, all together even while the Sturmfrost rages?"

The chiefwoman nodded. She looked around at the tribe, all seventy of them gathered in this great vault. A low fire, mere coals really, shed enough light to brighten each hopeful face. Nearby loomed an immense woodpile, timber gathered by Little Mouse and the younger children from the nearby grove.

Using charcoal, the shaman had sketched the image of Chislev, the bird's head and wings upon the fishtail body, along one wall of the cave. She had just led the tribe in the rite of thanks, traditional among the Arktos when they faced another Sturmfrost with shelter, food, and companionship.

In stark contrast to the dark hair, bronzed skin, and rounded faces of the Arktos, Kerrick Fallabrine's visage stood out in the firelight. He had combed his golden hair over his damaged ear, and his narrow face and large, almond eyes seemed to glow an almost supernaturally. He had lain, unconscious, for two full days after Bruni had carried him into the cave. Now he had awakened, though his eyes were haunted, his cheeks gaunt and hollowed. Little Mouse had helped him to sit up against the cave wall, and he had watched the thanksgiving impassively. Moreen thought she understood why.

"Bruni tells me that your companion's bravery might have saved your boat," she said, going to his side, kneeling next to the pallet upon which he sat.

His expression was desperate, and he clutched her arm

with fingers that tried to tighten, then fell limply away. "He saved me as well as the boat," he said softly. "I don't think he even understood the danger. It was madness! But, yes, because he got the anchor ashore, *Cutter* stayed in the water. I don't know for how long, though. I've never seen a storm like that. If the cove freezes, the hull will be crushed."

"Well, you're safe, at least," Moreen said in irritation. "Five women of my tribe were slain in that same time!"

The elf looked stricken. "I'm sorry," he said. "Yes, I am safe. And my boat is unimportant compared to lives."

"I am sorry about your friend," said the chiefwoman. She felt very tired and no longer angry.

"What can I do to help now? Anything?" Kerrick asked. He tried to push himself upright, but his strength failed, and he collapsed against the cave wall.

"Yes. You can rest until you get your strength back. After that, you can come to the mouth of the cave. We're going to build a wall of ice blocks, closing off all but a narrow doorway. If the tuskers come for us, we're going to give them a fight."

"Fight," he said numbly. His head slumped to the side, and only the weak rattle of his breath told her that he still lived.

18

Endless Night

ail Grimwar Bane, king of Suderhhold!"

The cheers rang through the hall, and the newly crowned king allowed himself to beam with pride.

"I *knew* you could do it, Your Majesty. I knew it all along!" Baldruk Dinmaker, standing on a chair beside the ogre king, leaned over to whisper hoarsely in his ear.

"Knew that I could recite the names correctly?"

"No! Knew that you could, you *would*, take the throne from your father. Why, I've been working toward that end since I came here, nigh on twenty years ago. Surely you appreciate that!"

Grimwar Bane was about to snort skeptically but stopped to think. Perhaps the dwarf *had* been working toward this end for all these years. Certainly he had welcomed the prince's ascension with manifest enthusiasm. Baldrunk's pride in Grimwar was evident even now as he stood at the new king's side, and they let the cheers wash over them, cheers that rumbled throughout the Hall of Blue Ice, proclaimed to all of Winterheim the dawn of a new era

Later, Stariz let her pride be known, though in a more cautionary fashion, as she spoke to him in their private chambers.

"You can be a mighty king of Suderhold, my husband, but you must be wary of threats on all sides."

"Yes, the elf," Grimwar said impatiently. "You have told me that the elf is due to come to Icereach. In the spring I will embark on a quest with my best warriors, and we will scour the shores of the White Bear Sea until we find this damn elf and kill him!"

"I pray that will be sufficient," the new queen said. She wasn't wearing her obsidian mask, but there was still a godly aura about her, although she was frowning, which Grimwar did not find reassuring. He sat and listened attentively because he dare not do otherwise.

"It may be, so far as the elf is concerned. But these is another matter, one about which my spells have raised a caution."

"And that is?"

"The dowager queen, Thraid Dimmarkull," said Stariz bluntly. Her small eyes narrowed to burning holes that bored into the king's face. "She is a threat," she said, startling her husband. "She has the power to bring your rule to an end."

"What would you have me do?" asked Grimwar guiltily. Indeed, he had just been thinking about his father's young widow, and not in the context of any danger.

"Perhaps she could be sent to Dracoheim . . . there to keep the Elder Queen company," Stariz suggested casually.

Grimwar gulped. He could think of no more awful fate for the young ogress, than to send her where she would be wholly within the power of Queen Hannareit, whom she had supplanted in Winterheim.

"I will consider it," he said noncommittally, rising to his feet and departing the room before his wife could make any other recommendation.

Soon thereafter, he met his protocol officer. Lord Hakkan bowed, then looked around to make sure that the two of them were alone. "Your father's widow awaits you in her chambers," he said coolly. "The slaves have been sent away."

"Very good," said the new king. He made his way through the royal apartment, and decided that, in fact, this was turning out to be the best winter of his life.

The Sturmfrost raged, expanding outward across the frozen sea, surging against mountainous barriers, curling back only when it reached the bottleneck of the Bluewater Strait. All Icereach lay buried beneath a blanket of deep snow, in some places five feet deep, in others even higher, its drifts burying houses, villages, whole groves of trees. This was a world of utter darkness, for even the faint twilight that might have brightened the land at noon remained masked behind the murky clouds, the constant, ice-laden winds.

Everywhere the landscape was frozen, except for one small speck of wetness, a pool of water in a steep-walled, sheltered cove, where hot springs fed small streams, bubbling upward from the bed of the sea. Around the shore the water froze and the snow piled, but enough warmth seeped up from the seabed to hold back the ice from the inner cove.

Cutter was now triple-roped to the Signpost rocks, and though ice crusted her decks, mast and cabin, the water beneath her hull had stayed warm beneath the continuous steam and fortunately the boat remained intact. The wind whipped, and the waves churned. The sun was absent. Sometimes Kerrick believed it had disappeared forever. He could barely make out his boat, pitching and rolling in the small circle of warm water.

Though it had been a full month since his landing here, Kerrick found himself still searching for the lost kender, kicking through the deep snowdrifts along the shore, staring into the dark water where the hot springs bubbled. Surely there ought to be some trace of Coraltop Netfisher! It seemed monstrously unjust that he couldn't give his friend a proper thanks or a hero's farewell.

He thought back to the landing, trying to reconstruct in

his memory as much as he could of that frigid night. The ring of his father had given him the strength to survive until Bruni had found him, but once he had been carried into the cave the magic had seemed to sap his strength beyond recovery. He barely had the awareness to slip off the ring and conceal it in his belt pouch.

He had lain in the same spot for a week, surviving on only gruel, while the Arktos—Dinekki and Little Mouse—nursed him back to health. During that period he had come to understand the fullness of his father's gift, and also his warning. Without the magic assistance of the ring, he would have certainly have perished in the Sturmfrost. Yet if he had worn it much longer, it might have killed him.

In the aftermath, he had vowed never to put it on again, but he doubted his own commitment. Once he had taken it out of the pouch and held it in his hand, ready to hurl it into the water, but he couldn't. He carried it still, tucked away, hidden from view but never far from his thoughts.

Sighing, shivering, he tromped back to the cave, seeing the narrowed shadow of doorway, all that was left after the Arktos had walled off the entrance. Already his tracks were half filled with drifting snow. Experience told him that by the time he came out tomorrow for his daily round of investigation, they would be gone.

The attack caught him in the forehead, a blow out of the darkness that knocked him backward and sent shivers of ice down his face. He flinched in shock, then chuckled as he understood what had hit him.

"Mouse!" he hissed, immediately squatting, compacting his own ball of snow with his gloved hands. His keen eyes, elf-sensitive to warmth, saw a flash of movement in the doorway. Little Mouse leaned out, trying to discern the effect of his snowball.

Kerrick uncoiled in a fluid motion, the hardpacked missile soaring true, splotching into pieces across the lad's face.

He arrived at the cave mouth and slipped through the narrow door. Warmth assailed Kerrick, and he shrugged out of his cloak with relief. He and Little Mouse were in the large entryway to the cave. One Arktos, often Little Mouse, remained on watch here at all times, peering from the narrow crack into the polar night.

Now the youth was laughing, wiping the snow from his face, pulling it out of his collar. "For someone who never threw a snowball before this winter, you've gotten real good at it," he said.

"Considering how many times you've ambushed me," the elf replied, "I can't believe I still get taken by surprise."

Little Mouse grew serious, looked out the door. "Your shipmate?"

"No sign of him," the elf said, "but the boat is doing fine. Thanks again for your assistance getting those extra lines lashed down."

"I'm glad to help," Mouse replied. "I think sailing on your boat, coming over here, was one of the most fun things I've done."

"It can get into your blood, the sea can," allowed Kerrick, somewhat wistfully. "I admit that I can't wait to return to open water."

He leaned against the small doorway, staring into the black, impenetrable storm. He wondered if the relentless roaring of the wind would ever stop.

"Tell me how you found him, again, at sea," Mouse said.

Kerrick settled beside the lad. "Well, I was sleeping, running with short sail and tiller lashed. I woke up when *Cutter* crashed into something big and hard. . . ."

He told the story in full detail, lingering over description of the monstrous dragon turtle, as the youth listened intently to every word.

Others of the tribe, Moreen in particular, had seemed skeptical of his tale, some even going so far as to suggest that the kender might not have existed except in his imagination. It helped, Kerrick thought, to be able to talk about his passenger with someone who did believe. He could reassure himself that, yes, his heroic companion had really been there, had sailed with him to the end of Krynn.

The Sturmfrost surged and seethed. In time that relentless

pressure spilled north, roaring through the Bluewater Strait to expand across the Southern Courrain Ocean, where—finally—it was diffused by distance and sunlight into a mere tempest. As the power of the storm waned, slowly, gradually, the Sturmfrost began to relinquish its grip upon the world.

Urgas Thanoi was the mighty-tusked chieftain of the Citadel of Whitefish. He had three fine wives, each of who maintained a delectable layer of fat even through the late winter months. His wives saw to his comfort, and two had already given him fine babes. As the chief bull in this fine place, his life was splendid indeed.

This fortress had been ceded to Urgas, personally, by a mighty ogre prince. Those same ogres had spent the past year exterminating the hated humans, the tribespeople who had made the White Bear Sea a dangerous place for the last four centuries. While routing a human attack, his tusker warriors killed four of the enemy. Those bodies had served as food for the Sturmfrost rites, before the tribe of walrus-men had settled, snug and comfortable, to wait out the worst of the winter storm.

For Urgas Thanoi, life was good, his position secure, his tribe stronger than ever before. Still, he was worried. He padded through the snowdrifts now, on the wall-top parapet surrounding his mighty citadel. Here and there sentries greeted him with tusk-bobbing bows. It pleased him to know that his warriors, alone among the peoples of the Icereach, could actually survive in the face of the Sturmfrost. Of course, he allowed his guards to spell each other every day or two, but no walrus-man would think of complaining merely because the wind was blowing icily or a snowdrift was mounting around his feet. The tuskers were blessed with thick, leathery skin, and, so long as they were well-fed, their underlying layer of blubber insured their survival even in the most bitter of conditions.

Urgas Thanoi finally came to the great gatehouse,

which—since it lacked an actual gate—was the weakest link in his citadel's defenses. He plodded down the stairs inside the tower, kicking through the snow that even here had drifted to a height of a few feet. On the ground he peered through the open arch of the great entryway. Once, he knew, a great slab of iron-strapped wood had secured this portal against assault. Of course, that wooden barrier had rotted away centuries ago. Perhaps, the tusker chieftain thought, he should capture some human slaves, as the ogres had done, slaves who could build him a new gate.

A round-shouldered shape moved in the darkness, and Urgas tensed, before recognizing one of his trusted lieutenants.

"Splitlip—you have returned from the shore. What did you learn?"

The second thanoi, nearly as tall as mighty Urgas, paused in the gatehouse, out of the wind. A long icicle draped each of his tusks.

"It is as you feared, my chief. The humans are still down there. They took shelter in the great cave, and they watch the entrance. They have built a wall of ice and seem prepared for any attack."

Urgas released a bleating, nostril-flapping explosion of disgust. They were his special curse, humans! Now they had followed him across the sea and seemed destined to camp on his very doorstep.

The thanoi chieftain peered into the storm, sensed that the wind was waning, that the peak of winter's onslaught had passed. He thought of what he must do, and he was unhappy, but he could see no alternative.

"Tell my wives I will return to them before spring," Urgas Thanoi said to Splitlip. "I am going to take this news to Grimwar Bane."

"The wind is dying. I think the worst is past!"

Strongwind Whalebone shouted the words over the

howling of the blizzard. He and Lars Redbeard stood atop the loftiest tower of Guilderglow Castle, staring into the eternal darkness of the Sturmfrost night. A comfortable amount of warqat burned in the king's belly.

"Yes, Sire, I believe it is!" shouted back his wolf-capped lieutenant.

Both men were bundled in many layers of woolens and furs, hoods cinched tightly. The king's beard was frozen, and his breath came in icy rasps. His hand were encased in two layers of mittens, sheepskin and lambswool, but his fingers felt frostbitten. He was anxious to move, to take action, to *do* something. After five weeks of sitting in his castle, drinking warqat, feasting, listening to the Sturmfrost roar outside his walls, he found he was unbearably restless.

He looked at Redbeard, was unable entirely to contain his scorn. "You have a wife, Lars. Home life has softened you, I see. You would be content to stay inside past the long winter, to grow weak.

"Sire, I can only say that I live to serve your command. Should you have a task for me, I would offer my very life—"

"Yes, enough, enough." The king moved to the edge of the parapet, as Lars followed. The blizzard howled around them, but perhaps the strength of the gale *was* fading slightly. No longer did they see rocks whirling past, icy boulders falling from the sky. No longer did black moaning cyclones tear at the land.

"She asked me if I knew about dragons," Strongwind said suddenly, turning and speaking directly to Lars Redbeard.

"Sire?"

"I mean, she was thinking about dragons. She must have been thinking about Brackenrock!"

"Moreen of the Arktos?"

"Yes, of course! Those barbarians must know the legend of the Scattering, the reason humans were driven from Brackenrock. She has figured out that with the dragons gone she might take her people there. That's where she was going, why she needed that accursed boat. She didn't want me to know it, didn't mention the place, but I'm sure of it now. She took her people to Brackenrock."

"A possibility," Lars admitted, turning his back to the wind and sheltering behind the wall. "Without a boat of our own we were not be able to pursue her. Once the weather allows us, however, we can embark."

"You are correct," Strongwind Whalebone said decisively. "But you are also wrong. There *is* a way. There is a way to cross the strait without a boat."

Lars looked askance at the king, and gestured to the storm. "You can't mean—"

Yes!" Strongwind cut him off with a fierce grin. "Yes, we can cross the strait before the ice breaks up. We will summon my priests, and they will send the word to all the clans. I am ordering the Highlanders to make a winter march!"

"Tell us something about Silvanesti," Moreen asked, as Kerrick sat with the Arktos at another meal of tough, dried whale meat.

He sighed. After eight weeks in the cave with the tribe, he felt as if he had exhausted every anecdote, every detail about his homeland. During the same time, of course, he had learned much about life in Icereach, about the ogres and their prince, Grimwar Bane, about the villainous dwarf who was his henchman, who had slain Moreen's father with his magical, poisoned blade.

They had also spent much time exploring the cave, which had proved to be surprisingly spacious. There was a wide entryway, mostly closed off from the outside by the wall of ice, and after a short, narrow passage the place widened into a large cavern where the whole tribe gathered for meals. A wide, fast stream of comparatively warm water churned through the center of this chamber, until it plunged through a deep hole. This was a vortex, the most dangerous spot in the whole cavern, and the Arktos took pains to keep their children away from it. Anyone who fell in would be swept into a lightless chasm and drowned somewhere in the bowels of Krynn.

Far back, the cave devolved into small passages, several cozy grottos with their own hot springs, and a few passages that were dark and dirty and seemed to twist around forever. Though Little Mouse had volunteered to spend the whole winter exploring these passages, Moreen had forbidden him to roam beyond the sight and sound of the rest of the tribe.

Their stay here had been comfortable enough. Their biggest enemy was boredom. As Kerrick chewed on the tough jerky, he thought that the food would make passable sailor fare, and he was reminded of another tale, one of the few he hadn't told yet.

"There was a time, not too many years ago," he began, "when Silvanesti went to war with the great human kingdom of Istar."

"What did you fight over?" asked the ever-curious girl named Feathertail.

"Lots of things," the elf admitted. "But mostly, it was about gold. . . ."

The Sturmfrost had relaxed its icy grip to the point where sometimes the wind barely gusted, and during clear spells the sky revealed a vista of stars. The midday hours were marked by a brightening of the northern horizon, like the promise of a dawn that had not, thus far, actually materialized.

It was no longer dangerous to go outside, and despite the deep snow, it was possible for the hardy to move about.

"Summon the clans," Strongwind Whalebone ordered, and the priest of Kradok, bruinlike in his massive fur robe and cap made from the skull of a great bear, nodded.

The two men were alone on the highest tower of

Guilderglow, and the king forced himself to curb his impatience as he watched the priest at work.

The man kindled a fire, burning seven sticks of coal that had been shaped into smooth rods and piled into a narrow-peaked pyramid. As blue flames began to flicker through the shafts, the priest chanted in the guttural tones of his ancient language. Strongwind stood back, musing that the man sounded like a bear as much as he physically resembled one of the great creatures.

The blue smoke spiraled upward from the coal fire, swirling like a corkscrew, rising through the still, frigid air. When the pillar of vapor was thirty or forty feet tall, it ceased ascending. More smoke rose from the fire, seeming to surround and compact the first spire, until the king saw a shaft of darkness so thick and lightless that it might have been mistaken for solid obsidian. Still the smoke poured from the coal, thickening the spume, and still the priest growled his incantation. The column of murk swayed this way and that, propelled by mysterious pressure, for there was still no breeze. Strongwind felt a tightness in his belly, a sense of impending release.

"Gather to your king!" cried the priest at last, reverting to the normal tongue of his people. "Gather on the Blood Coast, where the tall cedars grow!"

The cleric spread his arms wide, hands in taloned gloves reaching up like bear paws. Instantly the smoke pillar erupted, tendrils of darkness exploding into missiles that flew up and away, soaring through the dark sky.

Through the air the magical summons flew, arcing high, then at last soaring back to Krynn, one to each of the citadels of the Highlanders that lay within a week's march of Guilderglow and the sea. Each missive found a priest in its destination, and within minutes each priest was telling his thane or chieftain of the king's command.

Within seven days a force of one thousand Highlanders emerged from their winter quarters, riding great sledges pulled by their dogs, or walking on snowshoes, some sliding on skis. Each made his way by the fastest route, moving through the winter to the great mustering in the grove of tall cedars. These men of the Icereach were dour and fierce, ready to march.

When all had assembled, they started across the icy waste of the frozen sea, dogs barking, men grunting and cursing. It was a great gamble that the king took, for a late-winter blizzard could roar up from the south and wipe out the whole force.

Kradok seemed to smile on his chosen people, though, for the skies stayed clear and starry, the winds light. Like a great, furred snake, the column of the marching army moved onto the ice, bearing for the opposite shore, and the ancient realm known as Brackenrock.

19

Icebreaker

Though Thraid Dimmarkull Ber Bane put on an admirable show of grief in public, the widowed ogress left no doubt during her private moments with Grimwar Bane that she was very thankful indeed that Winterheim had a new ruler.

It was only Grimwar's fear of mortal consequences—not so much from his priestess wife but from her connection with Gonnas the Mighty, the Willful One—that caused the new king to exercise some discretion in his dalliance with his father's widow.

"She is expecting me for an augury session," he explained apologetically to Thraid, while his new mistress, beautifully, elegantly recumbent upon her huge, fur-covered bed, pouted coyly. The king looked into those deep, limpid eyes and fought surrender. With a sigh he reached out to wrestle his foot down into his tall boot.

"You have slaves for that sort of thing," Thraid suggested with a gesture, deliberately allowing the fur blanket to droop seductively off her shoulder. "Even the minor nobles don't have to put on their own boots."

"Yes, well . . ." The king grunted in irritation.

They had been over this topic more than once. At this point, only six weeks after the death of his father, Grimwar was taking no chances. He intended to keep the affair secret even from the most insignificant slaves who, it seemed, were almost always underfoot. Why did he have to repeat his explanations, every time the two of them stole an hour or two of privacy?

Grunting from the uncharacteristic exertion—it was not as easy to bend double as he thought it used to be—Grimwar reached for the other boot, his mood souring fast. When he was done wooing Thraid, he only wanted to be away from her, to get out of her chambers without being seen—at least by anyone who might report his activities to Stariz. Throwing his cloak over his shoulders, he leaned over the massive bed for a farewell kiss, but the voluptuous Thraid was sulking and had turned her back to him.

He muttered his goodbyes and slipped out of her sleeping chamber. The great hall was empty. He turned down a back corridor leading to the king's study, where he had ostensibly been poring over mining reports, after having left strict orders not to be disturbed.

"Spring will come early this year—soon, before you are prepared for its challenges," Stariz said, studying the knucklebones she had tossed in a large golden bowl.

"Pah! Spring comes, and the snow melts. Same thing every year. How is one prepared or not?" Grimwar retorted skeptically.

Stariz glared at him with an expression that insinuated he was rather a slow-witted child and she was working very hard to pass on her wisdom.

"Perhaps . . . perhaps our god means to tell you—" Strariz spoke painfully slow—"that when the spring comes, you should be prepared to *act*."

"To do what?" demanded the king impatiently.

The queen set her jaw in a tusk-baring scowl. "Well, that would be up to you, presumably, but we must keep our eyes open, our minds ready for signs of the god's will. Just last night I had a new dream—"

A knock interrupted the scrying session, and Grimwar raised his head, relieved.

"What is it?" he demanded, in a tone perhaps gruff enough that his joy at being interrupted would not be noted by Stariz.

"Sire, my deepest apologies for the interruption." It was Lord Hakkan, pushing the door open slightly but not stepping into the room.

The king waved away the apology. "What is it?"

"There is a messenger come to Winterheim. He wishes to speak with you."

"A messenger? Here? He has journeyed through the Sturmfrost?" Grimwar Bane asked in amazement, even as he welcomed the diversion. Stariz had been about to begin what would surely be a painstakingly detailed interpretation of one of her dreams, and that was reason enough for him to see the visitor.

"Who is it?" the king asked.

"It is . . . well, it is a thanoi, Sire," Hakkan said with obvious distaste. "He is waiting in the harbor well."

"The harbor will be fine," Grimwar said. He could just imagine how the ice cart, not to mention the air in the royal apartments, would smell if the fish-eating visitor was brought into the upper reaches.

"I'm coming with you!" declared Stariz, immediately rising and hurrying after him.

"This is a king's matter," Grimwar protested, as Hakkan tactfully withdrew, closing the door behind him.

"No!" Stariz said heatedly. "Don't you see—this is the sign from Gonnas. The thanoi has come to show you the will of the god!"

Urgas Thanoi was as wrinkled and fishy smelling as [G]rimwar Bane remembered. Yet the king tried to overlook those unpleasant features, for in this crude and tusked brute, he had an ally.

"The Arktos survivors have come to your citadel?" Grimwar asked in disbelief.

"Yes, a small tribe of women. They attacked my fortress, and we defeated them, drove them away with much killing."

"Of course." Grimwar wondered how "much killing" the walrus-men had accomplished. After all, their chief had come here, plodding a hundred miles through deep snows, to seek the aid of the ogres in dealing with the hated humans.

Grimwar was not displeased. Indeed, the tusker's news might provide the key to his wife's nagging and prophecies.

"Human women, do you hear that?" he asked Stariz, baring his tusks in a grin of pleasure.

"An elf—did they have an elf with them?" she asked anxiously, speaking bluntly and directly to Urgas.

"No, my Lady Queen. None was present in the group that attacked my castle."

"He must be there. He *is* there!" insisted the ogress.

"It is indeed possible." Urgas was hasty to agree. His piggish eyes tightened as he appeared to concentrate his thoughts. "My spies reported to me the presence of a strange watercraft, unlike either the kayaks of the Arktos or the great galley of Your Most Noble Highness. This boat arrived after the battle. It may be that the elf was borne in that."

"Yes. Most certainly, that is the elf's boat," the queen said, leaning back and glaring triumphantly at Grimwar Bane.

"Well, of course!" snapped the ogre monarch. "I never disputed your auguries! The boat makes sense. After all, elves cannot fly!"

"What are you going to do? Remember the augury—spring will come early! You must be prepared to act!"

Grimwar snorted. "Of course I will act, when it's

possible to do something! We can march to the citadel. I can take my whole army there, over land, down the Fenriz Glacier! And I will do so. We will enslave the humans, and exterminate this rumored elf. But ogres are not thanoi—we cannot march through snow for a week, and expect to reach the end of the journey with any hope of fighting a decent battle. So I will indeed act in spring! The snowmelt is months away!"

"When the Willful One demands action, he who would honor his god must act!"

"How?" demanded the king hotly. "By taking a thousand ogre warriors out where they will freeze to death?"

"Faith," Stariz said, her voice softening ominously, "sometimes require that we take chances."

"You have very fine weapons," Moreen told Kerrick, examining the keen metal sword he had brought from *Cutter*. Now that the winds had died down Kerrick was spending more time outside the cave, and, by agilely maneuvering himself from snowbank to rocks, he was able to get out to his boat, climb aboard, inspect it, and bring some of its contents to shore.

Moreen had accompanied him on his most recent trip out to *Cutter*, and he had enjoyed her company. Together they had looked at the sky, pointing out the stars of their respective gods, the emerald speck of Ziviliyn Greentree close beside bright Chislev Wilder, both stars in the zenith overhead.

"It occurs to me that, perhaps, you could teach my tribeswomen something about fighting," Moreen suggested.

She never ceased her planning or working, it seemed. Ruefully Kerrick stretched his sore muscles, reflecting on how she had recruited him on so many of her goals. Just yesterday a group of them had finished their biggest project ·et, a diversion of the warm stream that had run through · main cavern. Now they had a series of small pools for soaking and bathing, all of which were maintained at a comfortably hot temperature. The main stream, colder most of the time, vanished down a waterfall that still plunged through the hole in the center of the cave, but they had built a low wall around it to keep the children safe.

Those were nice benefits, the elf admitted. He considered the wall of ice they had built across the mouth of the cave. Certainly, if the tuskers were to attack, that would be an invaluable safeguard. What was the matter, though, once in awhile, with just resting and daydreaming?

He agreed that the Arktos women could use some training in combat and agreed to help. They tromped back through the snow, along a path now becoming a permanently worn groove. Back in the cave they gathered nearly thirty of the tribeswomen, as well as the enthusiastic Little Mouse, and filed through the darkness to a large, dry chamber lit by numerous oil lamps. A large, flat floor in the center of the room made the place ideal for training.

Kerrick set to drilling the Arktos with spears, the first type of weapon he had learned to use in his studies under his weapons master. Within three hours he had them thrusting, parrying, and blocking in relatively orderly sequence.

"If you can stay together when facing a number of opponents, they won't be able to get between you. Each of you only has to worry about your front. That's the way to prevail, even when you're outnumbered."

For another two hours they worked on hurling, using wooden shafts as spears, and charcoaled outlines on the cave wall as targets. Kerrick also let Moreen practice with his sword, showing her some basic maneuvers for attack and defense, pleased that she showed real aptitude with the weapon. In a short time she was carving big splinters out of the pine trunk he was using as a mock target. All of the women were breathing hard, faces glistening with sweat. Little Mouse alone still sprinted after his hurled "spear," racing back to cast his shafts, one after the other, right into the target.

"Good," Kerrick said approvingly, as with one final slash the chiefwoman cleaved the trunk in two. "Now we'll work on a few simple commands—"

He was interrupted by a dull *crunch* that sounded in the air and pulsed through the floor underfoot.

"Avalanche!" cried Little Mouse.

"Worse!" Moreen was already flying out the door, still holding Kerrick's sword. The other Arktos followed, and the elf ran after them, toward the great cavern near the mouth of the cave.

Even before they came around the last bend they heard cries of fear and panic. They charged into the hall.

Kerrick pushed through the Arktos women, who had halted in apprehension. Torches illuminated the great cavern all the way back to the bottleneck passageway and entry hall. Those brands were borne by men, bearded and tall, wearing thick furs and bearing axes, swords, and spears.

"Moreen Chiefwoman," declared a cold, imperious voice. Strongwind Whalebone held a squirming, elderly Arktos man by the arm. Contemptuously he cast the fellow to the ground.

"See how easily we take your people. Your pathetic wall of ice fell to a single keg of warqat, touched by flame. Our brew is quite explosive."

The Highlander king seemed very pleased with himself. More warriors spilled into the cave, scores of them spreading out to surround Moreen's people, while additional ranks of Highlanders thronged behind in the narrow entry hall. A girl screamed, Feathertail squirming in the grasp of a Highlander.

"Release her!" demanded Moreen, stepping forward, brandishing the elven sword.

"The kitten has teeth?" chuckled the king. He nodded at the blade. "A fine bit of silver steel for a beachcombing barbarian!" He lifted his own weapon, which was a massive sword held in both strong hands.

Kerrick saw Moreen grow tense, ready to attack, and he

quickly stepped to her side. "He'll kill you!" he whispered. "Is that what you want?"

"Let the girl go—for now," Strongwind said. Her captor released her and Feathertail sprinted over to the warriors. Bruni scooped her up and held her close. The big woman made a soft, soothing noise, but her eyes as they looked over the girl's shoulder were flat, dark, and angry.

The king continued, "Chiefwoman of the Arktos, I have a thousand warriors here, and you are defenseless. We claim this cave and all its squatters in the name of Guilderglow!"

Moreen drew a hiss of breath. More and more of the Highlanders pressed in, moving back along both walls of the cave, hundreds of them here now. Clearly there was no hope of resisting. Strongwind Whalebone swaggered forward, sheathing his blade, then snatching the sword from Moreen's hand with a swipe of his gloved fist.

"You Arktos are my prisoners. We claim your weapons and your food. You will remain here, under the guard of my warriors, while I decide what to do with you." He glared at Moreen, his eyes running up and down her body as if he inspected a haunch of meat for purchase. "I will think a while, before I decide."

The sun pushed its nose hesitantly over the horizon, each day lingering a little bit longer at the place called Icereach, where for a quarter of the year wind and snow and ice and cold had shut the world in darkness. Drifts shimmered and swelled across flat landscapes, while mountains and ridges were draped in vast cascades of white. Avalanches regularly tumbled down the long slopes, carrying rock and ice in crushing waves.

With each fleeting exposure to warmth and light, a small part of that snowy blanket shifted. Drifts softened, valleys began to trickle, streams flowing beneath the snow each day grew more vigorous. The wind still scoured across the lifeless world, but now, for a short time each day, that wind bore a hint of moisture and warmth. The winds of darkness were still killing and cold, but they were more tentative, lasting less long, than the gales that had raked the land for the past three months.

Now, at the base of Winterheim, Grimwar Bane gathered his ogre army and his dwarven adviser in the small hours before the next glimpse of that precious sun. Beside him was his wife, in her black obsidian mask. In her hands she bore the long-hafted and gold-bladed Axe of Gonnas, the most hallowed artifact of her great temple. She had explained her plan to the king, who by this time knew enough to keep his grumbling and his skepticism to himself.

Urgas Thanoi was there, too, incongruously dressed in the loin-cloth that seemed to be his only garment. In contrast, the ogres of the king's army, a thousand strong, wore long capes, high boots, leather gauntlets, and bulky, sheepskin hoods. If the ogres were bundled warmly, Baldruk Dinmaker was all but buried in furs, a hood drawn so tight that only his eyes and nose were visible. They were all prepared for a brutal march, though the warriors, as well as Grimwar Bane himself, were still not clear as to how exactly they were going to march anywhere, not when snow lay ten or fifteen feet deep across the Black Ice Bay and the rest of Icereach beyond.

The tusker chieftain, of course, had the advantage of his broad, webbed feet. He had explained that he had walked mainly on top of the snow when following the track of the Fenriz Glacier to Winterheim. If Stariz was right, the ogres could take that same route.

A horn brayed from high up on the city's atrium, the golden notes ringing through the halls, finally wafting down to the great gathering on the harbor docks. "The sun rises!" Stariz hissed, as if the king might have forgotten what the signal meant.

"Open the gates!" called Grimwar Bane. Immediately, four hundred slaves set to work, hauling on lines connected to the huge capstans. The rumble of the massive slabs shook the stone floor. The cold air blasted in as the gates parted wider. The sky in the north was pale blue and cloudless.

Black Ice Bay was a frozen swath of drifted snow. When the gates had opened wide enough, Stariz strode along the stone edge of the dock to halt before the wall of snow, perhaps twenty feet high, rising almost to the top of the Stormgates. She held the treasured Axe of Gonnas in two hands, high above her head, declaiming loudly. Baldruk stood beside the king, his pale eyes shining as they watched the priestess begin her incantations.

"Gonnas, our Immortal Protector, Gonnas the Mighty, Gonnas the Strong, show us thy will, and thy path!"

Grimwar felt awe as he looked at that gleaming axehead, saw it glowing with a light from within. Blue flame licked along the keen edge, rising and waving in a magical dance. When his wife swept the mighty weapon through the air, it seemed to make an audible hiss. Steam swirled through the air, like the moist gout of a hot spring, obscuring vision and slicking skin.

Stariz seemed to vanish into that mist, walking forward out of Winterheim and heading down toward the great snow wall. Grimwar and Baldruk hurried forward. The king saw her walking down a wide trench, making a deep gouge through the snow covering the sea. The axe struck, and more snow hissed and evaporated.

The ogre warriors, awestruck but disciplined, marched quickly behind their leader, the entire column snaking out of the city and onto the bay. Again Stariz gestured with her axe, and another great length of path was carved out of the snow. The icy drifts loomed to each side, but the base was solidly frozen bay, and the gap fully thirty feet wide—room for five or six ogres to march abreast.

The daylight was feeble, and only lasted for a few hours, but in that time Stariz was able to work wonders with her axe, and the ogre army crossed the bay and headed onto the smooth surface of Fenriz Glacier. They kept marching even into darkness, the arrival of which caused Baldruk

Dinmaker to snort with pleasure even as frosty air closed around them. The blue flames on the Axe of Gonnas flickered unnaturally bright in the night.

Grimwar announced their stops for sleep would be brief. The route of their march led northward between the mountains. A hundred miles away they expected to emerge at the sea very near Brackenrock.

"You Arktos will stay here while we explore your cave," Strongwind Whalebone declared. A dozen of his warriors, as well as the high priest in his fur and bear-skull raiments, stood back as the tribespeople filed into a small side cavern just off of the main chamber.

"You, elf. Stay here."

Kerrick halted, watching as the Arktos trudged through the narrow entry. Bruni turned to look back at him, then ducked to enter as a barbarian warrior raised his spear threateningly. Moreen was last, but she halted and then shrugged off a restraining hand, coming back to stand at Kerrick's side.

"He is not your enemy," she said, as the Highlander king narrowed his eyes. "We took him captive and coerced him into carrying us across the strait."

"Is this true?" growled Strongwind Whalebone.

Kerrick was strongly tempted to say "yes." Perhaps the Highlanders would spare him whatever fate they planned for the Arktos. Clearly they held the power here, and there was nothing to be gained by allying himself with Moreen's doomed tribe.

"It's true," the chiefwoman insisted, glaring at the elf, but he saw the hidden plea in her eyes, urging him to deny the Arktos, to seek whatever escape he could. It was that plea, more than anything else, that forced him to speak the truth.

"I helped the Arktos willingly," he told the barbarian monarch. "I consider them my friends."

Strongwind grinned in mocking pleasure. "It is as I suspected. With your skill with your boat, you could have escaped easily enough. You—go!"

Moreen slumped in defeat as two Highlanders dragged her away. Strongwind turned back to Kerrick.

"I have heard that elves are magical people. Search this one. Let us divide him from his treasures."

They ungirded his scabbard and set it aside. Rough hands lifted his knife, his small pouch of tinder and flint. Blunt fingers slipped underneath his belt, around his side. The hidden pouch was plucked away.

"No!" he cried, lunging, snatching back the small fold of material. The drawstring was tight—he couldn't get his hands on the ring—but he broke the hold of the burly warrior clutching his arm.

"Stop him!" cried the king.

Kerrick heard steel slip from a sheath behind him, and he twisted out of the way, barely avoiding a stab in the back. The other Highlander, the one who had been searching him, drew a dagger and thrust at him.

His training took over. Feinting left, Kerrick twisted to the right and seized the man's knife arm by the wrist. Pivoting, using his attacker's momentum against him, he pulled the man past, sent him tumbling into the other warrior waving his sword.

More hands seized Kerrick as a dozen of the king's men closed in. The pouch was yanked from his fingers. The elf was watching the two men who had collided and collapsed to the ground. The swordsman scrambled to his feet, looking in revulsion at his bloody blade. A groan of pain came from the other man. His chest was covered with blood.

"I . . . I didn't . . ." Kerrick stared in horror, conscious of being gripped so tightly he could hardly breathe.

"Nevertheless, you did," sternly declared the king of the Highlanders. He glared at the elf. "For that, you will pay the penalty customary among our people for the crime of murder."

He nodded to his men. "Put him temporarily in the cave with the Arktos. Let him try to stay warm in there, as we prepare a slab for the Ice Death."

20

King of the Highlanders

ap another keg, and fill my mug once more. Then shall we have some entertainment!" Strongwind Whalebone proclaimed with a wild flourish, to the deep, ringing cheers of this men. He stood in the center of the cavern, illuminated by two great bonfires his warriors had built, surrounded by a throng of Highlander warriors.

The Arktos were gathered together at the side of the big chamber, except for Moreen, who stood in the center of the room with Lars Redbeard and another bearded man flanking her. Along the wall was piled the great cache of supplies that had been unloaded from the Highlanders' dogsleds. Much of that pile consisted of the ubiquitous casks of warqat, which the men had been drinking steadily over the past few days.

The Arktos had been segregated in a smaller chamber, though they had often been able to hear the raucous laughter and crude jeers of their drunken captors. Kerrick suspected it was only a matter of time before the women began to suffer even baser abuses at the hands of the crude men. He had spent his own captivity in grim anticipation of the sentence pronounced by the Highlander king.

Even so, he felt no regret about declaring his allegiance

to the tribe. Contrasting the dignified captivity of the Arktos with the brawling revelry of the Highlanders, the elf found every reason to despise his captors. He was well aware that his contempt, unfortunately, did nothing to render these men less dangerous.

"You asked me about dragons," King Strongwind chortled to Moreen, "and thus I knew you were seeking Brackenrock. Though little did I expect to find you in such snug shelter. That was well done, that wall you built across the cave mouth. I have given the order that it be rebuilt. I intend no harm to your people, if things go well between us.

"You should know, however," he added with a harsh laugh. "Brackenrock was the ancestral home of *my* people, not yours!"

"That's a lie!" declared the chiefwoman. "It is said that the Arktos came forth from that place during the Scattering. From that time we have made our villages on the shores of the White Bear Sea!"

The king shook his head, pointing a finger right at her face. "You say this, but you have no histories, no books, nothing for proof. I have the stories of this period written by Highlander bards three centuries ago!"

"Because if you write it down, that makes it true," Dinekki muttered to Kerrick sarcastically, her voice too low for any of the Highlanders to hear.

The elf nodded, reluctant to attract attention to himself by making any reply.

Since the Highlanders had invaded the cave three or four days ago, they had not seemed in any great hurry to decide what to do with their prisoners.

Until now. Within the last hour, all of the Arktos had been summoned, then roughly herded into the great chamber. The bonfires had been lit, filling the air with lingering smoke that, at least, covered the smells of sweat and stink of many hundreds of unwashed men. The great stream of meltwater rushed along its trough in the floor, until it reached the chute in the center of the cave where it plunged downward and out of sight in a churning torrent. Several stones had been arrayed against the cavern wall, and it was on this makeshift throne that Strongwind Whalebone sat. For ten minutes he had been arguing with Moreen Bayguard, who stood before him under the protective watch of Lars Redbeard.

"Now," the king finally said, cutting off any further debate with a gesture, "it is time for you to learn why we have gathered you all. Bring forward the elf, the one who sails that boat."

Kerrick was quickly seized by two burly warriors, who brought him to face the king. Moreen stood nearby, looking at him with despair. He winked at her, trying to be encouraging, but was rewarded by a cuff.

"Save your attention for King Strongwind," growled one of his guards.

Kerrick saw that the monarch was looking downward, examining the thin gold ring he held between his coarse fingers. He raised his eyes as the elf was brought close.

"This seems a silly trinket to kill—and to die—for," Strongwind said. "It is too small for my own finger, but I will keep it, as a reminder of the only elf ever to come to the Icereach."

Kerrick uttered a strangled cry and tried to break free. Only the strong grip of the Highlanders holding him by the arms kept him from throwing himself at the king.

It gave him some satisfaction to know that the man was too much a fool to recognize the worth of his prize. If he tried hard enough to put it on, the magical band would expand to fit his finger. The ring was a mixed blessing, and a part of Kerrick hoped to see the king wearing it.

Strongwind scowled at the elf, narrowing his blue eyes. "I have sentenced you to an ancient punishment, one exceptionally fit for this splendid cave. Perhaps your Arktos companions will find it instructional. My men will find it entertaining."

Kerrick's anger faded, replaced by a feeling of dread.

"Bring forth the ice slab!" cried the king.

Four strong men dragged a large, flat object out of the

shadows, bringing it toward the center of the cavern. Kerrick saw that it was a massive block of ice, and that two chains, each with a manacle attached, had been embedded in the solid chunk.

King Strongwind laughed. "I give you a new boat, elf, one made by my artisans, just for you. It has been shaped with tender care and frozen solid over the past few days. They tell me it is ready, now."

Kerrick struggled wildly, but the Highlanders threw him onto the flat surface and in short order bracketed his hands. The water gushed past him, inches from his head, plunging into a hole that, even to his keen elven eyes, was lightless, airless, and cold.

"No!" Moreen twisted hard, breaking free from Lars Redbeard. "You're no better than the ogre!" she shouted, throwing herself at Strongwind Whalebone.

She reached out with every intention of clawing his eyes out, but the Highlander king leaned back in his makeshift throne and effortlessly struck her away. Lars and another warrior grabbed her again, and Strongwind laughed aloud.

"Hold her over here," said the king, rising, sauntering past her. "I would have her watch this business—probably it will be the last chance she ever has to look at one of the elven race." He wagged a mocking finger toward her. "After all, when I've got you settled in Guilderglow, I don't think you should plan on getting out much . . . darling."

The chiefwoman stared miserably at Kerrick, who was pale with fear. His arms were spreadeagled. Flat on his back, he lay shackled to the slab of ice. She had brought him to this end, she knew, just as surely as she had led Nangrid and Marin, young Banrik, and the others to their deaths. Her leadership had brought cruel death to many.

"Well, here, lad. It might be a cold ride," Dinekki said, hobbling through the ring of Highlander guards and approaching Kerrick. "May the blessing of Chislev Wilder see you through the darkness."

"Stop, hag!" cried one of the Highlanders, raising his hand to block her path.

"You stop, yourself!" snapped the shaman, poking a bony finger in the man's face. "Perhaps you dare the wrath of Chislev Wilder?"

"Kradok protect me," murmured the Highlander, recoiling and lifting both hands in prayer.

Moreen watched numbly as the old woman bent down to touch Kerrick's face. She said something quietly, then Dinekki stood upright, gave the nearest Highlander a look of undisguised contempt, and hobbled back into the assemblage of Arktos.

Strongwind Whalebone looked impatient and once again raised his voice. "Send the elf into the depths!" he roared. Numbly, the chiefwoman watched the burly warriors muscle the slab into an upright position. The elven sailor hung there, looking at her briefly before they tipped him, face first, into the churning waters of the subterranean stream.

Kerrick barely had time to draw a deep breath before the current snatched him. He felt the weight of the ice slab as a crushing burden on his back. Liquid filled his nostrils, and he fought against panic, knowing that would be the fastest way to death . . . and realizing that nothing he could do was likely to delay the end of his life by more than a minute or two.

Above him, for an instant, he spied the hole in the floor and the firelit ceiling of the cavern, then darkness swallowed him. The slab tumbled and spun, and he landed face down in water that seemed frigid. He felt pain, a bizarre burning sensation, as if he had been poked by a multitude of red hot irons.

Water filled his mouth when he gasped involuntarily. Complete darkness enclosed him. Head first, he continued to plummet, twisting violently around in the current. Water tugged at him, and the manacles chafed his wrists, wrenched his arms. His feet and legs twisted outward, and he used all of his strength to pull himself against the ice slab.

The tunnel bore him along with remarkable velocity. The elf was tossed about and scraped against the side of the shaft. He expected at any second to be smashed to bits, but apparently the water had worn a smooth channel through this abyss. He careened onwards with a series of jolts, still surrounded by water.

Only then did he wonder that he wasn't drowning.

He drew a deep breath without choking, though he was fully immersed. Again the slab pitched forward, tumbling down another chute, banging from side to side, then spinning lazily through a powerful current in a larger channel. Once more he took a breath, conscious of invigorating air flowing into his lungs—from the water!

The explanation came in a flash: Dinekki had cast a spell upon him. Somehow she had slyly given him the benefit of her magic, conveying Chislev's enchantment upon him, giving him the power to breathe water. In the midst of the nightmare, he felt a sense of profound confidence and peace.

A sense of weightlessness overwhelmed him as he fell through a waterfall. Again the ice slab plunged into a churning maelstrom, whirling him upside down. A hot spring made the temperature almost tolerable. Then he was rising, floating toward the surface, lying on top of the ice slab, feeling the raft push, gently buoyant, against him. He was drained of energy, unable even to clench his aching fingers. He lacked even the strength to lift his head.

He felt air—bitterly cold air. When he blinked the wetness out of his eyes he saw a green star and a white star, side by side in the heavens. He was still lying flat on his back, arms splayed to the side, still manacled. Now he shivered, for his soaked body was exposed to the wind. The drops on his eyebrows turned to frost. He saw that he was outside on a cold, clear night, and he knew that he would freeze to death soon, but he also felt strangely glad that he had such a nice view of those two stars.

Something else loomed against the sky, a familiar post rising from a wooden hull. He almost chuckled, inanely amused to realize that the undersea spring had spewed him into the pool of water where *Cutter* floated. How fitting for him to die here, under the shadow of his own boat.

Something else moved across his vision, a concerned face, with a shadowy topknot draped over one shoulder. Now he knew he was delusional, for Kerrick was certain he heard Coraltop Netfisher's voice.

"*There* you are!" the kender said, sounding rather vexed. "What in all Krynn kept you for so long?"

"This place will do nicely," Strongwind Whalebone declared in satisfaction, examining the grotto in the light of the oil lamps two of his men had put in place. Another pair of his warriors held Moreen, who had exhausted herself by resisting them during the long walk through the cave. The king gestured to his men. "Leave us here. Stretch a bearskin across the door and wait without. Don't worry if you hear a bit of a commotion—she's a feisty wench!"

The men gave Moreen a hard shove away from the narrow entrance, before they retreated. Quickly a great white pelt was raised across the aperture. The two were shut off in a small chamber crowded with ornate rock formations studded all over with tiny crystals that sparked and twinkled in the light of the lamps. Shadows leaped and danced on the wall.

When the chiefwoman looked around, she noticed that the Highlander monarch was taking off the gold chains that dangled around his neck, and slipping out of his tall, metal-buckled boots. He slid the chains into the boots and stretched, looking at Moreen with an expression of amused contempt.

"You'd might as well make yourself comfortable," he said. "We're going to be here a while. The more you cooperate, the easier it will go for you."

"I would die before I submit to you!" she spat.

"Did you consider that perhaps you don't have a choice? I am stronger than you, and much bigger. My men are in control of your stronghold. For once, Moreen Chieftain's Daughter, you would be wise to acknowledge the inevitable."

It was her turn to laugh. "Do you know that, when you were showing me your citadel. I actually allowed myself to think that, perhaps, you were a great man, a great leader. How foolish I was. Now I see you are a mere beast. The ogres at least had the courage to fight our warriors. You Highlanders, it seems, would rather wait till the enemy's warriors are gone, then come to force yourselves on the women. Perhaps you should call your two men back in here. If they held me down, you wouldn't have to work so hard."

The king glowered as he set his boots to the side. "You are rapidly destroying any intention I had of being gentle with you.

Moreen's eyes cast around the grotto, seeking something, anything, she could use as a weapon. She saw the king of the Highlanders shrug out of his tunic. His body was muscular and huge.

Now she saw her chance.

"You're looking somewhat worse for wear," Coraltop Netfisher said with a scowl, "but your skin is getting kind of pink instead of all white and pasty like when I fished you out of the water."

Kerrick wrapped his hands around the cup of tea, soaking up the warmth. At least he wasn't shivering as much as before. He could hold the deep mug without flinging the contents all over the cabin.

"H-how did you find me . . . and w-where have *you* been?" he asked. "You didn't spend the whole winter sleeping on the boat, did you?"

The kender shrugged. "It never got too cold. I think there's a nice hot spring under here."

"There is," Kerrick agreed. "I came floating right out of it. But you—how? When we crashed . . . I saw you fall in the water . . . I looked—I looked *everywhere*. . . ." He shook his head in disbelief, trying not to doubt his good fortune at finding his shipmate alive. "Don't tell me about that sleeping potion, again. I don't know where you got it, but you didn't have it with you when I found you!"

"Well, all right, I *won't* tell you about it!" sniffed the kender. "Maybe you'd rather get back in the water then waste your time with me?"

Kerrick groaned and shook his head, but when he probed for more details, Coraltop was adamant in his refusal to offer an explanation. Finally the elf desisted, lacking the energy to continue.

By the time Coraltop, with a few twists of a little piece of wire, had freed the manacles from his wrists and helped the elf aboard the sailboat, Kerrick had slowly pieced together how he had come up in the spring-heated cove. The stream that vanished through the floor of the cave obviously carried a significant flowage into the sea, including some of the warm water that had kept this little patch of cove from freezing through the bitter winter. His makeshift raft had been borne by the current, through the deep channel, until it emerged in the cove where it had bobbed gently to the surface.

"So, are we going to go sailing again very soon?" Coraltop asked. "I mean, after you've had a bite to eat and a nap."

Kerrick sighed. "We might be floating in water, but the last time I looked, this cove was still pretty well frozen in."

"Well, you mean the sea, yes. That's all ice and snowdrifts. But the whole cove is melted, now. We can float right over to the other side, where the road winds up the cliff. And the sun came out—why, it must have been up there for three or four hours today. Of course, I suppose it would be kind of boring, just sailing back and forth around here. Like my Grandmother Annatree used to say, 'It's not really a trip unless you go somewhere. Or fall down.'"

Kerrick chuckled. "I think we're a long way from getting out to the sea, or the ocean. I'm going up on deck to have a look."

Emerging from the cabin, Kerrick saw the sky was brightening from the midnight darkness. He noticed something else—people, *big* people, moving on the shore. They shuffled through the snow, cloaked in white, barely visible in the growing light. He saw a whole column of them, an army of warriors, larger and uglier even than the Highlanders. Several were gathered around *Cutter*'s anchor rope, and they pulled steadily on the line, hauling the sailboat toward shore.

"Stay right there!" growled a creature on shore that the shocked elf recognized as an ogre. He tried to think. The ogres were spread out along the shore, with several even now approaching the mouth of the cave where the Arktos and Highlanders were gathered.

"That's it—don't fight, and there's no need to kill you. Not right away," the ogre on shore said encouragingly.

The elf perceived that he had been mistaken about something—these were not all ogres. One squat figure pushed back his hood to reveal himself as a dwarf, a bristling-haired dark dwarf standing with the ogres who were drawing *Cutter* closer to shore. His breath steamed in the air as he snorted impatiently, and when the dwarf turned his face to look at the sailboat, the elf all but stumbled.

The last time he had seen that face, Baldruk Dinmaker had been looking over the transom of *Silvanos Oak*, as that mighty galley commenced her last departure from Silvanesti. His father Dimorian Fallabrine had been in command of the great ship, and this same bearded dwarf had served as second mate.

21

Wall of Ice and Blood

Sire! King Strongwind!"

The voice, from the other side of the bearskin, carried an unmistakable urgency.

"What is it?" demanded Strongwind Whalebone impatiently. He was just now glaring at Moreen, who held one of the oil lamps high over her head, ready to throw it at him. The other had just sailed past his head, and lay in shards on the floor of the cave, the oil still burning on one of the slick rocks. The king was out of breath, having spent several minutes chasing the woman around the small grotto.

"Ogres, Your Majesty! They're attacking the cave!"

Strongwind blinked, scowled, shook his head, then squinted at the bearkskin-covered doorway. "What?" he demanded.

"Ogres, you numbskull!" Moreen shouted. "Does lust make you deaf?" She put down the lamp and started for the doorway. "Pull down this bearskin!" she demanded. "Let us out of here!"

She gave the king a contemptuous glance. "Or do you want to continue? Flattered as I am by your attentions, I think an attack by ogres is a little more important."

Her mind was filled with horror. How many ogres were

here? How were they pressing their attack? She needed to find out what was happening.

There was a pause, a hesitant cough. "Sire?"

"Do it!" roared the king, who was shrugging into his tunic. He lifted up a boot, which jangled loudly. Impatiently he dumped it over, spilling his gold chains and bracelets across the floor, before sliding his foot in. "I'm not through with you," he growled to Moreen as he did the same with the second boot.

His henchmen pulled the bearskin away from the entrance to the grotto, and Moreen raced away. She muttered to herself, "Oh, yes you are."

The ogres roughly pulled Kerrick from the deck and threw him into a snowbank. He avoided looking at Baldruk Dinmaker. Until he understood what was going on here, he didn't want to dwarf to know his former shipmate's son had recognized him.

Other ogres scrambled aboard the boat, one even squeezing into the cabin. That one emerged a moment later with a shrug. "No one else here!" he called.

"Look again!" the dwarf snapped. "I heard voices."

The ogre disappeared, and for a moment the boat shook and thudded from the sounds of cupboards being opened, the bunk pulled apart, and other compartments investigated. Finally the ogre emerged, shaking his head. "Nope. Musta been talking to himself."

Coraltop? Shaking snow from his face and twisting to sit up, the elf shook his head in disbelief. He was glad his small companion had avoided capture, but he was more certain than ever that some kind of magic was at work. In any event, he had more immediate problems to worry about.

Three big ogres stood over him. Each wore a cloak of white bearskin, stiff jerkins over their torsos and clad in heavy leather boots. Their heads were hooded with sheepskin. Two carried big spears, and one a long-bladed sword slung casually over his shoulder. Nearby, a whole column of the brutes made its way along the shore of the cove, while a band of at least a hundred had gathered just out of bow range of the main cavern entrance. Enough of the dawn light had paled the sky that the rim of the valley, high above, was visible at this hour. Just beyond that crest, he knew, the walls of Brackenrock rose imposingly from the top of the mountain.

Kerrick observed a massive ogre approaching, the creature's square face with unusually small tusks locked in a scowl. With a shock he saw the straggled hair dangling from her scalp and realized this one was a female. In one hand, the ogress held a long-hafted axe that looked as though the blade was pure gold.

The elf had a feeling of dire apprehension as she looked down on him. With a sharp gesture she reached down, tore his hood away, and seized his blond hair in her sausage-sized fingers.

"It is an elf! The elf!" cried the massive ogress, hoisting him upward with a neck-twisting jerk. "My Lord King! He is here, our prisoner! The messenger of the prophecy!"

She dropped him. Another massive ogre plodded toward them, through the snow. This was a bull, tusks wrapped in gold, wearing a golden breastplate that gleamed across his chest. Around his shoulders was draped a bearskin—the only black pelt among this small army of cloaked ogres. The elf remembered Moreen's descriptions of Grimwar Bane, who had massacred her tribe and stolen the black bear pelt of her ancestors, and wondered if this could be the same brute—though she had referred to him as a prince, and the ogress had called him "king."

"You?" growled the monstrous creature, squinting down at Kerrick as if he could barely see him.

Any clever retort he wanted to make died in his throat as he looked upward in awe and dread. "Well, I am an elf," he admitted.

"What happened to your ear?" demanded the king.

"It was cut . . . by an elven lord," Kerrick replied. He

seized on a possibly helpful explanation. "I am an outcast, an enemy of my people!"

"Should we kill him now?" the king asked the female. The pale-eyed dwarf, Baldruk Dinmaker had come up behind the king, following in the deep footsteps the ogres had plowed through the snow.

"Not yet," said the queen, with a pensive look at Kerrick. "There is a mystery to his presence here. Now that he is in our power, I would question him."

"It will have to wait," declared the king. "We have the humans trapped in the cave. We found the camp of their dogs and killed most of the mutts and the guards watching over their sleds. From the tracks, though, it's clear that a great number of them have sought shelter in this barricaded cave."

"In that little crack?" the queen asked skeptically.

The bull ogre snorted in dry amusement. "That's a wide cave. They're tried to block off the entrance with a wall of ice blocks, but we'll see how that stands up to an ogre charge."

"Good luck, my husband," declared the ogress. She looked back at the elf, and Kerrick wondered if she was reconsidering the bother of keeping him alive.

Abruptly she picked up the axe. Kerrick flinched as she twisted her hands in opposing directions on the haft. Abruptly blue flames flickered along the edge of the blade. She lowered the golden head of the weapon, which hissed loudly as it made contact with the snow. Steam rose all around him.

"The Axe of Gonnas," she said grimly. "With the merest excuse, I will cut off your leg." She turned to the king. "Go to victory, my husband. I will watch the prisoner myself."

"Good enough," grunted the king. He drew a long, snuffling breath and shouted to the great, dark column of his warriors. "Pick up the pace, my ogres! We attack!"

"They're massing out there," Lars Redbeard said, as Moreen and Strongwind joined the panicked humans crowded into the great cavern. "There are at least a hundred of them."

"There's five hundred or more," Little Mouse declared loudly. The youth was standing in a dark niche off to the side of the main cavern, six or eight feet above the floor. "A column that goes for a mile, along the far shore of the cove. Some of them went and pulled Kerrick Fallabrine's boat over to the shore." He glared at Strongwind Whalebone as he made this last statement.

"What witchcraft is that, lad?" demanded Strongwind. "Do you have a crystal ball?"

"No," Mouse said. "I have a spyhole up here. The snow has melted in the last few days, and you can see the whole cove, even out to the sea, from up there."

"He's telling the truth," Moreen declared resolutely, though Mouse's spyhole was news to her. "Mouse is the best scout in our tribe."

"Five hundred ogres? Or more?" Strongwind Whalebone looked stricken.

"We have two hundred of our men posted in the entry, behind the wall built by the Arktos," Lars hurriedly explained. "I don't think it would be wise to move any more in there. We wouldn't have room to maneuver."

"No, you're right," agreed Strongwind. He pointed. "If they charge the entrance and take the front of the cave, we'll have to stand against them there, in the bottleneck before the main cavern. We can hold out for a while. . . ." His words faded. It was clear to everyone that the ogres had them in a nearly perfect trap.

"Is there any other way out of here?" he demanded, turning to Moreen.

She looked at Little Mouse, who had come down from the narrow niche to join the group on the main floor.

"Mouse, you know this cave better than any of the rest of us."

"The spyhole I told you about—one person at a time could squeeze out of it," Mouse said. "You'd come out on a steep, snowy hillside, maybe two hundred feet above the open water of the cove. Of course, the ogres will spot it sooner or later. Even at night, you can see someone against the snow."

"What else?" Moreen asked grimly. "Is there any other way out, is there a place we could hide?"

"Not hide," Mouse said, "but there is one narrow way, a sort of path that climbs up through a chimney way in the back. I didn't tell you about it before," he said apologetically, "because it probably leads up to Brackenrock, to the room where all those tuskers sleep. I knew you'd worry about it."

Moreen didn't know whether to laugh or cry at that piece of news—a possible escape route, but one that led straight into a barracks full of walrus-men.

"It's a tough climb, too," the lad continued sheepishly. "There's another reason I didn't tell you. You'd have been really mad, and told me I could have broken my neck. I guess you'd have been right, too, but I didn't! I'm sorry."

"No, you did well," Moreen said, giving him an embrace as her emotions choked off any more words. They had come all this way, and for what? For her tribe to be caught by surprise and held captive, and now trapped between an army of ogres and enemy tuskers.

"Brave lad you are," King Strongwind acknowledged with obvious sincerity.

"What of the tuskers up there?" asked Dinekki, who had hobbled up to join the conversation. "Do they know about this cave? Or do they just ignore it?"

"Well, see, they've bricked up a wall to cover it it up. I could see through some gaps in the bricks, and we—well, Bruni or somebody else really strong, anyway—could knock that wall down with a good push. So no, I think they might not even know there's a tunnel to a cave right underneath them."

The chiefwoman turned to Strongwind Whalebone, found his blue eyes meeting hers with a look of respect. That way lay hope, at least a chance. To stand and try to hold the cave indefinitely was a recipe for disaster. Even if they fought with skill and bravery, the ogres would inevitably prevail.

"Give me two dozen of your men!" Moreen declared. "I'll take them and some of my own warriors, and we'll head through the cave and come around at the citadel from the back. With a small force, attacking by surprise, we'll get the tuskers rushing out of there in a hurry! Your men can fight a rearguard action down here, hold the ogres long enough that we can get everyone up to Brackenrock."

"But . . ." Strongwind Whalebone's eyes narrowed.

"But what?" she demanded.

"It's risky," Strongwind said in a low voice, changing his tone.

"Can you get a rope up that chimney," Moreen asked Little Mouse. "so the rest of us can get some help on the climb?"

"Well, sure," he said. He lowered his voice and leaned close. "It will be tough for some of the grandmothers, though."

Dinekki's hand flicked out and slapped the boy on the back of the head. "You let us worry about that." She turned back to Strongwind Whalebone. "Surely you could assign of a few of these strapping fellows to help us elders get up."

"Of course," Strongwind said curtly.

One of the Highlanders was already rummaging through the supply cache. "Here's a rope," he said. Moreen recognized him as the man Strongwind had called Mad Randall, the berserker. Mad Randall smiled most pleasantly as he slung the coil over his shoulder and ambled forward to volunteer.

"Bruni, Tildey, all of you Arktos warriors, come with me," Moreen declared, then turned back to the king. "We'll need our weapons."

Strongwind seemed at last to regain his decisiveness.

"All right. Good luck to you. Your spears are over there. Arm yourselves." The king himself reached into the cache of Highlander supplies and brought out a gray-bladed sword. Holding it, hilt first, toward the chief of the Arktos, he asked, "Do you want to take this? It's one of my old reliables. The edge is keen, and it might be more effective than a spear when you're fighting inside the fortress."

"Thank you," she said, surprised at the feeling in his words. She took the weapon, felt the sharp edge and the weight of the metal blade and was grateful Kerrick had had time during the long Sturmfrost to show her a little about wielding a sword.

Strongwind gestured to Lars Redbeard "Take Randall, and twenty of your best men skilled with shortsword and shield. Let the boy show you how to get to Brackenrock. And—" he looked at Moreen and drew a deep breath "—I bid you follow the commands of Moreen, chief of the Arktos."

Grimwar led his ogres in a grand charge, his own roars mingling with the battlecries of his warriors as they hurled themselves at the cave mouth, and the crude wall of ice blocks erected by the humans. The monstrous attackers lumbered through the snow, the big ogre boots crushing powdery drifts and trampling the shoreline into flatness.

A stream of arrows arced from the narrow mouth of the cave, but the humans hadn't allowed space for more than a handful of archers to hold the defense. Several ogres roared in pain, plucking the vexing missiles from their flesh, and one hapless brute went down, stone dead, shot in the eye. Yet for the most part the light barrage had no effect as the charge was repeated.

This was warfare! A great roar of noise, an enemy who would stand and fight—if for no other reason than that he had no retreat—his whole army surging into the attack.

"Charge, my brutes!" Grimwar cried excitedly. "Kill the

humans! A fist of gold to the ogre who brings me the enemy captain's head!"

Already several warriors had boldly hurled themselves at the narrow entrance, and steel rang as unseen human defenders thrust their weapons through holes. One ogre lunged with his spear, then stumbled back and dropped his weapon, bleeding from a gash on his wrist. A second attacker quickly took his place, stabbing with his sword, then jumping halfway through the aperture to hack at the humans within. A moment later, he too fell, and as other ogres pulled his bleeding body out of the way, still others, just behind him, pushed their huge spears at the defenders within the cave.

"Knock down the wall! Use your strength, my warriors!" cried the ogre king. His troops had already set to work, chopping with axes and swords, bashing with hammers, surging against the ice wall with the considerable weight of their hulking bodies. A frenzied melee centered on the narrow doorway.

Satisfied for the moment, Grimwar stepped back and looked around. Across the still water he saw the curious boat and, on the bank, his queen, looming over the elf, who remained seated in the snow. He wondered, vaguely, why Stariz—who had been warning him for a year about the menace of this elf in Icereach—had not wanted to execute the prisoner immediately. Grimwar Bane took some pleasure from the fact that he had informed her, curtly, that interrogation must wait until after the battle.

At a safe distance from the battle stood Urgas Thanoi, watching the action with intense interest. Closer to Grimwar was Baldruk Dinmaker, grinning fiercely through his bushy beard. "A great day, Sire, a great day, indeed!" exclaimed the dwarf.

"Yes. On this day, we shall end the Arktos once and for all. Truly, Gonnas has smiled upon us."

He glanced again at his wife, standing guard over the elf, and added, "You know of elves from your years on the continent, no doubt."

Baldruk, spat disdainfully but nodded and agreed that yes, he had some experience with elven scum.

"Go to the queen. Be alert for elven treachery. See if you can discover what brought that wretched fellow to our land. The sooner we have learned what he can tell us, the sooner we can be done with him for good."

"As you command, Sire."

As the dwarf started away Grimwar was distracted by a loud boom. He whirled around to see that a sizeable section of the block wall had tumbled inward. Ogres poured through the gap, clawing and slipping, stabbing with swords, hurling spears against the suddenly exposed defenders.

These were no mere women warriors, the king observed. Instead of the small group reported by Urgas Thanoi, this was a full rank of strapping, bearded humans, who fought with skill and determination. "Highlanders!" he cried exultantly. "We've trapped a war party of Highlanders!"

The humans fought savagely. In moments the shattered ice blocks were slick with blood, and wounded warriors, human and ogre alike, thrashed and groaned across their irregular surface. More and more of the attackers converged on the breach, and the sheer numbers carried them through the line, burying the Highlanders under a wave of ogres.

Moments later, another huge section of the icy barricade fell away and, for the first time this day, Grimwar drew the Barkon Sword and waded into the fray. A desperate human thrust a spear that the ogre king swept aside with the tip of his blade. With a deft gesture he whipped the weapon around and stabbed the man clean through. Stepping over the corpse, the monarch entered the cave.

Another human advanced on him with a longsword. The king's tusks flashed in a fierce grin as he met steel with steel, blocking, parrying, pushing the human backward. The man fought with courage, even forcing Grimwar to retreat a few steps. Finally the Highlander overreached, exposed himself, and the king brought the Barkon Sword down in an overhand smash that shattered the human's sword, skull, and breastbone in a bloody splash.

Dead Highlanders were everywhere, and the survivors gathered into small knots, harried by ogres. A few of the men fell back toward a dark archway leading deeper into the cave, and with a triumphant bellow Grimwar pointed after them.

"They flee the steel of Suderhold!" he cried. "After them, my brutes! Pursue, and carry the day!"

"I've got the rope tied off," Little Mouse called in a hoarse whisper from the overhead darkness.

"Thanks be to Chislev," Moreen murmured, her knees almost buckling in relief. For the past half hour she had been dreading the sight of her young tribemate plummeting from the heights of the cavern's natural chimney. The sides were sheer, hand- and footholds barely visible in the dim light of the oil lamp they had brought along. Yet the youth had scrambled up the shaft without hesitation.

Now it was time to move. "I'll go first," Moreen said, as Randall held the rope for her.

"Of course, lady chief," he replied. "Just be careful."

She started up, climbing hand over hand, bracing herself against the rocky walls. Within moments she had passed beyond the illumination of the oil lamp and was fighting claustrophobic terror. Soon she could see a glow above from the small candle Mouse had climbed with. Shortly afterward she found herself sprawled beside him on a narrow, mercifully flat section of cavern floor.

"Next!" whispered the boy as she caught her breath. Soon Randall, then Tildey, had joined her, while the rest of their battle party—twenty Arktos she-warriors, and twenty of the Highlanders—made their way up, one by one. The newcomers gathered on the landing, crowding the rest back from the edge.

"Let's go have a look at Brackenrock," Moreen suggested.

"I'll show you the way," Mouse offered, and she was surprised at the relief she felt that he was here to provide guidance.

The youth led Randall and the chiefwoman up a steep corridor and around several bends. Abruptly Moreen caught a whiff of raw fish, and in another moment the smell was overpowering. She remembered that stink from her earlier battle with the tuskers and felt a flush of primal hatred. Unconsciously she tightened her grip around the hilt of her iron-bladed sword.

Soon they reached the walled-up place Mouse had described. From within the shadowy chamber they could see orange light spilling through chinks in the stones. When she pressed her eye to the gap Moreen saw a huge room, lit by several blazing hearthfires, and containing dozens of the big thanoi warriors. Some were sitting around listlessly or sleeping, though a knot of them were gathered around a big table, arguing over some kind of game.

It made no difference what they did, Moreen vowed silently, with a prayer to Chislev Wilder. They were doomed.

22
Rock and Snow

Strongwind saw immediately that his warriors would not be able to hold their defenses for long. His bravest swordsmen stood shoulder to shoulder across the bottleneck gap, but the ogres were too big, too strong, too numerous. All they could do was sell their lives for precious minutes of survival.

Already the Arktos elders and children had retreated deeper into the cave, toward the base of the shaft discovered by Little Mouse. Many of Strongwind's warriors had followed, though others remained at his side, ready to fight to the death in the big cavern. It was a fight that could have but one outcome. Already dozens of bleeding, wounded men were retreating past him, visible in the smoky light of the twin bonfires. Maybe a hundred of his men were already dead, an equal number grievously wounded.

Strongwind Whalebone was not an introspective man, but he found himself cursing the foolishness that had brought his army forth from Guilderglow. The Arktos woman had enraged him when she so rudely spurned him at their first meeting, then she had humiliated him by escaping from him. Most of all she had fascinated him in a way that no other person ever had. By Kradok, what madness had she worked, to bring him and his army to such a dolorous end?

The madness had come from within himself. His passion for her was a self-destructive delusion. Now, oddly, he found himself hoping that she might make it to Brackenrock, that she would be able to lead at least some of her people to safety.

"Here, you—King Strongwhistle!" He was startled by an elderly woman snapping at him.

"Strongwind!" he corrected the woman angrily, recognizing the cantankerous shaman of the Arktos tribe. "What do you want?"

"Are you going to stand here like one of those rock pillars, or do you want to do something that might give the ogres a little pause?"

"Tell me what you mean!" he declared, ready to seize on any possibility.

"Well, you have a god of your people, don't you? You call him Kradok the Wild One, we call her Chislev Wilder. But it's the same god—just like we're the same people, 'cept some of us are thick skulled."

"Do you have anything to say besides blasphemy?" demanded the king. For the first time he noticed, in the shadows behind the shaman, his own high priest, now garbed in his ceremonial robes. "Did you hear that foolishness?" he asked.

"Er, actually, sire," said the man, an elder cleric who had guided the faith of the kingdom since Strongwind's childhood, "there is an element of truth to her words."

"This wild goddess? You tell me Kradok is a woman?" The king couldn't believe what he was hearing.

"Such matters . . . really do not apply," said the priest, his bear skull helm bobbing apologetically. "That is, they are not important now. I suggest that you hear what the shaman of the Arktos has to say."

"Very well. What are you trying to tell me?" Strongwind said testily, glaring at the skinny old crone.

"Let's start simple, so you can understand. You see, our goddess deserves respect, and she has a kind eye for her humans, undeserving though we may be. She doesn't want to see us all butchered like fish in a barrel. So I think she will help us."

"How?"

The woman—she was called Dinekki, he remembered suddenly—pointed to a great row of stalactites jutting from the ceiling in the middle of the cavern. "Well, she might be willing to knock those down for us. That would hold up the ogres a bit, don't you think?"

"That could bottle up the whole cavern. It would take them a week to dig through!" He looked at his high priest. "What is your advice?"

"If the woman can form the framework of the spell, I will try to add my power to the earthquake. We may be able to cause quite a collapse—that is, I believe we can."

"It would halt their attack." Strongwind immediately saw the possibilities: A barrier would protect them from ogre pursuit long enough that possibly all of the humans could climb, or be lifted, up the chimney to Brackenrock.

"That's what I've been trying to tell you," clucked the elderly priestess. "It will take a little spellcasting from us, and a little distraction from you. We've got to hold the ogres at that entrance for a bit longer, til we can get ourselves set."

"How long do you need?" asked the king of the Highlanders.

"Ten minutes should do. Now, let's get all those people—all them that aren't fighting ogres, at least—deeper into the cave."

Kerrick's fingers probed at the icy snow behind him. The wet snow, where the Axe of Gonnas had touched it, was slushy and wet. For several minutes, he had been forming a fist-sized ball, compacting it into a chunk of ice as hard as a rock.

The huge ogress queen stood a dozen feet away, her back to the elf, looking across the cove at the battle raging around the mouth of the cavern. From here it was obvious that the humans were faring badly. The wall had collapsed in several places, and ogres were pouring into the cave mouth.

Kerrick saw a figure plodding away from the fight, coming towards them, and he recognized Baldruk Dinmaker. Several other ogres formed an escort for the queen, but they were a respectful distance away along the snowy shore. *Cutter*, still triple-roped to the stone pillar, rested in the placid water a short distance beyond the queen.

The ogress turned and clumped toward Kerrick, silhouetted against the purple sky paling toward brief daylight. He dropped the iceball, let it sit in the darkness next to his hip. The queen had that great axe in her hands, though the fire had faded from the edge of the blade. She turned her attention to the approaching dwarf. "What word do you bring?" she asked crossly.

"My queen, let me help you guard that wretch," suggested Baldruk Dinmaker, only dozen paces away. "These elves are ever treacherous, wickedly dangerous."

"You don't *look* dangerous," mused the massive, square-faced ogress, turning to look at Kerrick pensively. The water was now at her back, and the snowbank sloped sharply downward behind her. "Thanks be to Gonnas, we have warning of your wicked nature."

"I know I don't look dangerous," Kerrick said casually, wrapping the fingers of his right hand around the ice ball. "But I *am*."

He pivoted, sprang into a crouch, and threw the missile with all of his strength. He started a prayer to Zivilyn, but before he could complete the first word he saw the solid chunk of ice strike the queen between her eyes. She cried out and clapped both hands to her face, momentarily leaving the axe standing on its long haft.

Kerrick was sprinting, barely hearing the dwarf shout a warning. The elf reached the reeling ogress and smashed his shoulder into her gut, sending her staggering backward. His hands darted out and snatched the axe. Staggering under the weight, he raised the blade, sent it slashing downward toward the queen's neck.

She was already overbalanced. Hands flailing, massive feet sliding down the steep snowbank, she fell backward and plunged into the waters of the cove. Roaring, cursing inarticulately, she clawed at the edge.

Instantly Kerrick whirled around. He heard shouts of alarm, and saw that several ogres had observed his escape. The dwarf was rushing toward him now, shouting curses in a foul, guttural tongue as he drew a silver dagger from his belt.

Cutter floated close beside him, and Kerrick again raised the massive gold-bladed axe. With a single chop he cut the ropes that had bound his boat to this shore for the long winter.

The dwarf was almost upon him now but halted as Kerrick raised the axe high. A single downward blow would have split that hateful skull, ended that wicked life, but this was not his intention. Not yet.

"Drop your knife and get on the boat or die," growled the elf. "You have two heartbeats to choose."

Glaring hatefully, the dwarf let the weapon slip from his fingers. He took a step toward the sailboat, while a half dozen ogres scrambled closer.

Kerrick brandished the axe again. "Move now, or else!"

The dwarf leaped onto the deck, landing with the easy balance of an experienced sailor.

"Get to the bow."

Reluctantly, the glowering dwarf moved forward. A wild leap carried the elf, still holding the axe, to the boat, where he almost stumbled over the side. Catching his balance, he turned and waved the axe to hold the dwarf in place, and saw lumbering ogres a few dozen paces away, closing fast. With a smooth flip he planted the head of the axe against the shore and pushed the boat into deeper water.

One of the ogres stopped to cast a spear, and the elf knocked the weapon away with a sideways swipe. His luck continued, and before the next ogre thought to launch a weapon, *Cutter* and her two passengers were bobbing in placid water, safely out of range.

"Now!" Moreen said. Bruni threw her weight against the brick wall. The chiefwoman also pushed against the flimsy barrier, as did Mad Randall, Lars Redbeard, and several other of the big Highlanders.

In a clatter of dust and debris the wall burst inward, and the attackers exploded through the opening. Moreen carried the iron-bladed sword, and thrust it into the chest of a surprised thanoi as the brute scrambled to sit up on dirty straw mat.

"For Nangrid!" she shouted, a piercing cry.

"For Carann! For Marin! For Anka!"

The Arktos shouted the names of their deceased comrades. Moreen whirled into the tuskers with a vengeance, instinct wielding her weapon with surprising accuracy. She flew at another thanoi, dropping it with a vicious slash across the throat. She stabbed a walrus-man trying to scramble out of her way, chopped at one to the side. Everywhere the creatures were lunging to their feet, barking and shouting, reaching for their weapons. Many fell before the sudden, merciless onslaught.

One Highlander whirled among the tuskers like a deadly cyclone. It was Mad Randall. His voice was an animal howl, a nightmarish sound. His axe slashed through a circle of tuskers, and the survivors fell back, bleeding from cuts. Before they hit the floor the berserker had leaped over a table and charged another pair, killing one swiftly and sending the other tumbling backward into the fireplace, where it shrieked and flailed, trying to bat away flames. Thrashing desperately, the monster crawled out of the the blaze, but its fat was already melting, crackling into greasy flames. It died in a cloud of grimy smoke.

Moreen felt as though she was watching herself, a

stranger, as if someone else was enjoying this horrible violence. She killed with pleasure, with hatred, her movements quick, efficient, relentless. Even when her hands were doused with warm blood, when the fishy stink of thanoi guts choked her nostrils, she enjoyed the killing.

On the far side of the room, Bruni swung her mighty stone hammer, bashing one thanoi after another as the creatures struggled to collect themselves, to raise weapons or flee. Tildey stood near the fallen wall, shooting arrows at any tusker that offered a clean target. Already a half dozen lay dead or dying, pierced by the archer's lethal missiles.

After several minutes of frenzied battle, two score or more of the monsters lay scattered around the big chamber. Others had fled, ignoring the wide double doors, which were still latched, instead leaping out windows to the ground.

"Take the whole fortress!" cried Moreen. "Spread out and find the tuskers wherever they're hiding!"

The humans moved rapidly in pursuit. Mad Randall wasted no time in smashing the doors apart with a blow of his great axe. His strange, shrieking war cry rang in the courtyard now as he led the Highlanders through the doorway. The berserker's eyes were wide, his lips flecked with foam. He wielded his great battle axe with lightning blows, leaving one thanoi after another battered and bleeding in his wake. When a great bull lowered his tusks and charged him, Randall's blade effortlessly cleaved his enemy from crown to sternum. Without pause the Highlander vaulted over the fallen thanoi, landing on his feet and somehow bringing his axe up for a slashing cut at another scrambling walrus-man.

Moreen heard a familiar voice cry out, and turned in horror to see Little Mouse taking on a big thanoi. The youth had a thin knife extended before him, while the hulking brute was lowering its bestial head to bring its sharp tusks into line. With startling speed the walrus-man sprang forward, driving the heavy body with long, supple legs.

Little Mouse went down, but Moreen saw that he had

fallen and rolled, so that his knife could stab upward, ripping out a long cut in the monster's belly. The tusker fell with a groan and a kick, and the lad was on him in a flash, driving the keen blade deep. Then Little Mouse scrambled up, took a spear from a pile of thanoi weapons, and hurried to continue the fight.

"To the walls!" Moreen shouted, as the last of the tuskers outside the barracks was cut down and eliminated. "Follow me to the gatehouse!"

Daylight had brightened the sky, and she saw some thanoi were fleeing out the gate. Others paused to touch torches to a large pile of oily firewood, discharging a spume of black smoke.

Everywhere the attackers spread out, striking and killing. Moreen shouted, a furious cry of exultation, fury, and grief. Her bloody sword held high, she ran forward, her tribemates following.

"Chislev Wilder, in our sight, show thy signal, light the light!" chanted Dinneki.

Strongwind Whalebone, fighting beside his men, couldn't hear her exact words, but he saw a flash of brightness, emanating from somewhere behind the dozen Highlanders fighting here. The rest of Strongwind's warriors had already withdrawn beyond the stone spires where the shaman prepared her spell.

"That‘s the signal!" he cried, praying that the rest of Dinekki's magic worked as well as this light spell that alerted the Highlanders to retreat and stunned the ogres into momentary awe.

An attacker facing the king raised both hands to his tusked face, crying out as the magical light momentarily blinded him. Strongwind stabbed his enemy in his belly, which bulged beneath a metal breastplate. The ogre dropped with a gurgling moan.

"Fall back!" shouted the king.

His men turned and ran, for a moment opening up a gap between themselves and the attackers, who had been momentarily stunned by the brightness.

Strongwind held back, making sure that all of his men had escaped. When the last had passed he started after. Something hard struck him, and he sprawled forward on the ground. As he lay on his face, a weapon ricocheted into the shadows, and he realized that he had been hit by an ogre spear.

He tried to clear his mind, to leap to his feet and run, but could only rise to his hands and knees, groggy and stunned. Knowing he had to get away, he pushed himself up, then everything whirled. His men had reached the safety of the deep cave, and the ground shook to the pounding of ogre boots. Crawling behind a big rock, Strongwind sat up and tried to get his bearings.

"Chislev Wilder, through the gloom—bring these ogres rocky doom!"

The shaman's command resonated thunderously through the cavern, her voice impossibly loud for such a frail speaker. The floor pitched and buckled. Rocks splintered, and Strongwind smelled acrid dust. Shards of stone whizzed over his head, and a cloud of murk descended. The floor heaved, and more stone broke from the ceiling, crashing downward, piling onto the floor, rising upward to form a great barricade. Some ogres shrieked as the cascade crushed them. Most of the brutes stumbled backward, avoiding the rockfall but thwarted in the pursuit of the fleeing humans.

She had done it—that crotchety old woman had summoned up the godly power of the earth itself! For the time being, while the ogre army clawed through the rubble, the two tribes were safe.

Except for Strongwind Whalebone, who, as his head cleared, realized that he was on the ogre side of that barrier. He stumbled to his feet, seeing a dozen ogres within a stone's throw, but they were also off balance. Several of them stared dumbly at the pile of debris.

"Move it!" roared an ogre voice from somewhere. "Dig it out of the way! After them!"

Strongwind rolled to the side, staying low, realizing that there was still adequate light here from the bonfires his men had burned. An ogre shouted and pointed. He had been seen!

At the edge of the cavern he saw a shadowy wall, pocked with niches, and he remembered something—Little Mouse and his spyhole!

Wincing from the pain in his shoulder, the Highlander king drove himself on, finding the opening, crawling up to slip inside the tunnel, desperately pulling himself through a winding passage. Fresh, cold air bathed his face, smelling of melting snow, and he knew he was on the right path.

Loud noises came from behind: shouts, grunts, and metallic scrapes, and he knew the ogres had seen him and were hot in pursuit.

23

Citadel of Humankind

What happened to *Silvanos Oak*?"

Kerrick held the golden axe upraised. The weapon was heavy but perfectly balanced. He twisted the hilt as he had seen the ogress do and was rewarded by the sight of blue flames dancing along the edge of the blade.

The dwarf, backed into the very prow of the sailboat, glared at him. His pale, milky eyes narrowed.

"I never heard of such a ship," he said sullenly.

"You are Baldruk Dinmaker. You served as Dimorian Fallabrine's second mate for years, at least three voyages before the last. If you lie to me again I'll . . . I'll cut off your arm."

The dwarf chuckling ruefully. "Well, you've got a keen eye. I'll tell you, though it's not a happy story. The *Oak* came to these shores, and she was taken by ogres at her first landfall, captain and crew—including myself—all made prisoners. The ogre king had her renamed, outfitted her as his own ship. She's called *Goldwing*, now. That's what happened to the *Silvanos Oak*."

"And the crew? What of the elves and humans and kender who crewed her?" demanded Kerrick.

The dwarf snorted. "Elves and humans went to thc king

as slaves. The kender he butchered—who could blame him? Kender are good for nothing, not even ballast, if you ask me. Tell me something: Why are you so concerned about that doomed voyage?"

"Dimorian Fallabrine was my father."

Now those strange eyes came into tight focus, and the dwarf's hand scratched thoughtfully at his beard.

"You do look a bit like that old pirate, and I know Dimorian had a son. Never stopped talking about him, in fact. So that's you? Strange coincidence!"

Kerrick nodded numbly, but his mind was racing ahead. "The ones who became slaves—where are they today?"

Baldruk frowned. "They don't last long under slavery around here," he said bluntly. "I don't think one of them lived through the first two years, not the elves, at least. Who knows, some of the humans might still be there, working in the king's mines, or tending his harbor. Elves are too soft to make good slaves. The humans last longer . . . sometimes."

Kerrick sagged. The dwarf was right. Any Silvanesti condemned to perform physical labor as the chattel of ogres would inevitably perish before long. The degradation was unthinkable, the physical toll lethal. He addressed the dwarf in cold anger.

"But you—you're no slave, not one who marches beside the ogre king and who comes to counsel the queen. You're a traitor!"

"Now, wait, lad. I had a chance at survival and I took it! I never betrayed my crewmates. We were captured by ogres! How can you blame me for seeing my chance at life, taking a job that got me out of the accursed mines?"

"No, I remember the stories. It was one of my father's mates who convinced him to sail after gold. *You* were the one who planted the idea in my father's head. It was you who spoke of the Land of Gold, you who claimed you could lead him to riches!"

Baldruk's eyes were slits. His hand, unnoticed by the elf, slid to the back of his leg, touching the top of his leather boot.

"Don't jump to conclusions!" he urged.

The silver dagger flashed, clutched in Baldruk's fist. Kerrick couldn't believe his own stupidity. The dwarf must have caught the blade and secreted it in his boot. Too late, he recalled Moreen's tale of the weapon that had killed her father.

Even as he remembered this, Baldruk lunged at him, and Kerrick brought the fiery axe down. The golden blade bit into Baldruk Dinmaker's neck, sizzling as it cut flesh.

With a gasp, the dwarf thrashed backward. His knife splashed into the water. Blood spread across the foredeck as his eyes, wild and hateful, met Kerrick's. "Fool!" croaked the dwarf. "You still don't know the truth—and you never will!"

He convulsed, thrashing on the blood-slick deck, rolling over the gunwale. He splashed into the water and disappeared into the inky depths.

"No!" cried Kerrick. What did the dwarf mean? Was it possible that his father still alive? Why had the fool tried to attack him? Kerrick hadn't wanted to kill him!

"Who's that up on the snowfield?" Coraltop Netfisher asked, standing on the cabin roof, pointing excitedly. "Is it one of the good guys? How did the boat get all bloody? Are you okay?"

"What? How did . . . where?" Kerrick was trembling as he turned to confront his green-tunicked passenger. The massive axe was suddenly heavy, and after a twist extinguished the flames he dropped it onto the deck.

The kender hopped down from the cabin and sauntered forward, then yelped as Kerrick lunged, seized him by both shoulders, and shook.

"Tell me! Who are you? *What* are you?" demanded the elf. "How do you keep disappearing?"

"What, because a simple-minded ogre didn't find me? Have you seen those pig-eyes they have?" chuckled the kender. "It's like my Grandmother Annatree used to say, 'You can't see anything, unless you look.' "

"Not just the ogres!" spat Kerrick, with another, none-too-gentle, shake. "You couldn't have survived the winter out here! You couldn't sleep for five days on a crowded boat. I looked for you. You weren't on board!"

"Speaking of looking, who is that up there? I think he's in some kind of trouble."

Snarling in exasperation, Kerrick squinted, following Coraltop's pointing finger. A figure had emerged from a narrow slit in the snowbank and was poised on a steep slope, a hundred feet above the waters of the cove.

"It's a man," Kerrick said, as the lone figure started to move sideways along the steep slope, kicking footholds into the wet snow.

Up on the hillside, something else moved, a hulking shape. The drama focused the elf's attention once more on the present. A fist flailed out from the hole in the snowbank, and a long spear probed outward, though the escaping man remained just out of reach.

Kerrick felt a rush of sympathy for that desperate human. The fellow was undoubtedly a Highlander, but the appearance of the ogres had triggered a deep feeling of kinship with the humans—especially compared to the ogres and thanoi.

"I don't think the ogre can get out through that hole," Kerrick said. He peered at the shore, where more ogres thronged the cave mouth. The lone man was some distance away from them, but it was only a matter of time before the brutes fanned out in pursuit.

Kerrick dipped his oar in the water and pushed his sailboat across the placid, snow-bound cove. *Cutter*'s keen bow sliced through the surface, smoothly gliding closer. "Help paddle!" he barked. Coraltop willingly lifted the tiller, using it as an additional oar.

"And stay here, dammit!" added the elf, glaring at the kender who grinned and stroked with enthusiastic vigor.

"Down here!" Kerrick shouted, turning his attention to the hillside as they drew nearer to the snowy ground.

The ogres outside the cave had finally noticed the fugitive. Some lumbered along the shore, toward the place where *Cutter* approached, while others started climbing toward the lone man.

"Slide down to the water. We'll pick you up!" called the elven sailor.

The man looked down and cursed as ogres came closer, pushing through deep snow. One brute struggled to squeeze out through the narrow slot where the man had escaped from the cave.

"Hurry!" cried the elf, eyeing the ogres as they made their way along the snowy shore.

With another curse, the man careened down the steep slope, cutting a trough through the slushy snow, sending pebble-sized ice spraying around him. Kerrick pushed off with the oar, moving the boat a little way from the shore. The man tumbled in ungainly somersaults. He struck the water with a loud splash and vanished into the black depths.

Probing with the oar, Kerrick touched a squirming form, holding the blade so that the man could grab on and be hauled to the surface. The Highlander sputtered and cursed. With loud grunts and more curses he heaved himself onto the deck.

The elf recognized Strongwind Whalebone. "I should push you right back in the water!" he snapped. "Isn't that what you did to me?"

The Highlander king wrung out his braided beard, shook water from his hair and tunic. He did not look regal.

"It would be a reasonable act on your part in revenge for a foolish act on my part," said the man. "Strike me down if you must."

Kerrick glared. "How did you get out?" he asked after a moment.

"There was a spyhole. The lad, Little Mouse, found it. I used it to escape, after that shaman, Dinekki, and my priest worked a spell to collapse the cave. The ogres are stopped, at least for now."

"What about the tribe and your men?"

"Your Arktos friends might reach safety," Strongwind said. "Little Mouse also found a way up to Brackenrock inside the mountain. He took the Arktos and a band of my warriors up there. They're attacking the citadel, right now."

The elf glared at Strongwind for several moments before chuckling wryly. "Dinekki's the only reason I'm alive. She gave me a spell of water breathing before you dropped me in that hole."

"Yes, good for her," said the man glumly. "Good for you. It was a noble thing, to come back and rescue me thus."

"I didn't know it was you," Kerrick said bluntly. He was struck by another thought. "Coraltop," he called, "come and meet a human king."

"Who do you address?" asked Strongwind, looking toward the stern.

Kerrick craned his neck and looked for himself. The tiller where Coraltop Netfisher had been rowing hung slack. There was nobody there.

"Sire!" It was Urgas Thanoi, speaking urgently. "Do you see that smoke rising from beyond the ridge. That is coming from Brackenrock!"

The ogre king couldn't see the lofty citadel from his position on the shore, but the plume of black smoke was clearly visible, rising across the pale blue sky.

"What of it?" demanded Grimwar Bane, who was still furious about the cave-in that had so decisively blocked his army from a vengeful bloodbath. Furthermore, his wife, bleeding from a knock on the head, had just stomped over to report that the elf had overcome her when she wasn't looking, kidnapped Baldruk and escaped.

"That is the signal for trouble. They must be under attack!"

"How? From where?"

"Is it possible, oh wise lord, that the humans have discovered a passage from their cave to my citadel?"

"What is that?" growled Grimwar Bane. "A passage to your citadel? This is a fine time to mention it!"

"Begging Your Majesty's pardon," offered the thanoi, "but we're swimmers, not cavers. We've never explored these caverns, but legend holds that they twist and curve, rising beneath the floors of our citadel."

"Where's Baldruk Dinmaker when I finally need him?" The king frowned angrily. "He knows about tunnels and caverns and the like! The little runt spent fifty years living underground in Thorbardin!"

"He's dead, I think," Stariz said dazedly, rubbing an ugly bump on her forehead. "The elf took him on the boat, and I saw them fighting. The dwarf keeled over and rolled into the water."

"What good is that to me?" huffed the king. He squinted at the boat, drifting on the placid water with two men visible on deck. "Well, that elven rascal won't get far until the ice melts outside the cove. We can worry about him later." He looked at his queen, suddenly realizing that he wanted, even needed, her advice. "What do you think? Are the humans on top of the mountain now?"

"It's a very good chance," said Stariz slowly, regaining her composure. "That's clearly a big cave, warmed by the same steam that heats the tusker citadel." She nodded contemptuously to Urgas Thanoi "Even if the tuskers haven't discovered such a route, it's likely that one exists or could be forged."

"Well, then, we'd better get up there while we still have a chance to recoup our victory," snapped the king, actually enthused by the prospect of more action. "Come on, you louts!" he roared to his warriors, who were waiting around the outside of the cavern. "We've got a hard climb to make!"

He pointed to the road excavated into the side of the steep slope, beginning near the cave mouth. It curved along the mountainside, making its way higher and higher above the water in the cove until, on the far side of the valley, it vanished through a narrow notch, a pass flanked by a pair of brooding, cornice-draped cliffs. Beyond that notch rose the plume of smoke marking Brackenrock.

"Up! Let's go, my brutes! With luck, we'll have plenty of killing on the top!"

"More of the Highlanders are here," Bruni said, pointing to a throng of warriors spilling into the courtyard of the fortress, emerging from the door to the barracks chamber and the once-secret cave. Moreen lowered her sword and at last drew a breath. "They must be coming up the chimney now as fast as they can."

"Only one at a time," Moreen said, half to herself. She and Bruni were atop one of the two towers of the gatehouse. Five dead thanoi, bodies still warm, lay at their feet. The first rays of pale sun bathed them in light, but all Moreen could see was the slick, brilliant red of the blood that covered them and everything else.

The big oil fire in the gateway had been kicked apart by Highlanders and Arktos, but the smoke still lingered. It had clearly been a signal fire, and soon enough the chiefwoman expected an attack from the ogres on the shoreline below.

The fortress was mostly secured. The Highlander warriors, behind the berserker Mad Randall and the veteran Lars Redbeard, were here and there breaking into chambers within which the tuskers had barred themselves. One by one these strongholds were cleaned out. Against the most stubborn pockets of defense, the Highlanders tied burning rags to flasks of warqat and threw the flaming missiles with explosive effectiveness.

More Arktos warriors had reached the fortress in the last few minutes, fighting side by side with the men or going after individual tuskers on their own.

Tildey had led a group out the gates of the fortress, slaying the few tuskers who had tried to flee through the snow. The archer had gone all the way to the notch overlooking the cove before turning abruptly and heading back at a trot to Brackenrock, leaving four Arktos women standing guard at the pass.

"I'm worried," Moreen said. She and Bruni climbed down from the tower and met Tildey in the open gateway of the fortress. Lars Redbeard, his axe stained with tusker blood, also met them there.

"The ogres," Tildey announced, trying to catch her breath. "They're starting up the path. The whole column is on the march, and they'll be here within two hours."

Moreen nodded curtly. She looked at the slopes leading toward the gate, imagining what a charge of ogres could do. Her eyes fell on the narrow notch, where Tildey had posted her four sentries. Tall flanks of rock, each draped with cornices of snow in deep drifts, loomed to either side of the gap, narrowing the pass to a bottleneck.

"Let's get most everyone working on getting some kind of barricade across this gate," the chiefwoman said. "Use whatever we can find."

"Good plan, but it'll take the better part of a day," Lars noted.

"I said *most* of us should work on that. The rest of us will go there, to that narrow pass. It will be up to us to hold the ogres off long enough to seal the gate."

"Will you work with me against a common enemy?" asked Strongwind Whalebone

"I don't think we have much choice." Kerrick pointed at the steep slope, where the outline of the ancient road was just barely visible through the snow. "Up there is Brackenrock. You know where the cave is. The Arktos and, I suppose, the rest of your army are holed up in there. You say they were going to climb up to the fortress from inside the mountain?"

Strongwind explained about the narrow chimney, the hope that Moreen and a small force could rush the castle from within, and lead the rest of the beleaguered humans there to safety.

"If the ogres get there first, Moreen won't have a chance." Kerrick spoke grimly, pointing to the ogres massing outside the cavern. Already they were forming up and filing along the snowy road that gradually ascended toward the fortress, curving up the side of the valley until it disappeared through that lofty notch.

"That smoke must be some kind of signal."

"If we somehow delay the ogres, can the citadel be held against ogre attack?" Kerrick wondered.

"Yes, as long as most of my men get behind the walls before the ogres do. Brackenrock was impenetrable for generations, before the dragons came. It was the center of a blossoming civilization, and the ogres sent many armies to destroy it but could never breach its high walls. If we can seal off the gate, we can hold the advantage as long as necessary. From the towers we can harass them with bows and spears. But how can we hope to delay so many ogres?"

"There!" Kerrick said, pointing to a notch beneath the overhanging shelves of snow. "The ogres have to pass through there. If we get there first and get some help from your men, we might be able to hold them up."

"As good a plan as any," Strongwind agreed. He touched the hilt of his sword, secured in the great scabbard strapped to his back. "I have my weapon. What about you?"

Kerrick picked up the gold-bladed axe. "This will work," he said grimly.

Only when he and Strongwind made ready to jump to shore did Kerrick again remember Coraltop Netfisher.

"Your passenger?" asked the king, seeing the elf look back to the stern and hesitate.

Kerrick shook his head. "Forget him. He's gone." If he was even here in the first place, he added to himself.

He had maneuvered *Cutter* to a place directly under the massive shelf of snow. Reluctantly, he abandoned the boat, consoling himself that she couldn't drift far in the icebound cove. The ogres were on the other side of the bowl-shaped valley, slogging their way along the road that angled gradually upward, though they had yet to travel very far.

"It'll be a steep climb," cautioned the Highlander. "Do you think we can get ahead of them?"

Kerrick snorted. "I don't think we have any choice," he declared. "Anyway, we can go straight up to the notch, and they'll have to circle around half the valley." He left unsaid that the ogres would climb a smooth track on a gentle grade, while the human and elf would be going straight up a steep slope strewn with rocky outcroppings.

Together they jumped onto the snowy shore, the momentum of their leap shooting *Cutter* slowly toward the middle of the cove. Sinking knee deep into the wet snow, dragging the heavy axe behind him, Kerrick started to climb. Strongwind Whalebone kept pace at his side.

The snow was wet. At first the elf tried to drag the axe along, but he quickly realized the heavy weight of the weapon made it a liability. He used the long shaft as a climbing pole, jabbing it into the snow.

"No sense in both of us doing all this work," Strongwind suggested after a few minutes. "Why don't you follow me for a while? Use the path I make?"

The elf found it easier to follow in the human's bootsteps. Strongwind clawed his way upward with admirable strength, steadily ascending until finally he collapsed, gasping for breath. Kerrick passed him, taking a long stint in the lead. Within a few minutes they had risen as high as the leading rank of the ogre army, still across the valley, like a long, dark snake on the snow-covered trail. No doubt the ogres had spotted the climbing duo, though they hadn't visibly quickened their pace.

Once more Strongwind took the lead, and soon they were climbing above the ogres, but the steep grade took its own toll. Before long both again collapsed, gasping for breath, straining to find strength in their leaden limbs.

The ogres were close enough now that Kerrick and Strongwind could see the metal speartips in the long rank glowing with reflected daylight. The king and queen marched at the head of the column, and Kerrick felt the ogress's eyes upon him, sensed her fury, her desperation to regain her sacred axe.

"Got to keep moving," grunted Strongwind. "You follow."

Again he started out but after a dozen steps collapsed facedown in the snow. Kerrick clawed up behind him, his own fatigue like a heavy burden. He knew they wouldn't be able to push all the way to the pass.

Only then did he remember the talisman of his father. "My ring!" he croaked. "Do you still have it?"

"Yes." The human pulled a necklace from beneath his tunic and the elf saw the artifact dangling there. He looked at the strapping, muscular man, compared with his own slender frame, and knew what he had to do.

"Put it on," he said. "It will give you strength!"

"It's too small. You take it."

Kerrick waved him away. "It will grow. Put your finger through it, and you'll see."

Strongwind followed the elf's instructions, eyes widening as the circlet of gold expanded to surround one of his fingers. Slowly, he slid the finger through the ring. He sat up straight, and looked at his hand with wonder.

"It is powerful magic. Give me the head of the axe. I'll pull you along."

Looking more like a bear than a man, the king of the Highlanders set himself against the slope with heavy footsteps. His hand gripped the knob at the rear of the axeblade, and Kerrick held on to the hilt, feeling himself lifted almost effortlessly.

Strongwind Whalebone kicked and stepped, kicked and stepped, with fierce energy and determination. Higher and higher they climbed, the elf following along, the man straining and pulling and steadily ascending. Strongwind skirted the base of a tall cliff, then scrambled up and over a belt of wet boulders. Finally, Strongwind drew near to the notch, curving under the great overhanging cliffs of snow. Kerrick followed closely behind, helping himself as much as possible, leaning on the man's strength when his own muscles started to fail.

Finally the two reached crest of the ridge, where they were greeted by four Arktos spearwomen. More humans, a dozen of each band, were hurrying toward them from the lofty fortress. For the first time Strongwind and Kerrick got a good look at Brackenrock, taking in the sweep of the high walls, the formidable gatehouse, the towers and parapets lofting behind the outer barrier.

Closer, the elf recognized Moreen, Tildey, and Bruni. At the sight of Kerrick the Arktos halted in astonishment. Abruptly Moreen hurled herself forward and threw her arms around his neck.

"You're alive!" she cried. "But how—"

"There'll be time to explain later," he interrupted.

She nodded, already scrutinizing the ogre column which had ascended most of the way up to the notch. "The fort is secured," she declared. "We have everyone who can lift a rock working to block the gates. We'll have to hold them here, for as long as possible."

Even commanding the high ground, the odds of winning a long battle against the ogres were not good. They needed something else, some advantage to give them hope.

Kerrick lifted his eyes along the great drifts and cornices that flanked the pass overhead and loomed high above the outer slope.

"If we can start that snow falling," he mused, "we could knock a lot of the ogres right down to the water."

"How?" asked the chiefwoman. Then her eyes brightened, and she turned to the Highlander who had accompanied her. "Lars, your men have flasks of warqat, don't they?"

The warrior, his head capped by a wolf-skull helmet, nodded. "Most do. We used a few to burn out the tuskers."

"That's what gave me the idea. Strongwind said you used warqat to knock down the wall of ice. If we planted the flasks on those snowbanks, could they do the same thing?"

Strongwind nodded. "Yes, if we could ignite them."

"I know how to do that," Kerrick said. He lifted the axe

and twisted the handle, bringing the blue flames springing from the blade.

"We'll climb, then!" the king said, as the Highlander warriors produced, between them, ten flasks of the oily brew. Strongwind slung the straps of the flasks over his shoulder and turned toward the nearest cliff. He took a step, then staggered, falling to one knee.

"My strength is gone!" he groaned.

"The ring—take it off," Kerrick said urgently. "You'll need to rest. Here, I'll take the flasks."

By now the nearest ogres were several hundred paces away. The king and queen pulled back, prudently allowing a few dozen stalwart warriors to take the lead, but Grimwar Bane followed close behind.

"Go!" Moreen urged. "We'll hold them here!"

The elf scrambled up a jagged, steep slope of rock, quickly moving above the first of the great snowbanks. He dropped two flasks along the base of the thickest part of the drift, loosening the corks so that a bit of the flammable liquid could leak out and serve as a fuse. Then he climbed on.

A downward look showed him the first ogres lumbering into the pass. Bruni met one with a swing of her mighty hammer, knocking the brute in the head, sending him tumbling down the long, steep slope. Moreen stabbed another, the elven sword drawing blood. The Arktos and Highlanders in the narrow gap stood side by side, axes, swords, spears and hammers all thrusting outward, holding the lead ogres at bay. The rest of the column still advanced, passing directly under the elf's lofty position.

Higher and higher Kerrick scrambled, dropping two flasks along the top of another drift, then planting three at intervals of ten paces in the base of a huge cornice. The crest masked his view of the ogre army, but he could still see the detachment fighting to block the humans from the pass. Moving quickly, he placed his last three flasks at the base of a large shelf of icicle-draped snow.

He heard a scream and looked down to see the ogre

queen pointing at him. "The sacred axe! Kill the elf, and return the Axe of Gonnas to his priestess!" she cried.

Moreen lunged at the hulking ogress, her sword flashing. Kerrick gasped in horror as an ogre spearman slipped behind, his brutal weapon poised to strike the chiefwoman in the back. Then Tildey was there, knocking aside the blow, tumbling back as the ogre fist smashed her face. She lay on the snow for an instant, and before she could move the great spear plunged downward, piercing her belly and driving deep into the suddenly crimson snow.

"No!" screamed Moreen. She pulled back her sword, slashed it across the face of the ogre. Bruni added a hammerblow, and that hulking attacker followed several others on the long tumble down the mountainside. Tildey lay still amid a growing circle of red.

Near the top of the promontory, Kerrick lifted the goldbladed axe. He twisted the handle, and flames sprang into life. He touched those flames to the flask of warqat he had planted at the crest. Immediately the snow, saturated by the leaking brew, leaped into flames. He ignited the next two flasks, then quickly slipped downward, on the back side of the ridge.

The first explosion shook the valley with a muffled thump, followed almost immediately by two more booms. The icy drift trembled and began to slide. Kerrick was already lighting his lower charges. One after another flames surrounded the bottles, heating the warqat, licking eagerly toward eruption.

The elf climbed to his feet and looked outward, just in time to watch sheets of snow tip forward and roar down.

As the huge slab of snow and ice swept toward the marching ogres, Grimwar Bane knew in a sickening instant his army was doomed.

"Forward! Carry the pass!" cried the king, seizing his wife's arm and pulling her out of the way of the avalanche –

which meant lunging almost onto the blades of the furiously resisting humans in the narrow pass. Two of his warriors flanked him, cutting down a Highlander in the king's path, gaining for Grimwar as small space to stand.

They made it by inches as the slab plummeted behind. He turned back just in time to see dozens of ogres vanish in the first strike. The avalanche spread, as more of the snow cover broke free and toppled toward them, until it seemed as though the whole mountain was falling. White fury engulfed the slope, a cascade of powder and ice, burying everything in its path.

The wave of white swept the ogres away as though they were toys. Some of the warriors tried to flee ahead of the catastrophe, tripping and cartwheeling clumsily down the slope. They had little chance. The snow swept down crushingly. So powerful was the avalanche that it tore rocks from the mountainside, mixing these missiles into the mass of snow and ice.

Grimwar watched in horror, until the ogre beside him fell with a dull groan. He turned back to the battle, the Barkon Sword in his hands, to face an infuriated human woman.

"This is for my father, you bastard!" she cried, jabbing a sword with remarkable dexterity, a slashing blow that drew blood from the king's leg. He chopped back, but his blow was unbalanced, hacking only the trampled snow in the pass.

Another human woman, this one almost as big as an ogre, charged in with a huge hammer raised over her head. One of the king's warrior's intercepted her, buying Grimwar precious seconds before falling with a crushed skull. On his other side, Stariz screamed and tumbled against the king, her face gashed by a sword cut, blood spilling through her mouth and onto the snow.

Everywhere the humans were closing in. A trio of Highlanders cut down the last of Grimwar's ogre warriors, leaving only the king and queen remaining in the pass. The long slope of churned snow spilled downward behind them, and vengeful men and women closed in from the front.

Fear propelled Grimwar Bane into the only choice he could make. Seizing his wife by the arm, he pulled her with him, falling back from the pass, slipping and tumbling down the steep mountainside. With Stariz clinging in terror to him, he skidded and plunged and rolled down from the pass toward the bottom of the mountain. After many minutes—it seemed like hours!—both of them splashed into the icy water. In wild panic Grimwar kicked and grasped, feeling the weight of his gold as a cursed anchor. Somehow his hands dug into the snowbank, and finally he was able to crawl out of the cove, shivering and soaked. Stariz gasped and cursed at his side. She was still bleeding grotesquely, and he saw that half of her nose had been hacked off.

All around his warriors were gasping and thrashing in the cove, many of them slipping beneath the water. The avalanche had been relentless, sweeping away the road, smashing through the ogre ranks. Half of the army was gone, wiped out in the first instant of frosty assault.

Above them now was only a clean, steep mountainside. Around the king were the remains of a proud army, ogres drowning in the water, or clawing their way onto shore. The cove was spotted with floating bodies.

"We must attack, get revenge!" hissed the queen, leaning over Grimwar and staring into his face. Her eyes, staring from that mask of blood, were wild and terrifying. "They have the Axe of Gonnas! Lead your ogres up there again!"

"No!" Grimwar roared, with a look so fierce that, for once, even Stariz shrank back. "We will go back to Winterheim and wait for this accursed snow to melt. I told you, this is no time for a campaign!"

"The Willful One demands, *requires* vengeance!"

"I promise you this: Summer will come, and the snow will melt. I will gather the rest of my army from Winterheim, bring reinforcements from Glacierheim and Dracoheim, and demand troops from all of my tribute lords." Grimwar was making a grand plan already, a design for blood and victory. The humans had thwarted him, but they had not defeated—they would *never* defeat—him!

And the elf—that *elf*—would taste his vengeance!

"As Gonnas himself is my witness," Grimwar told Stariz, "we will return and take our revenge."

Dimly Kerrick heard the cheers from the gatehouse of Brackenrock. Moreen embraced him, and he was touched to see tears in her eyes. She turned to the Highlander king, meeting his abashed look icily.

"You're don't know how lucky you are. Killing him would have made me hate you forever. Our tribe owes our very survival to him."

"I was doubly lucky, it turns out," said the Highlander king with unusual humility. "His survival is the only thing that saved me when I came out on the snowfield below." He coughed awkwardly, looking down at the ground, then back into Moreen's eyes.

"My lady chieftain," he said bluntly. "I have acted wrongly in ways that, as you have correctly pointed out, are more suited to ogrekind than man. I would humbly and sincerely beg your forgiveness."

Moreen's dark eyes flashed, gleamed with a note of triumph. Kerrick watched her, wondering if she would unleash the crooked half-smile that he found so intriguing. Instead, her face remained tight, pensive, and Strongwind eventually lowered his eyes.

"We won!" Little Mouse said, running up to them excitedly. "I took a spear from a tusker! And I killed two of them. . . ." His voice trailed off, and he looked at the notch, still bloody and covered with scattered bodies, some from their side. "It wasn't quite the adventure I thought it would be," he admitted. Then his eyes widened in dismay. "Not Tildey?" he groaned, his voice cracking.

"Yes," said Bruni, kneeling beside her tribemate. She closed Tildey's eyes with a gentle touch of her big hand, as the big woman's tears mingled with Mouse's and Moreen's.

"We suffered much today, losses we will never replace," said the chiefwoman sadly.

Garta and several other Arktos came from the fortress to join them at the pass. The matronly woman, her handless arm draped awkwardly around Feathertail, looked at Moreen with tears of relief and grief in her eyes. "The Highlanders carried me up the rope," she said. "It's true, Moreen—you brought us here, to safety! You did it!" Emotion overcoming her, she began to cry softly. Feathertail offered her a small rag to dry her tears.

"Now, don't be carrying on like that!" snapped Dinekki, hobbling up to join them. "We've got plenty of work to do before that place is liveable! And I swear, it's going to take years to get the fish stink out of these stones."

"Welcome to Brackenrock," Moreen said, stepping back and gesturing Kerrick and Strongwind toward the tall towers, the still-yawning gateway where people were still busy gathering tusker bodies, and cleaning up rubble.

"It is warm here, and the sun is returning." She took the elf's hands and looked into his face. "Your coming was a message from the goddess to us. You brought us across the strait and here, at the end of the battle, started the greatest avalanche in the history of Icereach. I welcome your friendship and will do anything I can to repay you."

Kerrick flushed, suddenly ashamed of his base motives. She didn't know he had sailed on a quest for gold. Right now he couldn't bring himself to tell her. He nodded gratefully.

"I have a lot I want to say to you," Moreen added, before looking over at Strongwind Whalebone sternly. "You, too."

"I will listen," promised the king of the Highlanders, "but know that my people have paid in blood for this place, even as have yours."

"You told me that this is a place sacred to your people's history, as it is for ours. Perhaps we have more in common than we thought," Moreen said. "Perhaps now, with a shared victory, we can explore our points of similarity, instead of our differences."

"Yes," the king said sincerely. "Let us talk."

"You go ahead," Kerrick said, as they started toward the warm fortress. "I'll be right there."

The elven sailor wanted to check on his boat. He walked out to the very brink of the notch, until he could see the small circle of water that was the cove. He looked down, saw *Cutter* floating there still icebound and safe. The ogres in their chaotic retreat were vanishing around the shoulder of mountain at the shoreline, and they had left his boat alone. He waved, and was not surprised to see a small figure seated at the tiller, waving back.

He waved again and blinked, and there was no one there.

The Dhamon Saga

Jean Rabe

The exciting beginning to the Dhamon Saga

—NOW AVAILABLE IN PAPERBACK!

Volume One: *Downfall*

How far can a hero fall?
Far enough to lose his soul?

Dhamon Grimwulf, once a Hero of the Heart, has sunk into a bitter life of crime and squalor. Now, as the great dragon overlords of the Fifth Age coldly plot to strengthen their rule and destroy their enemies, he must somehow find the will to redeem himself.

Volume Two: *Betrayal*

All Dhamon Grimwulf wants is a cure for the painful dragon scale embedded in his leg. To find a cure, he must venture into the treacherous realm of a great black dragon. Along the way, Dhamon discovers some horrible truths: betrayal is worse than death, and there is something more terrifying on Krynn than even a dragon overlord.

June 2001

The Crossroads Series

This thrilling new DRAGONLANCE series visits famous places in Krynn in the pivotal period of time after the Fifth Age and before the War of Souls. New heroes and heroines, related by blood and deed to the original Companions, struggle to live honorably in a world without gods or magic, dominated by dark and mysterious evildoers.

THE CLANDESTINE CIRCLE

MARY H. HERBERT

Rose Knight Linsha Majere takes on a dangerous undercover mission for the Solamnics' Clandestine Circle in the city of Sanction, run by the powerful Hogan Bight.

THE THIEVES' GUILD

JEFF CROOK

A rogue elf, who may or may not be who he claims, steals a legendary artifact, makes an enemy of the Dark Knights, and rises and falls inside the Thieves' Guild in Palanthas.

DRAGON'S BLUFF

MARY H. HERBERT

Ulin Majere and his companion Lucy travel to Flotsam, get mixed up in a rebellion, and battle against a dragon terrorizing the local populace.

July 2001

THE MIDDLE OF NOWHERE

KEVIN KAGE

Kevin Kage's debut DRAGONLANCE novel tells a tale of irrepressible kender, a forgotten town, and an act of pure bravado.

December 2001

The tales that started it all . . .

New editions from DRAGONLANCE creators
Margaret Weis & Tracy Hickman

The great modern fantasy epic – now available in paperback!

THE ANNOTATED CHRONICLES

Margaret Weis & Tracy Hickman return to the Chronicles, adding notes and commentary in this annotated edition of the three books that began the epic saga.

SEPTEMBER 2001

THE LEGENDS TRILOGY

Now with stunning cover art by award-winning fantasy artist Matt Stawicki, these new versions of the beloved trilogy will be treasured for years to come.

Time of the Twins • War of the Twins • Test of the Twins

FEBRUARY 2001

Classics Series

THE INHERITANCE

Nancy Varian Berberick

The companions of Tanis Half-Elven knew of their friend's tragic heritage—how his mother was ravaged by a human bandit and died from grief. But there was more to the story than anyone knew.

Here at last is the story of the half-elf's heritage: the tale of a captive elven princess, a merciless human outlaw, a proud elven prince, the power of love, and how tragedy can change a life forever.

May 2000

THE CITADEL

Richard A. Knaak

Against a darkened cloud it comes, soaring over the ravaged land: the flying citadel, mightiest power in the arsenal of the dragon highlords. An evil wizard has discovered a secret that may bring all of Ansalon under his control, and it's up to a red-robed mage, a driven cleric, a kender, and a grizzled war veteran to stop him before it's too late.

DALAMAR THE DARK

Nancy Varian Berberick

Magic runs like fire through the blood of Dalamar Argent, yet his heritage denies him its use. But as war threatens his beloved Silvanesti, Dalamar will seize the forbidden power and begin a quest that will lead him to a dark and uncertain future.

MURDER IN TARSIS

John Maddox Roberts

Who killed Ambassador Bloodarrow? In a city where everyone is a suspect, time is running out for an unlikely trio of detectives. If they fail to solve the mystery, their reward will be death.